Praise for *A Book of Secrets*

A Book of Secrets is fresh and impressively researched. With its engaging heroine Nsowah positioned at the very heart of an Elizabethan drama, Morrison offers an intriguing and important update on historical novels where black characters have been either absent or confined to the margins. Morrison's rich and complex rendering of the interior of Nsowah's life shows her to be an empathic and talented new writer.

Colin Grant, author of *Homecoming: Voices of the Windrush Generation* and *Bageye At The Wheel*

A tale of religious fervour, loyalty, piracy, desire and identity, *A Book of Secrets* is a masterful piece of storytelling that draws you into a Tudor London you won't have visited before. Our guide, Susan (or Nsowah), who was born in Ghana but raised in Sussex, inhabits a world of printers, crypto-Catholics, Jewish conversos, pirates and Guinea traders. Her city is much more diverse and permeable than is often assumed: we learn that a Tudor 'Blackamoor' could also be a wife, learn a trade, and become an intelligencer. But this is no heavy-handed history lesson; Susan's quest to find security, happiness, and discover her true identity intrigues the reader from the start, has us rooting for her through her gripping adventures and leaves us wanting more.

Miranda Kaufmann, author of *Black Tudors*

A Book of Secrets

Kate Morrison

JACARANDA

First published in Great Britain 2019 by
Jacaranda Books Art Music Ltd
27 Old Gloucester Street,
London WC1N 3AX
www.jacarandabooksartmusic.co.uk

This is a work of fiction and all characters and incidents described in this book are the product of the author's imagination.
Any resemblance to actual persons, living or dead,
is entirely coincidental.

A CIP catalogue record for this book is available from the
British Library

ISBN: 9781909762695
eISBN: 9781909762701

Cover Art: S. Ross Browne
Cover Design: Jeremy Hopes
Typeset by Kamillah Brandes
Printed and bound in the United Kingdom

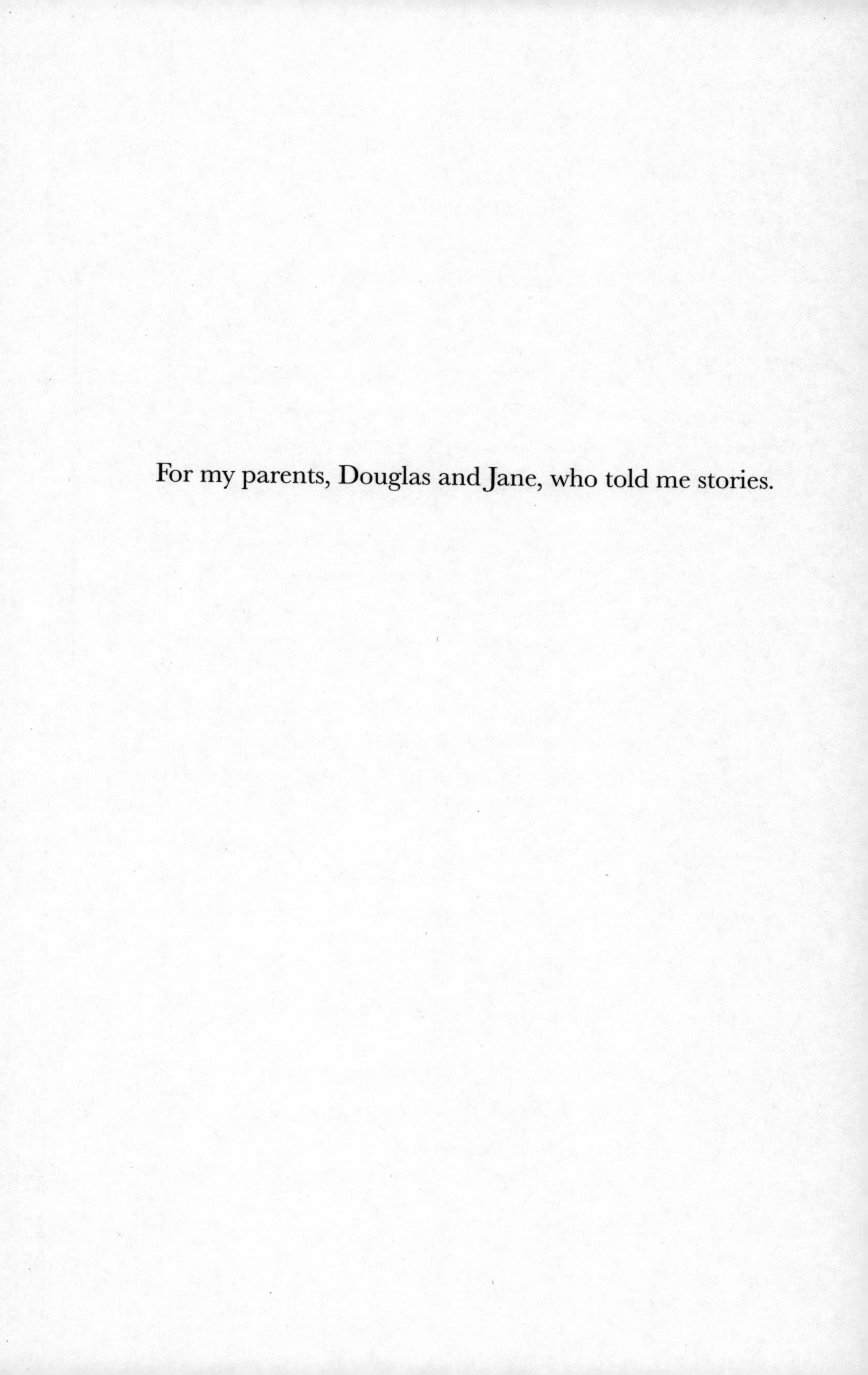

For my parents, Douglas and Jane, who told me stories.

'Every word is the word.
The word is easy
and difficult.
He who would speak
must speak clearly
and speak the truth.'

Traditional expression used
by Ivory Coast drummers before telling a story.

PROLOGUE

GHANA (THEN KNOWN AS GUINEA), WEST AFRICA, 1562

Ama stands in the shelter of the great shade tree planted by her ancestors. Beyond the cool shadow it casts, the earth soaks up the sun's fire. The sweeter air of morning slowly shimmers to heat-haze along the straight path through the village. The path leads to the far edge of the settlement, where the midden and the graveyard roar and hum. Here, a gate marks the boundary between civilization and the hungry forest, where spirits walk.

Beside her sits Ama's eldest son, Kofi. Yesterday he was a child; today he is a man. His new *dja*, complete with the scales, gold dust, figurines and weights, is open and laid out on the red earth. He turns the weights over, considering his new responsibilities.

Ama's baby, snug against her back in the sling, snorts and settles in closer to her with a fat, contented wriggle. Nsowah, her seventh child, is a gift. The cord had been around her neck when she was born. With sweating, bloody hands, the midwife freed her as fast as she could. Ama watched, praying for the child to cry, but when the cord was off Nsowah stayed still and pale. There was a moment of profound silence. Then, with all eyes on her, she suddenly came to life with a great sneeze and a creaking roar, waving her fists.

At nearly a year old she is full of life, and only still when she's asleep. She sleeps well, better than any of the rest. Kofi kept Ama awake most nights his first two years, angry and inconsolable. Now he is fifteen and after yesterday's ceremony he is no longer under her guardianship. He may begin to learn the full and complex meanings of his *dja* pieces and the proverbs that go with them.

Ama watches him handling the weights, murmuring to himself under his breath. He has always been an observer, the cleverest and quietest of her children. One day he will inherit her brother's title. When he is ruler of the region, the Omanhene, he will need to make his presence known more, put on a display. Will he be able to rise to it? She worries for him. Her people, the Akan, are strong in this country and they respect strength in a leader. Kofi is subtle, bright, and quick. People listen to him, but they don't follow him. His gifts so far are those of an advisor, not a ruler.

A wind blows up towards them from the forest, bringing the smell of green life and green death swirling in the red dust. Ama shades her eyes and turns her face away. The forest wind makes her uneasy. Tomorrow, she, Kofi, and Nsowah will walk back along the red paths to her husband's village and the rest of her children. She misses them, the rhythm and melody of their voices and bodies that fill her home. She misses being enveloped in the constant cacophony of laughter and screams, play-fights and real fights, but it is good to spend time with just these two, her eldest and youngest.

Again she feels Nsowah stir against her back and whimper, so she begins to walk about in the shade to soothe her back to sleep. She is astonished at how much she loves this one. She loves her best of all. She tells no one but Nsowah this, when they are alone, whispering against her daughter's little soft head. She loves all her children but sometimes Ama feels she and Nsowah are a complete universe in themselves, wanting nothing and no-one else.

The forest wind drops and the smell of earth and wood smoke

rises up again. Ama drinks some water and settles down again beside Kofi, closing her eyes to breathe in the familiar scents of her family home. She is at peace here. In her lifetime she has seen the shade tree grow taller and wider, blessing the village. She returned here to give birth to all her children. Her mother still cooks on the hearth in the Omanhene's compound and she will crown Kofi when his turn comes to rule.

This place has resisted all attempts by the forest to swallow it back up. Rains, droughts, enemy raids. Instead it has grown rich on the gold mines that run deep beneath the trees. Ama's people send gold south to the Portuguese in exchange for slaves to work the mines and fell trees. Over time the slaves earn their freedom and are absorbed into Akan families by marriage or through service. The gold, divine and dangerous, travels over the seas and the deserts, to be turned into bullion in faraway countries.

Kofi weighs out gold dust now, spoon by small spoon, testing his scales. The ladder weight now rests in the other scale, which rises slowly as the gold dust heaps in. This is the source of her family's wealth; a golden sea running beneath the red earth.

The wind rises again with more force and she looks up with a start. It is blowing the canopy leaves. Branches rise and fall and through the heat-haze something glints and flickers at the forest edge. Sunlight on a blade. Kofi catches Ama's startled movement and also looks towards the trees. Ama puts her hand on his arm as Nsowah breathes hot against her back. In her last seconds of peace, touching her youngest and eldest children, she has never loved them more.

PART I

LONDON & SUSSEX
1563 – 1593

CHAPTER I

I have a riddle in my hands that can kill a man. It may kill John Roberdine, who was once my lover and is now my enemy. If I tell the right person the meaning of this riddle, men will ride up to Roberdine's house and drag him away from it. His lands will be seized, his treasure forfeit. They will take him over the bad Sussex roads, through the Wealden clay and the woods where the iron forges smoulder in the night, all the way to London. He will ride in under the Traitor's Gate on Southwark Bridge and they will take him to a traitor's room in the Tower. There he will stay till they take him out to hang.

We made that journey to London together once, when he was a sunburned apprentice with a salt voice and sea-green eyes, and I was a little maid whose life and family had been swallowed up by a thunderclap.

Who am I now? Can I condemn him to death?

The paper that may hang him has only a few words written on it:

10 culver
10 robin
15 a bird.

Innocent enough, seemingly. Ten doves, ten robins, at a certain price. But Roberdine is no birdcatcher. He trades now in larger prey.

I have been sitting in the empty print room since sundown, burning precious candles, trying to dig wisdom from the thickest part of the night. Little flickers of reflected flame spark out from the cases of type, as all the letters sit in their allotted ranks, waiting to be formed into any words I choose. I could pick out a T now with my eyes closed. I know the place of every letter, comma and stop by heart.

The bronze heirlooms my mother brought from Africa lie on the table before me, stamped with their own secret language. I turn the little bird figurine over and over in my hand, trying to read deeper than words. I hold it up to the light and its eye squints gold in the candle flame. *Go back and fetch what you forgot,* it says. "Look over your shoulder and learn what the past has to teach you so you can decide where to walk next."

Can the past help me solve this riddle? Since I was born, other people have given me names and told me who and what I am. A stranger, a Blackamoor, a little labour-in-vain, a good wife, a whore. I don't remember my father or my mother and I knew almost nothing about the land of my birth when I was growing up. That has left me with a strange weightlessness, like the swifts that stay on the wing their whole lives.

I think of my son, who will know his place in the world. I imagine him in the future, a tall, curly-headed gentleman, reading aloud to his wife in a wood-panelled room, large and fine. I know this room. I can picture it exactly. One wall is full of his books and the others beautifully carved with birds and scrolls.

His head will be a store of knowledge and his house will be a store of good things. He will lack for nothing. Upstairs, a nurse will rock his own son to sleep.

I can make that future real for him, if I break this cipher.

I have had enough of people telling me who I am. I have had enough of the names they give me.

I will do it. I will look over my shoulder. I will go back and fetch it.

CHAPTER 2

We had a large dovecote at Framfield that we called the culverhouse. I used to like watching the white doves fly in and out, especially at sunset when the light turned them gold and I could imagine them phoenixes.

Framfield was the house in Sussex where I grew up. It overlooked the forest of the Weald, where the wind surged among the treetops in rushing waves and tugged away the autumn leaves. That forest was the source of my master's wealth. Sir Thomas Framfield owned one of the great iron furnaces that ate up the Wealden timber as fast as it grew and turned the iron ore from the soil into firebacks, cannon and shot. I was a maid and companion—almost a sister—to his daughter Anne, who I loved dearly. Framfield was my home and family, the only one I remembered, having been torn from my own as a very young baby.

That I am a Blackamoor is a book any man may read. Everything else about me has been put into a cipher so perfect I often have trouble decoding it myself. That being so, the plain and legible facts of my life are these:

I was born in Guinea where the gold comes from, on the coast of West Africa. My mother did not leave Guinea of her own free will. She and I were bought by Portuguese slavers who tore us from our home to trade for sugar in the Indies. They let me live. God knows why—I was a useless infant, still at the breast, and their most economic course would have been to dash my brains out against a post. They took my elder brother too, and what happened to the rest of my family, I do not know.

Our luck changed when the slavers were attacked by a ship captained by the famous John Hawkins. The English had no trade with the Guinea people yet, so all their gains in that region were got through privateering and stealing from the Spanish and Portuguese. Hawkin's crew killed the Portuguese and took all the bounty on the ship including us. Some of the goods and enslaved people they sold. Some, they brought back to the pale, wet, codfish country of England, so very different to the burning lands of Guinea. My brother was sold in Spain and died soon after, but they brought me and my mother home with them.

John Hawkins, who knew my master, sent my mother to him as a servant for the household. My master told me Hawkins' version of the story once:

"We put up some money for the voyage and he said the usual flowery stuff to me; anything I can do, any gifts I can bring you home. My wife asked him in jest for a blackamoor maidservant like those that serve the Spanish noblewomen, and a little one for the child—she was pregnant when Hawkins left. When he captured the Portuguese prize he thought it a very good joke to take her at her word and bring your mother home for her. I remember when you both arrived. He sent you with his servant and a letter. Your mother was sitting behind the servant on his horse, all hooded and cloaked, and when she took down her hood the stable boy screamed and ran. He thought it was the Devil come for him. And your mother showed no fright. She sat there like a queen and waited to be helped down. Then it was a whole new box of surprises when she took off her cloak and there you were, fast asleep in a sling around her back. Hawkins's letter just said:

> *As ordered; one Blackamoor lady & a child for the little one. She has learned English on board ship & claims she was a Princess in her home. I am told they must have been taken as prisoners of war—their clan are not usually sold as slaves and are too warlike to make good thralls, but treated well they will make excellent servants.*

Well, my lady was charmed by your mother's grace, so here you stayed. Sussex had never seen such a thing. We had every neighbour for miles visiting on all kinds of pretexts to see the Guinea princess and her baby."

The knowledge of the way we came to Framfield left a scratch in my own love for the place, like a burr working against my skin. My childhood was happy, my master and mistress cared for me as they did their own kin. Yet I baulked at the notion of my mother and I as goods, as an order that John Hawkins had taken down and fulfilled. I knew my mother did not want to come to this country, that she did not want to leave her own.

Stranded in another country instead of being returned to our own, deposited on a household's doorstep, offered as servants—what dignity did it leave us? We were not to become slaves, but we had no choice at all in our servitude. I grew up knowing nothing else but for my mother, a princess in her own country, it must have been a bitter transformation.

Whatever her private feelings, she took steps to root herself in her new home. She converted to Christianity and we were both baptised a year after we arrived. Susan Katherine I have been ever since.

She died soon after, when I was only three. The sense I have of her is like the scent of wild chamomile or primrose; it vanishes if I try to keep it. The more I rest my mind on her, the more she slips away. Anything I do recall comes to me unasked, when I am suddenly and vividly overcome by a feeling—her fingers, gentle on my cheek, or the sound of her voice singing a haunting, off-tone song with words I can't catch. Never her face.

My lady Katharine had planned a portrait of us all—herself, Anne, my mother and I—but my mother died before it was halfway done. I used to trace her absence in the finished piece, which hangs at Framfield still. My lady seated, with Anne and I standing at her knees, and the space where my mother should be filled with a wall-hanging. Sometimes I reached up to touch that colourful emptiness. I felt the roughness of paint under my fingers as if she was beneath it, and if I picked the paint away I would find her face.

Whatever my past was, princess or peasant, wherever we came from and whatever our life was like in Guinea, it was all expunged by our journey, as if the sea washed it away on the crossing. I was brought up as an English lady's maid, learning the ways of a great household.

The Framfield family were Catholic and so was I raised, as an enemy of the newly Protestant state, in a creed that from my earliest years demanded deceit and subterfuge. Loyalty, love, silence and secrecy were all sewn up together in the chambers of my heart, and so it has been all my life.

When I was young it was still just possible to be a Catholic and perceived as a loyal citizen, in the time before Spanish plots and Jesuit missions prompted the Queen to make opposing her faith a treasonable matter. Because my master did not openly rebel or refuse to attend church as some recusant Catholics did, he managed not only to survive but to prosper. He hoped that the Queen might by marriage or persuasion be reconverted to the true faith, and until that time he wanted only to be left to worship in peace within his household.

My master was a landed man with a good name. He was sanguine and ruddy-faced, a sturdy man of great energies. I never saw him sit still. Even when he was reading or writing, he flung himself about in his chair and he preferred to walk when he was thinking, pacing up and down the long gallery or in the lime walk. He spoke four languages and was a scholar of Greek and Latin besides. Lacking a father of my own, I took him as my model of everything a man should be.

"Render unto Caesar the things that are Caesar's; and unto God the things that are God's," he would say. "I give my temporal loyalty to the Queen and I will observe her laws, but my soul I owe only to God."

Over the years, priests stayed with us to offer Mass, lying in a concealed bolt-hole if strangers approached—for even in those days Mass was prohibited. They never set foot in the estate chapel, which had been whitewashed and stripped of bells, images, candles, and all its Roman Glory. When we knelt there on Sundays we said our prayers in English from the Book of Common Prayer, but the stories Lady Katharine read to us in the evening were the stories of Catholic saints and martyrs and there were rosary beads hidden among her jewels and sewing boxes.

"Elizabeth is a bastard," my lady told us, "and her mother Anne Boleyn was a witch and a whore."

She was the second kind of Catholic and believed that if England must return to the faith by force, through military invasion and dethroning of the Queen, then it was worth losing mortal lives in the endeavour in order to save immortal souls.

I clove to my master's more moderate faith, but it was my lady who taught me all my craft. Women are always less likely to be suspected of plots, intelligencing, and secret work, and that is a great advantage. My lady kept busy sending works of comfort or important messages to imprisoned Catholics and priests and she had many ways of concealing them.

I might have been seven or eight. I remember the smell of alum and vinegar in my nostrils and the weight of a white egg in my hand. Anne and I sat in my lady's private room. On the table, a bowl of eggs and two bowls of vinegar, one with an egg already sitting in it, looking fat and strange in its liquid bed.

"Keep careful hold of the new egg, Suky," said my lady. "Now Anne, fish out that egg there and put it on the plate. Gently now. Put it down softly, softly. There. Well done. How did it feel in your hand?"

Anne hesitated, in case her answer should be wrong.

"Soft," she said. "Not like a true egg. Is it a real egg, my lady?"

"Watch," said Lady Katharine, and took up a sharp knife.

We stared at the white egg, lying innocently on the earthenware plate, as she held it gently and cut very carefully into its shell, making a narrow slit.

"The vinegar makes it soft," said my lady. "A few days soaking and the shell is no longer a barrier to us. Now this is a message-box."

She took a slip of paper from her pocket, covered with letters written so small you could not read them with the naked eye. My lady's hand was steady and precise at such work, so the words looked like fine spider-stitches. She folded the paper carefully and tucked it neatly through the slit in the egg's shell, till it was quite concealed and the slit barely visible.

"Good," she said. "Now we leave this to harden again and in a day or so the shell will be as it was. Suky, put the new egg in the vinegar bowl to soak. This is a laborious method but a very safe one. Now listen to the recipe and repeat it back to me."

We said it back to her three or four times till we no longer stumbled on the words and she was satisfied. "Good. You will repeat it to me before evening prayers, and again every day this week, until I am sure you have it safe."

"Are the recipes written down anywhere?" I asked.

"Not all in one place," she said. "I would never be so careless. The safest book of secrets is the one you keep in your heads, no one may look at it without your knowledge, or steal it, or copy it. I am giving you an armoury, one that is fit for women to possess. This knowledge is a weapon in our fight. Keep it, hold it, never forget it. Now go. The morning is fine, you may ride out."

CHAPTER 3

The armoury my lady gave us was a strong one indeed. She had a dozen recipes for invisible ink and another dozen ways of smuggling the messages once written: in the eggs, on linen, in letters folded and refolded so tiny they could be tucked into a glove or pinned beneath a hairpiece.

We learned these arts as we learned how to run a great house. She was a stern teacher, my lady. She kept her silver hair hidden beneath golden hairpieces, and her pale blue eyes shone on us like two moons when she was angry. She kept a tally of all our slips and repeated them back to us, and where my lord's anger was hot, hers burned cold.

Yet she loved us—she loved me. She kept miniatures of Anne and I in a locket at her neck and sometimes, if we sat by her feet while she read to us, she bent to kiss each of our heads: one, two. I remember the feel of those kisses. I kiss my own son's head just so and I know it means love.

It was my great good fortune that my master believed girls should read and write and know the works of famous poets as boys did. Anne had tutors and she wanted me always by her side, so I learned with her. I learned faster than her.

Anne was more like her mother than her father. She was calm and quiet, but also gentler and more biddable than my mistress. She hated to be out of favour with her mother so if something went amiss—lost hairpins, torn pages, a broken cup—I took the blame. I don't recall her asking me to, I would simply speak up and say it was me. It was some unspoken pact. I was the maid and I could take a scolding. I was not so gentle as she.

Anne bore very patiently with her mother, who kept her far too carefully because Anne was the only surviving child. We were allowed to ride out on the estate but we never went out with the hunt into the wild wood beyond. She was not to get herself into a sweat, and if she caught a chill she was muffled up to her nose in a second. Kate said Anne had a phlegmatic nature. Though I loved Anne, her very patience sometimes maddened me—the way she could sit and smile through anything.

She liked me to read aloud to her; she was fond of my voice and preferred it to reading herself, so we would sit together while I read and she sewed. I have a quick memory and I learned a great deal off by heart, so even when the candles were out and we lay in bed I could tell stories until she slept. Once she was asleep I often propped a book on my knee and sat up late reading while she breathed beside me. There were not enough hours in the day for all the knowledge I wanted nor for all the books I wanted to read.

My master's library was a treasure-chest. Stocked with everything from Virgil to Chaucer, there were chronicles of history, books of secrets by natural philosophers and alchemists, guides to arithmetic and astronomy, sermons and devotions, and a whole shelf of travellers' tales. I loved Virgil and Homer in particular because my master would read aloud to us from them, translating as he went. I remember all those stories in his voice.

We had forbidden Catholic texts too, some printed and some

handwritten manuscripts that had been copied and recopied as they passed from family to family. We even had Protestant works by Luther and Erasmus, for my master said you must know your enemy's arguments through and through in order to counter them. I wished often I had been a boy and could have been trained up as his secretary.

I kept a notebook filled with anything I could find about Africa in the books I read—mostly stories from Pliny and Herodotus about monstrous creatures like the headless Blemmyae and the Ethiopian troglodytes who could not speak but squeaked like bats. There was very little about ordinary men and nothing at all about Guinea, so I made up my own stories about gold castles, and battles in which my father the King put the Blemmyae to flight.

Then my master obtained a manuscript copy of an account of the first English voyages out to Guinea in the Fifties, before I was even born. He gave it to me before even he had read it, thinking I would like to see words from someone who had actually set foot in my country. I took it away and curled up in the window seat of the library, turning the book over in my hands before I opened it, as a glutton surveys a pie before the feast.

I had to leaf through what seemed endless descriptions of elephants—were there no other animals in Africa?—before I came at last to a passage on the people of Guinea,

> *who were in olde tyme called Ethiopes and Nigrites, which we now call Moors, Moorens or Negroes, a people of beastly living without a God, law, religion or commonwealth, and so scorched and burned with the heat of the sun, that in many places they curse it when it rises.*

I read it over again: *A people of beastly living without a God, law, religion or commonwealth.*

And there was more:

> *All the regions of Guinea are pure Gentiles and Idolaters, without protection of any religion, or other knowledge of God, than by the law of nature.*

I put the paper down on my knee and stared out of the window, seeing not the green fringes of the Weald but those words, emblazoned in black ink, marching across the sky and marring the whole world. Then I did a dreadful thing, the only bad act of my childhood; I tore that page out and threw it in the fire. My master noticed of course and I could not explain why I had done it. After that I did not write in my book any more. I did not want to learn anything else about my country or my people. I told myself that Framfield was all the home and family I needed.

My master and my lady were as dear to me as parents, and almost dearer was Kate the housekeeper. She was a particular friend to my mother and she took charge of me when my mother died. She eased my pain in the motherly way she tended me, softening my skin with oils and gently twisting my coils into simple braids. Kate's hands inherited that knowledge from my mother, and in turn passed it on to me. It was Kate who nursed me when I was sick, mended my clothes and comforted me when I found myself in trouble. She never told me that she loved me but love proves itself in deeds, not words. By her actions I knew how much she cared for me.

Kate kept my mother alive for me in the stories she told about her. "Do I look like her?" I asked her again and again. "Tell me what she was like." I loved to hear how visiting noblemen had praised my mother's beauty and called her the Queen of Sheba. When Kate was in a soft mood she would sometimes stroke my cheek and say, "You have some of her looks. She is not altogether lost to you, my dear, you are made in her pattern." Believing praise would spoil me, she would then counter her kindness with the sobering admonishment:

"Now don't think that means you're a beauty and start growing proud. Pride is a sin and beauty dies with us."

How I wished the artist had finished my mother's portrait. There was no-one on the whole estate who resembled me, nowhere I could look to find a reflection of myself. Whatever Kate said about my mother's looks, I knew how much everyone admired Anne's gold hair and delicate complexion. Hers was the pattern of beauty most prized in the world I lived in.

Sometimes her mother came to help us dress her, taking charge of pinning up Anne's hair. It hurt me to watch them together, their two faces in the mirror, unmistakeably mother and daughter. Kate found me once, weeping in private after one such morning, and mistook the reason for my tears. "Envy is a sin too," she said severely, "We can't all have Lady Anne's looks."

I could not explain to her what I felt, that I did not envy Anne her beauty, only her mother. I loved my own skin and my coiled hair, as the last vestiges of my mother in me. I only longed to see her face next to mine, to feel her love and to truly know how I might look as a grown woman.

So I grew up walking the paths allotted to me. The whole estate was as beautifully ordered as a knot garden and I felt rooted in it. I was part of its pattern.

I used to go to sleep at night thinking of my place on the earth. I in my bed beside Anne, all the rooms of the house around us and the estate beyond filled with sleeping men and women, from my lord and lady in the big bed hung with tapestry, to the grooms above the stable where the horses nodded in the straw. The household might be at odds with the religion of England but Queen Elizabeth was far away in London and there were many others who worshipped as we did. I trusted my master and mistress to keep us all safe, knit closer together by the bond of secrecy.

Outside the walls of the estate the rolling Weald stretched out to the sea and the sea went all around the world, to Africa and the Americas. Beyond the earth itself the spheres curved around us in concentric layers like the rings in tree trunks, out and out through the realms of fire to Heaven. I was snug in the centre of it all and God was outside everything, holding us safe in His palm. Then one day, without warning, He opened his fingers and let me drop.

CHAPTER 4

One November morning in 1580 I woke beside Anne in a fever. It gripped me so fast that within an hour I fell into a raging, burning hell of sickness.

It was one long nightmare of screaming phantoms, my head banging with pain and the world spinning around me. I dreamed terrible dreams. I remembered my mother's face for the first time, saw her lying beside me in the bed, naked, with dreadful red eyes. I saw demons creeping towards me from the corners of the room. I had been dropped straight into Hell and I was lost in that maze of sickness for two weeks. When I found my way out of it, Anne was dead and my mistress was close to following her.

For some days I was too weak to move and the only people who came to see me were the physician and Kate. I was too ill and too lost in grief at Anne's death to wonder why. My sister, my bedfellow, my dear companion. I knew the body was only a vessel for the soul but I missed her warm presence as much as her gentle spirit. I used to love reading until she slept, keeping watch over her, then at last curling into the warmth of her back and hair and closing my own eyes. Now my bed was empty and comfortless. Even the faint smell of the lavender water we used on her linen had faded.

My sorrow was nothing compared to my lady's. She went mad with it. She had lost three sons and two daughters before Anne so her daughter was her very best-loved thing, her dearest hope on earth. She cared for Anne more than anybody or anything, and because Anne was not strong she feared all through her childhood that some illness would carry her off. Just as she thought she had her safe set on the next path in life, with a marriage to be arranged, something came for her.

She believed that something came from me. I was the agent of Anne's destruction. I fell ill first, so I harboured whatever seeds of sickness took root in her and killed her. I did not realise what all this meant when I first woke from my fever, but I soon learned.

Two weeks passed and while I was able to sit up in bed, I still spent most of the day sleeping, wandering in strange places. One day I woke from a dream with my mother's voice very clear in my ear, as if she was right beside me, calling my name.

When I opened my eyes, I sat up in a fright. There was a corpse standing in the room with me. A terrible old woman, wrapped in shrouds of white, glaring at me by the door. Her face was grey and sunken, her mouth pulled down, her eyes worse than empty.

When a ruby on her finger flashed in the light from the window I recognised her. It was my lady's ring. It was my mistress standing there, struck with some curse. As she took a tottering step towards me, the shawl fell back from her head and I saw she had lost half her hair. What remained had turned stark white and clung in thin strands to her scalp. Truly she was like a corpse, dragged out of the earth and set in motion.

"You bitch," she said as she came toward me, her voice a rasping whisper. "You black bitch, you. Throw you in the street for the dogs. I'll kill you myself; I'll tear out your eyes—"

She came crying and stumbling toward me, groping at her

shawls in an attempt to cast them away. I could not move. She was coming to kill me but I could not move from the bed. I was paralysed with fear at this apparition.

She was almost on me before I began to scramble away, then she grabbed at my arm and fell on me. Her thin hands grasped at my face and her white wrappings trailed over me, the smell of sickness rising from them. I flung up my arms against her as her nails scraped my face. She reached for my eyes, cursing me and dragging at me as if she was pulling me down into the grave with her.

"You cuckoo, your mother was a witch. Lilith mother of whores. Why should Anne die and you live. You ink, you night, you crow, you carrion crow. You peck at her eyes. I will take out your eyes, I will take them out—"

Suddenly the weight and stink of her was lifted away from me. My lord had come into the room and was pulling her back from the bed. He held her tight to him, but though she was too weak to struggle free she still cursed and wailed at me, stretching her arms out for me as he carried her out of the room.

I sat back in my bed trying to catch my breath. The horror of it all rushed over me, turning my stomach, and I lay over the edge of the bed vomiting bile. My body understood what had happened before my mind did.

I never saw her again. My master separated us, moved me from the house for my own protection and for his wife's health. I was taken to the porter's tower by the gate, where Kate and the porter's wife, Margaret, put me to bed upstairs in the little garret room.

With Kate's help, Margaret tended to me while I recovered. My lady had the best knowledge of physic but they could not ask her help. When I asked after her, Kate shook her head. "She's wandering," she said, without looking at me. "Not herself."

I slept most of the time. For weeks, doing anything more than sitting up and taking in some broth sent me plunging deep into exhaustion, my spirit lost in some murky abyss. I could not even go to Anne's burial. November trod sadly into December, the days like a funeral march. Christmas passed unmarked, another bleak day without her. Sometimes I could not tell if I were awake or asleep. My long, feverish dreams rambled out into the room and peopled it with devils, angels, and monsters.

One day in mid-January it was sunny and I felt a little better. I sat up in bed, watching tree-shadows dance on the wall and moving my fingers in my hair, trying to work out the knots. No-one had tended my hair for weeks and hidden under my nightcap it had grown out all tangled in clumps.

There were footsteps on the stairs, then Kate came in with a bowl of pottage. She drew in a breath at the sight of me.

"Merciful Mary, you look lightning-struck. Your hair is all a-pudder. Come, let me mend it. Where's your comb? Where is the oil?" And she set down the bowl and started to work on me.

The space was more private than any I'd had in my life, for the porter's wife worked out at the brewhouse and my room was right at the top of the house. We were all alone and peaceful while Kate worked at the knots and picked out nits, sucking in her teeth at the number she found—the linen in that room was not clean. As her hands moved in my hair I began to weep; her touch was so kind it hit my heart.

I tried not to let her see it but after a while she paused in her work and stroked my head. Kate was never usually so gentle and this unaccustomed softness from her only made me cry harder.

"Come, little lamb. Anne is with God, and weeping is no remedy."

Her own voice was unsteady but in a minute she began to search my hair again, the familiar movement a comfort to us both.

"My little labour-in-vain," she said, and I half smiled. Kate called me that when I was small, for the old proverb about labouring in vain to wash an Ethiop white. The nickname had always stung, though I knew Kate meant it affectionately.

"How I laboured with your hair, child," Kate said. "Your mother had so many ways of plaiting it and fixing it up. She tried to teach me, but my fingers lacked her speed and skill. I did try, after she died. I could only manage the braids and it never looked so well. Your poor little head under my fumble-fingers." "

The sun was warm on the coverlet and I closed my eyes, thinking of my mother. For a brief moment I imagined it was her hands in my hair, soft and swift. Kate hummed as she worked and a robin sounded its glass notes on the vine beneath my window.

At last Kate sighed and stopped. She smoothed my hair again and leaned her head against mine, then she turned me to look at her. There were deep shadows under her eyes and lines of exhaustion. Her tired face was as dear to me as Anne's had been.

"They took the master in last week," she said, "for harbouring priests. What cruelty, to do it at such a time. They did it on purpose, thinking to take him when he is low. He is released without charge, but he is not himself Suky and I doubt he ever will be again, any more than Lady Katherine will be."

The corners of her mouth tugged down as she spoke. She was fighting to keep the tears down.

"What did they do to him? Did they hurt him?"

"No rack, no manacles, nothing of that sort, but it was torture enough to take him from home with his wife sick and his daughter dead. And now they've made it plain he's suspected he's afraid for all the household."

"Oh, Kate... oh, Kate," was all I could say, and we held each other close for a while. I felt I sat in the heart of an earthquake, with my home flung in lumps and pieces of stone around me—my family broken on the ruins. I clung so tight to Kate that when at last she drew away a little I saw my fingernails had left marks on her arm.

"My lord is thinking of you, Suky," she said. "He has not forgotten you. He is coming to speak to you later."

She took out her handkerchief and wiped my face, drying the tears away even as more fell.

"Such a pretty babe you were," she said. "Fat and sweet as an apple. I remember the night you came here. Your mother looked like she'd been pulled from a shipwreck, all dripping wet in the hall and clutching you close. Her eyes were so fierce they scared people, but I could see she was afraid herself. The thought of being dragged over the sea to a new world, with a baby to care for!"

She sighed again, took in a breath and gathered herself up into briskness again. She gave me a last pat on the shoulder and said, "I must go back now. The master will be up soon. Remember Suky—he is not as he was."

She leaned in and kissed me once on the cheek, with that same unaccustomed gentleness, and then she was gone.

CHAPTER 5

I lay back down in the narrow bed and waited for my master with a feeling of cold dread. Until now Framfield had been a haven. I had believed the world beyond us would not breach our doors. Lost in my own wandering thoughts, I had been quite cut off from all the machinery of the world, thinking with the selfishness of youth that my own calamity had broken the whole mess of wheels and cogs.

Of course it had been turning coldly and smoothly without me, as it does. That freezing winter, while birds sucked snow from the ivy-leaves, the Privy Council sat in their furs round a polished table and produced a carefully worded trap.

The new Act declared it treason to withdraw the Queen's subjects from their natural obedience to her or to convert them 'for that intent' to the Romish religion. It turned faith into a crime against the state.

The trap had been laid to catch a particular pair of Catholics—Edmund Campion and Robert Persons—Jesuit priests who had come into England last summer on a mission from Rome to bring comfort to English Catholics. Other holy fathers might pray or hear mass with individual households but they had set up a secret printing press, from which they sent out words like cannonshot across the Queen's bows, proclaiming the Catholic cause from the very heart of the realm.

There had not been such a stir, such a spring of hope in my lifetime. My lady read their texts to us out loud as we sewed; manuscripts sent to us by other Catholics in a secret chain of hope, reaching from household to household. Some printed, some painstakingly copied out by hand. One I learned by heart. Campion's Challenge to the Privy Council, that read like a declaration of war against the Church of England:

> *...be it known to you that we have made a league—all the Jesuits in the world, whose succession and multitude must overreach all the practice of England—cheerfully to carry the cross you shall lay upon us, and never to despair your recovery, while we have a man left to enjoy your Tyburn, or to be racked with your torments, or consumed with your prisons. The expense is reckoned, the enterprise is begun; it is of God; it cannot be withstood. So the faith was planted: So it must be restored.*

It is of God; it cannot be withstood. I felt those words deeply. These men came prepared to die for us—for every soul in England—and they were in danger of their lives as soon as they set foot in the country. They claimed they came only to save souls, but the Privy Council saw two traitors, heralding a flood of priests come to burrow into men's homes, hearths, and wives like poison toadstools. Houses from York to Sussex were rumoured to be as stuffed with them and their Romish blasphemies as fleas in mattress-ticking, so that if Philip of Spain sent his armies over the Channel the whole country would collapse, undermined by Jesuit woodworm. Those Catholics like my master, who had tried to balance themselves between betraying their faith and offending the Queen, read the terms of the Act, heard its teeth snap, and shivered.

The sun was going West when my master came to visit me at last. I saw he was indeed changed too, though not so horribly as my lady. He looked older and paler, the red of his cheeks eaten away to a network of thin, rosy veins. His riding-jacket hung loose on his shoulders and his steps were slow, nothing like his usual bouncing walk.

He drew up a chair beside the bed and took my hand. His mouth moved, as if he were struggling to smile or speak, but only a choked sound came out. Then he put his free hand over his face and began to weep. He sat there with his shoulders shaking and the tears rolling out from under his hand. I was all emptied of tears but I pressed his hand with my fingers. His skin was cold and soft where usually he ran hot, his humours out of balance.

"Forgive me," he said at last, his hand still over his eyes and his voice all warped with tears. "I have lost you all. My lady—"

At last he looked at me, blinking teardrops from his short, pale lashes. His eyes were red and dim. There was no blame in them and no hostility, but there was no comfort either. A pit had swallowed his wife and daughter and he had no strength left to try and pull me back from the edge too.

It is a commonplace that the wheel of Fortune turns quickly and can drop you as suddenly as it raises you. Until it actually happens to you it is impossible to understand what that drop feels like. As I listened to him speak I felt as if I was falling from a tree at night, with no idea how far away the ground was.

"I have prayed and struggled for a way to see you safe out of this calamity," he said. "I have been praying for our whole household. They took me in, you know, to question me. There is a new Act passed, to catch us all. The times are more severe now, bladed and whetted. It grows harder for me to keep us all safe. I have not told the household yet but I—I expect to be arrested any day. My lands are to be held from me while I am in prison and my cousin Robert will run the estate."

I sat up in bed and held his hand tighter.

"Sir—how can it be? How can they take it from you?"

"Oh, it is all in law, little lamb, written down, sealed and signed."

We sat in silence a moment. This was disaster piled on disaster. What test of God's was this, to prove our faith? I was speechless.

"My cousin, you know, is an avowed Protestant now and unmarried," said my master at last. He did not look at me as he spoke. "He has offered for your hand, Susan."

I stared now. His cousin Robert was forty-odd, a stocky huntsman whose choleric features mimicked my lord's but were as brass to his gold. His smiles were feigned, his good humour false. I had seen him whip a servant boy to blood, for a trifle. To be his wife would be to take a cup of poison.

"No, sir," I said.

"You would be safe," he said. "He is Protestant, he cannot be touched. You could stay at Framfield. My lady—my lady will go to the Dower House, with her maidservants."

He stumbled on his words a little and I held myself upright in the bed, though my eyes were full and brimming. For a moment I felt suffocated again, as if my lady's skeleton arms were on me and her white robes swathing me like a shroud.

"Must I marry him? If I am to stay?"

"There is no 'must'," he said. "You might stay and serve in the house. But I will have no power Susan, none..."

"I see," I said. "I see." I saw myself serving a man I disliked and under greater surveillance from the pursuivants, now they had caught my master. Kate would try to protect me from cousin Robert's attention, but what if she could not?

"There is another path," he said, hesitantly. "There is a man in

London who sends me many of our forbidden books. John Charlewood, a printer and a staunch Catholic. You have met him, though you may not remember him. He stayed here once. His sister married a Lewes man. A dark, smiling sort of man who dresses like a player. He has an acute mind and he is busy about God's work. He keeps many Catholics supplied with words of comfort. He is a good man and a brave one."

"I remember him," I said. He had stayed with us two days over Michaelmas, bringing with him manuscripts he'd copied out himself. We talked several hours after supper and I had enjoyed hearing about his work in London, all the booksellers around St. Paul's and the rivalry between different groups of printers. He had read widely though he was not a gentleman or much educated. His work, I supposed, brought him many chances to read new philosophies.

"Well then," said my master. "His wife died last year. He has no children and he wants to marry again—a Catholic woman who can read and write and work beside him for our cause. He has already helped Campion and Persons in their mission and I have no doubt will continue to do so."

He looked at me now with an expression that was almost hopeful.

"If you were agreeable, Suky," he said, "you could marry him. You could do God's work in London. I think you would be safer there than Framfield. I know—I know it is not a match we would ever have considered but I fear for us all. Charlewood is a good man. If you could like him—I would see you happy, Suky, wherever you go. There is no happiness here and I do not know if there ever will be again."

I looked at him again, his sad broken face and his slumped shoulders, and thought of all the times he and my lady had stood together against the pursuivants, strong in their faith and made stronger by one another. There was a hole opening in my heart, black and burning like a fire in paper.

A man in London, not even a man in Sussex. When I thought of marriage, I had imagined a house near Framfield. Perhaps a servant on one of the other great estates, or even another Sussex ironmaster with enough money for a library and stables. Close enough for my children and Anne's to know and love one another. I could not imagine myself living in London. I belonged here, as much as the apple trees in the orchard, and if they dug me out of this earth I would surely wither away.

Besides, I had been brought up to run a large household. I should be matched to a man with such a state. To marry a printer, even one such as Charlewood, was not something I ever dreamed of. And he was old—twenty years older than me, at least.

Yet, what else was I to do? I could not marry my lord's cousin—a Protestant and a devil and himself at least 40 years on this earth. I had liked John Charlewood when I met him. He was courteous and kindly and a man of intelligence. Built on good lines, a man of energy. I told myself these things and tears began to run down my face. I let them fall and drip down onto the coverlet.

"Will you pray with me, sir?" I asked him. "I must ask for guidance. I cannot—I cannot see my way clear."

"Of course, Suky," he said, and he knelt beside my bed and clasped my hands. I bowed my own head and closed my eyes and called for help from the Blessed Virgin.

We stayed there a long while. So he had prayed with me since I was a little girl, when he called me little black lamb, for I was wild and skippish when I was small.

I took comfort from the warmth of his hands, from the sound of our breathing and the words I knew by heart—in my heart, in my blood and bone. *Ego tali animatus confidentia, ad te, Virgo Virginum, Mater, curro, ad te venio, coram te gemens peccator assisto. I fly unto thee, O*

Virgin of virgins my Mother; to thee do I come, before thee I stand, sinful and sorrowful. I called to the Virgin and to my own mother and they answered me. There in the darkness was a still small flame, a light to follow.

At last I opened my eyes and said to my lord:

"I will marry John Charlewood. I trust that a match you make for me will be a good one and I will remain your servant for the rest of my life, no matter where I live or work."

He nodded at me and blinked and I saw the tears filling his eyes again.

When he had left me I sat and tried to comprehend the change I was to undergo. I could not. I understood nothing but the agony in my chest, where my heart had burned away.

One of my lord's favourite phrases from Horace came to mind. It was supposed to be a comfort in hard times: *Cease to ask what the morrow will hold and count as gain each day that Fortune grants*. It thudded in my ears like earth clods falling on a coffin and brought me no solace at all.

CHAPTER 6

The day I went to London, Kate shook me awake in the early hours of a freezing January morning, repeating my name in a hoarse whisper. I hit out at her as I woke and she held me tight.

"Child, it's only me. Hush now. Come—come with me now. You must say goodbye to the master."

"Goodbye?"

"The men have come for him—he is being arrested. Be quick Suky."

She had set a lantern on the chair by my bed and in its light I saw her face streaked with tears. The night was deep and silent, mid-way between Epiphany and Candlemas. The heart of winter. I was too much asleep to be afraid, but as Kate pulled back the covers the cold struck me like sheet ice. I shuddered but let her help me out of bed and into my thick winter cloak. Downstairs by the door my boots waited for my freezing toes.

Together we crossed the lawn up to the big house. The grass was rimed with frost that sparkled in the lantern light, and the soft glow from the windows of the Great Hall and my master's bedroom. A hedgehog stopped still as our lantern shone onto it, curling itself into a spiny ball. I wished I could do the same. I was awake now and understood what was happening. I was desperate to see my master but also felt the cold point of a pick ready to shatter my home for good and always. This moment was the blow that would break us.

When we came into the Great Hall there was my master, standing, and four men with staves around him. They were Justices of the Peace—men who had dined with us, neighbours, but now they stared straight ahead with stern eyes and did not smile at me.

"Suky," said my master, and I ran to him. One of the men moved nervously but the other touched his arm to hold him back.

My master held me tight a long moment and kissed my forehead. "God be with you, my dear girl," he said. "God be with you."

I did not want to let him go. I clung on with my face against his coat, his old riding-coat that smelled of smoke and the stables and cold weather. He had carried me in his arms a hundred times, wearing that coat: when I was very small and scraped my knees on the cobbles, when I fell asleep by the library fire and he carried me off to bed though my lady protested I should walk, when he lifted Anne and I up one in each arm and roared at us like a bear. The smell was the smell of home and comfort. What comfort would he have, in prison? When his home was no longer his own, his wife exiled in her madness, his cousin sitting in his seat by the fire?

At last I stepped away. He kissed Kate, then nodded to the men. They walked him away down the Great Hall to the wide oak doors. We followed and watched as they mounted their horses and rode down the drive to the gates where I would soon be standing, awaiting my own journey to London. Kate and I held each others' hands tight as the horses trotted through the gates and away. I felt in my heart he would never come home again. I choked and sobbed but Kate squeezed my hand tighter.

"That's no help, Suky. We must be steel. We must be stone. Come, I must dress you properly for your journey, and I have some things for you. Oh, that they should take him from his own home! With Anne dead, and my poor Lady Katherine run mad!" All her resolve broke and she wept and wept in the freezing air. We were a pair of waterfalls then, holding each other close until our tears stopped at last. Then we made our way back to the porter's lodge.

There was an urgency now to my departure. They had taken only my lord this time, but surely they would return to question the rest of the household and I was one of the closest people to him. Kate helped me dress, cursing her fingers that stumbled in the cold air. I began to cry again and could not stop, and this rallied Kate a little.

"I have some things for you," she said, when her voice was calm again. "Your mother left them with me when she died. She told me to look after them and give them to you when you were full-grown. She was wandering somewhat by the time she gave it me, talking half in English and half in her old language but I understood the most of it.

"She said it is what's left of your inheritance and that they are precious. The only reason I've not given them to you before is I wasn't wholly sure they were Christian. I didn't want to hand on anything heathen. But I've seen you grow up and I know you're a good Christian. These might remind you of your mother—something to take with you. Something of your old home."

She reached into her pocket and gave me two small objects that fitted into the palm of my hand. They were about the size of our chess-pieces. One was a little, square, bronze block with what looked like a ladder done in relief on the top and the other was a bronze figurine. A long-legged bird like a heron, standing on a small pyramid, with its head turned gracefully back so that its beak met its tail-feathers.

I picked it up. It was about as long as my index finger. A solid weight, heavy enough and satisfying to hold. The dull bronze came alive in the candlelight.

"What are they?" I asked.

Kate shook her head. "I don't know. Such little things, but when she was dying she kept turning to them, making sure they were still by the bed. She told me a dozen times that I must give them to you when you were grown. I think she began to forget she was in England. She called you by your old Guinea name and it took me a while to understand she meant you—I'd forgotten it, it was such a slippery word to say."

"What was it? My old name?"

I had never thought to ask what I was called before they christened me. I did not even know I had a name when I was carried out of Guinea.

Kate closed her eyes and thought. "I can't remember the whole of it, it was such a babble of words. Shonwa. Shonowa? Pretty, but slippery. Susan was the nearest thing to it."

"Shonowa. Sho-no-wa. Susan."

The syllables were heavy and alien. A push, a hush, a negative; a lamentation. It sounded like a rush of grain being tipped into a pail. I wanted to put my hands into the letters and stir them. Sho-no-wa. It was not a name for me. Susan and Suky are workaday names. Shonowa sounded like sugar melting into butter, rain falling after a long drought.

I looked at the small bronze objects again.

"And she said these things were valuable?"

"I don't think she meant in money. But maybe it meant something more in Guinea. That's why I was afraid they were some Godless idols. Then I wondered if it could be something like your family crest? If she really was a princess, maybe you had a coat of arms like my lord and these were the pictures from it."

I gazed at the bird. Its carved eye peered back at me, opaque, giving nothing away.

"How will I ever know what it means?"

Kate put a hand on my shoulder. "Maybe you won't, child. Not all dying messages are clear or understood. But she left it with love, that's the thing to remember. Keep it for love."

I looked at the little things and was unsteadied by a surge of anger that rushed through me, so strong I almost threw them to the floor. I caught my breath and closed my hand around them so tight that they dug into my flesh. This was my mother's legacy, a puzzle I could never solve. I did not want it. I wanted her. I wanted Anne, and my lady, and my life here. I wanted living love, not some cold inheritance. I squeezed the things till my hand ached, and choked back my rage.

"Do you think she was a princess?" I asked Kate. She held up her hands.

"Lord knows. She held herself like one and many people here thought her proud and stomachy. If your crown falls off you must live like the rest of us, bareheaded. She acted as if there were still jewels shining on her forehead. She was dear to me, though."

I closed my eyes and saw my mother coming in from the rain to the great torch-lit hall that first night, walking tall and holding me to her for comfort. I said my old name aloud again: "Shonwa. Shonowa."

Lovely, whispery noises. Empty sounds, meaningless.

Kate looked at me with concern. "Let be, child. I don't want to add to your sorrows. These are only little gifts, that's all. Keep-sakes."

She glanced out of the window, where the sky was just beginning to grey at the edges.

"Suky," she said, and her voice shook a little. "It is time."

"No," I said. "I know it is God's will, Kate, but I can't, I can't!"

A sudden panic gripped me. Nothing around me was solid. The room tipped and swayed and the bed beneath me was air. Was this how my mother felt, when she was wrenched from her home into exile?

"I am falling, Kate," I said, "I am falling!"

Her arms came around me and she held me tight again.

"I have you, sweetheart," she said. "I have you safe. God is with you. You will not fall. You will not fall."

As she held me, the world slowly came back again. I felt my two feet on the boards, the bronze things pressed against the bones of my hand, Kate's arms holding me together.

"My lamb," she said at last, her voice rough with her own sadness. "You must make the best of this or bitterness will poison you as it has my lady, who is choked with such black melancholy. Put pain behind you. That is the only way to live with sorrow. Weep it out, then close the door and walk on with God's help. You have no mother on earth but the Blessed Virgin watches for you. She is watching you now and will walk with you wherever you go."

I nodded and rested my head against hers a moment. Then I tucked my mother's gifts into my pocket, wiped my eyes, and stood up.

"Let us go," I said. "I am ready."

Kate walked with me to the gate, and the porter carried down my trunk. Kate and I stood and waited, watching the moonlight glittering on the pale road beyond the gates. A thin crescent moon still hung in the West but a few birds were singing for daybreak.

As I stood breathing in the chill air, two of the estate foresters came walking down the path to the woods to cut firewood. I felt like a ghost watching the men go by. They began to sing as they walked out and I closed my eyes to listen. I wished I could dissolve there and then and vanish into the music. You cannot marry a song, you cannot hurt a sound.

I felt untethered from the world, altogether. My days had been very empty since I fell ill, partly because I was too weak to work and partly because I was no longer serving anybody. For nearly thirteen years my first and last thoughts of the day had been for Anne. I woke before her to prepare the clothes and jewels and adornments she would need for the day, and at night slept only when I had put them all away.

Now there was only myself. No-one to mould the day around, no mistress to fit clothes or arrange hair for. I felt often as if I might quite easily lose my grip on the earth and float away up to the spheres. I tried to bring my mind back to the day, the journey, and the destination.

I must have first seen London in my mother's arms. We travelled there from Plymouth to stay with John Hawkin's servant for a month and be fitted out with clothes and shoes and other gear before we went to Sussex. I don't know how we arrived but I imagine it was by water, on the long ferry from Gravesend, travelling up the Thames among the black river-dolphins. I imagine her holding me, wrapped in a shawl, looking up the river towards London Bridge with the sun coming up behind her. More likely there was no sun at all, everything wreathed in sea-fret and London mist and all she could see or taste was salt whiteness.

This time, my journey to London was to be by road. My master had paid for a carrier's cart to take us all the way to the city. I was to make the journey with Charlewood's sister, who lived near Lewes, and his new apprentice John Roberdine, a boatbuilder's son from Rye.

I did not know precisely what negotiations had passed between John Charlewood and my master, but I knew the dowry was paid, the banns were read, and the date was set. A week after I arrived in London, I would be married.

Now came the sound of wheels on the cold road, and a minute later the cart rounded the bend and drew up to the gates.

Up in the cart sat a woman all bundled up in blankets and a boy in a dark cloak.

"Are you John Charlewood's sister?" Kate called up to the woman.

"Mary Akehurst I am, and, for my sins, John Charlewood's sister," said the woman, "Is the girl here? We must be off, this cold is frightful."

"She is here," said Kate. "She has been ill, and is weak still. You must take care of her, you and your brother. I have friends in London and I will know if anything is amiss, do you hear me?"

"Well indeed, as if my brother would mistreat a wife, and him married twenty years before this without a scratch or slap and she was no milk pudding. Now put her up here—apprentice, you fetch up that trunk."

Kate turned back to me and we held each other tight one last time. She kissed my forehead and said quietly in my ear, "God knows if I ever loved anyone, I love you and Mistress Anne. Write to me, child, and I'll have it read to me. Write to me, if he is unkind. Safe journey. God be with you."

Then she pulled herself away from me with a gasp and set off up the lawns, walking fast and looking straight ahead. I watched her go and felt my whole throat swollen with the effort of holding back tears. Then I turned to face the cart and my future.

CHAPTER 7

I folded my hand around a letter in my pocket, which was my chief comfort on this bleak morning. It was from my master to John Charlewood and was all business, but on the reverse was a note for the priests, Campion and Persons, written in secret ink I had made up myself from one of my lady's recipes. My master sent them good will and a welcome in Sussex if ever they needed sanctuary. There was also gold for them. The coins were sewn into the sides of my bodice, so if anyone were to stab me, the knife would be turned back by a handful of angels.

The boy in the cart jumped down and helped the carter heave my chest in, the rest would follow after. The apprentice was only middling height and looked slight but he hauled the chest in without apparent effort. I let the carter help me into the cart and sat next to Mary while the men tied the trunk down at the back.

Mary pulled down one of her scarves and peered at me in the lantern-light as the carter climbed up behind the horse.

"Well met, sister Susan," she said. Then, reaching a hand out and taking mine, "You certainly are black—black as a burnt pot. Did you come from a very hot part of Africa? Why, your skin feels no different to mine," and she turned my hand back and forth.

I pulled my hand from hers, staring at her as if she had bitten me. I had never been spoken to so discourteously by a common woman. This woman, this low woman, was to be my sister. If one of our kitchen maids insulted me so, I would have slapped her. I was already so choked with sadness that it hurt to speak, and her insolence left me with no words at all. She looked away and settled her skirts over her knees, brushing away dust from the road.

"There now, I mean no insult. Only I never saw such a dark girl."

I had nothing to say to that, so I said nothing. I pulled my cloak around my shoulders and watched as the carter climbed back into his seat and readied the horses. The apprentice sprang back in too and sat down beside me.

"This is John Roberdine, but he won't answer to his proper name," said Mary, as if he was not there. "Only to 'Rob'. Fancies himself a seafarer."

I turned to nod at Roberdine, still unable to trust my voice.

"Good morrow, mistress," he said, and smiled.

His hair was cropped close to his head and he had no beard—he looked my age or even a little younger. His eyes were slanted and bold and he looked at me somewhat as if he recognised me, as if we were already familiar with one another and had no need of greetings. In the blanched light before dawn I could not tell what colour his eyes were, or his hair, but his voice was warm and he spoke well. He smiled at me and his eyes almost disappeared. I liked his face: he looked as if he would laugh often. I was still sore from Mary's speech but I thought of my lady, always so unflinching and brave before her collapse, and so perfect in her manners. I was to be mistress of a house now, and this boy was of my household. I found my voice and said:

"Good morning, Rob," as coolly and courteously as my lady

would have spoken, though it cost me dearly. Then the cart jolted as the horses began to move. Mary grabbed my arm to steady herself and I nearly fell sideways. Rob stopped us all from tumbling out, catching my hand in his. The touch of it set my pulse racing fast as a hare startled from the long grass, feet pattering the earth. I had never felt so aware of a person all through my skin and my lungs and throat. I had to look away from him and I glanced back at the house before I could stop myself. The starlight and faint moonlight shone pale on the glass window-panes, the new brick chimneys, the grey trunks of the beeches that grew behind the house. I felt a tearing in my chest, a sawing at the sinews of my heart.

I had told myself I would not look back, imagining that if I kept my eyes ahead like Orpheus leading Eurydice from the underworld, one day it would be restored to me. Like Orpheus, I couldn't help myself. I stared at my home, telling myself to remember every stone, until we rounded the corner and it was gone. I turned around again and sat up even straighter, fixing my eyes on the white ruts of the road ahead.

Before long the cart's jolting began to make my back ache, though it sent Mary to sleep. First her head nodded on my shoulder and then she slid down until she rested in my lap. I hated to be her pillow but it was more comfortable than her head banging against my shoulder so there I let her lie. We rode on as the moon and stars began to pale and birds sang in the hedges. In a while I saw that Rob was asleep too, his head nodding on his chest.

With no eyes on me, I let my tears fall, thinking of Kate holding me by the gate. I had always been loved at Framfield, lifted up and warmed in the certainty of that love. Now here I sat, flanked by strangers, on my way to marry a stranger. Anne was in her grave, my lady mad, my lord in prison. How had it come to this? What plan of God's was this? I prayed again for guidance, for all I could see was darkness. When I opened my eyes, Rob was awake again and watching me. I rubbed the tears away from my cheeks angrily and looked away from him.

"Charlewood's made in a different mould to that one," he said, glancing at the sleeping Mary. "They're nothing alike."

It stung that he was trying to comfort me.

"I know," I said. "I've met him."

"He and my father are old friends, somehow," he said. "He grew up with my mother. Now he's to make me into a printer and keep my boots on dry land. I like the man, but good luck to him."

"You would rather go for a sailor?" I asked.

"My father's a boatbuilder. I've been in and out of water since I was born, and I was born in the caul so I can't drown either. But now my father says I'm trampling on my mother's grave with the company I keep and so—off to London to find better company. What I've heard of London, it seems more likely I'll hang there than in Sussex but perhaps it'll please him if the rope is silk rather than hemp. I don't see why he cares either way—he hates me."

He spoke the words without rancour. I studied him closely. The sun was rising now, warming the winter sky with streaks of gold, and I could see him clearly at last. The light called out gold flecks in his green eyes and strands of red in his dark hair: cat colours, copper-beech colours. What was there to hate in him?

"Your father hates you?"

"I killed my mother. She died of some infection after I was born. And I have three older brothers, so what use is a fourth son? I don't take after him, either. My family's famous in Rye: the fighting Roberdines. Their fame has not reached the Weald? Well, they're great tawny brawlers, all of them except me. I'm not like them. Folk never believe I'm the fourth brother. I'm the changeling child."

Again there was no bitterness in his tone. He spoke as free and plain as if he were talking of some other person. His mother was dead, like mine, but he was not sad. His father wanted him out of the house, but he was not angry.

"Don't you care?" I asked. He squinted up at the cracks of gold in the sky as if he was pondering the question, then shrugged.

"What's the good of caring? I can't please my father. I can't turn myself into a charging golden bullock like my brothers. I could shed a sea of sweat and tears trying. I'd rather be free and do what I like and let them all go hang."

He spat over the side of the cart and tucked his hands under his armpits.

"If I don't freeze first. Aren't you cold, mistress?"

I shook my head. I had soft furs beneath my cloak and Mary's head was warm on my lap. My body was not cold, but the further we went from Framfield, the more frozen and stone-like my spirit felt. Heavy and cold and a thousand years old. Words felt like stones in my mouth too, hard and meaningless. Rob, with his bold talk and his quick movements, was a fire flickering beside me.

"Have you been in London before, mistress?" he asked now, and I tried to gather my wits.

"When I was a child," I said. "Once to the Shrovetide revels, before the queen."

"Was it very fine?"

"Very."

That was in the past, when the Queen still treated quiet and conformable Catholics almost as friends. The mistress had dressed us very carefully, Anne all in blue velvet and me in white, and she even bought little seed pearls to fix into my hair with wires. Everyone was dressed in such paradisiacal colours, their silks and satins and jewels playing tag with the torchlight.

The Queen sat in her chair at the far end of the hall, her face chalk white and her hair an autumn bonfire pile of red, framed by a ruff pinked with patterns as fine as frost. Sometimes she laughed and clapped and everyone around her laughed too, a ripple spreading out from her across the company.

She was the ruby at the centre of a gold necklace, the jewel completing the setting. You could not take your eyes from her sparkle and flash. She fascinated me in the same way as the spiders that lived in the wall at home. I would tickle their thick-spun webs with a grass-stem, then jump back screaming when they scuttled out of their holes, jaws up for the expected fly. I felt the same about the Queen, who was our ruler and the enemy of our faith. I wanted to run up and touch the wonderful crisped gold embroidery of her skirts and then run away again, screaming.

At the revels was a play, by one of the boy's companies—something set in a Sultan's court. I had watched it holding Anne's hand tight because there in the midst of the infidels, all Englishmen with their faces washed with coals, was a black musician, a trumpeter. A true African. The first black face I ever saw besides my own. *Is it your father?* whispered Anne, and I whispered back *No, my father is a king.* Still, I stared at him and wondered if he resembled my father. He was serious-faced and slender, and when he stepped forward for the fanfare the other musicians were silent.

I was so deep in my memories, the gold and pomp of that performance and the familiar feel of Anne's hand in mine, that I hardly noticed Rob was speaking again.

"The Gold Coast?" he said, and I stared at him, not fully taking in his words.

"Are you from the Gold Coast, mistress?" he repeated.

"Nearby," I said. "My mother was princess of a country inland."

"Is it so!" said Rob. "Do I call you Your Majesty, then, or no?"

"Do you see a crown on my head?" I said, suddenly irked by his talk, his light, mocking voice.

"No, but perhaps you travel incognito, like the Queen… I met a sailor who went out to Guinea on the first voyages, twenty years and more now."

"Indeed," I said.

"He came back with gold dust: he had some still, saved in a bag. He said the people there had chests and chests of it, nuggets of gold as yellow as the sun. They asked him if his mother washed his skin in milk and pinched his nose out to make it so long. Do you remember anything of the country, mistress?"

"I was a babe when they took us," I said. "I remember nothing."

"He said, way inland, there's even stranger countries," Rob continued. "The men have only one leg, or their eyes in their chests, or they file their teeth and eat people, like in the tales from Pliny."

"Those stories are old," I said. "No-one has ever seen such things with their own eyes. They're tales made up to frighten travellers."

"And why would they make up such horrors?" said Rob.

"It makes a better story," I said. "No-one wants to hear that men went all the way across the world and found other men just like them."

Rob laughed and looked at me sideways again, a swipe of those green eyes. He had a lithe energy and watchfulness about him, like a cat up in a tree keeping its eyes peeled for birds. John Roberdine would not be easily ruled and I wondered if my new husband realised the type of animal he was taking into his house.

"Aye," he said. "Sailors always add garnishing to their stories."

I knew very well that Roberdine was a danger to me and I should not converse with him alone. I had known it since the minute my hand touched his. But his voice was a Sussex voice that reminded me of home and it had a husk to it, a saltiness, like the sea.

The little bronze objects were safe in my pocket. I felt so strange about them—angry and helpless and yet also a kind of love. I could not bear to admit my ignorance about them. It was the fairy hour before day truly begins and we were still on the road. I was not yet a wife. Therefore I put the angels of my nature aside, brushing them away like so many dead leaves, and took out the little bronze bird.

I held it up in the early light, holding it tight so Rob would not try and take it from me. The shadows stood out in the lines of its feathers and it looked like gold.

"My mother left me this," I said. I hesitated, and then repeated what Kate had suggested to me. "It's a symbol of my family. It is a sign of my mother's royal blood."

Rob leaned in to look at the bird. He raised his hand as if to touch it and I moved my hand away again, putting it back in my pocket.

"A royal family," he said. "Were the rest of your family stolen away too, or are they still in Guinea?"

"I don't know," I said. "My brother was taken with us, but he died. For the rest, I don't know."

Suddenly exhausted again I said, "I must sleep now. I am very tired," and closed my eyes before he could say anything else.

The journey to London took all day, though we stopped to eat at a wayside inn stuffed with travellers. Our meal was a muddy and obscure stew with hard bread, the three of us fighting for elbow-room at the end of a long table. The smell of sweat and dust from the road, mingled with a hundred different perfumes and rotten breaths, was as strong as a punch in the head. I thirsted for the peace of my room at Framfield.

As we drew nearer London we found ourselves on the road with half the livestock of England, as if every farm in the South had come to bring tribute to the Queen. A herd of cows paced beside us, lowing and snatching at grass, while a cock someone was carrying crowed its head off. Despite the noise, Mary fell asleep again and snored.

At last, late that afternoon, we entered the city, through Southwark and over London Bridge. The stink of London reached us half a mile away, wafted on a cold north wind, and as we approached

Southwark it made a leap and plugged itself up my nostrils, as thick as bread.

Mary leaned out of the cart and, after haggling furiously, bought a bunch of lavender for us from a woman laden with herbs.

With the smell came something else. A crackle and jolt of life like the air before a thunderstorm, the pulse and breath of a thousand people moving about the city. I swear I could feel it before we even reached the houses of Southwark. It called to me and woke me up. It was not like the dream of London in my head, all glitter and majesty. It was rougher, more violent and more alive.

I sat up, my skin prickling all over. I glanced at Rob and saw he was sitting up too, like a cat sniffing roasting meat, looking all about him.

"London," he said.

"London," I replied, and taking off my gloves, stretched out my hands in front of me, easing away the travel stiffness. I broke off a sprig of the lavender and passed it to Rob, and as he took it his bare skin brushed mine again. My heart swooped like a fish rising, a swallow diving. I stared down at my lap and pulled my gloves carefully back on over my hands, breathing, trying to catch myself, but it was too late. I felt again as if I were falling. I closed my eyes and thought of Kate, and all afresh could not fathom that I had lost her, that I had lost Framfield, that I was truly in London and my life was changed forever.

"Are you well, mistress?" said Rob, his voice close by, and I shook my head a little.

"I am dizzy. I—"

"If you look now," he said, "you will see London Bridge."

I opened my eyes and looked, and the sight jolted me out of my giddiness. The sinking sun lit the coloured bricks and turrets of the high, noble houses built all along the bridge and the roaring water pushing through the arches. The red sunlight through the evening mists gave radiance to the wide river Thames and the crowd all around us. It was a marvel.

I held my lavender sprigs under my nose and stared at the river as it poured out from under the arches of the bridge and curled back, foaming like a lion's mane and roaring like the lion itself, a huge, belly-deep thunder.

As we approached the gate a black crow rode the wind above us. I followed its curving flight, remembering my mother's love for them. Everyone else curses them for carrion birds, killers of lambs, but she always saw them as omens of good luck. It's one of the few things I remember of her.

The crow swooped down to the gate and perched on a discoloured lump on top of the arch. I looked closer and saw that it was a leg on a spike. Discoloured and stuck full of holes, you could tell it was a leg only from the way the knee still bent. The crow bent to tear off a beakful of flesh. This bird did not look lucky to me.

With a jolt the cart began to move faster and away we rolled. I caught Roberdine's eye as we stared at the approaching gate and its crown of traitor's leg. The crow threw its head up and cawed.

"London is vile," said Mary, half to herself, pressing the lavender close into her nostrils, and in another minute we were on the bridge and fighting our way into the great city. The red light and the noble view vanished as the cart rumbled into a tunnel beneath one of the houses.

It was chaos. Shops and stalls along the bridge pressed in on either side, cattle bumped and shat beside us and buildings shut out the light. London buzzed around me, a humming, roaring, rustling beehive; dark with old, crumbling wax and fragments of death, and the people like bees crawling over one another in the honeycomb.

CHAPTER 8

John Charlewood lived and worked at the sign of the Half-Eagle and Key, in the street called Barbican in the north-west of London. Barbican lies outside the city walls and out of the city's jurisdiction, in the old liberty beyond Cripplegate. I had heard that the suburbs beyond London Wall were riddled with danger and disorder, and as we drew near Cripplegate and the day darkened I began to feel a pressing unease.

The streets were emptying, householders turning in for supper and the last traders from the surrounding villages walking towards the gates of London, baskets balanced on their heads and still crying their remaining wares. It was the last, straggling exodus of the roaring caravan that had swept us along that morning. Now it abandoned the city as the light did. Dusk came in fast, the low roofs overhead breeding shadows.

At Cripplegate the cart stopped. The gate's archway was too low and narrow for it to take us further. Rob waved at two boys idling beside the gate and I gave them a halfpenny each, one to help with the chest and one to walk ahead with a lantern.

"Not far now," said Mary as we clambered down from the cart

onto the mercifully dry road. "Are you hearty, sister Susan?"

"Very," I said, though the air had grown cold as a corpse's kiss and Cripplegate looked low and mean. I would have given my right hand if the carter would turn about and take me back to Framfield, away from this narrow road with my husband waiting at the end of it. But this was my home now, so I followed Mary and the boys under the arch of the gate and into the twilit suburbs where all the evils of London were said to lurk.

The ringing of bells nearby startled me and I turned to see a church-tower rising up against the sky. Was that St Giles Cripplegate, where I was to be married? The bells sang on, the ringers practising their rounds. Around us and over us leaned the houses, packed close all around.

I stayed with Mary as we picked our way along. Shops were closing, lanterns being taken from porches and windows barred, while over our heads the little first-story windows flared with rush-lights. Men sitting on benches outside a tavern rocked and sang. I pulled my hood up around my face to avoid the eyes of these my new neighbours, who cast curious glances at our procession.

John's house was at the very end of the row. Beyond it lay a flat expanse of fields where a mist was rising, white and chill. Marking the very edge of the city and beginning of the wild, a black, tumbledown tower slouched against the sky. It had an evil aspect in that light, looming taller than any of the houses pestered together around us.

"What's that great building?" I asked Mary, staring.

"The Barbican watchtower," she replied. "John says it was built by those old Romans. I hate the look of it. I wouldn't live so close to it, there's all kinds of vagrants and masterless men sleep there at nights."

At last we stopped outside John's house. It was tall, spindly, and knock-storied as every other building in that street but set apart by its position at the end of the row. There were no other houses facing it, and a low building jutted out from the side towards the fields, perhaps an outhouse or stables.

In the light from the boy's lantern I could just make out the wooden sign that hung by the door, proclaiming John's business. The sign showed a circle, halved, with an eagle on one side and a key on the other. Around the circle ran the words *Post tenebras lux*. After darkness, light. A good omen?

"Here we are, sister Susan," said Mary, not without malice. "This is your new home. A mite smaller than your old one, but I'm sure my brother keeps a good table."

She stepped up to the door and knocked firmly. I took a breath, and prepared to meet my husband. After a moment the door swung open, but the person in the doorway was a tiny girl wrapped in a vast white apron. She was even smaller than me but her eyes were huge and her expression fierce, like the young tawny owls that perch on fences and gates at dusk and shout 'Kewick!' as if they were ten times bigger. She looked us all over with suspicion.

"Grace," said Mary. "Is my brother within?"

"Yes, madam," said the girl. Her voice, small and sharp, matched her size. Grace was the name of John's maid, I remembered. "Come in, quick, there's supper on the table. Master's working just now."

"This is Susan, John's new wife," said Mary, standing aside so Grace could see me. Her face remained hostile.

"Madam," she said, without the flicker of a smile.

"God be with you, Grace, I am glad to meet you," I said. She blinked, and then ushered us through into the house.

"Up the stairs and to the left," she told Rob and the boy still hefting my chest. "And be quick about it. I must shut the house for the night."

She waited by the door until they came back downstairs again, then she shooed the boy out, banged the door shut behind him with surprising strength and locked, bolted, and barred us in.

"A man was stabbed at the Grapes last week," she said. "These dark nights bring them out like rats. Come through now."

She led us through a door on the right into a good-sized kitchen. A fire burned on an open hearth large enough for roasting on. There was a big oak table set out for supper with a long settle-back chair against the wall behind it, a dresser full of crockery by the hearth, and a chest under the window that looked over the street. The floor was wooden and strewn with rushes and the room looked clean and well-ordered. It was a pleasant cottager's kitchen, but its smallness pressed in on me. This was now my estate. No Great Hall, no Long Gallery. No lawns, no mare, no hawk. No library. No Anne. I could not breathe. I rested one hand on the table and held myself upright, clutching the bird weight in my pocket until the constriction at my throat eased.

Rob and Mary stood by me, casting glances at the bread and cheese and pewter jug of ale, while Grace hopped up onto the chest under the window and drew the shutters and bars across.

"Are there many thieves here?" I asked as she stepped back down again, brisk as a grasshopper.

"London's a nest of thieves," she said, not looking at me. "But it's middling bad here. Someone got in last year and made off with half the plate. We're hard by Finsbury Fields and that's wormy with beggars and coggars and old soldiers living under hedges. It's a pretty place for a Sunday walk though. Will you sit down and eat? The master will be up in a moment."

I sat down gratefully on the settle-back, next to Mary, and looked at the table in front of me set with ordinary kitchen things. A board for the bread, a knife, and a cup. My husband would be here soon. My mouth was dry and my lips cracked after the journey.

I put my hands round the cup in front of me while Grace poured the ale. The pewter was cool under my fingertips and when

I tasted the ale it was cold and good and grassy with hops. None of us spoke. Opposite me, Rob tore into the bread as if it was his last meal.

I glanced at Mary, who was biting into a hunk of bread and cheese. Strands of her straw-colour hair were escaping from her coif and the travel dirt had settled in the lines of her face. She looked like a peasant come in from a day's labour in the fields, thinking only of her stomach. What if her brother were like her?

I watched in a travel-weary haze as Grace moved around, preparing for the night. Everything was dreamlike and dim in the firelight. She went to the back of the kitchen, knelt down and heaved up a trapdoor, propping it up on wooden arms. She had said the master would be 'up'. Did he live in the cellar, in the dark, like a bat?

For a moment I thought of Mr Fox, the monster from one of Kate's tales who kept a room full of butchered wives. John Charlewood had my marriage portion. Was it all a ruse to take my master's money and then cut me to pieces and bury me here? I could see the black pit, walls dripping with blood, and the man waiting for me in the dark with the axe-blade. I shook my head; I was half asleep and spinning nightmares for myself.

A cold draught breathed into the kitchen from the hatch, and with it a faint scraping sound. I put down my cup and Rob swivelled round on his stool to look at the hole in the kitchen floor.

There were creaking steps and a wavering light shining up from the floor, and then a man's head suddenly appeared at floor level, rising up out of the hatch as if the Devil from Hell in a mummer's play. The lantern light from above cast strange shadows on him as he clambered out of the cellar. The scarce light whetted the angles of his cheeks and nose but his eyes were pooled in darkness. I thought wildly of Aeneas in the underworld, climbing up out of a grave.

Then came three loud raps at the door, and Mary jumped and gasped, spilling her cup. Amber ale flooded over the table but no-one else moved. The man at the hatch froze. The raps were not neighbourly knocks, but the banging of a stick or a stave.

Without speaking, the man clambered swiftly out into the kitchen, put down the lantern and closed and fastened the hatch. He came to the table and placed the lantern in front of me, smiling as he saw me. I stared at him. Not a devil, now he was in the soft kitchen firelight, only a lean, dark-haired man in the mid-forties with a neat, dark beard flecked with grey. My husband, John Charlewood. His eyes were hazel brown, his face was lined and weathered and the skin at his jaw was just starting to drape into slackness, but when he smiled his face lifted as if tugged by guy-ropes and lines fanned around his eyes.

There was another bang at the door, and Charlewood cleared his throat.

"Who's there at this hour?" he called out.

"Searchers," came the muffled reply from outside. "Open up, Charlewood."

My husband-to-be grimaced and muttered "Again?" Then he unbolted and unlocked the door and swung it open, letting in a wash of night air and two men with staves.

"Must it always be when I am at table, sirs?" he said. "My bride is this minute arrived from Sussex and she is tired and hungry. Did you not do your job thoroughly enough last week, that you must come beating down my door and disturbing my household after curfew?"

One of the men, a great, Dutch-looking, tow-headed fellow, looked over at us. He looked at me twice.

"Sussex?" he said. "Surely she's come further than that?"

At that Grace gave a hoot of laughter that showed her gap-teeth and transformed her whole face with fierce merriment. She stifled it quickly as we all looked at her, putting her hand to her mouth and turning aside.

"Susan is a native of Guinea," said John coldly. "Now, take your eyes from my wife and do your work as you must. You'll find no pirate copy here."

"Well then," said the smaller man, "let us go about our business, John, and we'll be gone as soon as we can—if we find everything as it should be."

"You are my honoured guests," said John with a sour grin, folding his arms. "Where will you start?"

"The cellar, please," said the small man, bluntly.

"Grace," said John, "Let these men into the cellar. Take the lantern, so they may see clearly there is nothing hiding in it but mice."

Rob, Mary, and I watched as Grace went to open up the hatch and the men followed her. John went with them down into the blackness, and there followed a great deal of bumping and scraping.

My mouth was bone-dry again. There was certainly something concealed in that cellar that those men must not discover. As the two searchers went down into the cellar, Rob suddenly swung back round on his stool and took another great bite of his bread and cheese. I had no appetite left for mine. I stood up instead and went to fetch a cloth hanging from the dresser to mop up the spilled ale.

This was a strange place but a familiar feeling. The fear of discovery and the need to hide the fear, to be calm and quiet and everyday so the hunting dogs could not smell terror or sweat, or catch the flicker of a guilty eye. We Papists are seen as predators, wolves and kites, but I have only ever felt myself to be prey.

CHAPTER 9

We three in the kitchen did not look at one another as we listened to the noises below. I have never lived in a home free from suspicion. A home where men do not come in armed with sticks, turn out your store-cupboard, strew your very clothes over your floors, and look into every private thing you own. I have never known what it is to live in a land where you are not the enemy. It must be a very sunny, carefree existence.

I settled almost gratefully into that state of fear I know so well while John led the men around the house and we pretended to eat our supper like an innocent, law-abiding, Protestant household.

At length they were done, and John let them out of the front door again with the sour grin still on his face. He locked the door behind them and then stood for a moment, staring at the planks in front of him, listening. Then he turned abruptly and came to the table.

First he kissed Mary, and then he came over and took my hands and kissed me on the mouth. His lips were warm and dry and set no spark in me. My heart did not jump but sat level in my chest, beating in time. Well, perhaps that was all the better. Love had brought me nothing but pain so far.

John stood back and studied me. I returned the stare, taking him in. I had remembered him well. He was drawn of lean lines and light movements, and the keen strokes of his face were pleasant. The lines at his eyes showed that he smiled honestly. That was good. What a small store of hope to grasp at, that a man's eyes show he smiles honestly. I was flooded with relief that he was not deformed or hideous to look at, but there was Rob across the table watching me and it was his look that warmed me, not John's.

"Well met, wife," said John at last. I wondered what he thought of me. Had he seen me clearly when we last met? Had he painted me a beauty, or was my youth enough to please him? "I am truly sorry for the poor welcome."

"Well met, sir," I said. "Your welcome is balm after a long journey." The words sounded too formal even as I spoke them, but how else could I address him? I did not know him.

"And the sight of you is balm after the sting of those insects," he replied. "Back they come, again and again, like wasps to rotten pears. *Sciocchi*! Fools. At least they have a season to their movements. If they have come once tonight, they won't come again." He rubbed his hands over his face, and looked at Rob, ending our stilted greetings.

"And you are Rob? Well, I suppose this is as fitting a start to your apprenticeship as any. Come. I didn't intend to bring you into the thick of things so soon, but Fate has thrown the dice for us. Grace, will you show Mary her room and keep lookout? Rob, Susan, come with me."

He gave me his hand to help me from the seat and led me to the trapdoor. Everything about him was unfamiliar. *Husband*, I said to myself as we approached the dark hatch. *Husband, husband, husband.* The word began to lose its meaning.

John went down the wooden steps first, holding up the lantern.

Cold, musty air wafted up, chilling my skin and making me shiver. At the bottom he turned and looked up at us, the light swinging and dipping.

"Can you see well enough, Susan?" he said. "Mind your head as you come down. Rob, leave the hatch open."

I shook the shadows away from me and went down the steps into the chill, earth-walled space. Despite John's warning I almost knocked my head on the feet of two fat ducks hanging from the ceiling. The cellar smelled gamey, meat and blood tempered by the meadows-worth of dried herbs also hanging above me. The ceiling was low and anyone much taller than Rob would have to stoop.

The lantern lit a square cellar crowded with printing paraphernalia and kitchen goods. Against the left-hand wall stood old barrels, more shelves, and a tipsy-looking tall cupboard, all stacked with tattered, unbound books and spare wood blocks.

John handed the lantern to Rob and went to the tall set of shelves against the left wall. He moved aside a book on the middle shelf, beckoning for Rob to stay close by with the lantern, then pressed his thumb onto a board at the back of the shelf. There was a click and a square hole appeared as he pushed the board up—there was some very clever mechanism built into it, like our priest-hole at Framfield. Peering at the space I saw, of all things, a keyhole in the back of the shelf.

"This house used to be a tavern," said John, "and the landlord used the cellar for a little smuggler's store as well as his ale. God rest his soul, he was a good friend of mine and he sold me the building when he'd had enough of the business. The drink killed him in the end."

As he spoke, John took a key from his pocket and fitted it in the lock. It was well oiled and clicked smoothly open. He held onto the side of the shelf carefully and swung back the entire set of shelves, revealing a narrow opening in the wall. It was a secret door—the shelves had simply been nailed into it to disguise it. Rob's lantern cast yellow light over the threshold onto another bare earth floor.

John held the door open for Rob and me. Rob went first, holding up the lantern, and I followed him, stepping carefully as John closed and locked the door behind us. The thick walls deadened sound and my ears sang in the silence as I looked about me.

The space, square and earth-walled, was about the same size as the cellar behind us. A wooden contraption shaped something like a mangle, standing on legs and with a long iron handle, stood in the far right-hand corner. Two long tables beside it were stacked high with printed pages and unbound books, and there were more papers pinned and drying above them.

Two unlit lanterns hung on the right-hand wall. John gestured to a high stool beneath them, positioned in front of what looked like two easels.

"Please—sit," said John to me, and I clambered up onto the stool.

"Well then," said John. "This pit, Rob and Susan, is my secret workroom. That is the press and these are the cases of type—but we are not here to print tonight. We are in possession of a new work from our friends Campion and Persons."

He took a roll of paper from one of the long tables and held it up so we could see it.

"This is a copy of *Campion's Challenge* to the Privy Council—that the Protestants call his *Brag*—that went out all over the country in manuscript last year. He never meant it for publication. He left it with a friend in the Marshalsea to release if he was arrested. Now that it is in general usage we are to produce a printed copy. In a month's time we will send it out across London to be distributed all on the same day. Other men will do the same elsewhere, so that it seems the text has sprung up in the night like field mushrooms. This is a new idea of Persons', to try and confound the Searchers so that they cannot tell where the text first originated. It will be placed in the homes and workrooms and public buildings of Protestants, so that it can't be said that only Papists have copies of an illicit text."

So Charlewood was in correspondence with them, and this was the work my master had spoken of—God's work, that I would be set upon too. Still I could not feel thankful. I did not feel anything at all. The paper in John's hand was stained with travel but the black ink on it stood out clearly. It was too much for me to grasp. I knew the perils of keeping a hand-written copy of such work. Ours had been kept well hidden. How much greater must the risk be of printing out a hundred copies? And the Searchers had come straight to the cellar tonight—did they already suspect John? I stared at the slim pamphlet, trying to take the measure of the danger it represented.

John must have seen my face. He took my hand, which startled me, so that I flinched before I could compose myself. I hoped he did not think I was flinching from him. "I am not known to the Searchers as a Papist, Suky," he said, "but as a thief who prints work licensed to other men. The books I publish must be registered at the Stationers' hall and if we print something registered under another man's name they may prosecute us for it. Some of us among the Stationers believe work should not be kept chained to one man in such a way, so we work to free it. This is where I make my illegitimate books; my unlicensed paper bastards. Come, is it not better than a mistress and a flock of fat by-blows over in Southwark?"

Rob laughed. I was exhausted. I wanted to go away from this dark room, lie down on a bed and weep. I felt like a piece of straw swept downstream between pebbles, but I could not rest yet. I pushed down my tiredness and took my hand from John's, feeling in my pocket for my own letter.

"Sir," I said, "I have a letter here for the two fathers. It is in secret ink on the reverse of this paper. My master wished me to deliver it safe to you as he knows you are in close conference with them. I also have gold for them but I cannot give it to you this minute as it is sewn into my bodice."

Rob and John stared at me. I held the letter out to John, who took it and read through the note from my master before turning it over and squinting at the blank reverse page.

"Your master told me he put great trust in you," said John. "Such a little creature! And you came all that way from Sussex with this letter and a bodiceful of money? Truly, God has sent me a brave wife!"

"And one with a bosom stuffed with gold," said Rob. "What man could ask for more?"

John rounded on him. "Watch your tongue, sirrah," he said. "I brook no insolence in this house." He eyed Rob, taking the measure of him, and Rob stared back.

"Your pardon, sir," said Rob at last, bowing his head. "I spoke out of turn."

"No more than I expected," said John. "I had word of you before you came here too, from your father, and nothing so flattering as what Sir Thomas wrote of Susan. Take him to London, he said. Keep him on the straight path and away from the sea. Don't let him near the river or the naughty men that run up and down it. Not a drop of water here, is there, or the sniff of a Sussex owler? I expect you're used to working in murky holes like this, too?"

"This is nothing," said Rob. "I've walked the tunnels at home a thousand times without a light at all. I know it all by touch."

"And what might a fine lad like you be about, wandering underground in the blind dark?" asked John.

"Helping out the excise men," said Rob, after a pause.

"Aye, lightening their workload by slipping a few spice-packets in round the sly way. I know you Sussex men," said John. "Well, that's why I hired you. I'm a Suffolk man myself and I grew up running messages along the estuary for gentlemen who work at night. I know your sort. We shall get along very well if you remember your courtesies and sweeten that salt tongue. Stay off the ships and on this side of the Channel and I've plenty of work for you, of a kind you'll take to well."

"Now—let's to bed like good citizens that love the light. I'll show you to our bedroom, Susan. Mary will be your bed-companion these three nights until we are married. Rob, I'll take the pallet beside you in the attic. Come, follow me."

Fatigue was now blurring the room around me and when we came up out of the cellar into the warm kitchen again, I felt I must surely be back in one of my fever dreams. Grace lit candles and led Rob and Mary up the narrow stairs to the upper floors, but John held me back a moment. Rob cast a glance back at us as he followed Grace.

"You're tired, I know," said John. "I won't keep you. I'm sorry the Searchers were your first guests in your new home. How is Sir Thomas?"

I felt tears prick my eyes. "I don't know. He was not himself, even before the arrest. I don't know how he will fare in prison."

John grimaced, watching me closely. I wished he would let me go to bed. He seemed to be concerned for me but all I wanted was to close my eyes and forget everything about this arduous day.

"There is one more thing I must ask you," he said. "Your master said you have great skill with secret inks and other devices for passing messages."

"I have some skill," I said. "My lady taught me and she was accomplished in all those arts."

He nodded. "Good—good," but the frown line between his eyebrows deepened. At last he seemed to make up his mind, and said:

"I need your help, Susan, to ensure some vital messages stay hidden. Can you make me up a very sure and certain ink? It must be quite invisible on the page, but clear to read when uncovered. I have agreed to pass messages between Father Persons and another man—they hope to work together to secure this match between the Queen and Alençon ."

That stirred me. Here was something more I could do in God's service that would help our faith and our country, and that would keep my lady with me, as she used to be.

"Yes," I said, "if we can come by all the ingredients. I will make a list."

"Thank you, Susan," he said, and smiled at me. Then he brought my hand to his lips and kissed it. I let him hold my fingers a moment before I pulled gently away. He cleared his throat and took up another candlestick from the side.

"Come," he said, "I'll show you to the room."

Grateful beyond measure that sleep was within reach, I followed him up the stairs to a room where a large bed curtained with faded red hangings stood. My marriage bed. My room. Next to the bed was a little window over the street, with a stool beneath it. Mary stood by it, splashing her face at an ewer. My chest was against the far wall, beside a small desk stacked with books and papers. To my right was a little fireplace, embers glowing in the grate.

The room was clean, neat, and small, like the rest of the house. Not a cobweb to be seen. It was half the size of my room at Framfield, with its windows looking over the lawns and its embroidered wall-hangings. I swallowed down tears and put my hand out to touch the bed-curtains, soft and worn with age. They had probably hung there since John's first wife came home a new bride.

"Goodnight sister. Goodnight Susan," called John, and left us. Mary blinked water from her eyes and glanced at me balefully. I did not even speak to her, but undressed at speed, clambered into bed, and fell instantly into deep, obliterating, glorious sleep.

CHAPTER 10

Sunlight woke me in the morning. A pale winter barb, striking through the little window and reflecting back into my eyes from the piece of polished tin that hung by the fireplace and did for a mirror. I rolled away from the brightness, blinking, and found my face against a broad back clad in faded, musty-smelling linen. Anne's linen was always neat and fine and smelled of lavender water, and it took me a few minutes to understand where I was and who was sharing my bed.

Then I rolled away again, quick as a cat, not wanting to wake Mary or speak to her. It must be late if the sun was up. I dressed hurriedly in my plainest things that needed no help in fastening or lacing-up and went softly down the stairs into the kitchen. There was no-one there, but the table was messy with cups and plates and breakfast crumbs, and from behind a door I could hear men's voices. I hesitated outside it, guessing the print room lay beyond. I did not want to disturb the men at work.

A cold breeze ran over my cheek and I saw another door was open at the back of the kitchen. More thin sunlight fell through it onto the rushes. I went to open it, putting off a foray into the print room.

"Oh," I said, astonished, as I took in the size of the garden. I had not expected a garden at all in the city but it was long and narrow with high walls—a good-sized kitchen garden. Although it was in its winter colours I could see fruit trees trained against the walls, rose-bushes, well-grown herbs, and a small vegetable plot. Rosemary, thyme, bay, mint, fennel, lavender, camomile, and leeks, sprouts, kale and cabbages. Enough for a good medicine cupboard and for the kitchen pot. The path was long enough to walk back and forth of an evening. I set foot on it, then stopped. Grace was kneeling by a big lavender bush, pulling off sprigs. She stared at me as fiercely as she had last night, her wide mouth tight as a button.

"This is such a fine garden," I said.

"The old mistress planted it well," said Grace, gathering up all the lavender in one hand and standing up to face me. "I've kept it up."

"You've managed it bravely," I said, looking about me. There was even a beehive at the far end, meaning honey and honeycomb for the house and maybe enough to sell a few pots too.

I turned back to Grace and caught a glimpse of her unguardedly contemptuous expression before she smoothed her face over. With her free hand she was switching a long grass-stem about between her fingers, exactly as a cross cat would twitch its tail. The cold morning sun picked out red lights in her thin hair and cruelly excavated pock-marks in her skin, making her look an odd, changeling person, sour at the mouth. Yet that raucous laugh I had heard from her last night indicated a generous wit.

"How long have you kept house for?" I asked.

"A year. Since the mistress died."

Perhaps she had been very fond of John's first wife, or had grown accustomed to running the house. Perhaps she had even hoped to win John as a husband for herself. I must find a way to befriend her. I needed Grace.

"London's a new world to me," I said. "Will you take me round the markets—show me which stalls to buy from and which traders I can trust?"

"You'll find it hard, coming from such a great house," she said, not answering my question. She let her grass-stem fall and folded her arms. "There's only us here to cook and clean and fetch firewood, not a whole army of servants. You don't look like you've ever scrubbed your hands raw."

I looked down at my own smooth hands, kept soft with my expensive oils, and then at Grace's red, cracked knuckles. "Come," I said, smiling, deciding to ignore her hostility and be pleasant. I was the mistress now. I thought of my lady before the illness, cool and calm, never letting her temper flash out, in control of the whole estate. This was only a little house with a little serving-maid, no cook or baker or steward to manage.

"Show me the house. Where is your linen cupboard?"

She shrugged, dropped her arms, and led me back inside. As we came through the kitchen John poked his head out of the door where I had heard men's voices.

"Suky!" he said, smiling. His voice was warm and his eyes rested on me with pleasure. I smiled back: his warmth was so welcome after Grace's coldness. "I hope you are rested? We let you lie abed after the journey. Come in, come in! Grace, clear the breakfast things and then wake Mary."

He reached his hand to me and I took it as he led me through into the print room. It was filled with light and busy with men and equipment. There was a sharp smell of lye, ink, and wet paper—the lye so strong it tickled the back of my nostrils and made me sneeze. There were two good-sized glass windows in the wall to my left, and two more in the right-hand wall. The glass must have cost a pretty penny and the sunlight made everything in the room look crisp and clear.

It was such a contrast to the dark pit where John's secret press lived that I blinked once or twice, wondering if I could have dreamed the dank earth room under the kitchen.

In the corner stood the wooden printing press with its arm and rollers. Two men I didn't recognise were working it, one holding what looked like two leather balls on sticks while the other set up the paper to be printed. Rob stood beside them watching, arms folded. He glanced at me as I came in then quickly looked back at the press, frowning. He looked as if he was not much enjoying his first lesson.

"How much do you know of printing?" asked John, observing me. "All this machinery—do you know what it does?"

"It is a press worked by hand," I said, stiffly. I was very conscious of the men and of wanting to have my answer correct, and my words came out a little stilted. "And the letters are on little blocks. That it may all be repeated and repeated, once you have a page, to save the labour of copying by hand."

"Very good! Very good. We are setting a piece by the man who will marry us, Suky, as it happens," said John. "Robert Crowley, the vicar at St Giles. He has written up answers to a challenge set by Thomas Pound—that Marshalsea Papist."

I looked up at him sharply. My master knew Thomas Pound—he was the man who had first copied out *Campion's Challenge*. He had been in prison for two years now. What was John doing, printing a work by a Protestant vicar opposing a staunch Catholic?

John caught my look and smiled at me. "I'll tell you more of Crowley later," he said. "Look—they're in the thick of it so I won't ask them to stop, but that is my press-man Gabriel and my inker John—those balls he holds are dipped in ink, so he can roll them over the type and ink it up—do you see? I'll show you the press workings later. This is Philip, the corrector and there behind the boxes is Tom, our compositor."

Philip leaned over a table laid with wood blocks in the centre of the room while Tom the compositor stood in front of two shallow wooden boxes standing on legs, like easels. Light from the windows behind him fell on the boxes. Tom, snub-nosed and with hair that stood up in tufts, smiled at me. Philip, sallow and bald, frowning in concentration, took off his cap in greeting and set it back on his head without moving a muscle of his face.

I followed John, my mind full of questions I could not ask him here. They darted about in my head like fireflies and preventing me from seeing what was in front of my eyes. Why print a work against Thomas Pound? Had I really dreamed the scene in the cellar last night—was my husband actually Protestant? I blinked and tried to keep my mind on what John was showing me.

He led me next to one of the wooden boxes on legs next to where Tom sat, catching light from the windows. Tom grinned at me again but did not stop in his task, snatching up letters as quick as a swallow on the wing snaps up flies.

"This is my new case of garamond type. Look. The individual letters are called 'sorts'. Do you see how the sorts sit: capital letters in the upper half, smaller letters in the lower?"

I looked at the case. It was divided into shallow boxes filled with letters. A rectangle filled with capital R's, a smaller square full of little e's, another square for punctuation.

"Pick out a sort and feel it. Pick an S, for Susan."

I scanned the case for the letters, reached out and took up one of the capital S's. It was tiny, stamped onto the end-face of a rectangular metal block. The whole block was only the length of my top thumb-joint, and the letter itself no bigger than an ant. I rubbed my finger over the S, feeling the raised bump of it.

"How is it made?" I asked, turning the cold type over to examine it.

"In a mould, with molten metal. We haven't the skill in England so we have to import the lot over from the Netherlands. We have to import the paper too—there are no paper-mills in this country. It's a stinking expense and causes great trouble."

I wondered if much of my marriage-portion had gone on the new case of type. The thought made me feel proprietorial towards it.

"So. Let's see if you might make a compositor," said John. "Tom, you can give your judgement on it." Tom looked up again and grinned at me, showing a mouth more full of gaps than teeth.

"This is the composing stick, which holds the type as we form the sentences," said John, placing a rectangular length of wood in my left hand, curling my fingers round it and positioning it carefully so it pointed upwards. A ledge ran along the bottom and one side of the device. His hand around mine was warm and it shook ever so slightly. I stood very still. I felt the men watching us. I wanted to take my hand away but I could not without jogging the type.

"Hold it just so, or the letters will fall out," he said, taking the S from me and resting it on the little ledge, where it sat snugly. "Do you see? It must be balanced. We form one sentence at a time, till the space is filled. Now, the trick with composing is that all must be done backwards and upside down. We will spell your name, and we will start with S, but you must place every letter facing the opposite way to how it sits on the page. Here are the spaces to place between words, in this box. You try it—spell out Susan Charlewood."

He left me then and went to look over Philip's work. I changed my grip on the composing stick, glad that he had gone. I felt ill at ease here in the men's space, like an indulged child playing at work. Surely John did not mean me to actually take on the labour of printing? It was illegal, for one thing, for I was not in the guild, and besides it would take work away from the men. Perhaps he just wanted me to understand how it all functioned. Or maybe printer's wives really did know the secrets of the trade.

The composing stick sat awkwardly in my hand. I felt as if all the men were watching me, seeing how this new strange mistress would take to the work. I looked at the hundreds of tiny letters in their cases, hunting for a small u. When I found it I took it out and placed it beside the S. This was a neat task.

Absorbed in the work, I soon forgot the other people in the room until Rob came over to where Tom sat, carrying a box. Tom peered into it. "That's the garamond," he said. "If you please mistress," he said to me, "will you make room for the 'prentice to sort the type back into those boxes? Every single one back in its right box," he said to Rob severely. "If one sort's out of place you may spoil a whole page, so go slowly."

I picked out the last few letters I needed, then moved the stool along for Rob. I placed in the last two o's and the d of Charlewood, conscious of Rob beside me muttering under his breath as he matched the letter to the box. His presence made me clumsy: I put the d in the wrong way round, took it out to correct it and fumbled it onto the floor.

Rob reached down to pick it up and passed it up to me, holding it out on the flat of his palm. I picked it up delicately, avoiding his eyes, and tucked it in beside its fellows.

"This is a finicking task," murmured Rob. "I haven't the patience."

"Perhaps it will teach you some," I said.

He stopped his work, holding one of the sorts up: a capital A. "So small," he said. "Such a little thing to cause such trouble between men."

"Hey," barked Tom. "Did I ask you to stand staring at the things like a moonstruck hare? Put it away and when you're finished with that lot, go and fetch a broom."

Rob went back to his task, scowling, and I looked at the compositor's stick. There was my new name spelled in small bright letters, backwards and far neater than my own hand. It looked strange, like a foreign name.

"Are you done, Susan? Quick work!" John came over again and took the stick from me, studying it. "All in their right place and not so slow. Tom, have a care, she might replace you one day. Good. When you have a few sentences in there, we transfer them to the galley—that's what Philip is poring over—till we have enough for a page. Then Philip will make sure the type is all set out properly in the galley before he fixes the chase around it to stop anything moving about. The chase goes into the coffin of the press with the type facing upwards, ready to be inked before we screw the paper down onto it and make the impression. Do you grasp that?"

My eyes followed his pointing hand, from the type to the table to the waiting press. Galley, chase, paper. It would take a while for it to sink in properly, but I nodded.

"Is that part of the press really called a coffin?"

"Yes," said John, "and if one of the men slips up we bury him in it.

"So, now you have an idea of the labour that goes into making a text, I'll take you to Stationers' Hall next. I need to register a book for print and I want you to meet the clerk. They will need to know who you are if I send you to register any work for me." As we began to leave he called over his shoulder, "Keep the 'prentice busy, Tom!"

Tom nodded and Rob paused in his sweeping to cast one of his pointed looks at John's back. It was not quite malicious but there was a reckoning in it. I sensed that Rob gathered up hard words and remembered them, like my lady.

John ushered me from the print room, through the kitchen and the hall and out into the street. I turned back to look at the building as we left and noted again the heavy wooden shutters at the windows and the bars on the door.

Now I know the route from the Barbican to St Paul's so well

that I could walk it blindfold. That day it was all new. The Barbican road felt less threatening by daylight. We walked past rows of tradesmen's houses with stalls outside, including some book-stalls and a few poor-looking taverns. It was a clear, cold day and the dust of the street scuffed up around my skirts as we walked, making my eyes itch. A little child sat with its bare feet in the gutter, making something out of sticks and string.

John took my arm as we walked. "I saw you took it ill that I am printing a Protestant argument," he said quietly.

"Not ill, sir," I said, "but it does puzzle me. It runs so counter to—your other work."

"It does indeed," he said, "and that keeps us safe. Good morning, Munday!" He waved at a pale young man who was leaning by one of the bookstalls, thumbing through a volume. The man looked up and raised a hand. When he saw me walking with John he almost dropped his book. He stared at us and seemed about to speak, but John pulled me firmly along.

"Munday's lately returned from living among the Papists in Rome," said John. "Writing up a famous account of his time in the Jesuit College that'll have the Pope chewing his beard off in fury. I'm printing it."

He looked down at me again and smiled. "Who knows what he was really doing in a Catholic priest's college in Rome? Was he bravely spying for his country, or did he just turn his coat to save his skin when he came home? Nobody knows, but he's made firm friends with spymaster Walsingham. That's good news for me. If I print work for men like Munday, it baffles the bloodhounds. They can't smell Papistry so strongly. Do you see?"

I looked down the road ahead. Cripplegate and the Roman Wall loomed up in front of us, the long stone arm hugging the city tight. There were no limbs waving on spikes above Cripplegate but the long march of stone still gave me a cold-feather feeling of fear.

I understood why John worked outside these walls, in outlaw land.

"Yes," I said. "It is a face you must turn to the world."

"That's right," he said. "Can you be at peace with it?"

He stopped before we reached Cripplegate. Two watchmen stood on either side with bored and weary expressions. They looked a little less bored when they saw us pausing at the gate. John studied me anxiously.

"Yes," I said. "I can."

John clutched my hand with relief and we walked on. He nodded to the watchmen as we passed and they did not stop us. John had to duck as we went under the gate's low arch, and when we came out on the other side we were in the City. The bells of Mary-le-Bow rang me in, as the bells of St Giles had rung me out the evening before. The street was busier than the Barbican, crammed with people of all degrees and in all manner of dress. I kept my arm firmly through John's.

"How did you come to be a printer, sir?" I asked. I found the crowds of people too much. All their eyes seemed to be upon me like a thousand-eyed Argus.

"In a roundabout way," said John. "My father was a grocer in Suffolk. I was apprenticed here to his old friend Richard, who was a wealthy man with a busy grocer's shop off Cheapside, and during the years of my apprenticeship I saw the bookstalls in Paul's Yard multiply faster than flies on meat. We sold books too and I made friends with the printer who supplied the shop. When Richard died I married his wife Liz. We sold the grocery business and set up work here the year Elizabeth came in."

So he had married his former master's wife. It was too soon to ask much about that.

"And you had no children?" I asked.

He was silent for a moment. "We had two," he said. "John Geoffrey and Lucy. They both took the smallpox and died. They were ten and twelve. They are buried in St Giles churchyard, next to their mother."

Chastened, I took his hand. "I am sorry, sir," I said.

"As am I," he said quietly. "And Liz and I were never such friends again, after they died. We had married too young, you see. We married in a passion and once it blew away we discovered we were not well matched. We were yoked together and we chafed and scratched at one another. When our children died we lived more and more like strangers in the same house. I worked and she planted the garden."

He put his hand on my own.

"You and I have better sense, Suky. We have used our heads to make a match and that is what will sustain us and build love between us."

"Yes, sir," I said. I left my hand beneath his for a while, thinking of the garden Liz had made so beautifully, laying out the paths and planting the flowers and herbs. That was where her heart had gone when she and John fell out of love. My heart was still in Framfield. I looked around me at the buildings crammed together and the street so clattery with street hawkers and loiterers. Being small, my skyline was littered with the baskets that street sellers hoisted on their heads and clusters of feathers bobbing like startled pheasants on the citizens' over-finished hats. Could love flourish in this place, with this man? God had directed me here. Now faith must light my way through these strange, unfriendly streets.

CHAPTER 11

Three days later, I was married. The morning of my wedding was the loneliest of my life. It should have been a day full of the people I loved best, but every moment of it reminded me they were gone. Anne and Kate should have been there with Lady Katharine, helping me dress.

If my mother had lived she would have been there to arrange my hair and place the new goldwork earrings, shaped like little bells, gently into my ears. She would have laced up my Venetian sleeves, puffed at the shoulder, drawn out with linen and tied with yellow ribbons. She would have smoothed down my new popinjay-coloured dress with the yellow sun embroidered on the stomacher, and kissed me before I set off to church.

Instead, I was attended by strangers. Charlewood's sister offered to help me dress but I couldn't stand the thought of her clumsy fingers on me. I asked Grace to tie up my sleeves, which she did well enough but without a smile or a word. When she was gone I stood by the bedroom window, alone save for a robin perched on the eaves opposite. Not a soul I loved stood with me. God had made me a path to walk and I did not want to walk it alone.

My chest felt tight and my stomach curled and twisted into a knot of snakes. I liked John Charlewood but I did not want to marry him. I did not want to lie beside him tonight and open my body to him without a woman of my own household to comfort me. I put my hands to my eyes and pressed them hard. *Mary is your mother now,* Kate had said to me. Our Lady was with me, if no-one else was.

Anne's portrait rested at my neck in its gold case and my mother's heirlooms were in my pocket. I touched both things, trying to draw comfort from them. They were warm from my skin and the folds of my skirt but they could not restore my loved ones. My mother was long gone, Lady Katherine died hating me, and Anne's portrait was a lie. She was under the earth and the worms would be on her face, burrowing through to the bone.

"Love is greater than Death," I said. "Love is greater than Death," but as I walked to St Giles Cripplegate for my wedding with Grace and Mary beside me, I thought far more of death than love.

John was waiting for me in church dressed up like a rainbow, proud in blue-and-russet striped doublet and padded trunk hose, with new buff stockings and a half-length cloak. There we stood in all our colours against the white walls of St Giles, with the congregation of my new parish packed in behind us. I felt their eyes in my back like arrows as we faced the altar and my voice sounded small and young when I said my vows.

Within an hour we were married and I was no longer Susan Framfield of Sussex but Susan Charlewood, a printer's wife and a parishioner of St Giles Cripplegate, where I would likely be buried when my time on earth was done.

Most of the people came with us to drink and eat afterwards at the Cross Keys, one of the inns with a playhouse yard. I could not eat a thing at first; I had felt sick all day and was dizzy trying to keep track of the great cluster of guests. The wedding party must have drunk London dry. Printers, playwrights, booksellers, players, intelligencers and poets: their thirst was extraordinary. The owner, Alice Layston, seemed to know John and she kept the wine and ale flowing like water. I drank more than enough myself, to disguise the fear behind my smiles.

The first man to come and congratulate us was a great, fat printer called John Wolfe, who kissed my hand Italian-fashion and gathered John in to embrace him as if he were the tenderest prey. I had been watching him. He was a sizeable man—not just in body but in his person. He filled up a room; he filled up the tavern hall now with his voice and his presence, pushing everyone else to the walls.

"Sweetling," he said to me, "look how you have brought the colour back to my friend John's cheeks. I told him to marry quick and marry young. He was wasting, pale as curd. 'Get another wife!' I said. 'Get a pretty one; get a young one. You haven't that many years left on earth—enjoy them.' Everyone else was pushing him to match with a fat widow with a fat purse of her own. I said, 'you'll die first and never get the benefit of it.' Now you are as good as *aquae vitae*. You'll add twenty years to his life. Make sure you keep him on his toes. Men don't die from nagging, they die from boredom."

"Lucky for you, Wolfe," said John, glancing at his wife Joan, who was as tall as her husband with a choleric eye and bright red cheeks. Wolfe barked with laughter and everyone turned to look.

I eyed him curiously. He and John were evidently fast friends but they seemed so different; John with his enigmatic, theatrical look and long, somewhat melancholic face, and Wolfe solid and loud as the bass bell at St. Paul's. I learned later he had started his career as a fishmonger and he brought to the fray all the attributes fishwives are charged with: sharp tongues, sharper elbows, loud voices and no morals.

Other friends followed in quick succession. It was a giddy blur of names and faces. Chettle, White, Kingston, Anthony Munday. The names flew past me like leaves in autumn, some that I recognised from my master's library at Framfield. Everyone laughed, declaimed, and bandied around words, snatches of new plays and poems I did not know, as well as bawdy songs. I smiled at guest after guest as they came to congratulate us.

Some spoke only to John and could not meet my eye, others enthusiastically kissed me, exclaiming me the Queen of Sheba. Some looked at me with the same deep mistrust I saw in Grace's eyes. I drank cup after cup of spiced wine till the sharp edges of everything softened and John's hand in the small of my back was not such a weight on me.

When you feel like an outsider in a company, you notice others who, like you, stay at the edges of the party or sit in corners and drink alone. Our little maid Grace was in the thick of everything, trading jests with young men. She must have a tongue on her—whatever she said had people in fits—but when I caught her eye she looked away from me. Roberdine, by contrast, leaned alone against a tall cupboard at the side of the room. The people he spoke to most were the tavern servants who came in and out carrying food and drink.

As I stood watching him I felt a touch on my shoulder. It made me jump, guiltily, for fear I had been caught staring at Rob. I turned around to see three ladies smiling at me. They had sat together all day and John had told me their names: Joan Jugge, Joan Kingston, and Joan Broome. Three Joans, all three stationers' wives, and all a good deal older than me.

"Come and sit with us, child," said the tallest Joan, who drew me over to their corner. Sitting on a stool, I looked between them. Joan Jugge with her white hair, tall Joan Kingston who had a man's long face and nose, and little black-toothed Joan Broome. They appeared as three fairies come up out of the earth to snatch me away. I waited for them to say something about my hair or my skin.

Joan Jugge smiled at me again and I tried to smile back.

"Any help you need, Goody Charlewood, only let us know. You're a young thing, I see, and you've only that little maid Grace to help you. Make sure you come and see me if you lack anything. My little grand-daughter is to be baptised on Wednesday at St Giles and we will have a gathering at home afterwards—come and share a toast."

"Thank you," I said. She was the first person who had proffered such kindness and I felt it deeply. I liked her strong, square face with its many lines, and her calm air. I wanted to put my head on her shoulder and rest for a moment, drinking in that calm. She was opening the door for me into the parish women's world of baptisms, weddings, and other festivals. I felt that she must hold a respected position in that world. If she vouched for me, the other women would surely look friendlier on me.

I did not quite understand yet what I had married into. John's friends among the Stationers were a band of rowdy rebels and upstarts, some of whom had travelled the Continent. They sat late in taverns boasting who had printed the most daring thought, the latest volume from the most controversial preacher, the news direct from war. Like John they printed work licensed to other men, risking fines and imprisonment, and thumbed their noses at the monopolists who clung to their privileges for printing ABCs, grammars and catechisms like a nest of elderly eagles.

We stayed late at the inn and it was near to curfew when we walked home, with a rabble of tipsy Stationers escorting us through the streets.

When we reached John's house they were baulked of coming in for the bedding by a watchman who bade them go back through Cripplegate before it closed for the night. John himself was almost too drunk to stand.

"Oh beautiful, beautiful, beautiful," he said, cupping my face in his hands as we stood by the fire in our bedroom. "Not a woman there could match you. African princess! Now don't fear, don't fear, I am all gentleness. Oh—" and he swayed and nearly toppled us both. I helped him to the bed, where he fell again and then scrambled himself in. I watched him, half in fright and half in disgust, as he wrestled off his doublet and shirt, laughing and muttering: "Don't fear, Suky, I'll master it, I'll master it. Mainsails up!" until he fell fast asleep with one arm still tangled in his shirt.

I studied him as he lay on his back, sprawled out on the bed with his free arm flung up and resting on the pillow. It struck me that I would probably never again have the chance to look upon him like this before we were entirely man and wife, joined together body and soul.

The bridge of his nose was very thin. His mouth fell half-open. He was not an ill-featured man, only some of his teeth were bad and his beard was not well-shaped. I reached out and touched the crows-feet at the side of his eyes, feeling almost guilty for watching him sleep, all unawares of me. He did not move when I touched him.

I sat beside him and ran my hand over his skin, feeling the shape of his ribs and sides. His skin was looser than mine and marked with moles, little red spots, veins and old abrasions; the dints and imperfections of the years. Another unholy thought came to me that if I put a pillow over his head now he would stop breathing and die, no-one would be any the wiser, and I would be a widow and free to marry someone else. I closed my eyes again and prayed for a clear mind. I prayed for strength, to bear what I must bear. There was nothing so dreadful here, but there was nothing that made my body quicken, either.

I did not feel sleepy at all, nor did I want to get into bed. I took off my ruff carefully, then undressed until I was in my shift.

I smoothed down my hair with oil, the familiar ritual calming me a little. I bundled my nightcap onto my head and sat by the fire a moment, shivering. There was a draught coming in from the door and I went to close it.

Floorboards creaked in the corridor beyond, startling me, and I opened the door wider to see Rob going up the stairs to the attic with his candle. He turned and saw me too and stopped. His look made me flush all over. He saw me, barefoot in my shift on my wedding night, with the dying fire behind me, and his eyes were fierce and hungry.

I dropped my own gaze and closed the door as a good wife should. Then I leaned against it for a minute, listening as Rob's footsteps trod up the stairs and into the attic above us. There were only floorboards, lath and plaster between us. My breathing came ragged and I felt as if my body trod the attic floor with him, beside him as he undressed and rolled himself up in the bundle of blankets on his pallet bed. The attic would be icy cold and his breath would steam in the night air. I put my fingers to my mouth, feeling my own breath go in and out. I wanted to lie down beside him and put my mouth on his. The curl of his lip, the warmth of it.

An ember flared up in the grate and John laughed in his sleep. I jumped back from the door in a fright and walked back to the fire. I needed to calm myself, kill this lust, make peace with my fate. I stood listening to the sounds of the house. John's breathing, heavy with drink. The hiss of the fire. Creaks and shifts of timber and that deep silence that floods a house at midnight, bearing the small sounds away with it like twigs and leaves. In that silence I think we are nearer to God and all our dead.

"I am in London," I said to myself. "This is my home. My name is Susan Charlewood. Mistress Charlewood." Then, more quietly: "Shonwa. Shonowa. Sho-no-wa."

John began to snore again, breaking my peace. It was too loud for me to sleep. The candle still had a way to burn so I took my translation of Horace carefully out of my chest. It was a birthday present from my master, bound in soft leather and already well thumbed. I climbed into bed beside John, tucking the blankets in tight around my legs, and began to read.

PART II

London
1581

CHAPTER 12

Now began my joint apprenticeship as a London Guild wife and an outlaw printer. My days were spent between dark and light, running from the legitimate work we did above ground to the secret heart of that house, the hidden cellar. In the kitchen I mixed herbs and spices, in the cellar I made up my trials of invisible inks.

It was all hard graft. There was no kitchen here staffed by the best cooks in Sussex and fed from a wide estate well-stocked with game and carefully-tended kitchen gardens, no laundry-maids to wash and press clothes, no soap-makers and distillers and bakers on hand.

Now I was up at dawn with Grace, directing her work, no longer a servant but the mistress. There was so much to do at the little bookstall outside the house, at the Stationer's hall by St. Paul's or with the account books at home, that though I spent my days surrounded by books I could only snatch odd moments to sit down with one. Candle stubs were too precious to waste on reading for pleasure.

I lived in a tall, squeezed house, all elbows and knees, in a cramped road in a middling to poor part of London among thousands of other squeezed houses. The low-ceilinged, narrow rooms were eternally full of authors or journeymen staying over to help John with a job and spending the night lined up on pallets on our garret floor, or even in the kitchen where Grace fell over them when she went in to stoke up the fire in the morning.

Everything in this new life felt teeter-totter, like a staircase with uneven steps, so that I was uncertain of myself and how to go about in the world. The house itself felt combustible, with Grace glaring at me as she pummelled dough and Rob making eyes at me as he prowled in and out on his many errands. Grace and Rob scrapped and played like puppies: he whistled at her, pulled her hair, and pretended to woo her, but she had four brothers and gave him cuffs and hard words in return.

Grace's hostility to me did not fade. She did everything I asked her to well and promptly, but with a sullen shrug and glare that made her look even more like an owl, one ruffling up its feathers against the rain. It stung all the more because with the rest of the household she was lively and loud. She had a quick wit and a scurrilous tongue, but she never laughed with me.

John himself could not have been kinder. I soon understood that he saw me as a kind of prize, captured from a higher plane and thereby lifting him up too. He would have preferred me to leave the hardest work to Grace and play the City wife, sewing in the parlour and showing off my languages to visitors. He was a good man, brave and generous, despite a taint of melancholy that marred him like a burnt edge of paper.

He had plenty of swagger, with pretensions to a higher state than the one he was born into, and he was willing to spend a good deal on the climb. His account books were a luxurious catastrophe, littered with items for spices, wine, French and Italian lessons with a private tutor, and painted wall-hangings for the parlour. Besides my wedding ring, which was yellow Welsh gold, he gave me goldwork earrings to match and a pair of entirely impractical embroidered slippers.

I had chosen a gift for him before I ever met him and was pleased at how well it suited him: a new translation of Piemontese's *Secreti* that he loved and pored over, reading out the most outlandishly expensive recipes for perfume and medicines and telling Grace to scour the markets for myrrh and ultramarine. He was only half joking—the rarest and most costly items held a fascination for him.

Part of me revelled in his love for court gossip, fats, and worldly treasures. I had grown up close to that world and I missed it. Besides, how could I not like a man who urged me to buy books until the walls of our bedroom were papered with them, or who insisted I continue rubbing almond oil into my skin rather than a cheaper substitute? But the part of me nurtured by my lady was horrified at his profligacy, and I went through his accounts as if I were picking out lice with a comb. He grumbled, but I could see he was pleased to have found a wife who would act as his economic conscience.

He was also pleased at my work with secret inks. My lady had a recipe for invisible ink she made with gall nuts, which I had only mixed once before. Luckily John's workshop was plentifully stocked with galls for common ink, so I was able to try my hand at it many times to get it perfect. I knew when it was right the ink was quite invisible, and would only came to light when brushed with calcined copperas (which John also had in good supply).

I worked in the evenings or after the first sleep, when the house was safely barred and shuttered. I still could not sleep well anyway. I could not grow used to sharing my bed with John. Awake, in the warm glow of the red bed-hangings, I did not mind him. I quickly realised that I had a strange power over him. My nakedness stirred him to raptures. He set aside my clothes gently, respectfully, like a man at work on a masterpiece. I watched his eyes widen and his hands move and felt myself changing. I had a new awareness of my body and its power, and for this I thanked him. Yet I could not sleep beside him.

Often I found myself prowling the house in the small hours, or sitting in the print room with the composing stick. I found composition calmed me and John did not mind me practising it.

"Joan Jugge is an excellent compositor," he said, "and I'm sure to die before you, Suky, so you may as well learn a widow's craft now."

In the print room upstairs we finished the work by Robert Crowley and Grace and I were set to stab-stitching the copies to bind them up. In the secret room, we began to assemble the type and the paper to print *Campion's Challenge*. It seemed so wrong—so unjust—that the false words of Nicholls flew so easily and glibly from our legitimate press, while Campion's precious, hard-won wisdom was pieced together slowly, painfully, in bitter cold and danger.

We never saw Persons or Campion themselves. Persons directed the work of his own press, which moved around and out of the city as it needed to, but Campion was out in the wider country staying with Catholic gentlemen and nobles.

Even assembling the tools for the task was dangerous. We could not use type or paper that could be traced to us so it all had to be smuggled in. The type was a rag-bag assortment that came to us concealed in bags of flour, spice, dried peas, and other household goods.

Rob fetched most of it, running up and down the city in his apprentice's blue suit, a bag slung over his shoulder and his pockets full of A's and O's. The paper came from a stock brought into the country in secret and held somewhere out near Spitalfields in an old Augustinian hospital, to be distributed to Catholics who might otherwise have come under suspicion for trying to obtain large quantities of paper. It was Rob, too, who often fetched the paper, bringing it rolled up around the arrows in his quiver when he went out to the archery butts on a Sunday afternoon.

Rob was not afraid though. He seemed to relish the work and he had no time or sympathy for weaker spirits. He seemed to settle into this new life with ease. He barely mentioned his family after our talk on the journey to London. John made him write to his father and tell him of his safe arrival, but he did so reluctantly.

"Do you miss your brothers?" I asked him as he wrote out his letter at the kitchen table. I was powdering up yarrow to make a salve, grinding the leaves down with pestle and mortar. Rob had a good, clear hand but took no care over the task. I saw him scribble a few lines then throw down the quill, leaving a blot on the paper.

"I miss the sea," he replied. "That's all. I've never in my life before eaten a meal without one of my brothers taking some of it off me and most likely hucking me in the head as a thank-you. How do you find London, mistress?"

The spicy smell of the yarrow was in my nostrils. It reminded me strongly of the kitchen at Framfield, where my lady had taught us all our herb-craft. I rested my hand a moment and tried to suppress the ache of longing for home.

"A great city," I said. "Too great to know yet. I like it in parts."

In truth, I found my greatest refuge in Paternoster Row, where the booksellers began. Stalls and stalls filled with pamphlets and chapbooks and loose ballads, the shops behind them showing off books bound in bindings plain, rich, and rare. Every time I walked along that road my fingers began to tingle, itching to rifle through the books for things I had not read yet and new copies of those I had. Every corner held new treasure.

There were more stalls clustered around St. Paul's like so many barnacles and mussels on the hull of a great ship, lifting upward into the light. This was the London I wanted to live in, one where the walls and the streets and the roofs were all built out of books and the roads paved with paper.

But even in this part of the city, where I felt at home, I could not get away from the people and their eyes. I had not realised when I first came to London quite how differently I would be perceived. In Sussex the colour of my skin was, if not truly invisible, at least less visible because everyone on the estate had known me since my babyhood. They looked at me and saw little Suky, who played with their children and was loved by Lady Anne and who happened to be a Blackamoor.

In London I was a stranger, a Guinean Black woman who happened to be married to John Charlewood, and people had to overcome whatever they thought of my strangeness before they began to know me.

This was despite the larger numbers of Moors and Blackamoors in the city, many of whom were servants to Spanish or Portuguese households. They had their own friendships and connections. I often saw the maidservants in clusters, laughing together, and once or twice they tried to speak to me in Spanish or Portuguese. I spoke a little of both but only enough to apologise for being English. Then they would laugh and walk on, leaving me staring after them, wishing I had a band of country-women of my own colour to walk the markets with, arms around each others' waists.

I worked hard to find my place with the Guild and parish wives. I was always smiling and courteous whether I met with friendly curiosity or outright rudeness. I smiled as I sat at baptisms and weddings, I smiled when I offered remedies for toothache or stomach-ache. I smiled as I walked down the Barbican road alone, because there was always someone watching me.

Once a stone struck me on the hand as I walked and a child's voice shouted: 'Black devil!'. I turned but could not see whose child it was, scuffling away down an alley in a cloud of dust and laughter. I walked on, smarting, angry at the tears that rose to my eyes. I blinked them away and kept smiling. A flung stone and a child's insult were little things, compared to the sufferings of saints and martyrs. Yet I found I could not shake these things off, and I took it badly indeed when Joan Jugge spoke hard words to me at one of the Stationers' dinners.

I had on my wedding dress with a new starched ruff that framed my face and my gold-work earrings, and I was very pleased with my appearance. I was happy to be seated by Joan, who was highly respected in the Stationers. Her husband Richard had been Queen's printer once. A widow managing four apprentices and a busy press, Joan knew a good deal about the company and how to get by in it as a woman. While those around us were busy talking, she touched my arm and said bluntly: "You must have a care, Goody Charlewood."

I looked at her, startled.

"You must have a care," she said again, quietly. "People are talking about you."

"Which people? Why am I talked of?"

"I know you are young, dear, but you dress very fine and you talk and look about you very freely. People say you are looking at their husbands."

"I am looking at no-one's husband!"

"Well, they think you are. You know how people say the Moors are so lusty and their women very free. People don't know you well enough, yet. They only know what they think they see and what they hear by rumour."

I stared down at my hands. My wedding ring was bright on my finger.

"I am not anything like that, Mistress Jugge. I only dress as other women in London dress."

"But you are not as other women in London. I don't mean to hurt you. I only say have a care. It will take only a little effort to make yourself seem more modest, plainer and more everyday, and it may save you trouble later. People gossip here. It may seem bigger than your old home, and freer, but there is always someone watching you. Two women have told me they saw you laughing with your apprentice as you came through Cripplegate last week and that you seemed very familiar with him. They are only light words but you must not let such poison spread."

Her speech was poison enough, though I could tell she meant it kindly. I picked up my cup and drank from it to cover my anger.

"Thank you, Mistress Jugge," I said. "I will be careful."

She smiled at me, her own white hair tucked neatly in under a plain coif and her ears and hands naked of jewellery. Her husband had held many privileges so it was more than kind of her to try and help me despite John's anti-privilege position.

I was conscious of the other wives all around me and wondered which of them had spoken of me to Joan. I felt my cheeks burn hot and sat up straight, suddenly uncomfortable in my popinjay dress with its sun-coloured embroidery. All the milky cluster of women looking askance at me, mistrusting me for my colour and my languages and my youth. I longed with a great ache for someone who knew me.

CHAPTER 13

One day near the end of February, a month since I arrived in London, I rose before dawn and sat in the kitchen, testing my latest batch of the invisible gall ink. I hoped the letters would stand out clearly when I brushed it. My first attempts had been weepish.

Grace had woken with a fever in the night so I let her sleep in and put more wood on the kitchen fire to build it up. I was wrapped in my housecoat but the chill still bit at me. As I watched the flames crackle and rise, I realised I had not thought of Framfield for some days. The kitchen had become familiar to me. I no longer noticed the low ceilings and cramped space. I was becoming accustomed to my new, lower place in the world. That gave me a pang and I poked at the fire fiercely. I must not forget who I was and where I came from. I must not sink into the commonplace and lose myself. I determined to write to Sir Thomas later that day.

I took out my bowl of ink, the quill, and some paper, and laid it all out on the kitchen table. I was so busy with my brush I did not hear Rob come down the stairs, and started when he said:

"How does it show?"

"Well," I said. "Look," and I showed him the paper, where

letters were forming.

"A kitchen alchemy," he said. "This makes them come out?"

"Yes. Here—take the brush and try."

I gave it to him and he dipped it in the copperas and brushed it over the paper. More letters came up until the whole sentence was visible. He read it aloud: "*O clemens, O pia, O dulcis Virgo Maria*. It is alchemy. How does the copperas bring out the letters?"

"An alchemist does not tell the secrets of his craft," I said, holding out my hand for the brush.

He handed it to me and I put it carefully on the table, making sure I did not touch his fingers as I took it, though the not-touching only made me the more conscious of him.

"I'm going to fetch water," he said.

I nodded and let him go. I tried to keep a cool distance from Rob, but it was hard. There's no older story than the young wife who finds comfort with the apprentice and I had no intention of writing myself into that hoary tale. But I was nineteen and my husband was forty and more, and I knew nothing of lust or love or even how to tell between the two. I only knew that nothing my husband did ever made my body kindle the way a word from Rob could.

The sun was up by the time he returned with the water-pails, and I was dressed and busy with breakfast. John and Grace were still asleep upstairs. Rob heaved the pails up on the table and took a folded paper from his pocket.

"A letter for you, mistress," he said. "The man was coming up the road with it."

It was my master's handwriting, I had not heard from him for a few weeks and I could not wait to read it. I opened it hurriedly while Rob carried the water into the pantry.

Inside was a paper puzzle, letters within letters. A note from my master was folded around two other letters, one on a fresh sheet of paper and one on paper that was browned and stained with water and that crackled when I opened it out. I laid the three sheets out on the table, one beside the other. My master's note said little, only urging me to read the enclosed letters immediately. I took up the fresh sheet first and read it through. It was from John Hawkins.

> *A remarkable thing. I enclose a letter. It's an old letter, by several years; the man who carried it has been kicking his heels in a Spanish prison. Now he is out and this came to me last week. I send it in hope it is not too late. It is from the Black boy I meant for Tipton, that we had all the trouble over & thought dead. If his sister still lives, send it to her.*

I read the note over again, not understanding. The Black boy meant for Tipton. If his sister still lives. Then I took it in all at once and swayed where I stood. I had to lean on the table to stop myself falling. Slowly I sat down, trembling. If his sister still lives. I was the sister and the Black boy must be my brother—the brother I thought had died on our voyage from Guinea. I stared at the final letter. Hawkins said it was from him. This was a letter from my brother—my living brother. I touched it with a fingertip. My brother was alive!

I unfolded it with great care and trembling fingers, as if it might crumble to dust in my hands, and read the short paragraph within. It was in English, with an address in Seville at the top, and dated 1576. Five years ago. The handwriting was clear and fine, the letters of an educated man.

> *My dearest mother and sister,*
> *These past twenty years I believed you dead. I was told you died before you reached England. Now, having learned that those who told me so lied about many other matters, I begin*

to hope they lied when they told me this too. I address this to Captain John Hawkins trusting that if you are living still he has word of you and will pass this letter on. I am in Seville and if you are living I pray to God that I will see your two faces again. I pray you remained together and were not parted. I send love and a great hope that this letter will reach your hands. If it does, write to me here and I will respond.

With love, your son & brother Kofi.

Francis Enriquez is the name I go under now.

I read the letter over again, holding the paper as gently as I would hold the hand of a child. Here were my brother's own words, in clear black ink. I could not take in the sense of it, my mind was in such upheaval. At last I truly understood that he was alive and he remembered me, and then I had to put the letter aside and sob into my hands.

"Are you well, mistress?" came Rob's voice, and I looked up. He was standing beside me, looking at the letters laid before me. "Is your master in trouble?"

I shook my head. "My brother. My brother is alive. We thought him dead these twenty years—he is alive! This—this letter is from him!"

I passed it up to him and he read it through, eyebrows raised. At last he handed it back to me.

"Why did you think he was dead, all these years?"

"I was told he died when the ship was docked in Spain, before we reached England. I don't understand—Hawkins says here, '*the boy I meant for Tipton.*' Who is Tipton? And my brother says someone lied to him."

I read both letters again; Hawkin's scrawl and my brother's neat hand. *The Black boy I meant for Tipton*. Something was amiss. My brother had been lied to. Had I also been deceived?

"I don't understand," I repeated. "He has been in Seville. He has been in Spain these twenty years and he signs himself Enriquez."

"Enriquez," said Rob. "That's a Converso name. Did he go to a Converso family?"

I knew the story of the Conversos, those former Jews from Spain and Portugal, forced into conversion or exile by the Inquisition, but I had never met one. Some had come to England, and if they came to England they would surely come to London.

"I don't know. It might be so. Have you met any here?" I asked.

"A few of their servants, " he said. "They keep many Moors and Blackamoors. I took books from the master to a house last week—the Lopes's. He's a great merchant and his house is fitted out for a king. They might know an Enriquez."

"I must write to my brother at the address on the letter," I said. "I must write at once. Fetch me the black ink, Rob, and I will send you to catch the post, right away."

Rob ran to fetch the ink and I sat with my quill, considering what I should say. Everything I thought of seemed too light, too trivial, for such a letter. I was conscious of Rob watching me; moments passed and my hand began to shake. *Dear brother,* I wrote at last, though I found it hard to form the words. I pushed the pen across the paper with none of my usual flowing ease. The ink spluttered and the nib creaked.

> *I am your sister and your letter has reached me. Our mother is dead. If you live still, please, come to me or send a sign that you are alive. You may find me at the sign of the Half-Eagle & Key, in Cripplegate. In London.*
> *Your loving sister, Susan Charlewood.*

The words were poor and thin, the letters inelegantly formed as a child's, but that was all I could write. I folded the paper slowly and sealed it. Rob and I watched while the wax cooled and hardened, and when John came into the kitchen, blowing on his hands and breaking the silence, we both startled.

"What's to do?" asked John, looking at us and all the sheets of paper on the table. "Suky, is there bad news?"

"No," I said, standing up and moving away from Rob. "No, indeed, good news! A letter from my brother that we thought dead—an old letter, from Seville, but it found its way here and he may be living yet. He may be alive! I have written to him. Oh God, if he is alive then I am not alone, I am not alone—"

I began to weep again and John came to hold me. I cried against his arm in an excess of feeling. That my mother was not alive to see my brother's words. That I had lived my whole life believing him dead, when he might have been a short sea-voyage away. That I had been lied to. And who had lied to me? Hawkins, perhaps. My master? I pushed the thought away from me, raising my head and drying my eyes. Rob was gone, left to catch the post while I was crying.

When I had recovered a little I went upstairs and wrote a reply to my master. I had to know the truth, though I did not want to.

> *Please sir, explain this to me. Who is Tipton? What was the trouble over my brother? Why did you believe he was dead? Dear sir, for the love I bear you, please tell me everything you know.*

I signed and sealed it and sat for a moment while the sealing wax hardened. My stamp has a bee on it: my master gave it to me once I was lettered enough to write my name and a greeting. I thumbed the end of the stamp, thinking of the bronze tokens my mother had left me. Had Hawkins lied to her? Had my brother been taken off the ship and smuggled away somewhere? My poor mother, having lost her home and family and then one of her only remaining children. I had always felt thankful to Hawkins for saving us from the Portuguese slavers, but perhaps I was wrong.

I put the letter to one side to catch the post later and then went to see John in the printroom before the men arrived for the day's work. He was looking through a proof when I came in.

"Sir," I said, "I think I have the recipe perfect for the secret ink," and I showed him my paper with the letters showing clearly.

"Well done, Suky, well done!" he said, holding it up to the light. "And this shows through with your mixture—not through heat?"

"If you hold it to a candle-flame the letters will stay hidden," I said.

"Perfect," he said. "It is perfect. Take this and burn it now, so that no-one sees your work."

"Yes," I said, taking the paper. "Sir—I believe my brother may have been in service to a Converso family, and Rob said he took books to a Converso house in London last week."

"He did," said John, cautiously. "The books were for Jeronimo Lopes. He's a very powerful man—his cousin is physician to the Earl of Leicester. The Lopeses control half the spice trade in London and Antwerp and they are fast friends with the pretender to the Portuguese throne, Dom Antonio, the fellow the Queen is backing. I hope to nurture him carefully."

"Next time we have books for him—may I take them?" I asked. "And may I ask if he knows the Enriquezes?"

John was silent for a moment, considering. "I am sure he will," he said. "Those Conversos have connections all over the Continent. They stick close together. If you nudge one in Cheapside their second uncle twice removed will hear about it in Constantinople the next day and send their lawyer to prosecute you for attempted manslaughter. Hmm, Suky," he said, and leaned back on his stool. "I don't wish to presume upon Lopes, or beg him for favours."

"I would not beg," I said. "And I might help your cause with him. I speak a little Portuguese. Remember, too, that my mother was a princess in Guinea and the Portuguese hold the Guinea trade. He might take an interest in me."

This was the first time I had needed to push John for something I wanted. He was too generous with his money and I rarely needed to ask for anything: clothes, books, jewellery were all given freely. Yet here, in something most vital to me, he was resistant. I understood his reluctance to presume on an important merchant, but I knew how to approach such people. Had I not dined with them a hundred times at Framfield and in other great houses, as a valued servant? When did John ever converse with great men, except as a supplier of books? I held my head up and looked him in the eye. He drummed his fingers on the table, and nodded at last.

"Very well. When I have a parcel for him, you may take them. But Suky—the thing must be handled delicately. I want Lopes's business, but I am wary of him. New Christian he may be, but his blood is Jewish. And it's not only Lopes. We have dealings with his man Domingo, who is a friend to Campion. Lopes knows nothing of that, and we must keep it so. Therefore, ask your question, thank him whatever the answer, and leave. Yes?"

"Yes. Thank you sir. This strikes close to my heart," and I came and kissed him on the cheek. He looked pleased.

CHAPTER 14

The next day I delivered the first of the secret letters to the Marshalsea with Rob.

We were to take a wherry across the Thames from Billingsgate to the Marshalsea. I felt as light-headed as a bubble, floating past the houses, tavern-benches and book-stalls in a suspension of terror and elation. The sky overhead was busy with clouds and sunlight, and a cold, high wind was blowing over the rooftops but barely ruffling the ribbons of my coif.

I had heard the tales of London prisons. Dark pits where the poorest prisoners lay one on top of another starving slowly and dying of the damp. Rooms filled with the bodies of dead men, where the warders might throw the worst offenders to choke on the reek or have their faces eaten by rats. I needed courage indeed to make the journey to the Marshalsea; not only my first visit to prison but the first time I would cross the Thames by boat.

But the Marshalsea was also a haven for Catholics. We could go there to make confession or hear Mass said by one of the imprisoned priests. Rob was to take me over the river to meet Grace by the prison, where her brother Barney was imprisoned for debt. The supposed reason for my visit was to scribe for him and write a letter to one of his creditors.

John told me before I left: "Barney works for us. Some of my best customers are in the Marshalsea: Sir Francis Tregian keeps a larger library there than most free men and he pays for Barney's upkeep, so that he may pass on the books we sell to prisoners and in turn the news they give to us. The Marshalsea is a very leaky gaol."

I took two sheets of paper with me on which to write the letter. One of them bore the secret message, which John had written out himself in the ink I made up for him. I did not know what it said: the message was not for my eyes. All I knew was to write Barney's letter only on one side of the paper. John had marked that side with a curious symbol, a small diagonal cross with a dot at the end of each arm. It was placed high up in the left-hand corner and looked innocent enough, like an idle scribble.

No-one would have guessed those innocent papers held hidden words, but I felt as if they were shouting their presence. I had sweated such a strong sweat of fear as we went down Cripplegate that morning that I never could scrub out the stains from my shift again.

"Rob," I called as we came down Cheapside, "wait for me." I had to walk fast to keep up with Rob, whose long legs took one stride for my two. He did not slow down to match my pace as John did. He was too set on his own quick progress; a young man impatient with the world and hungry to work his own will upon it.

He looked back at me again and slowed a little but I could tell he chafed at the delay. He had his own mission in Southwark. He was picking up the last few typesorts we needed to complete the setting of *Campion's Challenge*, but he looked as free and easy as if he was out to buy bread.

"Come, mistress," he said, "the river steps will be crowded out by now."

When we came at last to Paul's Wharf and the steps where little boats clustered, I let Rob go before me and hail one. I stood looking over the stinking river, watching the boatmen shout and compete for fares as the passengers jostled for position on the slimy steps.

Beyond them the great ships rode in the middle of the river and sailors went back and forth in dinghies carrying cargo from ship to shore. On the wharf behind me the boxes and barrels piled up. Salt fish, cloth, wine, pig-iron, the world's goods. Once my mother and I had been carried here and set down like so much cargo.

When Rob called me I went to the steps and let him help me down into the wherry. The water made the boat bounce and shift but I set my teeth and kept my balance.

The water of the Thames was thick and yellow with silt and a chill wind blew along the river. I drew my cloak in tight around me and tried to keep my skirts out of the dank water in the bottom of the boat. I was afraid of what we would find on the far bank.

The wherryman was a fattish man in his middle years who hummed loudly as he rowed, an off-key tune that grated on my ears.

Rob stretched out his legs and turned his face to a beam of watery sunlight. The light made his eyes a shade greener and picked out the copper threads in his dark hair. We were in mid-stream, London on either side of us and the sea down-river.

"Nonsuch House," said Rob now, nodding over at London Bridge. The towers and domes of that high-storied building reached up to the sky, their gilded vanes glittering. Built without nails, mortar, or iron, its fame had reached beyond London.

"I'll build a house to rival that one day," he said. "A home on London Bridge, better than Nonsuch. I'll captain ships that go out all over the world and come back to Paul's Wharf filled with good things."

He looked at me again as if challenging me to deny it, though he did not speak boastfully, only as if all these things were plain facts. His ambitions ran so far beyond his station that they should have been laughable, but I did not laugh at him. Sharing a household with him this past month had already taught me much of his character. I knew he was wilful and fearless, with a sharp mind and an abiding restlessness about him. He was not bound by the small house and the narrow streets of Barbican. His mind was set on far horizons. That only deepened my liking for him, but I could not show it.

"*They change the sky, not their soul, who run across the sea,*" I said, like any good housewife correcting an over-reaching servant.

Rob laughed. "So thinks Horace, but Augustine says: *The world is our greater book, what was promised in the book of God, I read in the world as fulfilled.* Is that not reason enough to go and see more of it?"

"The world is all around us," I said, "and God is in every leaf and tree. I don't need to stir further than London to see that fulfilment."

"My father agrees," said Rob. "He wants to keep me away from the sea. Well, if I can't be at sea, London is the only place for me. They say it's the whole world in miniature—and look, here I am in a wherry with a Guinea princess."

He smiled at me, teasing, but I did not want to talk about myself or my family. The wherryman was whistling softly but certainly eavesdropping on our conversation. I had not forgotten Joan Jugge's warning about people watching me.

"Where did you read Pliny and Augustine?" I asked.

"My father tried to educate me," he said. "I was supposed to go to Oxford and become what I know not—some shining expensive lawyer. I know all those old ossified Romans. But I am not made to sit at a desk and wield a pen and he has been sorely disappointed in me. I will see those New Worlds one day and come back rich enough to sit in my London Bridge house, watching the ships going out and the river running down to the sea. Did you never want to travel, mistress? To the new worlds—to Africa. Guinea. You could find your family."

He was leaning in too close to me, his slanted eyes on mine.

"Sit further away," I said, as calmly as my lady might have spoken. "You may only be playing at printer's apprentice, but I am a printer's wife. My place is here now."

He shrugged.

"A wife may play as well as an apprentice."

I looked across the river to the far bank, which was coming closer now, a higgledy-piggledy line of houses with St Mary Overie rising above them and the Marshalsea buried somewhere within.

"No," I said, "she may not. Nor may she go wandering free about the world. We are almost there now. Stop this talk and remember your place."

CHAPTER 15

At the Marshalsea we met with Grace and parted ways. One guard led Grace and I up a flight of stairs and into a narrow corridor—only the corridor of a sprawling house after all, with no skull-topped gates or mouldering stones—that led into an open gallery. The gallery was one of four on the first floor of the prison, all overlooking the garden where the prisoners took their exercise.

The garden was empty and the brickwork paths were flanked with beds of herbs and scattered with dead leaves. A small, sad space. Our guard stopped by a door and let us into the room where Barnabas sat, perched on the edge of a pallet. There were five other pallets in the room, but no other inmates.

Barnabas rose as we came in. He was lanky where Grace was tiny, but he had her same unmistakeable huge pale eyes and small beaky nose.

"Half an hour," said the guard, and closed the door again and locked us in.

"Sister," said Barnabas, coming to kiss Grace as the guard's key turned in the lock. We listened as his footsteps faded back along the corridor. "Are you hearty?"

"Well indeed, brother," said Grace. "This is the new mistress Charlewood. She has come to write your letter for you." Her voice had an edge to it when she said my name.

"God be with you, madam," said Barnabas. I took out my paper while Grace swept a quill and ink from her basket. Seated on the room's only joint-stool, and balancing the paper on the window-ledge, I wrote at Barnabas' dictation a letter begging for his release from a debt.

When I had finished writing and blotted the sheet, he folded it up and tucked it into his jerkin. Then he went to his pallet and from beneath the thin sheet that lay over the straw he took out another sheaf of paper. He handed it to me without a word. I looked at Grace for guidance, unsure whether I should write another letter on this paper. She shook her head and came to take it from me. Just as she whisked it away I saw that the paper was not quite fresh. In one corner someone had inked the same symbol that appeared on my own paper: the small diagonal cross with a dot at the end of each arm. It was almost as if it had been placed there to indicate where to start writing, save for those little dots which made it more than an ordinary cross.

"Goodbye, brother," said Grace, hugging him close to her. She came up just about to his armpit and he bent and kissed her head.

When she looked up at him, I was astonished to see tears on her cheeks. She sniffed and wiped them away on her sleeve. "We miss you dearly," she said. "Stay hearty, and be careful."

"And you," he replied. "My heart goes with you. Thank you for your help, madam," he added, nodding to me as Grace picked up the basket and knocked loudly on the door.

"Guard!" she called, and in a while the warder returned and led us back along the gallery. I was burning to ask Grace the meaning of that little mark on Barnabas' letter. In the lodge, the warder made a desultory search through the basket and waved us through.

We returned to the river to meet Rob as great ranks of cloud broke and reformed over London's rooftops. I watched Grace as she sat clutching her basket at the top of the steps, chaffing the wherrymen below. Like Rob, she showed no outward sign of fear despite the dangers of the paper she carried. I could not be easy and kept looking around for Rob. I wanted to be home safe, with all our perilous cargo stowed away in the cellar.

"Lucy Negro! Lucy Negro!" called a voice from among the boats below us and someone laughed. One of the wherries pulled away and the passengers waved up at us: two grinning apprentices. Grace's gaze flickered to mine and away and she shifted in her seat. I swear the corner of her mouth twitched into a smile. I wanted to slap her. The legend of this dark Southwark prostitute haunted the riverbanks. I had been called by her name a dozen times already since I arrived in the city.

"Do you laugh, when such river rats call your mistress by a whore's name?" I said quietly. Her face grew sullen again.

"No, mistress," she said.

We sat in silence, waiting for Rob. Grace's tears in the prison had wrong-footed me. I had been thinking of her as someone entirely hardened, like a pickled walnut, but she had a brother and she loved him. Let her hate me, then, if she must. What did I care for the ill feelings of an ignorant girl. If she continued in this vein I could tell John we must find a new maid and let Grace go. That was a power I had, and I hugged it to me.

Rob arrived at last, out of breath and clutching the proof for a playbill. This was his excuse for a journey over the river. I wondered where he had hidden the sorts. He folded the bill into his bag, cursing at the stiff buckles as we made our way onto the steps. His face was flushed and there was a swipe of dirt on his cheek. He caught me looking at him and laughed.

"Southwark mud," he said. "I tripped, running past the

bear-gardens. Don't fret, all's well."

He and Grace joked and pushed one another as we made our way into the wherry but I could not shake my fear. I knew the consequences of discovery. I could not forget the sight of my master being led away by those pikemen. Grace's brother was in prison so she must understand that pain. I sat upright and stared at the South bank as we pulled away, watching the passage of another boat behind us. Was my master comfortable in prison, like Sir Frances Tregian with his books? He told me in his letters that he was well fed and looked after, but would he tell me if he was not?

CHAPTER 16

That night we started work on the leaflets. There was one press-man and Rob to work the press, and I was called upon to read through the proofs for mistakes and help John with the composition.

The cellar was freezing. It was not possible for a compositor to work there alone for long periods of time in the winter. A compositor cannot wear gloves and after a while John's fingers would be too numb to pick out the letters. We carried down hot bricks wrapped up in cloth, and he clung on to those when he began to feel the cold. He was experienced enough to set up the type in the dark, knowing exactly where each letter would be in the typecase. I was not—but my eyes were young and better able to distinguish the letters by candlelight. So while he warmed his hands at the bricks, I carried on his work, slotting the letters into the compositors stick and then placing them into the forme. I went carefully. I felt it a heavy responsibility. Campion had entrusted his God-given thoughts to paper and ink. My hands took his words, letter by letter, and prepared them to be multiplied. In this small way, working in the dark, I might help bring souls back to the Catholic faith. I might help save my fellow men.

We worked until the bricks cooled and our fingers ached with the chill. Once we were done, Rob and the press-man Harold began their work: Rob inking up the type and Harold working the press. It was laborious work, for we did not have enough type to lay out all the pages at once. But by the time we went to bed we had one page laid out and printed on twenty sheets of paper—there was no room to dry more than twenty at a time in the cellar.

John and I sat by the fire in our room for a while, warming our fingers before we went to bed. It had been a long day, one of the longest of my life. My head was full of it. The Marshalsea, the deep cold of the cellar, and all our work to produce one small page of print.

"Thanks for your work, Suky," said John, taking my hand. "How are your hands? Ah, they feel cold still. Here, let me hold them."

He held my hands between his own and rubbed them, frowning. I watched him, noting how tired he looked.

"What was it like, sir, when we did not have to worship in secret—to live in secret?" I said. "You were young when Mary was on the throne."

He sighed and nodded.

"It seems such a brief interlude now. When I was a child, things were as they are today. I grew up under Edward and the last of Henry, when they were whitening the churches. There was a picture of the murder of Thomas Becket in our church. I used to sit and stare at it, being a bloodthirsty boy and thinking of the knights sticking their swords into his brain. One day they whitewashed it over and then all I had to look at was a blank wall, but I knew Thomas was underneath. I felt one day it would bleed through again, all the colours under the whitewash, that the saints would be stronger than the heretic fools who covered their faces. But the walls stayed white and we watched our priests persecuted, the abbey scattered, and land bought up by rich friends of the King. I was up in London, four years into my apprenticeship when Mary Tudor took the throne. We thought she would bring freedom to us poor Catholics who had been hiding like mice in church candles for twenty years, but—freedom was not all I had thought it would be."

He nodded towards the fire, which was burning down now to embers but still sending up flickers and spurts of flame. "I saw more than one of my neighbours burn—Protestants, who had lived beside me and known my family's faith and let us go unmolested. I did not take delight in watching those human torches."

"So you would not have Scottish Mary on the throne now?"

He was silent for several minutes, staring into the flames. At last he said slowly, "I have no power to choose a sovereign. I want only freedom to worship as I please. I trust that one day the truth will bleed through those white walls and my St. Thomas be restored. Let my noble friends the Howards play at kingmaking. We common men must go where they spin us, like tops."

He gave a final rub to my hands. "Are they warmer now? Good."

"Thank you," I said. Then, because he seemed in a soft mood, "Sir—I have something to ask you."

He sat up and smiled at me. "Go on. Your demands have been very few, Suky! I thought marrying a girl of your breeding would cost me a fortune in gowns and jewellery but instead you look at my accounts and tell me to buy linen, not silk. What is it?"

"It is not something you can buy," I said. I struggled with myself a moment, unsure whether to continue. What would my lady have done? She would have spoken to my lord, without a doubt.

"It is Grace," I said. "She is insolent to me. She dislikes me. I think it is because I am not English. I have spoken to her—I have corrected her—but it does no good. If she keeps on with her rudeness, I must ask you if we can find another maid."

John's smile had faded, and now he winced.

"Ah, I wish you had asked me for silks. I am sorry to hear this, Suky."

I waited. My lord always supported my lady if her grievance was just. Would John support me?

"Grace came to us when her parents died," he said at last. "She is the eldest of seven and she needed to work to put bread in the mouths of her brothers and sisters. My wife used to mother her, as our own children were gone. The youngest ones still need that money. I will talk to her, but I can't let her go."

So I must swallow my anger. I nodded. "Don't talk to her," I said. "I think it will make her hate me worse."

"Ah, she can't hate you!" said John. "How could anyone hate you? She has a tongue, I know, and she did love Liz, so it may be she finds it hard serving a new mistress. I swear she'll warm to you in time though. Tell me if she troubles you greatly and I will have words with her."

"Yes, sir," I said, but I knew I would not. If he took Grace's part, and if he could not believe she hated me, there was little point raising the matter again. I must endure her looks and her silences.

CHAPTER 17

Our work in the cellar continued through the cold nights of early March. Day and night I worked with and dreamed of typesorts, paper, and the creak of the press. I had not forgotten my brother's letter though. My master replied to me from prison, in a letter smudged with fingerprints and dirt:

> *I am more glad than I can say that your brother is alive, though I am furious we were lied to. Hawkins sent him to serve Hugh Tipton, an English merchant in Seville, along with a whole ship full of goods and treasure, but the Spanish impounded it and arrested Tipton. The boy went to a Spanish family instead and they would not give him up, nor would the authorities help recover him. We tried, but it was no good. There was a great deal of trouble with Spain over Hawkins' voyage. The Queen herself interceded to try and reclaim Hawkins' goods, to no avail. Then we heard your brother had died and there was nothing more to be done. It broke your mother's heart. I wish she might have lived to know it was not true.*

I sat shivering with the letter in my hand, sick with anger. Hawkins had sent my brother away. I never knew that. I never knew we were separated by design. What cruelty was that, from the famous John Hawkins? And my master. I felt the sincerity, that he had tried. But did he not think much of referring to my brother, my kinfolk, as merely goods? I pushed the letter away into a corner of my desk, but I could not shake off the anger. It made me more determined than before to find my brother again, to bring together what had been split. My family. My sibling.

My first step was to talk to Jeronimo Lopes, and as John had promised, he let me take the next parcel of books to him.

Lopes had a fine house not far from us, within the city walls, in Milk Street. His house sat cuddled up next to three or four other great merchant's houses like a row of ladies-in-waiting.

A sad-eyed Morisco maid opened the door to me and led me into the house, where burned, polished wooden chests lined the equally polished block wooden floor. The air was graced with sandalwood and other spices, aniseed, cinnamon, ginger, and the hall was quiet and peaceful. The maid pushed open a side door, letting the sound of men's talk and laughter out into the hall.

I could not stop myself exclaiming in pleasure as I came through the door. It was a library as extensive as my master's. There was not an unbound chapbook in sight. The bindings were all calfskin or leather, covers worked with gold and silver thread.

A man who must be Lopes sat by an applewood fire, leaning back in his chair. He was as elegant and richly bound as one of his books. A slender, olive-skinned man with curled black moustaches, he was dressed in plum-coloured velvet worked with gold embroidery. I curtsied to him and he nodded, while his eyes flickered over me and took the measure of me.

"Thank you, Sofia," he said, dismissing the maid. "Thank you, Goody Charlewood. Domingo, will you look through and make sure the titles are all present."

A man stood up from the chair opposite him, which had its tall back to me. I had not seen him sitting there and when he revealed himself I started and almost dropped my parcel. He was a Blackamoor. That was not so unexpected, for as Rob had said the Spanish and Portuguese kept many African servants, but I had not yet seen so dark a man in London. He was as dark as me—not a Barbary Moor or a Morisco but a man who might even be from my own country. And this was the man who John said had dealings with Campion.

He was richly dressed, all in black velvet, with the doublet he wore slashed to show the white silk beneath. The black velvet against his skin was the richest fashion I had seen—richer, somehow, than gold thread or silver-work. A bold choice, to pair black with black.

I could see him studying me as I studied him, and his eyes were wary, almost a little afraid. He stayed by the chair a moment before coming over to me. He took my hand with a little bow, and I curtsied in return.

"*Bom dia*," I said, and he checked a little, perhaps surprised at my few words of Portuguese, before responding:

"*Bom dia*. The books, if you please?"

I handed him the parcel, noting as he took it a skull grinning from a *memento mori* ring on his left index finger. He was tall, at least a head taller than me, and his face was ageless. I could not tell if he was twenty or forty. In his velvets and silks he looked like a star-cut night with slashes of moon.

His skin had a polished gleam to it. He had a strong nose, not flat like mine but broad, and a short upper lip—a humorous curling mouth. His cheekbones were high and broad. His eyes were almond-shaped and a little slanted, like my own, and his eyebrows surprisingly delicate for a man, winging upwards. A round beard and full lips. I had a mad urge to put my hands on his cheeks to be sure he was flesh and blood. The even madder thought came to me that against all odds and by some impossible fate, he could be my brother.

"Are you from Guinea?" I asked, forgetting all my courtesies.

"I am not," he said, his English only lightly accented. "The Gambra was my birthplace, but I lived in Spain since I was a little child."

His voice did not invite further questioning, so I only nodded, ashamed of the disappointment that flooded me and brought tears to my eyes. Why should I expect to find a brother here, when the last I knew of him was in Seville?

He moved away from me to a nearby table, where he set about unwrapping my parcel of books and leafing through the pages.

"Are you a Guinea native, Mistress Charlewood?" asked Lopes, who had now risen from his chair and stood beside Domingo, looking at the titles as Domingo held them up.

"I am," I said, remembering my purpose there. "I am. My mother was a princess in that country, and John Hawkins brought us to England from his voyage twenty years ago."

"Indeed," said Lopes, interested now. "And you grew up in London?"

"In Sussex," I said, "in the house of Thomas Framfield—the iron merchant."

"I know the name," said Lopes. "Yet you speak Portuguese?"

"Only a little, sir. My master had us learn many languages, but Portuguese was not among them. I wish I had more, for I could speak to you then in your own tongue, which I think very fair. I have a question to ask you sir, though I am afraid to ask it. You may think it too bold in a woman."

"Ask, ask," said Lopes, nodding at Domingo as he held up the last book. "I see you have brought me all my titles, even those I thought untraceable, and so I am in a generous mood."

"I am looking for my brother," I said in a rush. "He was twelve or so when we were taken from Guinea, and Hawkins left him in Seville to be page-boy to an English merchant—Hugh Tipton. But the Spanish took all Hawkins' goods from the voyage and gave my brother to another family, who told us he had died. Now I have a letter from him—an old letter, but I believe he may be living still, and he signs himself as Francis Enriquez."

"Enriquez?" said Lopes, and his expression hardened a little.

"Yes," I said. "I think he served a Converso family. I have replied to his letter, but he wrote it four years ago and I don't know what may have become of him since. I wondered—I hoped—you might know the Enriquez family. You might know if they had such a servant or be able to ask if he is still living. I have no right to ask such a favour of you, nor any hope that you would have time to fulfil it, and I could only repay you with my very humble gratitude—but I ask because I must, because my heart will not let me stay silent. My mother died when I was a child and I have no other family."

I watched his face, desperate for some sign of hope. The Enriquez name had made him angry, for some reason. Perhaps they had a feud and he would refuse me and put me out of the house. Domingo, at the table, was silent. When I glanced at him his face was as forbidding as Lopes's. He caught me looking at him and shook his head a little.

"It is true, you have no right to ask such a favour, or hope that it may be fulfilled," said Lopes at last. "You presume upon me, Goody Charlewood. But I thank your husband for his service, and I will send payment soon. I have another list of titles for him. Domingo—the list."

Domingo brought me a sheet of paper, which I folded up and put into my basket. I did not look at him. The hostility from him and from Lopes, when I had come in such hope, was unbearable. The room which had felt like home to me now seemed cold and strange.

"Thank you," I said. "*Obrigado*. I am at your service, sir," and I curtsied to Lopes, and went back out into the sandalwood-scented hall. I walked home fast through the streets, blinking away tears. I kept seeing Domingo's face and hearing Lopes's words: *You presume upon me*. So he had reminded me of my place. A little Guild wife. It was bitter to be treated so and all the way back to the Barbican I longed for Framfield and my former status.

When I reached home, I knelt down by the chest I had brought with me from Sussex and took out my mother's heirlooms, the little objects wrapped in cloth. If I found my brother, perhaps he could tell me what they represented. I wanted to hold them again

I unfolded the cloth and there they were, looking even smaller than they had in Sussex and just as alien. I picked out the bird and balanced it on my palm, holding it up to my eye-line so it loomed bigger, like a golden statue. It was very beautifully wrought. Its wings and feathers were clearly delineated and its backward-bending neck was long and graceful. Its eye looked amused to me, as if it were laughing at my ignorance.

"What's that?" said John behind me and I jumped in fright and almost dropped it. I had been so absorbed I never heard his footsteps. He came closer and bent down, leaning in over my shoulder.

"That's a pretty thing."

I felt guilty as a child caught stealing apples, and then angry with myself for feeling such guilt. What was the harm in it, truly? Why shouldn't he see it?

"My mother left it to me," I said. "It comes from Guinea." I hesitated, and then repeated the lie I had told Rob. I felt more secure in it now. No-one knew what these things were. If I gave them an identity who was to say it was not true? They were mine. I could make them what I liked.

"They are family symbols," I said. "The bird is my mother's

crest—a stamp of royalty. I don't know what the ladder is."

I held up the cloth to him and he picked up the ladder piece, squinting at it.

"What were they used for? As ornaments?"

"I don't know, exactly. I only know what they stand for."

"They look like pieces from a chess game," he said. "Let me see the bird." I passed it up to him reluctantly and watched as he weighed them in his hands, studying the work.

"Well, well. This fellow's had a long journey, wings or no. There's craftsmanship in this. If you inked this up, it'd make a good clear stamp."

"I don't know," I said. The same disproportionate, sad, and violent passion I had felt when I first saw them flooded through me again.

"May I try inking this?" he said, holding out the ladder to me, "I need to mark up some particular work that must travel secretly."

"No!" I said and stood up, taking the pieces out of his hands and clutching them to me. "No, you may not. They are not for inking or working or anything. They stay here, in this chest."

I was trembling, shocked at my own anger. The bitterness I felt towards the little objects was matched by the strength of my feeling that they should not be taken, used, or violated by the everyday. It was as if John had seen an open wound on my arm and deliberately pushed a thumb into it. My blood and bone cried out against him.

John looked down at me as I held the objects close to my breast like children.

"My pardon, Suky," he said. "They are from your mother and therefore precious to you. I'm sorry, I didn't think."

I turned away from him and wrapped my things up in the cloth again, placing them carefully back in the chest. I did not want him to see my face. I felt as if I was swaddling a child and placing it into a grave. The things lived and did not live. They burned with meaning and I could not read them. Every message that came to me from my birth country was incomprehensible to me—a funeral service for a stranger, sung in a foreign tongue.

CHAPTER 18

Spring came and I missed Sussex. Crocuses and primroses blossomed in our garden and the leaves came out on the chestnut trees in Finsbury Fields. Everything was blooming but our household lived for the nights, toiling in the dark cellar. The sunshine could not reach there and the old stones seemed stuck in perpetual winter.

With the printing at last complete and one hundred copies of *Campion's Challenge* stacked up, Grace and I were set to stab-stitching the pamphlets together with their endpapers. It was not skilled work, stitching cord along one edge of the paper to form a simple binding. It might have been companionable, with a different girl, but we mostly sewed in silence.

By mid-March all our work was complete. The printed and bound copies of Campion's work sat in the cellar, waiting for Father Persons to set the date they would go out into the world. When he gave the word, we would distribute them in bundles of five to Marshalsea priests and others who would all place them about the city on the same night. I thought of the pamphlets often, concealed in our house like caterpillars waiting to break out of the cocoon.

Then our compositor was arrested. Rob brought the news,

having witnessed it with his own eyes. I was at the bookstall when he tore up to the house in a sweat. It was nearly dusk and I was starting to pack the books away. The cold March air smelled of rain, fresh on my skin. When Rob ran up I tried to hand him a stack of books to take into the house, but he pushed them away.

"Is the master in the print room?" he said between breaths.

"Yes. Why? Rob, what's happened?"

He looked around us then pointed inside. I led him into the parlour and closed the door. He blew out his breath and put a hand on his ribs, wincing.

"I ran so fast I have a stitch. Mistress, we are in trouble. The pursuivants took Adam. In Paul's Yard. He is taken, and he was carrying type with him—our type, from the pamphlets—to go to Father Persons. If they torture him and he speaks—" Rob shook his head. My body flooded with cold fear.

"Stay here," I said, and I ran to the print room to fetch John. When Rob told him the news, he said nothing at all for a few minutes. He stood staring out of the parlour window into the street, while I fetched ale for Rob. He gulped it down in one thirsty mouthful and set his cup back on the table with a gasp. John looked round at us again.

"Persons is out of London now," he said. "It will take a few hours at least to send a messenger to him and to hear back. I can't wait. We must act. Rob, fetch the copies up and pack them in two bags. You and I will take them to the lime kilns and burn them. Suky, search the cellar for anything that might condemn us—any dropped sorts or scraps. Tip away all your inks: you can make up new ones. Grace can take down the bookstall and keep watch up here."

"What!" I put my hand out to him. "Sir, all our work!"

He shook his head. "If they find the pamphlets here, we will hang. I can deny whatever Adam says—even if they find the press I can show them I use it for printing pirate copy and they may let me off. But if they find even one of those pamphlets here, we are done for. It will take too long to burn them in the hearth, and the kilns are close by. Come now Suky!" He spoke sharply, seeing the disbelief in my eyes. We had already risked so much to print these copies out. Hours and hours in the freezing cellar, cramped backs and aching eyes, only the glow of faith to light the way. All of that, to burn up Campion's words in a furnace and send them into the sky as smoke?

I followed John to the cellar, bitterly angry at the ruin of our plans. As John and Rob packed our work away into bags I went up and down with a lantern, studying every inch of the floor for the glint of a sort or a pale manuscript leaf. Nothing was out of place. We swept the cellar carefully every night and the cold earth floor was clear. I went over the press, the stools and the tables too while Rob and John hurried out of the cellar into the twilight of Finsbury Fields.

When I was sure everything was safe I carried my bowl of gall-stone ink upstairs and emptied the liquid out in the garden. Then Grace and I set out supper, startling every time a board creaked or someone went by outside. We did not eat, but sat waiting at the table for John and Rob. Grace twisted a lock of her hair around her finger over and over again and I stared at the water in my cup, watching it tremble at every movement of my hand.

It grew dark outside and Grace lit the candles at the kitchen fire. As she carried them back to the table the front door scraped open at last. Grace gasped and dropped a candle. It rolled, still alight, into the corner and I jumped up and ran to save it from setting the house on fire. John and Rob came into the kitchen, bringing cold air and the acrid reek of the lime-kilns with them. I stood with Grace at either end of the room holding up our candles like two statues. John stared at us, hollow-eyed and smoke-smudged. Then he wheezed into silent laughter, bent double and hooting at the floor.

"Oh," he said, "Oh Lord, defend us from all perils and dangers of this night. Suky, you stared as if a lion had come into the kitchen. There are no lions, no devils. We are whole and hearty and everything we carried is flames and ashes. Oh, I am done. I am done. Let me sit down. Bring us wine, if you love us!"

I sent Grace for the wine and set the candles safely on the table while John and Rob took off their boots and ate a plain supper. John kept breaking into laughter again in between bites. His mirth only made me more sombre. I could not comprehend how he could laugh at the destruction of our work and the danger that still threatened us.

I did not want anything to eat and after a while I excused myself and went upstairs. I thought I might read but could not settle and found myself walking up and down our bedroom in agitation. At last I came out into the corridor and sat halfway up the attic steps in the dark, listening to the others talking below. John was the loudest, almost shouting, and soon he began to sing. That meant he was probably drunk. I felt like crying. This work had given me purpose since I arrived in London and now it was smoke. The city was cold and cruel and I did not belong here.

Footsteps sounded on the stairs below. John was still singing so it wasn't him, and it was too heavy to be Grace. Rob, then. I stood up to go into the bedroom, then sat down again. He saw me as he came into the corridor and walked slowly up to the steps, carrying his candle. I looked at him. Our eyes were level: his were a little red with smoke and his hair still bore specks of white ash. I wanted to reach out and brush them away. Instead, I folded my hands in my lap.

"My cat used to guard the garret steps like that," he said. "She'd scratch me unless I stroked her. Do you have a toll to pay, mistress?"

"Why is John laughing?" I said. "There is nothing to laugh about. You might both have died tonight. All our work is destroyed and Adam is under arrest."

"Have you never laughed out of fright?" he said. I stared at him blankly. I knew I should move aside and let him up the stairs, but I stayed, smoothing down the folds of my blue wool skirt. He sighed, and sat down on the bottom step with his back against one wall and his feet against the other.

"I can always sleep here," he said. "I could sleep anywhere, tonight." He set his candle down on the step below my feet, but it rocked as he settled it and a few drops of wax fell onto the pointed toe of my slipper—one of the ridiculous, embroidered pair John had brought me for a wedding gift.

"Ah," he said. "Your pardon, mistress."

I looked at the clear wax hardening and whitening, daisy-coloured blots on the fine swirls of green and yellow needle-work.

"It will scrape clean," I said. "What do you think will happen, if Adam talks? John said the cellar press isn't proof enough."

"I don't know," said Rob. "I think it would depend on how much they want to hang a Catholic this month. Or three. Me, the master, and Adam. The best-looking corpses at Tyburn this year."

"Stop it," I said, violently, and began to push myself up off the step. "Let me past."

He looked up at me, smiling. "Would you weep then, mistress, if I swung? I'd have thought you'd laugh. Wait—don't go yet. I'll get this wax off."

He moved the candle, putting it carefully on the boards of the corridor. Slowly I sat back down again as he took hold of my slippered foot and began to scrape at the wax drops with his thumb. White wax-flakes pared away and fell to the steps. His hand was warm around my foot. His left thumb rested at my ankle and his right pressed into my toes through the canvas and silk thread of the slipper as he scraped at the wax. It was a transgression. The heat of his hand set warmth up my calf, my thigh, all over my body. My chest was tight with held breath, breath that wanted to form his name. I should have pulled my foot away and I did not. I let him hold it and I looked in his eyes as he brushed away the last curls of wax and set my foot back on the stair. His fingers still rested at my ankle and his gaze was hungry and sweet. I tasted honey in my mouth and my lips parted. Then there was a crash and a curse from the kitchen. Rob pulled his hand away and I jumped up from the step, nearly kicking him.

"Out of my way," I whispered. "Get out of my way. Go to bed."

He stood, scooping the candle up from the floor, and moved aside to let me pass without a word. I swept into the bedroom, shutting the door tight behind me, and leant against it listening for his footsteps on the garret stairs. Then I finally let out the breath I had been holding and sat down by the fire. I was too dizzy to think. I took off my slippers and held them in my lap. I traced the embroidery on the shoe he had touched, finding small, shining patches left by the wax. I still had the slippers on my lap when John came up to bed, much the worse for wine.

CHAPTER 19

I was dog-weary all that spring, dragging my feet past the cold, old stones of London Wall through Cripplegate. We were in stasis. Adam was questioned and released, though they impounded the type-sorts. John thought they let him go in hopes he might lead them to Persons. Searchers came to the house, knowing he had been working with John, but John was able to show them the legitimate texts he had also laid out. So the shadow passed over us again—and we might have kept all those pamphlets without harm. It seemed the most sinful waste to me.

John remained unbearably sanguine, reminding me we were lucky to be alive. Persons and Campion were now working on a new text so there was nothing for us to take on. My secret inks were still required for our Marshalsea messages, but that was all. This sudden absence of purpose left me restless and snappish.

My one consolation was a letter that arrived for me from Jeronimo Lopes. He had been so discouraging at our meeting that I had not expected to hear from him again, but one fine May morning Rob came in twirling a neatly folded paper, sealed with a great red wax seal.

"For you, mistress," he said. "It's from Lopes—his servant found me in Stationers' Hall."

"What's that?" said John, who was still at breakfast. "Is it not for me?"

"He said Susan Charlewood," said Rob. "He was particular about it."

I seized it from him without ceremony and stared at it a while before breaking the seal. It was so beautiful. The paper was thick and cream-coloured, and when I finally opened it I saw that Lopes wrote in an extravagantly curlicued hand, leaving careless, expensive spaces between words. I almost stroked the letter as I read it. It spoke of the world I had left behind in Sussex, of power and position and men with the influence to see a business through.

It took me a while to understand what Lopes had written, I was so taken with the message sent by his stationery. When I did, I put my hand to my mouth and read the letter over again without speaking.

"Well?" said John, rising from the table and coming over to me.

"He may have news of my brother," I said slowly. "He has traced the little page-boy Hawkins sent to Hugh Tipton and he—he was certainly alive five years ago, when the Enriquez family left Spain. He says he will continue the search, which he believes may benefit us both, and will write when he has news. And he sends his regards to you, sir."

John stared at me. "'Benefit us both'? How may a search for your brother benefit him?"

I shook my head. "I don't know. I don't see how it could—unless he had dealings with the Enriquezes. Perhaps they owed him money and my brother could help recover it?"

John held his hand out for the letter and I gave it to him reluctantly. He read it through, chewing his thumb.

"I don't like this," he said at last. "Why doesn't the man say plainly what he means?"

"I don't care what he means," I said, suddenly angry. "He's offering to help me. Christian, Jew, heathen, whatever he is, I don't care. If he can find my brother I will shake his hand and thank him."

"Hmm," said John. "Remember what I told you, Suky. Have a care. These people are not our people."

I did not reply, but held my hand out for the letter. He returned it reluctantly and I folded it into my pocket.

The letter raised my spirits for a few weeks, but it could not shift my tiredness. The heat fogged my brain, and most days I found myself ready to drop by the afternoon. Of course it was Grace who guessed why I walked around half-asleep—Grace with her army of younger brothers and sisters.

We were sitting in the kitchen at the end of a fierce June, shelling peas into a bowl. I had no appetite for them in their hard green cases, though I used to love picking out new peas for their taste of summer and the softness of the cushioning pod with its silky lining. Grace was working twice as quickly as me, pushing the peas from the pod with a practised thumb. I stopped for a minute to yawn and she cast a sharp look at me.

"That's the fifth one. I've been counting. You've turned into a dormouse, madam."

Her tone towards me I felt to be both wary and accusing. I took that comment as a slur on my capability for hard work, and suddenly found myself as stung as if she had pushed me into a bed of nettles. I had suffered six months of hostility from this small carbuncle, this wart on the city's back with her thin hair and fishwife tongue. Who was she to pass judgement on me?

"I am sorry you must work for a black mistress, Grace," I said, shocked by the venom in my own voice, "and I am sure it irks you to take orders from me but I am your mistress and I will be obeyed.

I will not be sniped at by a little maid who has got all her learning from the gutter. I yawn because I have not slept, not because I am lazy. I work as hard as you and if I had spoken to my own mistress as you speak to me I should have been whipped."

Grace stared at me, her hands among the pea-pods, struck still by my outburst. The kitchen was quiet and warm and the silence after I spoke was tense as if I had slapped her face.

"I don't ask for a ladies' maid," I said, still lit up with fury. "I only ask for your respect: the respect that is due to me and that I give to you. This is the order of the house and it is your duty to keep to it. And how should you like it, to always be known for the colour of your skin, which is tainted by the things people choose to see in it—the devil, night, carrion birds? Your whiteness is invisible, no-one looks at you and thinks of leprosy, shrouds, ghosts and white-furred mould. I would like, just for a day, to walk around as you do without looks and stares. I would like to be so unremarkable."

I stopped abruptly, trembling. My whole body was hot with rage. I had never let fly at anyone in such a manner. My lady would never have spoken so to a servant. I put my hand to my mouth and sat back in my chair, appalled at myself.

Grace blinked again and began slowly opening another pea-pod. We sat without speaking for a moment as she pushed the peas out and put the stripped pod to one side. I had never seen anything as green as that bowl of peas, I could almost taste the greenness of them. It made me feel ill.

"I think you are used to grander servants," said Grace at last. "I meant no insolence by what I said about the yawn. I'm sorry you took offence. I only meant to say that you look a little fatter about the face—and that anyone can see how tired you are—and now you are angry too. I wondered if you had bled this month?"

I stared at her with my mouth still open. It was no apology, but the implication of her words knocked the rage right out of me with shock. Why it should have shocked me, I don't know. Life had been too full of other great matters.

"Yes. No," I said.

"And the month before?"

"I don't remember."

"Better start adding up the weeks, mistress."

She smiled, watching my face as I tried to think back. I picked up another pod and opened it, counting the days. I had not forgiven her, but I would have my apology another time.

My attention suddenly turned all inside myself, away from the world. I usually liked to know all the news and everything that was happening in the land but I began to rest my mind more on my body and the signs it was writing for me.

This secret hope gave me comfort in what became a bleak year. In June we celebrated an audacious feat by Campion and Persons. They managed to do what we had planned with the *Challenge*, secretly printing out and distributing a hundred copies of a new work by Campion. It went out all over Oxford, even in Great St. Mary's Church, so that every student coming in to service could pick up a copy, and under the very noses of every professor there.

The text, *Decem Rationes*, was a trumpet-blast to English Catholics, a light in darkness—and Campion's death-warrant. In mid-July the summer was snuffed out for us like a candle when the pursuivants finally caught up him. He was caught at a house near Wantage where he had been hiding and dragged back to London. Father Persons had fled the country, for which we heartily praised God, but the mood in our house was both sorrowful and fearful. The Treason Act left little hope for Campion. His life was likely to end on the gibbet at Tyburn in the most horrible fashion, and his quartered limbs set up on the gates of London.

And what might become of us, who had been working for and with Persons? If anyone discovered our part in his mission, there would be no clemency. The rest of my pregnancy played out against Campion's approaching death, my belly swelling as hope for his survival thinned to nothing.

There were other risks for us, too. John sourced books for other Catholic gentry and noblemen besides my old master, and these connections had won him printing work from no less a person than Philip Howard, the Earl of Arundel, who had just come into his title.

It warmed John's heart to style himself printer to an earl. He craved recognition from those high-born bull-pups who pattered about the Queen's skirts, playing at chivalry. The power they wielded often far outstripped their merit. Every belch and fart of theirs reverberated around Whitehall, gaining grandeur from each echo till it was a very hurricane by the time news of it reached us at the Barbican.

But the pleasure of gaining a noble patron was edged with risk. The Queen herself had Howard blood from her mother Anne Boleyn, but she viewed these persistently Catholic relations with a cold eye. Philip's father Thomas had been executed not ten years previously for making a play to marry Scottish Mary. So our household was publicly linked, however loosely, to one of the greatest and most notorious families in the land.

I said nothing to John about the baby until we were into August. I did not want to raise his hopes without certainty. Perhaps I was only fatter because we were eating well in the fullness of summer. Perhaps it was the sun that suddenly dissipated my tiredness and sickness and awoke a kind of glowing heat in me, a flush of vitality.

One lazy, warm morning I was in the garden picking herbs when I felt a stirring inside me—a strange fluttering and a kind of rising heat, a surging sensation almost like desire. It was like nothing I had ever felt before. Life. Something that was not me, moving inside me. I dropped the bunched thyme I was holding and put my hands on my belly.

The movement stopped but it had been unmistakeable, as present and quick as the smell of the herbs or the sun on my neck. For a moment all my thoughts flew to my belly and the child in the darkness there. The sun, the blue sky and the garden scents vanished and I was in the dark with it, blind and deaf to everything but the pulse of my blood.

Then my senses rallied and strengthened and the world rushed back in a hundred times stronger. The sun struck me, the green smell of thyme jumped at me and all the colours in the garden roared hallelujah. I stayed there until the feeling subsided, smiling at nothing. It was a wholly new feeling, but it tugged at me with something like recognition, as if I had just seen someone I loved for the first time after many years apart.

I said nothing to Grace, waiting to present the news to John like a gift. He was out with the printer Richard Rowlands all day and did not come home until I was already in bed, sitting quietly with my hands on my belly and waiting to see if this small being would stir again. John came in noisy and a little drunk, scrambling into bed and reaching for me. I resisted.

"Go to, sir," I said, pushing him away. "No, listen—I have news. Will you listen? In the garden today, I felt a quickening in my belly, a stirring. I think I am with child."

He was quite still and quiet for a moment, then he eased himself up till he was sitting beside me.

"You are sure of the feeling? It was not an indigestion—an ill humour?"

"I have never felt anything like it before. And I am fatter, lately, and my breasts ache. Grace thought it might be a baby."

He reached a hand over and placed it on my stomach, over my nightgown. His hand was warm. The night around us was very still. Outside the streets were silent, no-one stirring except night creatures moving between flowers in the garden.

"You are plumper," he said. "I had not noticed."

He caught at my fingers with his other hand. "Tell me if you feel it again. Tell me straight away. To have a child in the house—"

He broke off. We sat for a while, our hands resting over one another on my belly, waiting to see if it would stir again. Such a small thing to be invested with such huge hope. I knew John was praying for it to be a son, a boy to inherit the business. The baby had been growing unobserved inside me, telling no-one it was there—not even me. Now it had announced its presence and would never again, for the rest of its life, be free from the weight of its parents' hopes.

CHAPTER 20

John's mood was always uncertain these days. He was constantly looking over his shoulder now Campion had been taken. He had immediately began shoring up our defences and covering our tracks. He took a commission to print a carefully worded account of Campion's arrest, penned by Anthony Munday and authorised by Burghley and Walsingham, that made Campion sound like a coward, not a hero. John went in person to watch one of Campion's debates against the Privy Council and saw he had been cruelly tortured. The thought of that heroic man under torture was repulsive.

"They've racked him," said John as we sat by the embers of the bedroom fire talking one night. "His hand trembles so much he can't lift it. I tell you, when they kill him, they'll make a martyr. People are disgusted at the way they have used him, a man of such intelligence and grace. God above, it sickens me. It sickens me to print the lies Munday writes about him. Sometimes I feel a traitor to my own cause. But I will keep us safe—I will keep you and the baby safe, Susan, don't fear."

Despite his reassurance, as autumn came in and the days grew darker, I began to feel a strange dread. I could now see the outline of a small foot or a hand when the baby kicked out uncomfortably and pressed against my belly. The sight of the child moving made me terrified that I was going to die—that his birth would herald my death. I dreamed about it over and over, always the same dream. Someone took the child from my breast and I faded backwards into darkness, the light fleeting away and bells ringing in the distance.

On the first day of December I set out to market with Grace. In just over a month I would go into confinement and closet myself in my room, stop up the keyholes and draw the curtains round the bed to keep the light out and the warm dark in. Before I shut myself away I wanted to walk outside as much as I could, even though the days were raw and my feet ached.

"I wonder what the child will look like," she said to me as we stepped around the slush on the roads, squinting in the thin, cold mizzle. "What colour he'll be. Will he come out black or white? Or a mixture? Will his hair curl like yours?"

"God knows," I said, pulling my scarf further up over my head. I was sick of folk speculating on what the child would look like, as if we were trying out some new recipe for syllabub rather than making a living person. Grace had in some small ways been friendlier towards me since I fell pregnant, but I disliked her questioning. "He'll come out hale and hearty, God willing. Beyond that, I don't care what he looks like."

As we walked along Cheapside a cacophony of voices and the ringing knock of horses' hooves began to rise behind us. We turned and saw a crowd walking before and around three horses: a bay, a grey and a piebald, each led by a Tower guard. Other guards walked with the horses and among the crowd. As the procession drew closer the shoppers and traders moved aside to watch it go by.

I stood back with Grace, trying to avoid the greatest press of the crowd. The horses came slowly, stepping through the mud. The guards in their blue and red livery were the only bright spots between the heavy sky and the churned sludge underfoot. Rain clung to everything, misting on my eyelashes. People along from us began to shout and jeer as the horses passed them and I saw the animals were each dragging a burden behind them—men tied flat onto a wooden hurdle. The men's heads were at the lower end of the hurdle so the dirt and wet of the street splashed over their faces and into their eyes and mouths.

As the horses walked by, and the hurdles scraped runnels in the mud, the woman next to me leaned out to spit at the closest man. His head was spattered with mud and filth and a flung stone had opened a wound on his forehead. The flesh was gaudy with blood. His eyes were wide open, staring straight up at the sky, and his mouth moved as he jolted over stones and cobbles. He was praying. Despite the dirt and blood his face was familiar but for a moment I did not recognise him.

When I did, I clutched at Grace's hand. How could I have forgotten? It was the day of Campion's execution. It was Edmund Campion lying with his head in the mud beside his fellow traitors, being dragged through London to the Tyburn tree where they would hang him, cut him down breathing, slit open his belly and pull out his entrails to burn before his eyes, slice off his cock and stuff it in his mouth, and at last give him release by cutting off his head. These men were on their way to die.

The thought sickened me. I tried to turn away but someone jostled me from behind and I stumbled. Thinking of the babe in my belly I looked for a way out, but the press of the crowd was too great. Afraid the people would push us with them all the way to Tyburn, I turned to Grace.

"Can you see a way out?" I said.

"We're best to wait till they've passed by," she said. "I can't budge an inch."

So we stood together while the horses slowly pulled their

condemned men past us. I prayed for them—for Campion in particular—asking for God to be merciful and make their suffering quick. At the tail of the procession I caught sight of a dark head, standing out in the crowd like a poppy in wheat. Lopes's servant Domingo was in the crowd, walking next to the printer Richard Rowlands.

I watched Domingo as he approached. His face was expressionless, his eyes fixed on the horses dragging their burdens. He turned his head just as he passed us and stared straight at me. For a moment the look on his face did not change, set hard like packed ice and his eyes blank stone, then he recognised me and it flickered into a kind of raw grief. He turned away again and looked back at the man in the mud and I pulled my cloak closer in around me.

The rain began to fall more heavily and as soon as we could move we hurried home, where Grace wrapped me up and put me to bed. I was relieved to feel the child moving about as before. My nipples were already ringed with milk, coming ready for him. Campion would be at Tyburn by now, dying a holy martyr for the glory of God. I sent up a prayer that my baby would never make a martyr. Glorious it might be, but the thought of watching my child dragged through the streets to his death was appalling. I wondered where Campion's mother was, and how she was comforting herself on this day.

I came down late to breakfast the next day and found John sitting at the table with his head in his hands.

"I am commissioned to print Anthony Munday's account of Campion's death," he said as I came in, and looked up at me. "And a very rich pamphlet of lies that will be. What a hypocrite I am, Susan. I am trusted to print these things. I am trusted as a man who can turn Francis Walsingham's designs into paper and ink and send his lies out across the country. Everything Munday writes will run counter to my faith, but printing it is our best insurance against discovery."

I sat down opposite him.

"God knows your true intention, sir."

"I wish God would put the world back in balance so that I don't have to twist myself and hide myself and live in fear for my family," said John. "Then he wouldn't need to look into my soul to judge my loyalty."

The wind blew a scatter of raindrops against the kitchen window. I looked out at the grey murk of London and remembered the leg stuck up over the Bridge gate when I first came into the city. Campion had not twisted or hidden himself and as a reward his head and limbs would be set up on those spikes, a fleshly advertisement for martyrdom. Rain driving down on him. God's eyes watching him die. God's eyes watching me and my baby.

CHAPTER 21

My baby was born in the dark hours of Epiphany morning, in the year of Our Lord 1582. When the midwife first handed him to me, naked and bawling in the firelight with splayed, angry fingers, he smelled strongly of life—of heat and blood and my body.

I rocked him a little and said: "There, there, sirrah, the world is not so bad." He opened his eyes in between yells and looked right at me. His eyes were dark, the same shape as mine, and they said, plain as day, *Are you mad, woman? This is a terrible place.*

When the afterbirth was out and he was washed and swaddled and the cord cut, he grew quieter. The women and I sat and stared at him as if he were a new comet in the sky. There were black curls of damp bloody hair on his head and his little ears were perfect. He had curled his hands into fists like a fighter, but when I uncurled them his palms were pink and soft.

For a while all the women were out of the room and I was alone with my son. John was in Kent, not due back until the next day, so that night the baby was mine alone to worship. His hands moved, pushing at my breast, saying: *come here, go away*. He did not know who or what he was, but he was full up and brimming with spirit.

His eyes were my colour exactly. Perhaps my mother's too. I never thought of it before but the stamp of my parents may have been in this child, even if I didn't recognise it. My family. My eyes filled and blessed and never filled enough with the sight of his sweet, sleeping face. I was infatuated.

"My little heart," I said to him. In his perfect ear I told him what he was to me; my little heart, my little love. Holding him against me I felt my own heart beating slow and strong, counterpoint to the faster flutter of his own.

Outside time ran on. Snow fell and bells rang the hours of his first day. The men were in the print room catching pages as they flew from the press. The tide of the Thames ebbed and flowed and all over London people were writing down stories and recipes, proclamations, death warrants, sermons and ballads. Other babies were born and beggars clutched rags over their chests against the cruel wind. I told my son he would never go hungry, never beg, never be cold. In our small room we slept and woke through the warm, dark hours and time moved slow as sleeping breath.

When Grace woke me in the morning for the first feed, he was sleepy and would not hold his mouth to the nipple for long. Every time we turned him to my breast he moved his face away and dribbled out the milk. If we held him there he choked and snuffled. Joan Jugge, who had stayed with us overnight, shook her head over him. She made me squeeze milk out into her palm and tried him with a finger, giving him a little at a time. That worked better but he still turned his face away. All he wanted to do was curl up at my breast and go back to sleep. His lips were dry and pale.

"He's not getting enough," she said. "Perhaps your milk's not come in properly yet. We need to get him stronger. I'll go down the road and talk to Nell, the wet-nurse. Try and keep at it while I'm gone."

I tried, though it seemed cruel when we were both so tired and the day was so raw. It was cold in the room despite the fire and his little fingers grew icy. I swaddled him up again and sent Grace to fetch more kindling, holding him close against me to warm him till the fire was ablaze again. When she had piled on more logs and the flames leaped up I thought I would try again, but when I looked at him his face seemed pale, even in the ruddy firelight.

"Grace, come and see him. Does he look pale? His fingers are so cold. I fear he has a chill."

She came over and took him from me. He was asleep again and barely opened an eye. She carried him over by the fire and unswaddled his arms, feeling his fingers.

"He's cold indeed. Oh, little man! 'Tis cruel to be born in winter. I'll keep him here awhile until he's warmer. Oh, mistress—" She had lifted him up to her shoulder, and now looked at me with concern. "He's breathing very quick." She dandled him up and down and rubbed his back, then held him up to look at his face.

"I do fear he is ill. His colour isn't good. Come, you try and warm him. I'll see if I can fetch Joan back. Keep rubbing him and chafe his arms and legs like this; he seems very chilled."

She brought him back to me half unswaddled and then left the room. I heard her running down the stairs and felt afraid. I huddled the blankets around us, listening to his breathing. It was shallow and quick as she had said and he was very still. I clutched him tight to me, rubbing his back. I breathed on his little fingers with my hot breath and rubbed his hands. As I held him I felt his heart beating fast, surely faster than before. His eyes were half open, bright but unaware, not searching or fixing on me.

"Come now, little one," I said. "What ails you? I am warm, take heat from me. Wake up now, my little heart. Are you hungry? Is it milk you're lacking? The milk will come, it will come. Come, let me warm you. Oh, dear child, let me warm you."

In a minute I heard Grace's feet on the stairs again and she came quickly back into the room.

"Is he any warmer?" she said. "I've sent a boy up the road for Joan Jugge, and the midwife if he can find her."

She came back over to me and we both looked at him. My heart stopped. His eyes were still half-shut and his colour was ghastly. The beautiful brown had faded to ashen grey. His breathing came fast and laboured now.

"Oh, God, what's wrong with him?"

"I don't know, mistress," she said. "I don't know, but I've seen sick babies and I've seen them get better. Let me take him a minute."

I gave him to her and she began again to rub and chafe him, walking over to the heat of the fire and kissing his head.

"I've seen infants come back before. We thought my own brother was stone gone but my mother rubbed him and patted him and he choked and then he came back again. Come back little one, come back, you're only just arrived. Come back, sweetness."

My terror rose and rose. "Grace, he's not dead? He's only cold, surely, or he needs more milk?"

"No, no, he's not dead but he's grievous sick, mistress. Come on now, little one. Oh God, where is the midwife?"

"Give him to me, Grace. I'll try feeding him again. Grace, give him back to me!"

I heard my voice shake in panic but could not stop it. I had to have him back in my arms. I reached out to her and she handed him to me carefully. He was limp now and his fingers still so cold. His chest worked and rasped but he was barely drawing breath.

Other steps sounded on the stairs now and in came Joan Jugge and the midwife. They knelt down beside me and the midwife put a hand under his head, turning his face to her. Grace stared at them. "Where is Father Crowley? Did the boy not find him?"

"No, Grace," I said. "No, surely we don't need a priest. If we can only feed him. It must be the milk he needs."

Grace held me gently as the midwife took him back to the warmth of the fire with Joan Jugge. They patted and rubbed him, gave him a drop of wine. I tried to stand up and go to him but my legs were too weak and I nearly fell. I had to sit back on the straw with my hands over my mouth, trying to stifle the sounds I was making. I watched the flurry and panic of movement around him until at last it slowed and ceased and the midwife carried him back to me and put him in my arms.

"I can't help him," she said. "Some killing spirit has him. Something is suffocating him, he cannot breathe."

He seemed shrunk in on himself. He was so grey and small, fighting for sharp, wheezing, irregular breaths. It was dreadful. I held him and looked around from face to face.

"Fetch water, quick," commanded Joan Jugge. "He must be baptised—I will do it."

Grace ran to scoop water from the ewer. I held him to me. I could not believe he was dying. I looked back at him, counting now his every breath, matching each breath with my own as they grew shallower and fewer and fewer and fewer. Joan raised a hand for the baptism but even as she did the light went out of his eyes and the wheezing stopped. We waited for another breath, even a little one, but it never came.

CHAPTER 22

A terrible hole opened in my chest, darkness eating me from the inside out. Some blowfly breeding maggots in my heart. I held my baby too tight for the women to prise him away and when John returned later that day we were there still, curled in the corner together.

He died nameless, before we could baptise him, before we could catch at the heel of his soul and save him from eternity in limbo. I would not see him again in Heaven. I could not bear the thought of it. I was astounded by how much it hurt and how deep my grief was, for a child that barely lived two days. I could not find peace. My mind lurched here and there like a butterfly with a wing ripped off, unable to fly, turning back again and again to the one moment that made the difference—the difference between his living eyes and his dead eyes. Only a blink's difference.

I was like a cat with lost kittens, wandering about and looking in odd corners as if I might find my baby there. My breasts still leaked milk. I dreamed about feeding the baby and I ached. My whole body felt raw and weak.

Outside the freeze ended at last and a thaw came. It rained

till there were standing pools in the roads and a stink coming off everything and the only creatures thriving were creeping things like slugs and snails. It was dark until eight in the morning and dark again by four.

I developed a milk fever that gave me shakes and chills and prevented me from attending the baby's burial. Father Crowley at St Giles allowed him to be buried in consecrated ground, though no bells rang for him, and told John that if we prayed for him God would take him in to Heaven. But Crowley was Protestant and for him, Limbo did not exist. For me it was a real and vivid place, barren and cold on the fringes of Hell, where my baby would lie alone forever. I never knew how cruel that would be for a mother, to think of her child somewhere without her—without anyone—where she could not take it into her arms and comfort it. Now I understood, and I questioned a God that would allow this eternal punishment, so woefully unearned.

When John came home from the burial he sat with me an hour without speaking, holding my hand as he did when I told him I was pregnant. His son was dead, who should have been baptised and given a place in the world: John Geoffrey Charlewood, a child of London, of Cripplegate Ward and the parish of St Giles. A son of the Stationers' Company.

At last John said:

"God has cursed me. He takes all my children. I don't know how I have offended him, but he has cursed me."

All his bravado was stripped away, his theatrical manner and flourishes, the ring of his voice. His tone was dull and dark, like graveyard earth. It frightened me.

"I have sinned somehow and I must make amends," he said. "Pilgrimage, oblation, whatever is demanded of me." Abruptly, he put my hand aside and stood up.

"I will go to the priest and find a remedy for this. Sleep, Susan.

Recover yourself."

I watched him go and then turned my face into the pillow and wept.

John could not look his grief full in the face. He never spoke to me again with such honest sadness. Instead he turned away from his sorrow and went back to work, driving himself even harder than before. We were separated at night, too, while I was still in confinement. I slept on the straw bed and Grace lay in our bed in the same room, so I could call her if I needed her. I never called for her. John and Rob slept by the kitchen fire for warmth in this bitter weather.

When John did come up to see me I could often tell he had been drinking. His skin was yellow and there were dark swags under his eyes. I begin to think he blamed me for the baby's death. Silence put a blade between us. I had hoped a baby would somehow glue my marriage firmer, when sometimes it seemed to be based on little more than paper and ink. I could not sleep, lying wide-eyed into the small hours.

John paid a physician to see me a week after the baby died, to make me up a sleeping-draught. A large smiling man, recommended by Joan Wolfe, he seemed to me like some kind of awful visitation. He asked me questions to decide which herbs to use. What was my dominant humour, he asked—choleric or phlegmatic? When and where was I born, under what star and aspect? Was the baby hot, or cold, when he died?

"Cold, cold, cold," I said. "We tried to warm him by the fire but nothing worked."

He sat cogitating a while, peering down at me as I sat propped on my pillows. "I will make you up a draught," he said. "And I wonder—I might make a suggestion for diet, for your future fertility? I have been making something of a study of this. I understand that your colour goes deeper than the skin—that it may be an inherited infection of some kind. Perhaps from the curse of Ham who betrayed his father Noah. If so, it must surely affect other parts of the body too. Also the climate of your birth country is very fierce indeed. Perhaps the humours of your womb are too hot and dry for a seed from an Englishman—given also that your temperament is choleric and that you have a masculine bent for learning. Perhaps the mingling of your two natures—the African heat and the English cold – produced something out of balance in the child—"

I could not believe his cruelty. I sat up in the bed and stared at his grinning face.

"He was not a *monster*," I cried, "He was well-formed. He had all his fingers and toes, his eyes and ears and the hair on his head, all shaped fair and fine. His skin was a beautiful colour, like a little new chestnut and so soft. He was a lovely baby and you should not—you should not—" I could not continue. I was wild with anger. If I was strong enough I would have torn his tongue out of his mouth by its red roots and flung it in his bloody face.

"Get out of this house," I shouted. "Grace!" She came running in, hackles up, ready for a fight. I think she had been listening at the door. She manoeuvred her small person behind the physician and drove him sheep-dog-like to the door.

"Out you go, sir," she said and closed the door behind her.

I buried my face in the covers and howled till I thought I might vomit up my own lungs. In a while Grace came back and sat beside me, stroking me until I was calm enough to speak.

"Don't you believe a word he said," she said. "Not one bloody word. There's a living child up at Aldgate, seven years old or so, born of a Blackamoor silkweaver and a white seamstress. I've seen the boy with my own eyes, healthy as you like, running about in the street. That man knows nothing. That man can't see with his own eyes, he knows nothing unless he's read it in a book.

"I know his sort," she went on scornfully, "Such as him are not fit to make you cry, mistress. Babies die for all sorts of reasons every day, white, black and every other colour under the sun and up their souls go like feathers on the wind. My mother lost three, all in their first months. He won't be alone among all those other infants."

She raised my hand and kissed it. "You don't need his sleeping draught, neither. Piss and brimstone at twelve pounds the ounce. I'll go and boil you up some chamomile."

Whether it was Grace's chamomile or her kind words, something eased me back into sleep again. But a week later, I woke in the dark of early morning to hear scraping and rustling above my head. Too heavy to be rats or our cat Tib, or even Rob moving about on his pallet. Then there were voices, very low but audible, and a muffled groan. I sat up and listened intently. Footsteps sounded on the garret stairs, then the bedroom door opened and John came in with a candle. Grace was still asleep in the big bed, the curtains drawn around her.

"What's happened?" I asked John. "What is that noise in the garret?"

He set the candle on a chest and came over to the bed, sitting down beside me.

"Are you well enough to get up and move about?"

"Yes—of course." The milk fever had left me a little light-headed but the pain was gone as well as the fits of shivering.

John glanced up at the ceiling.

"You know the printer Rowlands? He has published an account of Campion's execution, written by a Catholic priest. A true account, which the Privy Council did not wish people to see—you know what was in Munday's version. Now Rowlands is wanted for arrest and he's had to flee London. Rob and Lopes's man Domingo helped him escape, but the Watch were in close pursuit and Rob and Domingo both took stab wounds. Rob's downstairs—his is only a slash—but Domingo is laid up in the attic, and he must have his wound dressed and stay there until tonight. He thinks the watchmen may have recognised him. He has passage on a ship early tomorrow, but we must keep him safe until then."

"Will he be safe in the attic if Searchers come? Should he go into the cellar?"

"It's warmer in the garret," said John, "and there is another secret space up there. I had a door made into the roof in case I needed to hide books there. A double insurance, if anyone ever found the cellar. It looks as if there wouldn't be room to place a sheet of paper but you can fit a man up there if need be. This filthy weather aids us too. The streets are knee-deep in slush. It's not the season for hunting criminals."

"Is he badly hurt?"

John looked me in the eye at last. His own hazel eyes were bloodshot and exhausted.

"No. He'll live. But your skill with physic would be very welcome. Will you dress his wound, and Rob's, and make sure they are not infected?"

I pushed back the covers from the bed. "Yes. Let me put on my slippers and my housecoat, then I'll go to them. Will you find me a bowl of water and my bandages too—the dressings are in my chest. And my yarrow salve."

John nodded and put his hand over mine.

"You are the greatest comfort to me, Suky," he said. "Our child is dead. Campion is gone too. There is no hope that the marriage between Elizabeth and Alençon will ever come to pass. God is truly testing us, but I am glad to have you as a wife."

I nodded but turned my head aside. All kindness made me cry. He fetched my clothes and the dressings, then helped me from my bed and down the stairs to the kitchen. Rob was at the table with his hand wrapped up in a torn strip of fabric. He looked pale in the candlelight. John brought water to the table in a bowl and set it down.

"I'm going to take water up to Domingo," he said. "Come up when you are done with Rob's hand, Susan."

"Show me your hand," I said to Rob. "May I unwrap that cloth?"

He nodded, wincing as I peeled away the linen from his bloody hand. There was a slash across his palm, not deep but it must be painful. I washed it very gently and the water in the bowl slowly turned pink. When it was clean I dabbed on the salve and began to wind the bandage round. Rob was unusually quiet. He did not joke or cast his eyes at me. He seemed chastened.

"Did the men who did this see your face?" I asked.

He shook his head."I don't think so. They must have followed Rowlands back to his rooms. Domingo had been helping him and I had come to fetch more copies to distribute, when all these men came piling in shouting. We were well muffled up and Rowlands had a back door into an alley so we ran for it. There was a fight, though, and they were well armed. Ouch!"

"Your pardon," I said. "I must bind it tightly." I finished my bandaging and tucked in the ends.

"It may bleed through," I said. "Try to keep it still."

There was a little blood on his fingertips and his face, too. I wadded up a cloth and wiped them. Touching him like this would usually send a jolt singing through my own blood, but in my grief for the baby I was absent, seeing everything from underwater. He was different too. I had never seen him so quiet, even after grave danger. When I finished sponging his forehead, he wiped his face on his sleeve and sighed.

"You know what they did to Campion, at Tyburn?" he said.

I nodded.

"I don't want to die like that," he said. He flexed out his bandaged hand. "At least this time they have only taken a little blood. This feels better. Thank you, mistress."

"Don't stretch your hand like that, it will set the wound bleeding again," I said, and reached out to stop him, holding his hand upright. "If you keep it like this, it will help."

He nodded, then said softly, "Mistress. I'm sorry the baby died."

My mouth twisted and I looked away from him. I had barely spoken to him since the birth, having been confined in my room. Rob to me was the wide world, adventure and peril. I had been on a different journey, full of its own dangers. He was always so outwardly unafraid of death, so dismissive of those who had not his appetite for risk. Somehow, I had not expected sympathy from him. He squeezed my fingers gently and let my hand go, saying, "You should go up to Lopes's man—he's worse off than me."

"I will," I said. "Thank you, Rob."

CHAPTER 23

In the attic I found Domingo sitting on Rob's pallet, reading our *Book of Common Prayer* by candlelight. He looked up at me and put aside the book.

"Forgive me if I do not stand, mistress," he said quietly. "The roof was not built for men of my height. I knock against the tiles."

"No matter." I set out clean water, my bandages, and the salve on the bare boards next to him.

"I am sorry to bring trouble on your household at this time," he said.

I looked at him sitting with his legs folded up, and his face and clothes smudged with dust from the roof. There were hollows of exhaustion under his eyes, but he retained his formality and composure, that appearance of being set slightly apart. He had abandoned his habitual black for grey, perhaps as a disguise, in a poorly cut rough wool suit that made his skin look ashy and dull. His diplomat's glow had gone, that air of richness. He looked very different from the man I had met at Lopes's.

"You have brought no trouble," I said. "Be at peace. May I see the wound?"

He nodded and rolled back his right sleeve, showing a bloody, makeshift bandage of linen wrapped around his lower arm. I unwrapped it carefully and found a deep slash running down all the way to the skin on the back of his hand.

"You're lucky it wasn't the underside, where the veins nest," I said. "Are you hurt anywhere else?"

"I took a cudgel here," he said, inclining his head towards me. A lump stood out at the back of his skull—it looked painful but had not broken the skin and when I felt it gently the bone around and beneath was firm.

"I have a thick pate," he said, "and their stroke was off. It aches like the devil, though."

"I'll clean and bind the wound," I said, "and I'll make you up a comfrey poultice later, for your head."

"Thank you, mistress," he said. He winced once as I began to swab around the cut gently but did not pull away.

It had begun to rain again and the drops drummed softly on the roof. Dawn was coming in, and grey light began to show through the small garret window. I felt almost at peace, lost in the familiar rituals of healing. I was glad to be hidden away up here. I was sick of pity: the pity that came from every guest, from John, even from Grace. Domingo's quiet detachment was calming to me. The thought came to me that I had never nursed a person of my own colour before. I had never worked to heal black skin. The thought brought tears into my eyes and I blinked them away. Why should that make me cry? But the sight of my hands washing his wound made my heart ache. I realised suddenly that his skin might be ashy because he had no oil for it.

"Are you wanting almond oil, for your skin?" I asked him. "I have some."

He looked at me and smiled. "Yes—thank you, that would be a kindness."

I nodded. "I will bring it with the comfrey poultice."

With the wound clean I began to smooth on the salve. The spicy, comforting scent of yarrow filled the air and Domingo breathed it in. I think the smell of the herb heals as well as the leaves. It mingled with the scent of dried lavender and meadowsweet from the rushes. We had renewed them before the baby came. It was the warm, sleepy scent of summer, sunshine and bees in the long borders. Domingo rested his hand on his leg and leaned his head back against the wall, closing his eyes.

"What do you remember?" he said suddenly and I looked up, startled. "Of your home country," he added. His eyes were still closed. "Anything at all?"

"Nothing," I said, shaking my head. "I was so young. I hardly remember my mother—she died when I was three."

I gathered up my bandages to begin binding the wound and took hold of his arm. His skin felt cold. I hoped my hands would warm it a little.

"Do you remember anything?" I asked.

He said nothing for a moment, then shook his head. "I was young too. Four or five. I remember when they took me from my mother."

He stopped abruptly and I waited. He still had not opened his eyes. Perhaps he was seeing it all again. "I didn't realise what was happening. They had dressed me in a suit, to be a servant, all blue and gold, you know, and I was very happy with my suit. They told me—"

He broke off a moment. When he continued his voice was rougher, raw with pain.

"They told me I could go to choose oranges and bring them back to the ship. Oranges. For my mother. Then the sailor led me down the gang-plank and there was this screaming, this sound like a knife in the ribs, and I looked around and there was my mother. I can't imagine she was meant to see me. Her scream was like a stab. No, worse than a stab. It was as if someone pulled my heart out of my chest. The way she was screaming. I knew they were taking me away forever. I never felt such terror, before or since. I began to howl too and the men gripped me tight and carried me away. It was cruel, cruel, cruel. How she must have felt, I cannot imagine."

Tears blurred my eyes and I blinked them away until I could see his face clear again. I could imagine how his mother felt, watching her small son carried away from her forever. All innocence, dressed up and smiling, holding the hand of his betrayer. I shook my head at the horror of it, knowing now fully the pain of a mother that loses a child. Though, was I even a mother? Could a woman be mother to an infant that slipped away before it ever came to earth—before it claimed a soul?

"I am so sorry," I said. "At least my mother was with me, even if I don't remember her. I cannot fathom the cruelty of tearing you away from her. Do you know—do you know what happened to her afterwards?"

He opened his eyes at last and turned his head to look at me. His cheeks were wet and his eyes shining with tears.

"She died," he said. "Perhaps her heart was broken."

I nodded and stopped my binding for a moment, looking up until I was sure I would not cry. I did not want to wet the bandage.

"I'm sorry," said Domingo. "I never talk of these things. I forget how much it pains me still. Please, carry on your work. Let's talk of something else."

I wiped my eyes on my sleeve and went back to bandaging, looping the strips carefully around his arm until it was neat and fastened up well.

"Where do you think the soul lives, in our bodies?" I said, still thinking of my baby.

He looked at me a while, then very slowly shook his head.

"I do not know," he said. "I am asking myself, and I do not know. I saw my friend Campion anatomised, opened from throat to thigh, and I am no nearer knowing where his soul was kept or when it flew out of his body."

"Perhaps the soul lives behind the eyes," I said. "You see it fluttering there and when a person dies their eyes grow dull. When my baby died... Perhaps the soul goes out with the light and lives in it, too, in the air."

I felt the familiar pricking behind my eyes. I was so sick of crying, but I could not help it. This time I could not stop. Tears fell on my dress, my hands, the dusty floor of the attic. The rain on the roof grew heavier. Perhaps I and the rain together could drown London.

"Campion's heart," said Domingo, and paused. "I'm sorry, I shouldn't."

"Please, talk on," I said. "Nothing you say can hurt me."

"His heart kept beating," said Domingo, "in the executioner's hand. As if it were trying to make something live, still. The sleet, or the air. The smoke rose off it in the cold. It was an awful thing."

He stopped and sat, staring at the wall opposite, as if the whole scene played out again for him on that blank space. Campion's crushed head and face, his lolling cullions and prick waved in front of him before they tossed his fertility into the fire.

"What was the point of it all?" he said wonderingly. "Did God ask him to die, for that?"

He leaned his head back against the wall again and held up his good left hand, where his *memento mori* ring winked on his ring finger, the little skull's amber eyes catching the pale light.

"This ring was Campion's," he said. "He gave it to me, in token of friendship."

It was a beautiful piece of work. Campion's own ring, now a martyr's relic. He and Domingo must have been very close. Now I understood the look on Domingo's face as he followed that ghastly procession to Tyburn.

"He lives in glory, now," I said.

He nodded, turning the ring about in the dim light.

"They called him a traitor and they hacked him to pieces," he said. "He was never a traitor. I understand why John printed Munday's account, he needs to live and he wants to be in favour with the lawmakers, but that text was a rank calumny. Munday twisted everything to make my friend sound like a coward and a criminal. He put words in his mouth and damned him and now those lies have been sent about to—to ruin Campion's name throughout England."

"But what else could John do?" I said. "Those lies may save us, if they keep suspicion away from this household."

"I know, I know, but—I am so sick of lies. Rowlands published the account of his death so they could not lie about him as they have already lied and so people can see what manner of man he really was. Is there any greater purpose than the truth?" said Domingo. "I don't know. I thought I knew, and now I find I know nothing."

He put his hands together in his lap, one bandaged, one healthy. The ivory skull stood out against his skin.

"I watched them kill him," he said. "I watched every second of his dying because I hoped he would see my face and take comfort from it. But now when I sit in this garret alone I find I cannot see what all of it was for. Did he need to die? Did it mean anything to the flames that burned him and the sky that took the smoke? To the worms that ate his bones? Did they know it was a sacrifice? Did God know? Does dying for your faith mean anything more than dying in a street brawl? And his soul, you see, it troubles me. How can his soul find its way back to that broken body at the Resurrection? I have been trying to pray and I find I cannot. God is not listening to me. He is not answering."

He broke off again, staring at the wall. The rain muffled the house. I heard Grace singing downstairs and realised I should have left the attic by now. It was daybreak. At the same time we both moved, looked around us and came back to the present moment.

"Mistress, I have said too much," said Domingo. "What I have said about Campion should not be for your ears. I am talking heresies. Stuff my words back into my mouth. O my tongue..." He stood up, hunched under the sloping roof, and helped me from the pallet. I stood up slowly, my hand in his.

"I cannot put the words back, but I can strangle them here," I said. "They die between us now and walk no further."

He looked down at me and nodded.

"Thank you, Mistress Charlewood."

"And what of Persons?" I asked him. "John told me about the meetings you arranged for him. He has escaped. He has also been called a traitor. Is his name ruined too?"

Domingo did not answer for a moment. When he did he spoke hesitantly, searching for the right words.

"Now their mission has failed, I am not sure what he will do, but he will not stop working for the faith. I—may see him again. I am leaving England for a while. It is better I am out of the way after this, though I have hopes they did not recognise me. Englishmen struggle to tell one black face from another, I find. And there is business I must attend to on the Continent, for Senhor Lopes. I will leave here tonight to sail out—but I will return next year."

"Yes," I said, though I was dismayed he was leaving. We had spoken of such deep matters. I wanted to ask him more about his childhood before he left Africa and his life in Spain. Now the conversation was to be abruptly broken off.

"Yes," I said again. "We will be here when you come back. I will come up again later today, with the oil and the comfrey."

"Thank you, mistress," he said, and smiled.

When I came down from the attic I found I was suddenly exhausted. I sat on the bed to rest a moment. I stared at the floor, seeing Campion on the hurdles again, all spattered with mud and blood. I remembered the look Domingo gave me as he followed the hurdles, the grief in his eyes.

I thought also of Campion's soul and body meeting again. How would the soul come back in at the Resurrection? Through his mouth? Back into his eyes in a beam of sunlight? Into his ears like music? Souls clustering in the high clouds and pouring down on earth like rain, funnelling into the bodies they left, re-animating the dust and shaping it round themselves.

Thinking of this, I found that my eyes had closed. I was overcome with tiredness, pressing on me like heavy cloth. I could barely move my limbs to tuck myself under the covers, and I was asleep in seconds.

When I woke, it was dawn the next day and Domingo was gone. I had slept through almost a full day and night. I railed at Grace for letting me sleep, and then cried my eyes red raw because I had never taken him his oil or the comfrey for his head. I had failed him, as I failed my baby.

CHAPTER 24

I was churched and let back into the world early. Robert Crowley, the vicar at St Giles, let me come in at Candlemas-day. Leaving the warm, closeted interior of the house, pungent with cooking smells and the fug of well-wrapped winter bodies, was a shock. The cold air poured over me in a drench, and the icy light hurt my eyes.

I walked to church with all the household, and neighbours and gossips joined us as we went towards St. Giles. I walked with my arm through John's, stepping carefully over the frost-cracked ground, glad that Grace and Joan Jugge were beside me. It was a new feeling, to be glad at Grace's presence. We had mourned together over my baby's death, and somehow it had changed her. She had thawed towards me.

Grace and Joan stayed with me as we entered the church and I went to the bench at the front for women waiting to be churched. St. Giles was full of people for the Candlemas service. Although I was now a settled and familiar parishioner of the church, kneeling with the rest every Wednesday and Sunday like any good Protestant, I suddenly felt like a stranger all over again. I was conscious, as I had been at my wedding, of all the eyes around me.

I knew exactly what the people would be thinking. They would be sorry for me and they would be wondering if there was something wrong with me, to have borne a child that died so swiftly after seeming so healthy. Perhaps they would be wondering, like the doctor, if it had something to do with the colour of my skin. Susan Charlewood, little black lamb. Little labour-in-vain—Kate's nickname for me, now prophetic and most horribly embodied.

When the time came for my churching I rose a little unsteadily and walked the short distance up the nave to the altar. Our vicar Robert Crowley, a fiery Protestant and a good man, took my hand and helped me kneel. Then he cleared his throat and rang out his beautiful bell-voice, the tone of which made his sermons some of the best-attended in London. Even those who utterly opposed his views came to hear him; your ears always took some balm from his speech.

"For as much as it has pleased almighty God of his goodness to give you safe deliverance, and has preserved you in the great danger of childbirth: ye shall therefore give hearty thanks unto God and pray."

I closed my eyes while he spoke the words of the Psalm over my head, willing God to let my next steps in the world be easier. He squeezed my hand gently to remind me the prayer and response was coming and I opened my eyes again as the congregation spoke together at his prompting.

Somehow the sound of their voices comforted me as the thought of their eyes had disturbed me. All the different tones of the parish mingled in a ragged music of bass-notes and trebles, from the youngest to the oldest. Whatever they thought of me personally, they spoke to pray for me. I was as much part of the parish as they were; the Londoners, the Huguenots, Flemings and Italians, the new arrivals from Devon and Norfolk and Wales. The secret Catholics—for there were a dozen of us at least in that parish who lived that double life. All of us clustered in this church built up alongside London Wall, each of us a part of London as each stone helped form the wall. I was one of them, after all.

As we left the church, many of them stopped to greet me or give their sympathies, especially the women. Some hugged me with tears in their eyes—even some of those who were not that friendly to me. I think every mother there had lost at least one baby. They understood, and that was something.

After the churching, I went into the graveyard to see the place where my baby was buried. The earth was bare and brown over him but at the wall of the churchyard snowdrops were just coming up, little pale green spikes and tender white flowers against the grey stone. I stood for a moment with my household and friends around me and said a prayer for him.

It was very hard to think of him there, small and alone with the soil packed in around his little body so cold and hard. I tried to think of what Grace had said about the infant souls like feathers dancing upwards, but I could not summon the feel of his warmth. All I could see was the implacable earth and his empty eyes.

It is such a common thing, for a mother to lose a child. What, then, makes us love them so? And what was I to do with all my love, the love that was born with my baby? He was dead, but my love for him was alive and strong in my body. It wanted the shape of him, the smell of him, his warmth in my arms. As long as I lived, I would hunger to cradle him again.

Shut the door and walk on, said Kate's voice in my head, and so with a great effort of will I did. I closed the door on him, opened my eyes again and looked at the snowdrops.

CHAPTER 25

Spring came, and with it the Plague, and suddenly everyone was dying. Out reached the plague's long white arm and where it touched, people blistered and oozed and died and rotted, quicker than they could be buried. The infection rode invisible currents in the poisoned air. We feared each other's very breath. A kiss from someone struck with the pestilence could set dark bubbles warping your flesh within the hour and your body in a civil war against itself.

I went to the drapers early one morning to order a length of cloth for a new dress, and when I came back that afternoon to collect it the shop was closed and the door slashed with red chalk. The draper's wife had died while I was walking up Cheapside making my other purchases.

Those red crosses, like pockmarks on city doors, tracked the disease's path and the Mayor ordered the streets to be washed morning and evening. The city was full of mourning sounds: weeping, funeral bells, and the burial carts coming around with the man singing "bring out your dead," as he passed. Yet the spring air was soft and all the trees tipped with green leaves. The pale sunlight mocked the hideous sights it illuminated.

All those who could afford it packed up and left for the summer, leaving the great merchant's houses empty and the city devoid of lawyers and wealthy doctors. Those of us who remained found ourselves in a kind of reckless, jittery fever, looking at Death over our shoulders and living as hard as we could, in case the next time we turned his scythe was at our necks.

In the midst of all this horror I had two pieces of good news. First, a letter in my master's own hand saying he had been moved from prison in Winchester back to a place in Sussex, nearer Framfield. There was hope he might be freed by next year—if so he hoped to negotiate with his cousin and regain control of the land again. The thought of him back in Sussex was so good that I wept, and I prayed that his cousin would prove conformable.

Not long after this, I received a summons to Jeronimo Lopes's house. That sent my spirits flying up. I retraced my steps to Lopes's door through the charnelhouse city with a scarf about my face and a bunch of herbs held to my nose.

I arrived early but knocked at the door to be let in. I wanted to be out of the plague-ridden street and away from the awful moans and sobs that erupted here and there from shuttered windows. No one came for a while and I knocked again. At last the door opened. It was the maid, Sofia, her head hidden under a scarf and her dress beneath an apron. She looked at me for a moment without recognition.

"Susan Charlewood," I said, "to see Senhor Lopes?"

She glanced behind her, bit her lip, then opened the door a little further and ushered me in. "We are spring cleaning," she said. "Please excuse. Please, sit."

I settled myself again in the hall as she went away. The hall was clean as a pin, and as cold. I could hear voices upstairs singing and a sound of bustle and stir. Perhaps they were cleaning to keep infection out. It was a pleasant change from the unease and feeling of miasmatic sickness wreathing the streets like fog outside. I sat breathing in the perfume of the house and listening to the maids chat as they went about their work.

When at last Sofia returned to show me into the library, Lopes and a tall man with a pipe in his hand were talking by the fireplace.

"Good morning, good morning," said Lopes. It was quite a change from his cold demeanour at my last parting from him. "Thank you, Sofia—you may go. Goody Charlewood, I am so glad you could come. This is Anthony Dassell, the merchant, whose ships go out across the world and bring back the best of it."

Anthony Dassell came forward and kissed me, enveloping me with the smell of tobacco. He was dressed soberly for a merchant—even for a seafaring man—but his height and the shrewdness of his grey eyes gave him presence.

"Now please sit and I shall unfold a tale to you," said Lopes. "A little sweet wine?"

I sat in the chair opposite him on the other side of the fire as he poured wine into a silver cup—no pewter here. The luxury of the room and the smell of books and bindings brought back afternoons in my master's library, very different from the raw, sharp smell of paper and lye in the print workshop.

I sat carefully on the edge of my chair, my hands folded in my lap, and watched him. There was a little table beside him where an envelope and ornate paperknife rested. He kept his hand on the envelope as he spoke.

"So," he said, "when you asked me your question last year, I was angry. I thought your request would likely cost me much effort for little reward and I did not want to pursue it. This family you spoke of, the Enriquezes—they have revoked their conversion and returned to the Jewish faith. I cannot afford to be tainted by communication with them. I speak frankly. I hope you understand. Besides, my time is not my own. I have several businesses to run in several countries, a family, and other duties. A man enslaved for so many years, like your brother, will have lost his history, his name, and everything he was before. Finding him again would be a long quest. Why should I go to much trouble to hunt for the brother of a woman I have met once? Again, you understand me?"

I nodded. "Perfectly, sir."

"Good. But then fate brought me a changing wind. You know Dom Antonio, who is recognised by France and England as King of Portugal—the pretender to the throne?"

"I do, sir," I said. "He was exiled in France, I believe?"

Lopes leaned back further into his chair, crossing one leg over another.

"He has been staying in England, at the invitation of Queen Elizabeth. He grew up with my cousin, the good Dr Lopes who attends on the Earl of Leicester, and my cousin has helped him forge links with the Queen. Now, as King of Portugal he has land rights in the Azores and along the coast of Guinea. In his generosity he has invited English merchants—including Mr Dassell here—to benefit from these rights, if he can be helped back onto his rightful throne."

"A trading agreement, you mean?" I asked, looking up at Dassell, who had finished his pipe and was taking out tobacco to build another one. He nodded.

"We will have the right to trade in Guinea if we pay duty to Dom Antonio."

I watched him, wondering if he knew John Hawkins. Hawkins, who had saved and then split my family. Given us away as gifts to his friends. For a moment the hairs on my neck stood up. I felt cold and weak, a shadow falling on my spirit.

"What goods do you hope to trade?" I asked.

"Wax, hides, and gold," he said. "I want to make it as smooth and safe a business as I can. Lost ships and men cost me money. The early traders in the region went about their work without all due respect for the Guinea chiefs and some of them suffered for it. We'll have enough to contend with from the Spanish, who'll set cannon at our heads if they think we're barging into their markets."

"No slaves?" I asked. "You will not buy slaves there?"

"No. It isn't worth the trouble," he said, and set the flint to his pipe. It sparked, and the tobacco took. Up curled the first plume of smoke, sailing out into the air and vanishing, adding the scent of tobacco to applewood. He smiled at me and coughed, and I looked away from him.

Lopes cleared his throat and sat up, reaching for the poker to riddle the fire.

"As Mr Dassell says, English merchants trade in Guinea, they pay duty to Dom Antonio, and we are all very happy—the English, the Portuguese, and the Guinea rulers. Now, when you spoke to me before, you told me your mother was of royal blood—yes?"

"Yes. That is what I have always been told."

"And do you know where in Guinea you were taken from?"

"Not the exact place, but it was in Upper Guinea. The Portuguese slavers bought us at El Mina, from traders who took their slaves inland and then walked them to the coast."

"Yes, yes," he said. "Yes, just so. Now, imagine my surprise when I make careful inquiries about the family you mention—you understand I cannot say how, or to whom I spoke—and I discover that they did have a slave who came to them from Hawkins' ship. It was easier to trace, because of the trouble at the time over the impounding of Hawkins' goods.

"They bought this slave, a little boy, to be a page, because they were told—guaranteed—he was of royal blood in Guinea. They wanted the prestige, you see. He grew up with them and worked as a secretary. But when they left Spain, six or seven years ago now, they gave him his freedom and left him behind."

"So," said Lopes again, "it became of great interest to me, to find your brother. If you both were truly taken from a ruling family in Guinea, it would be very—ah—beneficial to me and to the merchants who travel out to Guinea. I set my friend Dassell on the quest for him."

"Why?" I said. "You said that in your letter. How does it benefit you, or the merchants?"

Dassell spoke up again:

"I want to make friends with as many Guinea lords as I can, and there are regions that will be hostile to us because they trade with the Spanish and Portuguese or because the first English traders came blundering in like bullocks and made enemies of them—taking subjects without license from the kings in that place. If you truly are part of a royal family and we can find out which, I hope the news that you and your brother survived your journey will mend some fences and build up my profits. So you see, I should like to find your brother as much as you would. I have ships that go often to Spain, to Seville, and to Lisbon, and as we know your brother's name I put out word that I am searching for him."

I watched him slowly filling up his pipe again, yellow fingertips tamping down the tobacco, and tried not to show how avidly I was hanging on his words. I understood very clearly that this was a business deal, that both these men were helping me because they believed it could profit them, and I had learned from John that in business you should never give away how badly you want a deal. I waited and said nothing, though I wanted desperately to ask if he had heard any news. Finally, when he had lit the pipe and taken the first puff, Dassell spoke again.

"There was certainly an African of his name working as a servant for a Spanish gentleman in Valencia, not long after the Enriquezes fled Spain. One of my factors had dealings with him six years ago when he was setting up a deal for exporting wine. He remembers the African and his name because of his facility with languages—he acted as translator between men of several different nations. The factor liked him so well he tried to poach him but he said he was happy with his master."

I felt my lips trembling as I held back a smile.

"And is he still working there—in Valencia?" I asked.

"We do not know," said Lopes, breaking in. "This is why I called you here. Perhaps you would like to write to your brother. Anthony has a ship going out soon and can take a letter for us. If Francis is still there, he can pass it to him as proof he has a sister living in London. "

"I would like it above all things," I said. Lopes fetched me paper and pen and I sat at the table and wrote another note, the same as the first I had sent. Another message sent out in hope. Would it reach my brother? I folded the paper slowly and handed it to Lopes to seal up.

"Let us hope this finds its mark," he said as he stamped the warm wax. "The difficulty, of course, will be in finding out exactly which family you came from, but perhaps your brother knows more. Was he older or younger than you?"

"Older, I believe," I said. "So yes, he might remember." I wondered whether to mention my bronze tokens. They might indeed be proof of my royal origins, as I had told John and Rob, but they might be nothing at all. I decided to keep my mouth closed for the time being.

As I left, Sofia looked out from a side door and came to me with a parcel. She held it out to me. "We made too much bread this week. Please. It's a Portuguese bread, very good."

"Thank you. *Obrigado*." She smiled. The scarf was gone from her head and I saw that her hair was braided into tiny plaits, looped and coiled around her head. It looked wonderful, far more complex than the simple braids I managed on my own She saw me staring and put a hand up to her head, patting the braids.

"Your hair," I said, gesturing to it. "It's beautiful. How do you arrange it so?"

"Ah," she said, "our kitchen maid has good hands for hair!"

"Is it hard to do?" I said. Sofia shrugged.

"For English maids, yes. Impossible! You have someone to do yours?"

"No," I said.

We looked at each other a moment. I wanted and did not want to ask if their maid could work my hair so.

"Come and ask, if ever you want Beatriz to work with yours," she said. "Not this week. But—another time."

I shook my head a little and hugged the parcel of bread to me.

"Thank you. Good day," I said, and Sofia smiled and opened the door for me. I went away feeling something fluttering in my chest; hope or fear, I could not tell which. The two are birds of a feather, at least when they beat in my breast in the early hours of the night.

PART III

LONDON
1583

CHAPTER 26

On Epiphany morning in 1583 I rose even earlier than Grace, who had a fever, and came into the kitchen to make breakfast. It was a year to the day since the baby died. I said a prayer for him, quietly, while I moved about in the half-dark.

When I opened the door to throw out the slops, cold air rushed in. The sky was pale rose in the East and a crescent moon still hung in the night-blue West. The Barbican tower stood black against the lightening sky. Sometimes thieves and wanderers took shelter there, lighting fires among the stones and parcelling out their stolen goods or scraps of bread. Wild men and Bedlam beggars, with straggled beards and dirty faces, haunted the place. One of them barked like a dog when people passed by, another would stand shouting at the sky and waving his fist, starting a fight with Heaven he would never win.

Two men had been found frozen to death in the street below the tower the week before. The January days were bright as bells and cold as charity, frost feathers garlanded our inside window panes and icicles threatened the heads of passers-by.

I stood at the door for a moment despite the cold, thinking of the tramps and beggars huddling across flat fields barren of colour, warring with robins for bitter sloes, hips, and haws—thorns and frost piercing their fingers as they moved from one cold place to another.

While I stood watching, as if I had called him up from my mind, a walker appeared. His black shape peeled away from the dark bulk of the tower and his breath steamed in the air as he stepped over the frozen mud-ruts towards me. As he drew closer, I saw he was tall and broad in the shoulder, and there was something familiar about his gait. I waited, breathing quickly, as he approached. There was no-one in the street but us. If he were Death himself come to fetch me away, I could not have moved.

He drew his hood back as he arrived at our door and the scarce light gleamed on his beautiful, black skin. Wide cheekbones, a curling mouth, and bright eyes looking at me as if I were the ghost, not him. It was Domingo. The sight of him brought back every raw feeling from last January: grief, fear, and my deep, terrible love for my baby. It was too much. I made a sound, a whimper of loss. He put out a hand to me and drew me into an embrace. The wool of his cloak was cold and rough on my cheek, smelling of snow, but his breath against my hair was warm. It was comfort, all comfort and understanding. I rested my sadness on him and when at last I moved away, I felt more awake, more alive, than I had done in months. Perhaps for the first time since the baby died.

"I came so early," he said, "I was not sure you would be stirring."

"It is good to see you," I said. I could not stop smiling. I knew I should invite him into the house and step back into the warmth but I wanted to keep this brief, pre-dawn interval to myself. The stars overhead still, ice in the air and this man who understood me in some way the rest of my household could not. I honestly felt a kind of love for him. It was not the feeling I had for Rob, that lightning strike that lit me up through and through. It was a sense of home and familial kinship. Guinea and the Gambra are different countries but we must have been born under the same stars. He too had lost all his family. He too both belonged and did not belong in the place where he lived.

He looked up at the shop-sign hanging above us, the half-eagle rimmed with frost and little icicles clinging to the board.

"*In tenebras lux*," he said. "It has been a dark year. I missed London. How are you faring, mistress?"

I blew out another dragon-breath of steam and shivered.

"More in shadow than light," I said. "Come in now, I am letting midwinter into the house."

In truth, it had felt like midwinter this whole dreary year. John and I nursing our sorrow, me holding myself away from Rob. Even Grace had been quieter. I could not remember the last time we all laughed together.

My body quickened and failed again in August. One ferocious, sticky night I woke wracked with stomach cramps and sickness, my skin cold and clammy as if in defiance of the heat. In a little while the sad blood came. I rocked and sweated through the long stifling night, as with each shattering cramp the life that had been growing in me seeped away.

The loss drove me further into melancholy, but it hit John harder. It bred a bitterness in him that could not be sweetened. He seemed pressed by invisible weights that grew heavier as the year went on even though outwardly the business was thriving. He began to stay out later and later and often in the mornings I could still smell drink on him. Grace learned from Roberdine that besides the usual evenings plotting with Wolfe and the rest he was spending more time with the players at the Curtain Theatre, who drank like heroes.

"It's not all wasted time, though," said Rob. "That's how he won the agreement to print all their playbills. You have to go out and about and drink with people if you want to get their trade. Women shouldn't nag men to stay in at nights if they want bread on the table."

"Women need to know where their men go at night," replied Grace, "if they want to be sure the bread's not all getting drunk away."

The secret press had lain idle most of this year, and only a handful of Marshalsea messages came through marked with the dotted cross. We were chastened and wary after Campion's death. The seven priests who were arraigned with him were all executed at Tyburn in June. A bloody stack of martyrs. They were a terrifying, deliberate example to us all.

John still had not told me who was behind the Marshalsea messages, the 'particular man' that Persons was communicating with, but I suspected it is one of the Howards, Henry or Philip. They were the only nobles we had dealings with and who would have an interest in the Queen's affairs. I watched the stray messages come through and could not bring myself to care. Perhaps they indicated some new machination over the Queen's marriage, or lack of it.

Nor did I have any news of my brother, either from Lopes or my master. Lopes wrote to me in September saying that Dassell had discovered the man who had employed him died five years ago and his household was broken up. He had no luck tracking down my brother but was seeking out the other household servants to ask them for information.

I replied to Lopes thanking him, but since then I had heard nothing at all. I knew that Dom Antonio's fortunes were down after a defeat by the Spanish in the Azores and he was kicking his heels in Paris, so perhaps the Guinea trade agreement had gone to the wall and Lopes had no need for me any more. I knew that our agreement was purely a business one, he told me so very clearly—but his silence still smarted.

I had begun to feel that everything I did came to nothing. The fruit of my body withered and so did the fruit of my labours. Our work for Persons had all gone, burned in the lime-kilns. The messages we passed for him had failed to cement the Queen's match with Alençon . My brother was still lost to me and my marriage felt fragile as lace, filigreed with silence.

Now here was Domingo at my door and I felt the smallest shift towards Spring. I led him in to the kitchen and sat him by the hearth to thaw out. His boots were crusted with ice and he was well muffled up beneath his cloak.

"Is your husband at home, mistress?" he said as he unwound a nest of thick scarves from his neck. "I have a message for him."

"Yes—of course. Should I wake him?"

"Please. I cannot stay long."

"You'll break your fast with us, though? I will go and fetch John now."

I left him warming his hands at the fire and went to wake John. He was fast asleep under the heap of woollen blankets we piled up on winter nights, his face barely visible between the covers and his nightcap. I shook him gently till he coughed and opened one eye. It was bloodshot and his breath smelled of wine. He had come to bed late again last night.

"God's blood, Suky, what hour is this?"

"Early. There's a visitor downstairs. He wants to see you."

"Who, at this hour?"

"Go and look."

He growled and pulled the blankets up further. "If it's Wolfe tell him his wine is poison and he can wait out in the street."

"It isn't Wolfe. You must go and see him, he can't stay long."

I heard him cursing as I left the room to go and see how Grace was. She was down with another fever, asleep in her narrow bed in the little room opposite ours. Her forehead was damp but cooler. Asleep, with pale wisps of her hair clinging to her cheek, she looked younger than her years—barely more than a child. She had flung off the blankets in her sweat and I tucked them back over her to stop the chill getting in.

When I returned to the kitchen John had drawn up a stool beside Domingo and they were conferring together, my husband listening intently as Domingo spoke quietly to him. They looked up as I came in and Domingo broke off his talk. John, still in his nightcap and slippers, looked crumpled and unkempt beside Domingo. The firelight and shadow called out the hollows under his eyes and the deep lines around his mouth. He looked haggard as an old man in a play. The thought shocked me. I forgot John's age much of the time, his appetite for life made him seem younger. This unkind light and the ravages of wine showed he was not young. Even middle age would soon be left behind.

"Suky," he said hoarsely. "Get the breakfast things. And ale—a quantity of small ale."

I nodded and went to cut the bread. I listened out as the knife broke through the hard crust of our rye bread but the men were talking too softly for me to hear. Domingo stopped speaking again and rose from his seat as I carried the plates over to the table.

"May I help, mistress?" he asked.

"Not at all, you are a guest. Sit down and eat, please. I will bring ale next."

The noise from the kitchen must have woken Roberdine who came rattling down the stairs as we began to eat. He stopped short when he saw Domingo at the table, spreading butter thickly onto the brown bread. Domingo raised a hand in greeting.

"Master Rob," he said. "How fares your flesh wound from the Watch?"

Rob came over grinning and held both palms up. A thin scar

traced the line of his cut, so faint it looked like another life-line on his hand.

"Very well, thank you sir," he said. "And yours?"

Domingo rolled up his sleeve and displayed his forearm, which was marked with a silvery line like a spider's thread.

"Also well," he said, "thanks to Mistress Charlewood's physic."

"What happened to Rowlands?" said Rob.

"Safe in Antwerp," Domingo replied. "I've seen him."

"Are you safe here, though?" said Roberdine. "You're sure they won't come after you?"

Domingo shrugged.

"There are no warrants out for my arrest. No one followed me out to the Continent. I am safe as any Catholic can be in this country. I must leave you now, though. I have an early meeting with Senhor Lopes. Thank you for your kindness, and the food."

He took a last draught of ale and stood. I gathered up his things for him and he wrapped himself back up in scarves, gloves and cloak. His leavetaking was far more formal than his greeting had been: he kissed my cheek but said only a quick, "Goodbye, and see you anon." I watched him go feeling rebuked and unsatisfied. I wanted more time with him. I remembered our conversation in the garret last year when we were both lost in death's labyrinth—our heretical conversation. "God is not listening to me, he is not answering," Domingo had said. God had not been listening to me either.

All that year I had tried to reconcile myself to the thought of my baby in Limbo, but I couldn't. It felt like a glass splinter lodged in my skin that I could not dig out. The place had always been in my map of the world, Heaven and Hell, but as an obscure county my thoughts never visited. Now I felt as if I was trapped there myself.

I had prayed to God for comfort and guidance and got neither. I spoke to Marshalsea priests and re-read a hundred texts by dead theologians arguing for and against the existence of a place no-one had ever seen or mapped. I could not turn Protestant purely to save my own baby from the fringes of Hell, but my whole body rebelled when I imagined him there. I had not spoken to John about it, but perhaps Domingo would understand my feeling of loss.

When the door was shut and bolted again I sat back at the table, next to John, who looked a little healthier after his breakfast.

"What was Domingo's message, sir?" I asked. He shook his head a little and spoke low enough that only I could hear.

"Nothing of importance. Persons thanks us for our help. Rowlands is safe and well in Antwerp. The intrigues and machinations go on and on and we are no nearer to freedom. The Queen keeps her course. Priests hang; those who harbour them hang; we who print their words hide in our burrows and wait for the terriers to pull us out by the rump."

I looked at the grey glints in John's dark hair and thought how little I truly knew him. I did not believe that was Domingo's only message. A man does not cross Finsbury Fields on a freezing January morning before sun-up to pass on a thank-you.

CHAPTER 27

John grew more secretive and snappish with me even as the winter ice melted and the world began to open up towards Spring. He should have been in good spirits as outwardly the business was thriving. Together with John Wolfe and John Kingston we were printing a book on the art of memory by an Italian exile and philosopher, Giordano Bruno. It would appeal greatly to men like Philip Sidney that John was keen to cultivate—high-born, well-educated, and competing to be seen reading the latest thoughts from the Continent.

Bruno's philosophies tiptoed close to heresy so we printed it in Italian with a Venice imprint and claimed it had been imported, both to increase its appeal and to act as a shield in case any trouble arose from Bruno's theories. I helped read through the Italian proofs and found I enjoyed working in the print room more and more. It was a refuge from my sadness over my lost babies and somewhere I could use my languages and my aptitude for learning.

We were also pitching to print the playbills for Walsingham's newly formed theatre company, the Queen's Men, and John was busy wooing their leader Richard Tarlton with greater tenderness and extravagance than he ever wooed me.

Winning their business would be a great feather in his cap, and not just for the money it would bring in. Tarlton was the greatest clown of the age and at ease with people of all stations, from the lowest to the highest. That had made him friends in very starry places. Philip Sidney himself was godfather to Tarlton's small son, and Sidney had just married Francis Walsingham's daughter.

Tarlton seemed to favour John so he should have been in fine humour—he was never so buoyant as when a deal was waiting to be struck. Yet his smiles seemed forced. He pushed himself to be merry in company, but at home he was sombre and sometimes almost spiteful. I had to take such care with my words that often I avoided speaking to him at all, though even silence could cause offence.

It could not be chance that during this time we carried and received more books and letters through the Marshalsea than ever before. I was always busy making up secret inks, and Grace, Rob, and I went back and forth to the prison weekly. I began to watch for the dotted cross as a shepherd watches the hills for the quick black creep of a wolf. I had not feared it when I knew its purpose, but now John would not tell me what it signalled.

I asked him one night as we lay in bed, and he said, "You act as messenger, Suky. A messenger does not read the letters he carries."

His voice was calm but prohibited further questioning. I absorbed the rebuke, and said:

"I was always trusted with such matters, before. Women may be weaker vessels but surely I have proved to you I am made of good clay? I will not suddenly break and spill secrets rolling here and there like peppercorns."

"Go to sleep now, wife," he said, more coldly, "and trust in me."

I could not sleep, and I found I could not trust him. By withholding his own trust from me, he bred suspicion instead. I could not understand why I was shut out from his plans. The sight of the little cross made my skin tighten, even more so when Sir Thomas wrote and told me that Richard, the estate steward at Framfield, had been imprisoned for possessing an *Agnus Dei*—no bail to be given. That would be a great blow. Richard had been on the estate since Sir Thomas was a child. The recusancy fines must be mounting up too. England was growing a colder and colder place for Catholics, as cold as Hell. The freezing winds blown by Walsingham stripped us and flayed us, took our goods, and broke up our families. I was afraid for our household and I feared John was at some business that would bring us all into the teeth of those cold winds.

One evening in June, I found myself alone in the printroom with Rob, tidying at the end of the day while Grace prepared supper. Rob stood washing used type while I redistributed the clean, dry sorts in the compositor's case.

I watched him swash water over the type, the muscles rolling in his arms. He moved easy and fluid like all good workmen, making hard graft look like grace. He was so young compared to John, his face unlined, all his bullish arrogance plain to read, free of a past, free from whatever obscure meshes John was caught in.

I had kept my feelings for Rob pressed down for so long, never allowing myself to admit them, but the crushing had not killed them any more than crushing a dandelion will stop it pushing back up through earth and stone. I felt that gold rising up in me once more as I looked at him, that golden weed desire.

"Have you carried any papers to the Marshalsea this week?" I asked.

Rob was finished with the type. He stood upright, stretching out his back, and dried his hands on his apron.

"Not to the Marshalsea," he said, "but messages have gone downriver."

"Downriver?" I said. That was not a route I knew. What else was John keeping from me?

Muffled noises came from the kitchen: scraping chairs, Grace and John talking, and the clink of pewter as Grace laid the table. I listened for a moment as I put the last sort back into the typecases, then softly pushed the print room door, leaving it open just a chink. Rob watched me.

"What messages do we send down the river, Rob?" I asked quietly.

"That I don't know," said Rob, "but I know how they come and go from us, and that makes me wonder who sends them."

"Why?" I said.

"Because they don't hang you down at Wapping with your boots in the water for pirating other men's licensed copy," said Rob now. "Some of those books and papers come to us by pirates who work with knives and muskets, not paper and ink."

"And how do you know that?" I said. "Are they the Sussex owlers your father wanted to keep you away from?"

Rob flicked his hand in the trough water which rocked and rippled, awash with rushlight glimmer and ribbons of ink that sifted into it. He leaned against the wall beside me, at his ease.

"Something like," he said, "but that the Thames isn't the sea. Easier to hide in but it's a creeping kind of work. I hate those stinking bogs but there's nowhere like them for losing men, or goods, or anything else you need to make disappear."

He took up the rushlight that sat on the side-board and held it up. His breath made the flame waver and duck as he spoke.

"They send signals up and down the river with lights, like beacons. The lanterns talk to one another, as it were. If you saw them you wouldn't know what they were saying. You'd think it was marsh-light or a house lantern all a-flicker in the wind. But anyone who speaks the language would understand it. Sometimes those long black marshes look like stars in the night sky, all spotted with talking lights. And if anyone goes after them those lights vanish as if they've sunk straight down in the mud. They haven't. The men who hold them know their own paths, but you would think they've vanished. I would, too."

As he talked he moved a finger's breadth closer to me, so close I could hear his breathing as clearly as I felt my own. He smelled of ink and sweat and metal, like a printroom spirit made flesh.

"I like to know my master," said Rob, "and I like to know how close I'm standing to the gallows. I used to know well enough what the game was and my part in it. This I don't have the measure of, but it feels to me about the length of a gibbet rope."

I watched the rushlight move and found I was shivering. Rob had talked the river and the long mudflats in around us, conjuring the loneliness and dank marsh-smell. More than that, he had some other witchcraft about him, some kind of summoning that called my body to him. I closed my eyes a moment and tried to steady myself.

"Could you take one of the marked books to read?" said Rob, and I was awake again at once.

"No!" I said. "How could I ask for his trust if I steal and lie to learn his business?"

"Stealing and lying is allowable if the business is a hanging sort," said Rob. "You want to make sure that his work isn't coiling hemp about your own neck, mistress."

He was so close that I could feel his breath on my cheek. From the kitchen I heard chairs scraping. Grace was arranging the table for supper. Somehow I gathered the will to move and break the spell. I must get to the firelight and the solid, everyday world of the kitchen. I let my own breath out, and the blood roared in my ears like the sea.

"I must help Grace," I said abruptly, closing the conversation. "Close up here, please, before you come in."

CHAPTER 28

I slept poorly that night. I dreamed of lights out in the marshes, a line of them running down to the sea. I was running past them along the black river. My feet were light and I half flew over the rushes, awake and alive as a night-bird. Rob was running beside me, both of us at the same pace, passing lantern after lantern till we came to the yawning mouth of the Thames and the sea huge as night. Then I tripped and fell into those waters and woke up in a sweat. I sat up and flung the blankets away from me, gasping.

John did not wake at this turbulence, only rolled onto his side. He smelled of drink again. I could not bear the heat and stink of the bed. Scrambling out into the gentle dawn light, I splashed my face at the ewer, trying with cold water to wash away my sweat and the dark drag of the marshes. I dressed hurriedly and went downstairs to cut chives for a stew. I wanted to be out in the air and alone. I could hear Grace moving about in her room and I hoped Rob was still up in the garret.

My hope was thwarted when I saw the garden door stood ajar. I hesitated a moment before going outside, then stepped out boldly. I still wanted air, and it was my garden.

Rob stood in the middle of the path, holding a letter in his hand. He was not reading it, but staring across the garden at our russet apple tree, trained against the wall and heavy with ripening fruit. He stood very still. I had never seen him so motionless. Usually his movements were quick and constant—his stillness now was all wrong.

"Rob?" I said. He turned his head slowly and I saw he had taken some shock. His eyes were distant, his skin pale. I walked closer to him, the gravel loud beneath my feet in the quiet morning air. I said his name again and he looked at me as if he did not recognise me.

"My father is dead," he said.

"Oh, Rob—" I held out my hand to him but he did not take it.

"He took an apoplexy on Friday," he said. "My brother writes that he fell down suddenly at the yard and struck his head on a block. He's dead."

He gave the letter to me and turned away again, putting his hands in his pockets. I did not know what to say to him. I never quite knew what Rob was thinking or feeling, but I knew he would not want those soft words of sympathy we give the bereaved. I read through the letter he had given me. It was a short note, in a small, cramped hand. His brother wrote what Rob had told me, and that the funeral would be this Thursday. Rob should come. It was signed simply, *Your brother, Henry*. No words of affection. I folded the paper up slowly. Rob, the changeling child who believed his father hated him. My heart went out to him.

"They'll need an outsize coffin for him," he said. "He always said we should put him to sea in a boat, when he died. Pack one of the dinghies in with brandy bottles, nail a canvas over it and send it into the Channel for the French to puzzle over."

He reached for the flowers of a tall fennel growing beside him, running his palm over the soft fronds.

"I never had the skill for the work, or the patience," he said. "When I was small I liked to watch him, though. Sitting on a barrel down at the yard, watching them build up the ship-frames. He could heave up whole timbers as if they were nothing, as light as a flower stalk. He was the strongest man in the yard. I never thought he'd die before—"

He broke off a frond and rubbed it between his fingers, releasing the aniseed scent. When the green strands were all crushed, he flicked them away from him into the herb bed.

"Before I'd done something," he continued. "Before I made my fortune. Showed him what I am. That he was wrong."

"Are you so sure that he hated you?" I asked. "Fathers can be severe, it is their duty. That does not mean love is lacking."

Rob looked at me sideways. "Runt. Devil. Toad. Lackwit. Are these words of love?"

I reached out to him again but he moved away, shaking his head.

"Give me the letter," he said. I handed it to him and he tucked it into his pocket. "I've an errand at the Hall," he said without looking at me, and he set off back into the house.

"Rob," I said, "stay a while," but he walked on as if I had not spoken, closing the kitchen door behind him. I stood staring at its blank wooden boards for a few minutes. Death can come as suddenly as a door closing between you and another person. Only the door is locked forever, and they will never hear the words you meant to say. I felt a sudden awful thrill of sickness, that dizziness of loss that overwhelmed me after Anne died and my lady turned against me. I ran to open the door, but even as I came into the kitchen I heard the slam of the front door. Grace looked at me in surprise, the water-jug in her hand, then almost dropped it when I burst into tears, leaning against the dresser as my old grief rushed through me again like a spring rising.

Rob went to Sussex for the funeral and returned a week later. He kept to himself for some weeks afterwards, his natural energies all muffled. I asked about the funeral and his family, but he would say nothing beyond: "They are well, mistress, thank you." I felt he was avoiding me in particular. I wanted to show that I understood, but I could never catch him alone. We said prayers for his father nightly to speed his stay in Purgatory but apart from that Rob never mentioned his name.

Then John came home in good humour one night after a meeting with Tarlton. He had wine with him and insisted on pouring it out for us all while Grace was preparing supper.

"Go and tell Rob to come up from the cellar now," he told me, "Supper is almost ready. If the floor isn't swept clean yet he can finish after."

I went down to the secret room, glad of a chance to talk to Rob alone. I expected him to be cloaked in the same silence he had worn since his father's death, but when he saw me come in he stopped for a moment and beckoned me closer. He began sweeping again, the scratch of the brush-bristles covering his voice.

"I have one of the marked books," he whispered. "He sent me to the Marshalsea today."

"Rob, have you run mad!" I said. "He will know. He will guess. You must give it to him."

"Oh I did, I did. I gave it to him in here and he sent me straight upstairs, but I crept down quiet as a cat before you and Grace came home and watched him. He always leaves that door open a crack so he can hear us. I saw what he was at. Then I crept away again and came stamping down the stairs to tell him there was ink spilled on the galley proofs, so he hadn't time to finish. He whipped me for spilling the ink but I can take a few stripes."

Rob sounded entirely back to his old self, full of wild spirits. It sat so oddly with his recent melancholy that I could not quite believe in it. He seemed almost a little feverish.

Just then there came three thumps on the floor above us, the signal that Searchers were at the door. I cast a glance at Rob and went swiftly to leave the room. We always came back up into the kitchen or at least into the cellar if there was time, so that none of the household were unaccounted for. My hand was on the door when Rob came up beside me. He held the door shut and swiftly locked it.

"What are you doing?" I whispered.

"Come and see," he said.

"We must go up!" I said, but even as I spoke I heard a confusion of voices upstairs. The Searchers were already in the house. Rob went to stand by the lantern that hung from the wall and held the book up for me to see. I motioned to him to blow out the light, but he shook his head and beckoned me over.

"Mother Mary," I said, "dim the light! If they see it through a crack—"

"We'll hear them if they come down to the cellar," he said. "Look here."

He took a book up from the table: an edition of Rothomagi's *Jesus Psalter*. Rapidly he turned to the blank page at the back. Boots tramped on the kitchen boards above us as the flickering light fell on pale-brown curves and marks just visible on the paper.

"Invisible ink," I said, and Rob nodded.

"I saw him holding the candle to the paper," he said.

"That's not my recipe," I said, "the lines are too faint." I squinted at the lines, which formed one word and a series of numbers. "*24. Epistle: 2:4:6:1*," I mouthed the sequence out loud. "Epistle 2. It must be the Epistles in the Bible surely—it must be One Corinthians. But what is the 24?"

We kept a copy of the Bishop's Bible in the secret room. I snatched it up from the side and leafed through to One Corinthians, chapter 4, verse 6:

'And these things brethren, I have figuratively applied unto myself, and to Apollo's, for your sakes, that ye might learn by us, that no man conceive in mind above that which is written, that one swell not against another for any man's cause'

"What does the '1' mean, then?" said Rob, peering over my shoulder. "The first line? The first word? '*And these things, brethren.*' It makes no sense."

I stared at the page, then picked up the psalter again. "Epistle. Perhaps—" and I turned to the second page of the book, the last of the epistle to the reader. It looked quite ordinary. There were no marks, no underlinings, nothing to show that it might be the number 2 indicated by the secret ink.

I separated it from the other pages with my fingers and held it close to the light to see it better, in case there were faint markings I had missed. There were none. I flicked through to page 24, and when I reached it Rob clutched my arm and pointed. Dotted about the page, only visible because the light shone through them, were tiny pinpricks under particular letters. Elated, I turned to the fourth page and held it up, but there were no markings—nor were there on page six or one.

As we stared in confusion the sounds from above grew louder. Someone was coming down the steps into the cellar. Rob closed the book, replaced it on the table and blew out the candle. We stood side by side in the dark, listening.

"Doesn't it make your heart jump," he whispered to me.

"Hush," I said, putting out my hand and finding his arm.

"They can't hear us," he said. "We're safe, unless someone has given them a tip."

I clutched Rob's arm tighter. I could see nothing at all in this lightless place; my face might as well have been swathed in sacking. In the darkness Rob moved. He took my other hand and drew me close to him. I resisted, but he leaned in and whispered in my ear:

"What would you do now, if this was the end? If in a few minutes they were to break in and find us, and it was Tyburn tree for us all?"

"We're more likely to be hung if you can't stop your tongue!" I whispered back.

"I would tell you how rare you are, how soft you are, how your skin glows," he said. His cheek rested against mine, his mouth right beside my ear.

"Go to, boy," I said, but I did not dare move away from him in case we were heard. That is a half-truth. I did not want to move.

"Where's the harm in saying it?" he said. "When does he ever say it to you, the old man?"

On the other side of the door there were men's voices, bumping and scraping and knocking along the walls. My heart felt as if it was thumping in my chest and my head at once, my body itself only a heartbeat swelling and dying over and over. I felt his breathing and my own rise and fall, our bodies pressed together, and did not know if I were flying or drowning. For certain, I was not moving in ordinary air. He did not try to kiss me. He did not need to. I stood with him until the voices outside began moving away again as the Searchers left the cellar.

"Do you love me?" whispered Rob, in the dark.

"No," I said fiercely. Desperately I pulled away from him and patted down my clothes, sure that John would take one look at me and know what had happened. I had upended the natural order of things; master, wife, apprentice. God knew what retribution would follow.

"God forgive us," I said, crossing myself. "Rob, your father is not a month in his grave."

"And there let him lie," he said with passion. "He is dead, not I. What good does mourning do him? Let me live, grow rich and buy him up a purseful of indulgences to hasten his path to Heaven. I'm done with grieving. And God forgives everything, if you repent of it."

I had nothing to say to that so we stood in silence, waiting for someone to come and let us out. In a while, Grace came to the door and we climbed back up the cellar steps to the kitchen, where my husband was waiting.

CHAPTER 29

It is easy to condemn vices when you have none of them. I had never been greedy or gluttonous. I had always been loyal. I had fought against my feelings for Rob ever since I came into the household. Now they were in full flood and at last I understood how hard it is to fight the devil when he tempts you. I understood Eve in the Garden of Eden and the irresistible glow of that forbidden apple.

I was tempted every day by Rob. I counted each minute I spent with him as if it were a minute of sunshine, yellow sand falling grain by grain through an hourglass. His hand brushing mine for two seconds in the print room, a look he gave me as we passed on the stairs. I felt the warmth of each encounter and then the cold shadow of the sin it threatened. Our bodies shared such little time but Rob took up hours of my waking and sleeping life.

Every time I lay with John I conjured Rob up. In the darkness my husband became my lover, as day after day Rob and I exchanged glances that left me flushed and giddy. I prayed to be released from this lust but my prayers were lip service and did not come from the heart. It was not only the enchantment of mutual desire binding me to him but the secrets we shared.

I contrived to read through the marked book again while I was practising my composition in the cellar. The endpaper had been torn out but page 24 was still there. I turned to it and wrote down the sequence of letters marked by the pinpricks. As the sentence formed I realised it must be in cipher. It made no sense at all, a wrong turn in a maze. *llffimffgfhqnmpcqwyicx*. The meaning was double-locked. It made me shake my head. What waters was John dabbling in that required such a complex concealment? I told Rob the letter sequence too but it meant nothing to him.

The message about the Epistle must be the key to translating it. I spent hours poring over the Epistles, earning wry words from John about my sudden piety, but I could not fathom the meaning of that sequence.

In mid-September, Tarlton wrote to John confirming an agreement for him to print all the playbills for their winter residence in London at two inn-theatres, the Bull and the Bell. John nearly burst when he read the letter.

"Printer to the Queen's men—that's only four letters off printer to the Queen!" he said. "Dust off your best dress Suky, we'll go to the Royal Exchange on Saturday to peacock about and put John Wolfe's nose out of joint."

I've always loved the Exchange by candlelight, when the merchants have done trading for the day and musicians set up in the galleries, when it becomes a gathering-place for citizens rather than a marketplace for the wealthy. I was happy to see John happy, too. I clutched at any good mood these days as proof things could not be as bad as I feared.

But on Saturday morning, John went to the Marshalsea and then straight down to the cellar when he returned. When Grace went down to fetch him to eat he sent her back up again muttering angrily under her breath.

"He's in ill humour," she said. "I never saw him look so black or speak so harsh. Let him starve, then, if he wants no food."

"I'll take him something," I said. "Give me the bread." I had to know what was gnawing at him. I had to see what he was doing with that Marshalsea book. I began slicing bread and cheese to take down to him, when there was a knock at the door. Grace went to answer it and came back to the kitchen with John Wolfe behind her. He was breathing hard and sweat stood on his forehead. He looked as if he had run up from Paul's and John Wolfe was not a running man.

"Is John here?" he said. "I must speak to him, and quickly."

I saw my chance. "I'll go and fetch him," I said. "Grace, pour ale for the men."

Down the steps I went and found John sitting at the typecase, putting sorts back into place from the composing-stick. He looked up as I came in and paused in his work.

"I told Grace to leave me be," he said.

"John Wolfe is here, sir," I said, coming over to stand by the typecase. "He says he must speak with you."

I could see the text open on his lap. It was not the book from the Marshalsea but my wedding present to him, Piemontese's *Secreti*.

"What does he want?" he said, sharply. "I am busy."

"I don't know, sir, but he looks afraid and you know nothing frightens Wolfe. Will you come up sir?"

I reached out my hand to touch his arm but he jerked it away and grabbed at my wrist so hard that I cried out. The composing stick fell from his hand and the type-sorts scattered across the earth floor. I tried to pull away but he held on to me. He had never hurt me before and his face frightened me. Then it changed, and he stood up and let go my wrist.

"I am sorry," he said. "Jesus, have mercy on me." He put the Piemontese on the table and bent down to collect the sorts.

"Leave them, sir, I'll put them back," I said. "Wolfe cannot wait."

He straightened up, looking at the tumbled sorts, and nodded.

"Leave the light," he said. "I will come back down after," and he left the cellar.

Alone, I went straight to the table and looked for a new book. There it was, a book of three catechisms by Robert Harrison. When I found it I turned straight to the endpaper. The ink marks were still there. John must have just revealed them and had not had time to burn them. *17. Epistle 5: 15: 3: 1.* I turned to page 17 in a fever and held the page up to the light. There was the first pinprick, under the *J* of *Jewes*. I took a stub of pencil from the table and my notebook from my pocket, and wrote down each letter as quick as I could, praying I had not missed any. Then I replaced the book and the pencil and flung the sorts back into their cases.

I ran back upstairs, hoping to God John had been so occupied with Wolfe that he would not notice how long I had been in the cellar. When I came into the kitchen, Grace made a face at me. Rob was standing by the table, alert.

"They're in the parlour," Grace said. "Something's very wrong."

The next minute, John came into the kitchen and went straight to the trapdoor. I heard the front door close as Wolfe went out again. John did not even look at me. He was as pale as Wolfe had been and he did not speak as he went downstairs. Rob and I exchanged glances, then I looked away. Grace was watching me.

We all three stood listening, waiting for John to return, while the bread and cheese sat on the table uneaten, the knife lying harmless on its side. I wondered how many Catholic households had been left just like this, wives and husbands snatched from ordinary meals and taken away to die, leaving the bread to go stale and the cheese to mould over and a dropped cup rolling into the corner.

In a while John came back up again, carrying two or three books. He closed and locked the trapdoor and looked at us, standing as if

Medusa had turned her eyes on us. He actually laughed at the sight.

"Come," he said, "John Wolfe is no constable, only a watchman come to warn me of wolves in the distance. I am not dead yet."

He went to the kitchen fire and began tearing up the books, feeding them in a few pages at a time so they would burn well. Grace started back to life and went to put the sliced bread and cheese out on plates.

"When I am done here," said John, "I am going out. Meet me at the Exchange at five, Suky."

"Yes sir," I said. "But then—all is well?"

He turned his face from the fire to look at me.

"No," he said, "it is not. But we'll speak at the Exchange."

I nodded and went to join Grace at the table. I had no appetite at all but I made a show of eating some bread while John was still in the kitchen. Once he was gone, I pushed my plate away from me and put my hand to my mouth. I thought I might be sick.

"What do you think it is?" said Grace. "I never saw either of them look like that before. Wolfe or the master."

I shook my head. "I don't know. He tells me nothing. I must make ready—you take my bread, Grace, I cannot stomach it."

I met John up in the high galleries while the Wolfes went to buy drinks. When I reached him he was alone. He was leaning on the gallery rail, drumming his fingers and staring down at the people below. He glanced at me as I drew near him, but did not smile. Here was the reckoning, then, at last. I came to lean close beside him on the rail and looked down at the floor below, filled with people decked out in their finery. Feathers and hair-jewels nodded in the light as the women's dresses formed bright circles of colour.

"What is it?" I asked. "What was Wolfe's news?"

"Henry Howard has been arrested," he replied.

"On what charge?" I asked.

"There are rumours of conspiracy against the Queen," he muttered. I gripped the railing tight.

"Does it touch us? Would they find links to us if they searched his books?"

He shook his head. "I don't know."

I had never seen him take bad news so ill. He was sweating and the sharp smell of fear came off him in waves. Usually, the threat of discovery or danger sent him up, alert and angry and alive. His drinking and his slumps were not linked to risk but to sorrow; grief for our lost baby or his other dead children, or some past sadness he had not shared with me but that still dogged him. This moping reaction was new. All my fears ignited again and burned before my eyes in the shape of that dotted cross.

"Great men," he said, "we hang on to their coat-tails and when they fall, we fall."

"Walsingham knows you," I said. "We have done good work for him in the past, through Munday. Is that not insurance enough?"

He snorted. "Walsingham knows me well enough. God above, I wish that he did not. What more can I do? I have given all. I used to relish this game. Running back and forth, keeping everything balanced just so. Doing my bit for Walsingham and thumbing my nose at him behind his back. Perhaps I am too old now. Fighting for your faith is for young men. I should be wise by now, and politic. God save me, Suky, I am no martyr. Death should hold no fear for me but it does. It does."

I put a hand on his arm. He looked at me but his eyes were far away, focused on some distant horror: his head in a noose at Tyburn tree.

"What have you done?" I asked quietly. "What have you been doing for Henry Howard?"

He still did not seem to see me fully. He did not answer me directly.

"I saw what they did to Campion," he said. "They broke that

man. They broke his body completely. They could not answer his arguments, so they broke him and lied about him, and I spread those lies for them. I had to do something to make amends."

"And what did you do?" I said, more insistently. "Please, for God's sake, tell me what you have done?"

He looked at me in the eyes at last and I saw a weary darkness in his own and the pallor of exhaustion in his skin. He looked very different from the man at our first meeting, three years ago, the bright activity and uplift in his face all dragged down and rubbed out. I felt tears swelling my throat and moved my hand to rest on his own, my fingers on the warm gold of his wedding ring.

"We have not been good friends, you and I," I said, "since the baby died. I would be friends again, sir. You have been in a black humour these past months and it is poisoning the household. You are the head and you determine the mood of the house. We cannot dance around your melancholy forever. Please tell me what ails you. I am your wife and it is for me to help you bear your troubles."

He stared at me for a moment, then slowly shook his head.

"I have told you not to ask questions, not to look beyond your allotted place," he said quietly, almost despairingly. "Why do you persist in disobeying me?"

"Because I love you as a wife should," I said, "and a good wife should help her husband. You tell me not to ask about the things which are most important to you, so how can I ever know you or help you? I see that mark on the books and letters and to me it seems like the Devil's mark."

At that he moved his hand away from beneath mine. His face frightened me.

"I say this for the last time. Wife, don't question me. I tell you to shut your eyes: be blind. I tell you to shut your ears: be deaf. This is what I ask of you. And this is how you can help me. Now stop your tongue, the Wolfes are coming."

I bit my lip till it hurt, then turned to smile at John and Joan, while the musicians played and everyone around us laughed and nodded, a bright flock of birds, beautiful in the candlelight, that could in a second turn to a mob of carrion crows and come for us, ready to peck out our eyes.

CHAPTER 30

I knew John would drink the next day and so he did. I went up to bed early, leaving him drinking in the parlour.

Safe in our room, I took out my notebook and my Bible and pored over the jumbled sentence I had taken from the Marshalsea book. I could make no sense of it, still, though I went through every verse of the Epistles. I did not hear John's heavy, stumbling tread on the stairs until near midnight. I blew out the candle as soon as I heard him coming and folded myself up in the blankets, listening until he fell into bed beside me, snoring.

I waited a while longer until I was sure he was quite out, then I got up and went downstairs. I often went down to the print room or the kitchen in between the first and second sleeps, so there was nothing to make him suspect me if he woke and found me gone, or if Grace or Rob happened to come down too.

In the print room, I sat at the typecases and laid out my piece of paper with the penciled letters again. It was a jumble of nothing with no marks to show word breaks:

jflfissectmsgcthflclsctbfhwfijgefsgjgebjfflctbsoefhfict

I stared at it, willing light to shine in and the letters to rearrange themselves, but nothing happened.

In a while I heard a creak from the stairs and thought someone was coming down. I folded the paper into the pocket of my nightgown and took up a composing stick so that it would seem I was only practising composition. I began placing letters in the row, listening for more sounds, but none came. Perhaps it had been only the wind.

I put the composing stick down and took the paper from my pocket again, and even as I did so something shifted in my mind, a gentle nudge that brought back the image of John in the cellar, sitting at the typecases with Piemontese's *Secreti* in his lap.

Why did he have my wedding gift open at the typecases? Not for sentiment, surely, and not for printing, we had no order to print a new edition. I thought he had pushed my hand away so I could not touch him, but perhaps he did not want me to touch the book... I considered the way a typecase is laid out and the order the letters take, and almost dropped the paper in fright. I looked at the row of letters again. Could it possibly be?

The Piemontese was in the print room, on the side. I went to pick it up, suddenly sure. *Epistle: 5:15:3:1*. I turned to the Epistle in the Piemontese. Page five. Line fifteen. The third word: judgement, the first letter: J.

The first box in the top left-hand corner of the typecase holds the Js. What if J became A, and the next box of letters B, reading along left to right? That was it. That must be it. I had the wind behind me. The air hummed and the little sorts winked in their cases as the rushlight flickered. I smoothed the paper out where I could see it, then took up the composing stick again and put back the few letters I had laid out. Looking at the paper, I laid out the letters that were written there, making a long row of nonsense. Then I set about creating another sentence on top of that one.

The first letter of the jumbled sentence was a small 'j'. I replaced it with an 'a' and then counted along to the 'fl' box. I worked quickly, stringing the letters together, until I began to build something that made sense. The words all ran together without spaces, but I slotted them in as I made out each word.

The sentence that formed in my hand made the blood thump in my ears. With each letter added I felt as if a crack in the floor beneath me was splitting wider and wider until an abyss gaped at my feet, a cold wind springing up from the depths to wind round my throat.

I read the sentence through twice when it was done. There was no mistake. *Agreed. Twenty five thousand men and half the cost.*

Twenty-five thousand men was nothing less than an army. I did not quite want to believe it. What was John doing with this message?

I sat staring at my broken cipher with a dry mouth. This was either high treason, or John was working for Walsingham and it referred to some movement of troops in the Netherlands. In either case, my husband was not the man I thought him to be. John was caught up in great men's intrigues. No wonder he wanted to keep me well away from them. This must be some plot of Henry Howard's. It explained John's terror at his arrest. But if this was a plot against the Queen, he might be risking my life and the lives of all the household. What could I do?

Slowly I began to redistribute the sorts in the cases. The rushlight was burning down and the chill of deep night had descended. I had a sudden yearning for the warmth of the fire in the library in Sussex. I used to sit on my little stool by the great fireplace while my master read to us on winter nights, my mind wandering the world from the safety of that firelit room. I could not go back to Framfield, but Sir Thomas might still be able to offer help if a crash came, even from his prison cell. Yet if I told him I risked condemning my husband. Where should my loyalty lie?

I stared at the rushlight flame and prayed, hoping that I would feel God listening, but there was nothing. Only my own voice came back to me from the abyss. God had left me alone to decide.

I wrote to Sir Thomas in pale ink the next day. *I think the Howards move. I am afraid.*

The next week was curdled with dread. I knew I should fire up my courage and confront John and every day I ducked it, telling myself I would do it once my master had replied. In truth I was afraid of what John might do to me, when I had deliberately gone against his wishes and when the stakes were so high. When my master's reply came at last, written in milk in his neat hand, it did not reassure me as I had hoped.

> *Do nothing and tell no-one. I will not let harm come to you.*
> *Do not write of this again.*

I threw the letter on the fire when I had read it, tearing it up first in frustration. I seemed to do nothing but wait and watch. A woman's place, yes, but should a woman wait and watch as the sea came in until it washed her all away, or should she pick up her feet and run? I felt the tide coming for me. I heard the waves in the distance, but for the moment I obeyed my master and did nothing.

A letter from Richard Tarlton had arrived the day after we visited the Royal Exchange, announcing that the first performance of the Queen's Men at the Bull, on November 1, was to be *The Famous Victories of Henry V*. He asked us to commence printing the bill and advised that he would come to collect them in person when he arrived back in London.

In the weeks before the players returned to London we were run off our feet printing bills and distributing them around the city. Tarlton came by the print room a week before the first night to pick up a bundle, wearing an outlandishly theatrical pair of red boots, and brought news with him.

"Did you hear of the lunatic that came to shoot the Queen?" he said as he gathered up the playbills with a flourish.

"No! Christ. Is she hurt?" asked John, leaving the correcting-stone and coming over to him.

"Not harmed at all. They caught him long before he even reached London. John Somerville—his family seat's at Edstone in Warwickshire."

"Yes, they're ancient Catholics," said John. "God's bones. John Somerville, run mad?"

"He must be," said Tarlton. "He set out to walk from Edstone two days since, telling everyone he passed he was on his way to London to shoot the Queen. Of course the Watch took him up and I would think there's a noose already set up waiting to be tied round his fat Papist neck in a hemp bow. Good news for us. Such a thing puts people in the mood for patriotism. You'll come to the first night of course? Then you must come to supper, too. We're having a meal at the Bull after the first performance. Nothing grand, only the scrapings of the street; lords and ladies and bishops and the like. Wolfe is coming, and your new friend the Italian charlatan, and maybe my son's godfather. Come and dine on the Queen!"

"We will—we will. Thanks Richard, we'll see you anon."

Tarlton left with the playbills packaged up and clutched tight to his chest. When he was out of the door, John stood for a moment staring after him. Then he suddenly hooted with laughter, bending over almost double with mirth. When the laughter subsided, the tension had gone from his face for the first time since we heard of Henry Howard's arrest. His levity raised my spirits. If he could laugh at this, surely the message I read could not mean what I feared?

"*The Lord giveth and he taketh away,*" he said. "Things look bad for Henry Howard. Things look bad for me. But I am invited to a supper at the Bull with Philip Sidney and all the scrapings of London's richest streets. Run to Cheapside now, Suky, and buy yourself one of those spangled hairnets, on credit. Wear your gaudiest gown, wig yourself up and deck yourself in finery, we are to dine like royals."

CHAPTER 31

Two days after Tarlton's visit a man came to the house at twilight. I answered the door to him. He was muffled up to his eyes, and the eyes looked wild. I almost slammed the door in his face, his demeanour frightened me so, but he said: "Hold—I beg you, mistress. Is this Charlewood's house?"

John was down the road at James Roberts's; I did not know how to answer. I looked over my shoulder. Grace was busy in the kitchen and Rob tidying the printroom.

"They said he had a Blackamoor wife. Is this his house?" said the man more urgently. "Speak English? *Parlez-vous*—"

"Yes, yes, this is his house," I broke in. "What is your business here?"

The man drew a thin packet from his cloak and passed it to me.

"For your life," he said, "give this to him and tell no-one. Tell him to await instruction. Remember: not a soul!"

Then he pulled his hood further round his face and set off at a pace towards Finsbury Fields. I looked at the packet in my hand. Papers, with a seal I did not recognise. I went into the parlour and closed the door behind me, then stood for a moment by the fire, weighing the packet in my hand. If I broke the seal and read these papers John would know I had been meddling. So be it. I wanted the reckoning. I could not wait any longer, not after having seen that message in the book. I took a sharp breath and broke the seal.

There were two sheets of paper inside. I opened them out, squinting at the rough handwriting. On one was a sketched map showing a coastline full of inlets and rivers, with a list of places—all Sussex havens—on the reverse. On the second sheet was a list of names. The names were all Sussex too, Catholic gentry and nobles, and near the bottom was my old master's, Sir Thomas Framfield.

A map of the Sussex coast, a list of havens, and a list of Catholic men. My throat closed and I could not breathe for a moment. I dropped the papers onto the table as if they were a nest of snakes. Taken with the message about 25,000 men, it could be nothing less than a plan for invasion of England. I wished to God I had never broken the seal.

I stood staring at them, wondering wildly what to do and how, in Jesus' name, John had found himself caught up in such a plot. God knows it was hard to be an Englishman first and a Catholic second. God knows I prayed for the Queen to change her heretic ways and return to the true church. God knows I wished we could save the souls of all the Protestants who had left it, but I always hoped it could be done without bloodshed on this earth. Now here was my husband, up to his neck in a plot that would inevitably result in the murder of English men and women. And there was an end to my hope that Sir Thomas could save me if John's part in this was uncovered, for he was part of the whole enterprise. That tore at my heart. No wonder he told me to do nothing. Had it truly come to this, that even my moderate master could see no way for us to live under the Queen's rule?

I refolded the papers, tucked them into my pocket, and went to help Grace finish setting the table for supper with my mind in a storm. I moved round the table in the familiar order, laying out the bread on a board, fetching the cups and feeling the coolness of the pewter on my fingers, seeing nothing but that list of names with my master's standing out at the bottom as if it were written in flame. My mouth tasted bitter, my tongue dry.

I sat through supper somehow, and afterwards John went down to the cellar for a while. I poured out two cups of wine and sat up waiting for him at the kitchen table.

At last, when I had sat the space of two hours, he came up from the cellar. When he saw me he paused before closing and locking the trapdoor.

I thought you didn't care for wine," he said.

"I dislike it when you drink it, sir," I said. "Please, sit with me. I have something to give you."

He came over slowly and sat opposite me, and I drew the papers from my pocket and handed them over.

"A man brought these to the house this evening," I said. "It was I who broke the seal and read them."

He opened the papers and looked through them, and his face slowly stiffened. When he looked back up at me his eyes were hard and mistrustful. He had never looked at me that way before, not even when he was deep in his cups.

"Why did you open this?" he asked.

"Because I was afraid of that man, and afraid of what business you have been at behind my back. Now I am more frightened than ever."

He closed his eyes for a moment, then leaned back in his chair and took a sip of wine.

"I told you to leave well alone," he said. "I told you a hundred times not to ask questions. Why did you disobey me?"

"I had to know," I said.

"And now that you know, Pandora," he said, "what do you

think?"

"Where have those papers come from," I asked, "and what are they? Why do you have them?"

He swallowed down another mouthful of wine and looked at me, then spoke, suddenly more animated, as if there was no point holding back any longer.

"Walsingham arrested a gentleman called Francis Throckmorton last week," said John. "Throckmorton is a friend to Howard. This is from his house. It was slipped away without notice while the men were searching. As for why I have them, that is not your affair."

"Is this what it seems to be? A plan for Spanish invasion? John—this is high treason. You cannot deliver this. You never wanted a part of this! You told me yourself—"

"I told you what I felt after they killed Campion," he said. "I had to decide, am I a true Catholic, or no?"

"What is a true Catholic?" I said, picking the papers up and fanning them out in my hands. "This is not a deck of cards; this is not only paper. These words mean death, slaughter. Our neighbours burned as they were under Bloody Mary. Perhaps civil war—children killed, our child, if we have another—" My voice broke there and I had to stop a moment before speaking again, as calmly as I could. "And if you are caught, they will hang you. They may hang all this household! You told me you could never make a martyr. John, please, don't risk us all. And my master—my master's name is on here. All these men on this list—if it is found, you will kill them all. Burn them. Burn these papers now."

"I can't do that," he said. "I have made a promise."

I could not believe what he was saying.

"This is a death sentence, John. I will not die for you." Then, suddenly realising the further implications of these papers: "I will not die for you and nor will I give up my brother. This goes directly against everything that Jeronimo Lopes is working for—against the bid to put Dom Antonio on the Portuguese throne and win it back from Philip of Spain. He will never trust me if you are found to be working in this way! I will lose my brother all over again."

"And what have you to do with politics?" he said, staring at me. "What have you been meddling in with those damned Jews? Such things should not concern you. What manner of woman are you? Will you turn me over to Walsingham and save yourself that way?"

"No, never!" I said.

"You are my wife, Susan," he said, and his voice was as hard as his eyes. "You have vowed to love, honour and obey me. What did I marry you for? Not for your beauty, any more than you married me for my youth. Do you think I am a fool? I married you for your wit, your education, your superior understanding, and your faith. What use is a wife to me who does not believe what I believe and work with me to advance it? This is a battle for souls, not bodies, and sometimes bodies must suffer to save souls."

Not for your beauty. That cut to the bone. I smiled at my own vanity even as I flinched. He had always called me beautiful and now I knew it was a lie, a flattery. And what a light, frivolous creature I was after all, that those words were what hurt me out of everything he said. I thought of the other thing he might have said but had not: that I had not yet given him a living child.

I looked down at the papers on the table. My hand rested just by them and the warmth from the kitchen fire was on my back. My finger twitched. I kept my eyes down and did not look at John, desperate not to give away my intention, but I sensed him shift and tense. I felt the moment bulge like an egg, violence ready to crack through the shell.

Gambling, I snatched up the papers, but John flew out of his seat and grabbed my arms across the table, sending the wine bottle and cup spilling over the wood. His hands clamped tight round my wrists.

"Let go, Suky," he whispered. "I am in earnest. Let go those papers. If I must break your wrist, I will."

"Sir, you are not in your right mind," I said, but I knew the words were fatal as soon as I spoke them. He pulled me toward him over the table and pinned down my left hand with his elbow, leaning his full weight on it, while he tried to pull the papers from my right. I choked at the pain in my crushed hand but I clung to the papers until he bent my fingers back as if he would break them. I yelped in pain and felt him pull the papers from my hand as I flinched. Then he grabbed me tight about the shoulders, pinning my arms to my sides, and propelled me across the kitchen, stumbling, into the dark printroom.

"I am sorry," he said in my ear, desperately, "but this is God's work. Stay here and pray. Ask God for guidance and you will see that I am right. You will see your error. I am locking the door, and you will not raise the household, or we will all hang. You will keep quiet and leave me be."

Then he was out of the room and the door was locked before I could say a word. I was alone in the darkness of the print room. I put out a hand to find the wooden panels of the door, and I turned my back to it. I sat leaning against it in the dark, alone, breathing hard.

I sat there a long time, thinking. Not praying. The shock of John's violence and his actions was as great as the pain in my wrenched fingers. Had his mind really been bending this way ever since Campion's death? Perhaps it was a soft heart that kept me from turning onto the same path, but I had always hoped—trusted—that God was behind us and would one day right the balance, that words of truth would finally convince the Queen and other Protestants they were wrong.

How could they not, when it so clearly was the truth? True faith shone like the sun. Their eyes were clouded and one day God would break through and they would see clearly again. I used to pray for it every day. But for the past year I had been engaged in my own struggle to see through the clouds. I felt myself without God's light for the first time. When I prayed, he was not there. The sky was closed. My own grief kept me from the wider world and from seeing how my husband's thoughts were changing.

If he were arrested—if I was thought complicit in his treachery—I would never have the chance to find my brother. I would die or rot in a cell before I could see his face, when I had come so close, when the path was opening up before me. Although the darkness around me was already complete, I put my face in my hands, unwilling to see my fate clear.

Despite all this, despite everything John had just said to me and the way he had abused me, I knew I would not betray him. I could only try and stop him. I guessed he had been given those papers in order to pass them on to someone else, but without knowing who they were going to or where and when he would pass them over, the only way to do it was to find them and burn them before he handed them on.

Even as I thought it, there came a gentle scratch and click somewhere above my head, and then an equally gentle push from the door behind me.

I scrambled further into the print room, fearing John had returned. Light fell through the door-gap and I saw it was Rob, carrying a rushlight. I tried to stand but found I was shaking too hard with fear and relief. Rob was barefoot, his nightshirt tucked into breeches. He closed the door carefully behind him and came to squat down beside me on the floor. I put my finger to my lips and he nodded.

"He's snoring upstairs," he whispered. "I waited till I knew he was asleep. I was listening, earlier. I heard a fight, and the master come up alone. What's to do?"

"John is carrying papers for Henry Howard," I said, bluntly. "It is a treasonous plot and if anyone discovers it he will go to the gallows, him and maybe me and all of us."

Rob set the rushlight down on a stool. He was very close, close enough to whisper in my ear. What if John woke and came down to find us conspiring? But I must tell someone, I must have an ally.

"I knew he was stepping into deep water," said Rob. "What is it—what is he carrying?"

"Plans for invasion," I said. "He would not destroy them so he must mean to pass them on to someone, but I can't guess who. We must find them and burn them. He mustn't suspect I have told you anything. This is too much for me, Rob, I won't die for this!"

Rob sat still for a moment, thinking. The rushlight burned straight and still in the cold night air. Its yellow flame reflected as a cats-pupil flick in Rob's own clear eyes.

"If I found you passage on a ship, would you leave England?" he said.

I looked at him and did not know what to say.

"Passage to Spain, to Seville to find your brother, and then beyond that to Guinea."

"How would I—and why—"

"I am going soon," said Rob. "I've had enough of this life; it's not for me any more than it is for you." He smiled at me. "My father left me some money in his will. Less than my brothers, so now I know the exact measure of his regard for me, but more than nothing. Enough to keep us both, for a few months. I can crew with Thomas Dassell when he goes out on this Guinea voyage, and he is willing to take you with us. We'll look for your brother in Seville, and if we find him and he wants to travel with us, there is room for him too. If we can find your family in Guinea, which Dassell says we will if they are traders, then you have your family again and we will set up a trade agreement with them that will make us all rich.

Come with me, and a fuck for the rest of this poor city. I've had enough of working in the dark in holes and cellars, with paper and ink. I don't want to watch them burn my prick in front of me at Tyburn. I want to see the world. I want to live."

I stared at the shadows on the floor cast by the rushlight, the press turning into a wavering monster, all arms and head. God knew what course John was set on. What made up my life here? Stationers' Hall and all the bookshops and stalls at St. Paul's, Joan Jugge, John Wolfe, and Grace, and Framfield still in Sussex. My duties. My marriage vows.

I never let myself feel that here was my safety and my home forever. I kept my eyes open all the time, feeling my position as precarious as the swallows that nest in the eaves of Nonsuch House on London Bridge, hanging over the Thames. Sometimes their babies or their whole nests fall down into the river below, which smacks its lips and gulps them down saying yum, a little sweetmeat. I did not intend to fall blindly like that ever again, as I had in Sussex, trusting in my place and the kindness of my masters. Yet at least here I had a nest. Rob offered me nothing but the air over the open sea.

"I can't leave John," I said. Rob looked at me, his green eyes dark in the dark room.

"You don't love him, though, do you?" he said.

I looked at him, and my heart jumped the way it always did when I looked at him, and my stomach dropped. I couldn't answer him. He was looking at my mouth and the look was like a kiss. Then he leaned towards me and the kiss was real, his mouth on mine. I made a sound. I couldn't help it. His mouth was hot, and as he kissed me his hand touched my hair, my neck. The desire for him was almost painful. I never wanted anything so much. Then he began to pull me in towards him and I pushed him away so hard he nearly toppled over. He just caught himself and we sat looking at one another, breathing hard.

"No," I said, and meant it. "No."

"Why," he asked, "if you don't love him?"

"It's a sin," I said, "a mortal sin."

"And isn't lying a sin too? Don't you sin every day? Don't you lie to him every time you fuck him and think of me?" he demanded. I looked away from him.

"At least this is honest," he continued, "more honest than swearing in church that you will love a man forever, when you can't know that is true, and slipping a ring on your finger."

"I won't do it!" I said. "I won't make a whore of myself, and I won't burn my life behind me to see my brother. I can't. I have already started anew once. The Dassells will bring him to me if he is alive. I don't need to abandon my honour and go to Seville myself."

I stood up in one movement, stepping away from him. He stayed sitting, looking up at me with one arm leaning on the stool. He was such a lithe, dark creature. I folded my hands in front of me and dug my nails into my palm.

"Go now," I said. "If you see the papers John is carrying and you have a chance to take them and burn them, please do it. Or if there are any messages from the Marshalsea marked with that cross. I have the cipher now but John doesn't know that. Leave me here, he will let me out in the morning."

Rob looked at me for a moment longer. I turned my face away, terrified he would try to kiss me again. At last he picked up the rushlight and stood.

"If you change your mind, you have only to let me know."

I nodded without looking at him and he left the room as quietly as he had come in, locking the door and leaving me alone in the dark again.

CHAPTER 32

John came and let me out before dawn, when the shuttered print-room was still in full darkness. He stood in the doorway with his candle, looking at me where I sat on the floor, my arms wrapped round my knees for warmth. His hand shook and the candleflame shivered.

"The papers are well hidden now," he said, "so don't think to hunt for them on my person. But I hope you have had time to see light?"

I knew I would not be able to lie to him about my true conviction, so I spoke the half-truth I had been preparing.

"I have not changed my mind," I said. "I still oppose your actions. But I will not speak or act against you. I will honour and obey you as a wife should, but I can't force my mind to bend into league with yours."

"As long as you will not speak of it to anyone," he said, "and you will act as if you are quite yourself."

"I will paint myself the very picture of a good wife," I said, without smiling.

Over the next few days I watched John as close as I could

without arousing his suspicion again. I made sure not to be caught whispering with Rob. John kept to the house and did not drink, making it almost impossible for me to search for the papers. I had still found nothing by the day we were to go to the Bull to watch the Queen's Men play.

The Bull is at the heart of London and on the first day of the Queen's Men's residence it was overflowing; roaring and riotous and stuffed with people. Following Somerville's attempt on the Queen's life the whole city was buzzing with rumour and fear of attack, so there was an edge to the day. The crowd was alive with the pulse that can start riots if one fool panics.

John was standing with the Wolfes at the entrance, where we greeted them. John and I must have looked a poor couple, our drained faces markedly at odds with our holiday dress. I did not know if he had the papers on his person or at home, but I felt that any minute someone in the crowd would point to him and cry treason, and we would be hauled away to the Tower.

I stayed close to him, feeling miserable and helpless, as we pushed through the doors with men and women of all degrees. Rob and Grace went through to the pit with the groundlings, and we and the Wolfe's set off up the stairs to the gallery seats.

If I had tripped and fallen on the way up to the galleries, the press of the crowd would have kept me upright and simply carried me on up. The crush was just as bad in the gallery overlooking the stage. As we approached our seats a man pushed in between John and I, moving against the flow of people, and almost knocked us both down. I had been looking the other way, searching the crowd for anyone suspicious, and was only saved from a tumble by John Wolfe's bulk on my other side. I turned to rebuke the pusher, who had caught John by the arm to steady him.

"Your pardon," he said, and I made a stuttering sound. It was Domingo. His eyes flickered over to me as I stood open-mouthed.

He smiled when he saw me, then he pulled his hood further over his head and shoved on through the people to the top of the stairs. I kept looking over my shoulder for him as Wolfe barged forward and secured us our four seats, but he was gone.

John kept turning about in his chair, knocking Wolfe with his elbow and almost toppling the man sitting on his other side.

"Where is Sir Philip?" he said. "Susan, can you see him in the galleries?"

"Sidney will come incognito," said Wolfe. "He hates a fanfare. You won't spot him. God's bones, John, will you stop all your jiffling about?"

I ignored the pair of them bickering. The low, bright winter sun lit the banners hanging around the stage and the glints of silver and gold thread on the clothes of the men and women in the gallery audience. It shone in my eyes so that I had to squint and lean forward, shading my face. It was a cold day but the bodies around me kept me warm and our steaming breath rose up into a speedwell-blue sky.

All that brightness, and all I could feel was the cold lump of fear in the pit of my stomach, an indigestible ice-block in which all the events of the past week were frozen. Those words on the paper, the shock of John striking me, Rob's offer of an escape. My reverie was broken by the fanfare announcing the players' entrance, as all the heads in the yard below us lifted and the theatre roared at a pitch that would shame a lion—the roar of a London crowd.

If Elizabeth had needed an army to march against the French that very day she could have recruited every man in the Bull in an instant. The audience cheered her ancestor on every stage of his progress from rascal prince into the great victor of Agincourt. Yet under the cheers, the brave words and the battles, there was a small cold voice in my head whispering *treason*. What battles would be fought this time, if the Spanish came?

When the fight was won and the players had been cheered and stamped through the rafters, Wolfe led us through the tavern's mazy corridors to a low-ceilinged dining room set with two long tables and an extravagance of beeswax candles. I wondered who exactly was footing the bill. Either the company had already seen spectacular success on their tour or somebody's private purse (Walsingham's?) had been opened.

As we came in Wolfe bowed to a slim, tawny-bearded man dressed in black velvet threaded with gold.

"That is Sidney," said Wolfe as an inn servant ushered us lower down the table. "I'll introduce you after supper."

"Good man, Wolfe," said John. "A courtier to his marrow, hey? Look at him. Look at his ruff, you could cut cheese with the pleats. Ah, wine. Hey! Boy, fill my cup."

John's mood had shifted to a kind of furious, glittering good humour. Sweat stood on his forehead and he spoke too loudly. People looked at us as he called for the wine. I feared he would give himself away, he looked half mad. I put my hand on his.

"Sir," I said, "are you quite well? You seem feverish."

He looked at me without quite seeing me, his eyes too bright. He shook off my hand impatiently.

"Are you my wife or my nursemaid? I am hearty. Look to yourself, drink and fill your plate."

His voice broke loudly into a sudden silence. The hum of conversation around us had stopped and was replaced by the sound of feet tramping over the floor. I turned around to see four Tower guards marching towards us. Not comic constables, not Tarlton playing the Lord Justice in a bad wig, but tall, strong men carrying pikes. They were led by the landlord of the Bull, Matthew Harrison, whose forehead gleamed with sweat in the candlelight. People moved out of their way as they strode by. Harrison came to a halt right in front of us.

He pointed at John, avoiding his eye. "This is John Charlewood – this is the man you want."

"Me?" John stepped forward, his hand at his dagger-belt. "What for? What is this?"

I felt the whole crowded room turning its attention to us, as if we were an epilogue to the play. I saw Wolfe sidle discreetly closer.

One of the pike-men stood forward, saying:

"You are under warrant of arrest and are to be taken to the Tower at once for questioning with regard to seditious and treasonable plots."

John went white. "Indeed I am not. I am not coming to the Tower. I am no traitor."

"If you will not come with us quietly and in good order, then we must bring you there by force," said the guard.

"Go," said Wolfe. "Go with them. This is a mistake. We will speak for you."

John looked for a moment as if he might dash his wine on the floor and leap at the men anyway. Then Wolfe cleared his throat and inclined his head towards the corner where Tarlton, Bruno, and Sidney stood together, giving a very gentle reminder of the company we were in. John took his hand from his belt.

"God curse your bones," he said to the pike-man. "I am innocent. I come with you freely as proof of my innocence, and I will prove it further when I am there. Wolfe, look after Susan."

The guard who had spoken looked at me.

"This is your wife?"

I glanced at John and we both stayed silent.

"Goody Charlewood, you are to come with us too," he said. A frost of fear bloomed over my whole body, but I stood straight and spoke without a tremor in my voice.

"I come freely also," I said. "I have nothing to hide."

If John still had those papers on him, we had no hope; I was as good as dead. I fixed my eyes on a candleflame as two of the guards took position on either side of me, and I followed John, also flanked by two guards, out of the room, down the stairs and out into the day. But once we were in the street, John's guards took him walking one way and mine turned me the other. John turned, trying to see me, but the guards took his arms and turned him back again. I looked back too and was also set back on my course, one of the guards holding my arm firmly.

"You may put your hood up and cover your face, if you wish," he said, and I did so, confused and afraid.

"Sirs," I said, "where am I going? Why may I not go with my husband?"

They did not reply, but only kept me walking

"Where are we going?" I repeated. "And what is the charge? What has my husband done?" I asked over and over again, but they told me nothing. They walked me fast through the streets with my cloak bundled over me and my hood up, as if they did not want me to be seen, and they took me down side streets and alleys until I was quite lost. At last we emerged into Westminster Yard.

At the gate of a fine, big private house the guards handed me over to a man dressed like a porter with a bunch of keys at his waist. For a moment my spirits lifted. This was no prison.

"Is my husband here, sir?" I asked. "Please, I don't know why I am here or what for—I don't know why they took my husband. Please, at least tell me why I am here!"

But the man only shook his head. He led me through corridors like those of the old house in Sussex. I saw through the kitchen door where a boy was turning a pig on the spit, and even caught a glimpse of the garden laid out with knotwork hedges. The everyday sights only made my inward terror worse.

Then we came to a door in the wall, made of new oak timbers. The porter unlocked it and pushed me through into a wide, low-roofed, windowless room lit by torches. Chains and manacles hung from walls and pillars and all around were tables laid out with metal instruments, blunt, spiked, and pincered. Some were stained orange-brown with what might be rust. A horror slowly dawned in me. It was some nightmare workroom, businesslike and well-arranged as our print room but laid out for human torture.

CHAPTER 33

"What prison is this?" I asked, dry-mouthed. The man laughed without humour.

"These are Mr Topcliffe's private rooms, in his house. It is more convenient for him than the Tower."

I had heard the stories of Topcliffe, the Queen's torture-master. He was renowned for his cruelty. People said he was bestial and took pleasure in his work. I looked around me, revolted, my heart beating so hard that the blood rang in my ears. It was worse than a prison. To think that this vile place was hidden in an ordinary house, full of servants going about their daily business. Did they not hear people screaming in here? I tried to rouse up my courage but I could imagine what every one of these hellish devices would feel like, applied to me.

"I thought they did not torture women?" I said. "Please, sir—whatever my husband has done, I am innocent of it. Please, let me not be hurt."

"It's Mr Topcliffe does the hurting, not me," said the man.

"Oh, Jesus save me," I said, and then I shut my mouth and said not another word. I would not cry. I would not beg.

"Stand there," he said, and put me by a pillar. A pair of manacles were nailed high above my head and there were chains at my feet. He fettered my ankles and wrists and the chains hung so heavy that they dragged my arms down toward the ground. I stared ahead of me, waiting for whatever horror would come next, but nothing happened.

The man lit a candle on a nearby table then turned about and left the room, leaving me alone to anticipate the pain to come. Why had he lit the candle? The torches cast grim light enough, on metal teeth and spikes. A candle-flame can burn flesh through. I closed my eyes so I could not see it burning. I tried to think, to reason out what I could and should say.

I could think of nothing that would save John, if they had found the papers on him. Could I save myself? I was not brave enough to die a martyr. I knew it in that moment. I knew I would not uphold my faith and go to the scaffold and die in honour, whatever glories waited for me on the other side. I was no Campion. I would protest my womanish ignorance of theological battles, of politics and even of letters. I would deny every accusation and unless John gave me away, they would have no proof I knew anything.

I had thought the man would come back quickly but no-one came. I was there for several hours, the fetters rubbing my wrists and ankles and the fear growing worse and worse. The candle burned down until it was only a stump. At last the door opened and closed. I turned my head and saw the guard and another man came in. The new man walked slowly towards me and stopped several feet away.

He wore a cap on his head and a padded doublet, both richly embroidered with green and scarlet thread and silverwork. He was clean-shaven and looked in his middle forties, his face choleric and small-eyed, with a pock-marked nose and cheeks. He stared at me for a few moments, looking me up and down, his face full of disgust and some kind of horrible suppressed excitement.

"I am torture-master Topcliffe," he said, and smiled. "I expect you have heard of me."

He came nearer and put his face close to mine, his small eyes a pale, dull blue. Then he kicked me in the ankle and I yelped, though I had determined I would not make a sound. The spite and unfairness of it hurt me as much as my bruised skin. It was a mean, schoolboy's trick. He leaned in so close to me now I could smell the wine on his breath, the perfume in his hair and the human smell underneath that.

"Now tell me," he said, "as a true Catholic, if the Pope brought his armies to England to restore the faith—as you hope he will—whose part would you take? Would you be for the Pope, or for the Queen? Answer me!"

It was an impossible question to answer, and a trap. The Bloody Question that had been put to others before me. Could I deny my faith when it came to the point—when so many other Catholics had suffered and died for speaking the truth? And if I admitted to it but said I would take the Queen's part, he would call me a liar. This was it. Here was my death, waiting for me and smiling. I smelled the fire. I could not breathe. They would burn me. They would burn me alive, and I could not face such pain.

"I am a woman and ignorant of such matters," I said, "but I am a loyal subject of her Majesty. If such a thing ever happened, I would act as a loyal subject should."

"Loyal?" he said. "Don't think about denials, you lewd, fornicating, Papist whore. Others may be taken in. Others may think you have a black face and a white soul. I know you are soot through and through, that every inch of you is tainted by the Devil. I know what you have done. Your husband has confessed it. I know every when and where you have opened your legs to these Jesuits, these Spaniards who would rape our country, while he watched and took their coin. I know where you have fornicated like beasts while you deny God's name and plot the downfall of our Queen. Why would you not? What do you care for England's safety—a stranger and a Papist? What do you care if the Devil's own army lands on these shores and slays every living Protestant? You would welcome them in and fuck every one as they passed through London's gates."

The onslaught of his words stunned me, assaulted me. The violence of it silenced me. I had no defence for such a bludgeon.

"I am a Christian," I said at last, though it was hard to draw breath. "And I am no whore."

"Don't compound your sins with lies!" he shouted. He pulled open my mouth and dug his nails into my tongue. I kicked out and turned my head away, biting his hand and trying to shrink away from the pain, but he pinched my tongue with his sharp nails until it bled and my mouth filled with the iron taste.

My wig and hairnet slipped from my head and fell to the ground, exposing my bare head. Topcliffe snatched up the wig and ripped away the hairnet, shaking the dark hair out of its pins till it fell down and rippled. Tears sprung into my eyes. I was bewildered by his intimate brutality. He was like some drunken bully abusing his wife. It was hate, he hated me.

"Christian? Your people are not Christian, they are idolaters just as the Papists are. You say you have converted: lies, lies, lies! Vanity! Borrowed hair—borrowed beauty, a whore's tricks."

I swallowed blood and choked, my breath rattling.

"You are a Godless whore, punk to every Godless man who crosses your door. Are you not? I know you are. I know everything. I know who has planned the invasion, I know where it will come, and I know who your husband has helped. Throckmorton is arrested and we took the papers on him. So now you will give me more names. You will tell me exactly your husband's part in this and give me names, or I will have the skin stripped from your back. I will have you racked and stretched till your hands are too broken to touch a man again. I will see you beaten all the way to Tyburn, naked and branded, before they break your neck. Who have you sent your Catholic books to? Who have you bared those little paps to? Speak!"

"I am innocent," I said, thickly, though my tongue was raw and painful and I had to spit out blood. "I don't know an invasion. I don't know Throckmorton. Who is Throckmorton? You are mistaken—you are mistaken. I know nothing of this—"

"Liar!" said Topcliffe and pushed his thumb into my mouth again. I set my teeth against it and he took me by the throat and squeezed until I choked.

They kept me there for hours. Topcliffe ranted and spat, held his sword to my throat, asked me over and over again for names of plotters. He pinched me and kicked me, he struck me in the belly and made me vomit. He called me whore and said he would turn me over to his men to do with as they pleased. I wept, but I denied it and denied it and denied it. I denied everything.

At length I must have fainted from the pain and exhaustion and could not be roused. I woke to find myself alone in the dark, with no idea where I was.

Feeling about myself, I discovered my feet were still in chains and fastened to the pillar. I lay in the dark, trembling and trying to count the sore places on my body to see if I was badly hurt. Every part of me was in pain. My hands and arms ached fiercely and my tongue was horribly swollen in my mouth.

I curled up around the pain and tried to think. I was terrified. Topcliffe was as bestial as people said. He took pleasure in hurting and tormenting. I was very afraid that he would rape me or turn me over to his men.

It was not only the torture. His words were so brutal I felt violated to my very core. He spoke to me as if I was something to be trampled on, as if I was dirt on the ground. I did not think I could keep my spirit through much more treatment, but I knew I must try. He wanted to terrify me into a confession if only to make the pain stop, but I felt that if I admitted anything, false or true, he would use me even worse after.

I lay in the dark for hours with no sense of whether it was day or night, my whole body poisonous with pain, desperately trying to think of a way to survive. I kept thinking of my baby and his grave in St. Giles. He had bunched his small fists and fought for every last breath, and so would I. I would not give in.

When I heard the key in the door again I huddled away against the wall. Light fell through the door and the guard came in alone, carrying a lantern.

"Please," I said. My voice came out whispery and rough. I had torn my throat with screaming and my tongue was thick and painful. "Please, no more. He is a monster. This is not God's work. Please let me go."

He set the lantern down on a table and came over to me. He began unlocking the irons at my ankles and I closed my eyes. I could not bear to know what they would do to me next.

"You get your wish," he said, grimly. "Aren't you the lucky one? Mr. Topcliffe's done with you. You're free to go."

I clung to his arm as he helped me to my feet. It must be a trick. "Is it true?" I whispered, disbelieving. "I am free?"

"You must have good friends somewhere," he said. He led me stumbling out of the cell and into the corridor. "It's true enough."

I was dazed at the change from dark to light as we left the room. It was unreal to find that I was truly still in a gentleman's town house and not the deepest dungeon in the Tower. I was shaking, so weak I could only shuffle along, and I knew I must look like a corpse freshly dug up from the grave. Yet the sun was shining on Topcliffe's gardens, on his beautiful knotwork and his fruit trees. As we walked through the corridors of his house I could hear the sounds of everyday work, going on just the same as it had when they took me in. A hiss and sizzle from the kitchen, someone beating a rug, servant girls calling to one another upstairs.

Here was I, a cursed soul dragged back up from Hell onto Earth, astonished at the light and the clean air, disbelieving in a freedom so carelessly and suddenly offered and expecting any minute to be thrown back in the pit. Every step hurt and my mind worked slowly. Could John be free too? I did not want to ask the guard anything in case I betrayed myself.

I shrank back as we neared the entrance to the house. There were people going to and fro outside and I did not want anyone to see me so desperate and broken. My dress torn and dirty, my bare head and bloodshot eyes.

"How am I to get back to my house?" I said. "I can't walk that far."

The guard nodded to a small doorway in the shadows and a slim figure stepped out, dark-haired and grim-faced. Relief engulfed me and Rob came forward to take my arm.

CHAPTER 34

When we reached home I went straight to bed, with Grace's ministrations, and slept for twelve hours. When I woke I was stiff and painful and my tongue still horribly swollen. I could barely whisper. There followed three anxious days of waiting for news of John, while I stayed mostly in bed and let Grace go about the house. Rob and John Wolfe went daily to the Tower, asking to see John, but they were refused entry.

My body healed quickly. After three days my tongue and throat were working and my stiffness had worn off, but the abuse Topcliffe had thrown at me was slower to work its way from my system. I had never faced such hate. His words stuck and festered, poured over me like a bucket of night soil. I felt as I had when my lady turned on me in her madness. Angry and despairing and ashamed, as if the words of hate were spells, turning me into the thing they said I was. A Papist whore. You ink, you night, you crow.

Once I could speak again, I found I had nothing to say. John was in the Tower and I knew I should be doing more for him but my mind moved slowly and my tongue not at all. I waited for Rob to come and let Grace fuss around me while I stared blankly at the walls. I woke sweating in the night, spitting and choking, with the sensation of Topcliffe's hand in my mouth.

On the fourth day, Grace came up to tell me that Rob had news at last. She helped me dress and I made my way downstairs, where I found him sitting at the table, staring at the fire as if it might suddenly spit out a pardon for John. Grace set out bread and cheese and poured us ale, then left us for the Stationers' Hall: she had been running all my errands while I was in bed.

Rob tore into the food but I could not touch it. I settled myself opposite him, my hands folded in my lap, and did not return the smile he gave me. Rob looked wilder and more alive than I had ever seen him. I could see he was starting to shed the skin of printer's apprentice, his true nature emerging from beneath it. In contrast I felt numb.

"Tell me what is happening," I said.

"John is still in prison," said Rob. "I don't know who gave him away, but Walsingham knows he was carrying papers for Howard."

"Were they still on him when he was arrested?" I asked.

"No, he'd already given them to someone. It was at the Bull. He says he doesn't know who took them: he was told to sit in a certain place and the papers would be taken from his pocket. He sat in the gallery, and by the end of the play the papers were gone."

I thought of John in a cell in the Tower. Would they treat him as they had treated me, or worse? The rack—the screws.

"Was it Howard's mark?" I asked. "The little cross?"

"Mendoza's," said Rob. "The Spanish ambassador. It marked messages from him. The master was delivering letters from Mendoza to other men—Howard and Francis Throckmorton."

"So Walsingham knows this is treason," I said bleakly. "It is treason, and John could hang for it."

"He could," said Rob.

We sat in silence, staring at the oak table between us where we had drunk and eaten with John countless times. The sturdy wood was burned and stained as evidence of the many meals it had served and there was a little pool of hardened candlewax near my hand. I began to scrape it away with my thumbnail, paring it off. I did not want to rest my mind on John's fate and see it clearly. In spite of everything, he was my husband and I cared for him.

I worked at the wax to keep a picture of the gallows at bay, building up a little pile of white flakes. The motion reminded me of something. For a moment I could not remember. Then the memory flashed through me, so strong it was almost painful. Rob's hand on my slipper, scraping away the wax he had spilled. Abruptly, I stopped.

"Have they been watching us, then?" I asked. "How did they catch us?" Then, suddenly realising our position fully, "And why are there no Searchers in the house? Why am I free? Why are you free? Why did they let me go, if this is treason?"

Rob did not speak for a moment, but stared at the place on the table where the wax had been.

"John's turned," he said abruptly. "He's offered to help Walsingham. He swore to him you knew nothing about the secret work, that none of us knew. I don't know if Walsingham believes him, but he's offered the master—all of us—a way out. So there's a nail-paring of hope."

"Oh, John," I said, and put my face in my hands. What it must have cost him. What had they done to him, in the dark rooms of the Tower? I saw Topcliffe's rooms again. I felt his hand at my mouth, and I retched. My hands shaking, I took up my cup of water and drank from it, trying to drown my disgust. When I was calm again, I said:

"What is this nail-paring of hope for John?"

"We may be able to retrieve the papers John passed on at the Bull," said Rob. "If we return them to Walsingham the master's life may be spared."

I looked at the little pile of wax in front of me. My master's name was on those papers. Returning them to Walsingham would save John, but condemn him. A sword at my chest, a sword at my back. Could I turn one of the blades aside? I brushed the wax into my palm and threw it on the fire.

"How?" I asked.

"Walsingham seized papers from Throckmorton's house that gave names of plotters and descriptions of havens for an invasion landing," said Rob.

"The same as those I saw?" I said sharply. If they were duplicates then my master's name was already in Walsingham's hands and it was too late to save him.

Rob shook his head. "We don't know. The master must know but he swears he can't remember. That's why they used the rack, to make him give the names, but he told them over and over he can't remember. They didn't break him."

"It was a map," I said slowly. "One of the papers was a map, not a written description. It sounds as if they are different."

"Well, Throckmorton's servant has confessed that the master's papers were destined for Mendoza," said Rob, "and Walsingham thinks he will want to smuggle those papers out of the country and into Spain for King Philip's intelligence as fast as he can. Walsingham wants those papers back, but without causing a row with Spain. He's still gathering evidence about this plot and he can't accuse Mendoza openly."

"So what on God's earth can we do?" I said.

Rob smiled again.

"The master must have had a presentiment when he hired me as apprentice. He's told Walsingham everything he knows about the men who smuggle books for him, the routes they take and the ships they use. Those papers are leaving London by water, and I've been working like a terrier to dig up the courier. Now I've found it: a nice, fat Spanish rat stashed on board a ship. Maria Padilla, who is cousin and waiting gentlewoman to the wife of the Seventh Duke of Medina. She has been staying with Mendoza for the past month and the household has much complained of her temper and sharp tongue. Yesterday she announced she was cutting short her visit for no good reason.

"Then I met a Flemish sailor who was also bellyaching about a Spanish gentlewoman. She's booked a late passage on his ship, which is sailing from Ratcliffe tomorrow at dawn. A Flemish merchant ship carrying a cargo of cloth out to Seville. The first mate is being shifted out of his cabin to bunk with the men, to make room for this woman. The captain made no bones about it. She is paying some fabulous sum for the voyage and must be put up, but the mate is raging. I know that ship and that captain and he'd smuggle the Pope himself through Westminster if you paid him well enough."

I felt a sudden pang of hunger and realised I had eaten nothing yet. I reached out for the remains of the bread and broke off a crust, softening the hard grain with ale.

This whole tale felt unreal to me still. It was so far removed from my life. Our work with illicit books was something we did at the kitchen table, surrounded by pots and pans, the secrecy of our faith so ingrained in my life it was commonplace. Now Rob was bandying about the names of great people, kings, ambassadors, statesmen, and John was embroiled in a conspiracy that reached far, far beyond the lanes of the Barbican and that sounded like the plot of some grand tragedy. It was as if I was reading it in a book and in a moment I would mark my place and lay the book down and go away to make bread or do some sewing.

"So what is your plan?" I asked when I had swallowed my crust.

"None of this is evidence enough to accuse this woman," said Rob. "And Walsingham can't afford to arrest her; it would break these webs he is weaving so carefully around Mendoza and others. The Queen is adamant that we must not provoke open war with Spain. None of this must be seen to have moved under Walsingham's direction, so we must somehow steal the papers back from this woman without the theft being traced back to him."

"And how do we do that?" I asked.

"Look," said Rob. He picked up his cup and placed it in the middle of the table.

"That's Ratcliffe, where this woman boards the ship. The end of the table is the mouth of the Thames." He reached for my cup and took it round to the far end of the table. "This is Leigh, the last harbour before they reach open sea. Two days journey if the wind's behind them and you don't stop along the way. A week if they have to tack against the wind or pick up provisions."

"A week!" I said.

"I doubt he'll stop," said Rob. "He'll want to fly as fast as he can. Now. We'll have men following the ship and more joining them at Leigh. The crew will only see fishing boats and other river traffic, but they'll be watching. At Leigh our men jump that ship when the crew are sleeping. We shut the hatches on them so they can't get out, we rob the cabins and take everything that woman has on her—jewels, papers, money—so it looks like plain old river-pirates out for the passengers' gold. The papers go back to Walsingham, the master steps out of prison and this Maria Padilla can stamp her fat Spanish feet till they fall off."

He reached out for the two cups and brought them back together in the centre of the table, placing them so they were touching. Then he took mine and handed it to me, saying in a different, more hesitant voice:

"And—if you want to, mistress—you may come with me. From Leigh we can take ship with the Dassells."

I stared down at the patch of table from which I had scraped the wax. It had more of a polish to it now than the wood surrounding it. Rob said John's only hope was to retrieve these papers. John's only hope and perhaps ours too.

It sounded like a flawed and desperate plan but what else could we do? Yet I had an interest in those papers not being returned, or at least not with my master's name still on them. And even if I ran away with Rob, I could not abandon John altogether. If he was hanged and I fled that would be a stain on my conscience I could never scrub out. Somehow I must ensure that those papers went direct to Walsingham and with my master's name removed from them. The other names—the other men—I would be condemning to death. Whatever choice I made, I bore a heavy burden of guilt. I was foggy with exhaustion and I did not know what to do. I needed more time.

I lifted up my head. "Your plan is a gambler's plan," I said. "What will you do if you can't find the papers on this woman? What if she hides them too well, or hears the attack and destroys them before you can snatch them?"

"There's no other way," said Rob. "I can't go on that ship as crew, the captain knows me too well, and even if I was on board I'd be bunking with the men. We couldn't get close enough to the woman."

"But I could," I said, suddenly certain. "I could board the ship as a passenger and perhaps they would even have me share a room with this woman, if space is short. Then I would have more time to watch her and find out where the papers are hidden, and stop her destroying them when the men come on board."

Rob stared at me. I almost laughed aloud at his expression of disbelief.

"Don't mistake me," I said, "I am no intelligencer, but it seems to me that unless we recover these papers the last journey of my life might be along the road to Tyburn, strapped to a hurdle with my head in the mud like Campion. I had rather risk a week on board a ship than die for my husband's mistake."

Rob was smiling. "You're a rare woman, mistress," he said. "I believe you could do it. You have the wit, you can dissemble under threat. I will talk to Walsingham. This Maria Padilla is travelling without a maid so perhaps she'd like a woman to take passage with her. It is a risk though, mistress. What if she guesses the truth?"

"I was brought up as a lady's maid," I said. "I don't need to act that part, I lived it for thirteen years. I think God calls me to do this. I would rather go than sit here waiting."

Rob took my hand. His own were ink-spotted, like John's, and calloused from hauling the arm of the press. They were restless, too. He lifted my hand and bent it back at the wrist, kissing the life-line that forked across my palm. The kiss struck through me like lightning.

"It's perfect," he said. "I can't stay—I must go—but it could not be better. I thought to bring you down to Leigh in a fishing-smack but that ship will take you there in more comfort than I could manage. I can snatch you up at Leigh and take you to the Dassell's ship, and we will start anew."

I watched him, a chill flickering at my neck and wondered what a life with Rob would be like. Far-ranging and reckless, perhaps violent. Well beyond the encircling walls of London: outside marriage, laws, and Guilds. I was travelling further and further from my orderly beginnings at Framfield. Another step on the road. Gently I pulled my hand away from him again.

"I have promised nothing," I said.

"Maria Padilla's ship leaves in two days," he said, as if I had not spoken. "When I have passage booked I will let you know."

He rose, and went to leave, pausing at the door. "A fair wind for your journey, mistress, I'll see you again at Leigh."

I sat with my eyes closed when he was gone, feeling the warmth of the fire on my face. I knew what it would mean if I went with Rob and I knew what manner of man I would be casting in my lot with. Something in him had always called to me. When he touched me, it felt like a holy sin. That was blasphemy, but those were the words that came to me. I wanted him, body and soul, sacred and profane. He was brave and determined and full of fierce spirit, but Rob was wicked. He had never tried to disguise his desire for me, though my husband gave him shelter, bread, board, and apprenticeship. He was ruthless but honest. Perhaps that was better. Rob wasn't safe but he would always tell me the truth.

How could I abandon John, though? I am not ruthless. I could not run and leave him to the hangman, however much I wanted to find my brother. However much I wanted Rob. And if I returned the papers to Walsingham to save John, every man on the list, including my old master, would die. Both John and my old master had betrayed me, used my life as a pawn piece to be ordered across the board, but I still could not stomach doing the same to them.

It was impossible. Was there any way out of the maze? All day I went over and over the problem, my mind running here and there with no safe way forward. The list of names scrolled up and down before my eyes, men's lives to be blotted out.

As dusk fell I went out to help Grace bring in the books from our stall and to clear my head in the evening air. A full frost moon was rising in the East, over the houses opposite. I stopped to watch it slip free of the rooftops and ascend into the plum-blue sky, as shadows softened the border between the street and the wild grasses of Finsbury Fields. Soon all the land would be one darkness, like a pool of spilled ink.

The thought arrested me. I put down the book I was holding and watched the shadows deepen. Suddenly I felt calm. I could see my way clear. If I could retrieve the papers I had a path to follow, made of nothing more than moonlight, but at least it was a path.

I would follow a track of faith, a moon-road over deep water, and hope it led me where I needed to go.

PART IV

LONDON
1583-1584

CHAPTER 35

Rob sent me instructions the next day. I was to meet a wherry at Billingsgate steps the following afternoon at four o'clock. "You can't miss the wherryman," he wrote, "he is six foot at least and hairy as a bear."

I was still putting off my other decision that must be made: whether to go with Rob or stay with John. I told myself that I could only make that choice once I had the papers. I must retrieve the papers. The alternative was too stark. I fixed my mind on the task ahead. One foot in front of the other.

I packed that evening in a daze. Whatever my destination, my life was once again on the cusp of great change.

I told Grace to give out that I had gone to the Tower in person to plead for John and that Rob was visiting his family in Sussex. I did not tell even her where we were really going and she did not ask. She only nodded and told me to be careful.

At three the next afternoon I gathered up my bundle of things and stood staring at my chest for a moment, trying to think if I had left anything behind. My mother's heirlooms were tucked carefully into my pocket. I wondered suddenly what would happen to my belongings if I did not come back? John might die too and we had no children—everything might go to his sister.

I went to find Grace, who was sweeping out the hearth in the kitchen.

"Stop a moment," I said, and motioned her to put down the brush and stand up. She did so, looking confused.

"Grace," I said. "If everything should go against us and I die, I would like you to have my clothes and the things in my chest. The books too. You can give them to your nephews. I have not made a will but it is my wish. Do you understand?"

Grace stared at me. I must have looked quite wild, though I was making an effort to speak calmly.

"Of course, mistress," she said. "But you will come back safe, I'm sure you will."

I put my hand on her narrow shoulder and looked at her pinched face. There was a smudge on her forehead and her usually pale cheeks were pink with the heat from the hearth. I kissed her on the cheek and held her close to me for a moment, almost over-balancing us both. Then I stood up and went out of the kitchen before I started crying, leaving her standing on the stone hearth and staring after me with wide eyes.

I hurried down to Billingsgate steps, which were crowded with other waiting passengers. Half a dozen boats jostled at the foot of the steps, the boatmen shouting up to try and win fares. It was a cold day and a low mist was forming on the river as the day declined towards evening. I stared at the boatmen, looking for Rob's bear-like friend, and saw him at last right at the back of the pack, holding an oar up in the air. He was tall; a wild looking sailor with a thick beard. If Rob had not told me he was a friend I would never have ventured into a boat with him. He pushed forward as I hurried down, and helped me into the wherry at the foot of the steps. I was used to the tilt and swing of the little river-boats by now but I never grew accustomed to the stinking Thames miasma that struck when you clambered into one.

I pulled my scarf over my nose to block out the stench and sat clutching my bundle in silence as we struck out into mid-stream. The Tower swung by us on the left bank, pennants fluttering from the turrets and the ravens spiralling above it. John was there somewhere, perhaps lying in the black Pit. All his ambitions crumpled up like so much blotting paper, all his hopes cut short. I stared back at the great building as we moved on, leaving it behind us. The stone walls looked impregnable, ancient as London and impossible to escape.

The heavy clouds above were clearing as evening approached and they moved down-river faster than we could, gold-edged and piled high. Blue sky opened up between them and the sun behind us sent out long shadows over the dank-smelling water.

I had never been so far East on the river before. The widening water curled past Rotherhithe, Bermondsey, and Wapping, taking us further and further from Cripplegate and from John lying in the Tower. I was running away to sea, leaving my life behind me. I threw back my head to stare up at the clouds again as they poured overhead like a sky-river and for a second the weight of guilt and fear lifted from my shoulders. The golden light struck me like a bell; the freshening wind rushed over me. I felt dizzyingly free. This must be what Rob loved about his wild life, the giddy feeling of hurling certainty away like a hat and running headlong with the wind pushing you onward.

We reached Ratcliffe just before sunset. The docks were still teeming with people. They had a different air than the wharves and quays within the city, where I watched cargoes being unloaded. There, the world came in to London and brought its riches with it. That was journey's end. Ratcliffe smelled of departure and the start of new voyages. The ships' hatches were open for men to fill with provisions, not for cargo to be unloaded. Gulls clustered overhead in screaming swarms, gathering where the stones were slippery with discarded fish-guts.

Moored along the harbour, many of them of tall-masted, ocean-going vessels, were multitudes of ships. I wondered where they were all bound. Then we were in among them and the world shrank again. The tall seafarers rocked high above our little wherry, blocking the sunlight. Their shadows turned the river cold, dark and opaque, and we had to watch for slops being thrown overboard. I felt very small beneath their looming hulks and I clung on tight to the bench beneath me. I cannot swim a stroke and the thought of tipping out into the water and sinking under one of those great ships was appalling.

The ship I was travelling on was called the *Jonas*. When we passed it the last of its cargo was just being loaded by men throwing bundles of cloth hand over hand in a line up the gangplank. We carried on until we reached the steps up onto the jetty. Rob's friend jumped out and secured a line to one of the jetty moorings, then helped me out and up the slippery wood steps.

Then I was standing alone on the jetty and the wherry was moving away again, out into the busy river. I stood for a moment with my bundle at my feet, collecting my thoughts. Sailors passing by stared and muttered at me, making me suddenly conscious of being a woman on a dock overrun with men. I picked up the bundle and walked to the *Jonas*, trying to look purposeful.

A man stood by the boarding plank, watching as the last bundle went up onto the deck. He was dressed soberly and looked plain enough, a middle-aged, straw-haired Fleming with a sailor's brown skin and sun-wrinkled blue eyes, but he must have been earning a good fee to afford the silver whistle hanging round his neck and the gold rings in his ears.

"Master Derickson?" I said.

He looked me up and down and nodded.

"I am. You are our late passenger, Susan Charlewood?"

"Yes—I am sorry the notice was so short."

He shrugged. "I have been paid well for the berth, so no apologies. It will be snug, though. Your other lady tells me she is always sick at sea. If you are well, you may dine in my cabin. I advise you not to wander about the deck or speak with my crew. They are good sailors but rough men and to have a woman on board is a temptation, especially one who is young and a stranger."

"I will be more than happy with my own company," I replied. "Where is my cabin, please?"

"This way," he said. I followed him up the gangplank carefully, clutching my bundle, and stepped onto the broad deck of the *Jonas*.

The ship felt alive. It shifted and dipped and creaked around me, the masts and ropes lifting up overhead, running up into the sky. I put a hand to the great mainmast. The wood was good oak, cool and wet to the touch. The rope of the rigging was thick and bunched in hairy knots that would rip soft hands to shreds.

All over the deck men were busy tightening ropes, closing the hatches and going about a hundred other unfamiliar tasks that would somehow make this construction of timber and nails, rope and cloth, ready to go forward and ride the water to her destination.

"This is the aftercastle," said Derickson, stopping as we reached a structure built up from the main deck, with an upper deck and another mast on the top. There were two doors built into the timbers facing us.

"This is my cabin," he said, indicating the right-hand door. "Supper is served there at six."

"I have eaten already, thank you sir, but I will gladly dine with you tomorrow," I said, hoping that if the Spanish lady ate with the master I would have a chance to look through her things.

Derickson shrugged. "As you wish. And this is your berth."

He knocked on the left-hand door, which after a minute opened inward. A woman stood there, eyeing us both with hostility. She was short and dumpy, about thirty years old, with a lumpish nose and huge, beautiful dark eyes. She was dressed in a loose black travelling gown and looked as cheerful as a scissor-wielding Fate.

"Your cabin-mate, *Señora*," said Derickson, calmly. The woman looked me up and down, rolled her eyes to the heavens, and nodded.

"I'll send in folded blankets for you to lie on," said Derickson to me.

"Enter," said the woman. "You speak Spanish?"

I shook my head. If I feigned ignorance, I might catch something that would help me in my task.

"Well, what should I expect from this Godforsaken country," she said impatiently. "Come in, come in!" Then she opened the door wider and let me in to the cramped space.

"You will not have a pleasant voyage," she said. "As soon as the ship starts moving I will be sick and I will most likely stay sick until we reach Seville. You will be sleeping on the floor. Prepare yourself for discomfort."

The room was tiny, with just room for a narrow raised bed to the left with a shelf above it and a small porthole to the right of the shelf with a ship's lantern hanging from a nail beside it. Next to the bed was just enough bare floor for me to sleep on, with my head under the porthole so that rain could fall in onto me.

The woman climbed up onto the bed, took out a jewelled psalter from her pocket and began to read aloud in muttered Spanish, ignoring me entirely as I set down my bundle and peered through the porthole at the ship moored alongside us. The wherryman would be long gone by now. I wondered where Rob's river-pirates were hiding. There were plenty of little fishing-smacks and other small river traffic nuzzling in between the tall ships. They would be watching me. I was not entirely alone.

There was a knock at the door and a man came in at the woman's barked "Enter!" carrying a thick roll of blankets for me. Seeing him, the woman broke into voluble Spanish. This must be one of her servingmen. I kept my face blank and busied myself by rolling out blankets, hoping to catch something of use with my small stock of Spanish. From what I could hear, she was only berating him for forgetting some item of luggage.

The light from the porthole was fading now, the sun almost gone. As the man departed, Maria Padilla reached out and lit the lantern. The small space glowed. I stretched myself out on the blankets, lying at full length so I could see under the bed. Beneath it was a space where the woman had stowed her chest.

Even in the dim light I could make out a sack, and a lidded chamber pot wedged into a square made by four blocks of wood roughly nailed to the floor, clearly to keep the slops from leaking out when the ship was in motion. I wondered if I would be seasick and prayed not. I would need all my wits about me. She had said nothing yet of the secret purpose of her voyage, whether for safety or because she did not trust me fully, I could not tell.

"Can you read?" she said abruptly. I considered; was it better to be ignorant of letters? Most likely.

"No, my lady," I said, "but I can write my name."

"I will not want you attending to me on the voyage," she said. "I trust only my own maid to arrange my hair and my dress. As she is not here I shall manage it myself. I ask only for you to empty the slops and to bring me water and food, if I can eat at all. Do you understand?"

"Yes, my lady," I said.

From what I saw, the documents must be hidden either in that jewelled psalter, the chest, the sack, on the woman's person, or concealed somewhere in her bedding. That was a daunting list of places to search.

"Now, goodnight," she said, dismissing me.

"Goodnight, my lady," I said. I unpinned my coif and carefully tucked it into my bundle, then I looked out the porthole at the water below while she read her book.

In a while she began to make preparations for bed. I undressed to my shift, put on my night-cap and rolled myself up in the blankets with my hip-roll for a pillow and my skirt for another covering. I pretended to close my eyes but watched what I could from between my eyelashes. She was clearly unused to undressing herself, even in clothes designed for travel. She struggled with her lacings and made a great buffle of undoing her sleeves, before bundling up her small clothes beneath her pillow and laying out her skirts as extra blankets. Everything would be horribly crushed by the morning. I itched to help her but stayed where I was. I had been given my orders.

She closed the shutter over the porthole and blew out the candle, then sat for a moment praying. She spoke the Lord's Prayer in Latin and the familiar words calmed me. I closed my eyes and joined her quietly, thinking how strange it was to join in prayer with a woman I planned to rob. When she had finished her prayer she shuffled down beneath the covers and within minutes began to snore, quietly at first then louder and louder. I realised that I would get very little sleep for the duration of the voyage.

I lay in the dark, wide awake, listening to her gurgling snores. The boards were hard below the blankets. My neck was cold and the little squeaks and groans of the ship's timbers were very goblin-like in the dark. I thought again of John in the Tower and Rob, somewhere out on the black water, and shivered.

John, always talking and planning, out in the taverns and playhouses finding new friends and customers. Spending money carelessly on rich food and drink, always looking for a step up in the material world even as he turned out pamphlets and sent out secret messages aimed at restoring our spiritual world. Rob's ruthlessness and ambition, tempered by his warmth towards me. His yearning for wider horizons. With Rob I felt that I would only know him entirely if I gave into him, if I stopped pushing away my feelings and accepted the full force of them.

How far I had come since I left Framfield. It was not quite three years since I stepped into the cart at dawn and watched Kate walk away from me. I had not quite believed I could survive my banishment, but somehow I had. I had found my place in London. I knew the ins and outs of the printing world. I knew how to compose and set a text and all the parts and machinery that went into creating it. I had learned my brother still lived. I had watched the light fade out of my baby's eyes and still found hope within myself, a way to live with that loss. I had fallen into Topcliffe's hands and come out alive. Now, somehow, I was working for Francis Walsingham in the service of the Queen and against a woman of my own faith. Where was God's hand in all this? I turned my face into the pillow, trying to recover the certainty I had felt watching the rising moon two days ago. I must trust in God and put one foot in front of the other. That was all.

I turned my mind from this spinning wheel of thought to other things, wondering how hard it would be to search the woman's possessions unobserved. I felt sure the papers must be in the psalter as she kept it so close to her, but how was I to reach it?

If I were found prying and pinned as a thief it would ruin the whole enterprise. I would simply have to watch and hope for a chance. I sent up a prayer to the Virgin for help and protection, and tried to close my ears to the woman's snores.

I must have fallen asleep despite the noise. When dawn came I was jerked awake by a deep, shouting, rhythmical song from the deck above, the creak of timbers and rattle of chains. The sailors must be hauling up the anchor. I scrambled out of the blankets, winching at the crick in my neck, and unshuttered the porthole again. It was a grey, chill dawn with misty drizzle wafting past the window. If I craned my neck I could see the water below, choppy and dull-coloured.

With an effortful, noisy lurch, the ship yawed and began to move. As the sails caught the wind the water below began to foam, curling away in our wake, and we were on our way. That was it. I was truly alone now, with no escape to be had. I squinted out of the porthole, feeling the breeze freshen and blow. I licked my lips and tasted salt.

There was a loud groan behind me and I turned to see the woman leaning out of bed, scrabbling beneath it for the chamber pot. She opened the lid just in time and vomited up a stream of yellow bile, heaving again and again till her stomach was empty. The sour smell filled the cabin. She groaned again and lay back, her face grey.

"It begins," she said. "Fetch me something to wash my mouth out, please."

I quickly rolled up my bedding, stowing it on top of the chest beneath her bed so that even if the pot overflowed it would not catch it, and went out to try and find water for her.

The woman did not stop puking and retching for the next three days, except when she was snoring. The weather worsened as we travelled, with cold driving rain and rackety winds. The wind was behind us for the first day, then switched and blew against us, increasing the rock and yaw of the boat when we had to tack across the river.

The vile weather trapped me in the cabin with Maria Padilla except when I joined the captain for a silent dinner in his much larger cabin or carried the pot out to empty it, doing my best to tip it into the bilges or over the side without falling in myself.

The cabin reeked of vomit before the first day was out and

that evening the woman's monthly terms began. The small space was soon merry with stink: piss, shit, bile, and underneath it all the metallic smell of her drying menstrual blood. I, sleeping on the floor, was right beside the pot and its filthy miasma. I tried to raise my spirits by thanking God for the opportunity to practice endurance, but my thanks were not heartfelt.

Opening the porthole helped but we could only do it for seconds at a time or the rain drove in and wetted everything. It was warm for November, but still cold enough that I shivered through the nights in my bundle of blankets, miserable and red-eyed from lack of sleep.

Now I realised the sack under the bed was for her rag-rolls, I tried to give her privacy to change them, but in such bad weather and in such a small cabin it was impossible. I almost felt sorry for her. If she really was transporting the papers she was undergoing a horrible ordeal to do so. Even when we anchored at nights the ship kept up a rolling and dipping motion and the woman lay muttering to herself, praying for the sickness to end.

As the days passed I was no closer to finding the papers. The whole expedition felt quite unreal. I did not feel like a bold intelligencer and the plan began to seem more and more absurd. I had no chance whatsoever to search the cabin because the woman was confined to her bed. She kept her chest locked and the psalter under her pillow, and it was impossible for me to go anywhere near her things without attracting a fierce glance from her dark eyes. Even at night it was not safe because she did not sleep soundly.

I kept my eye on her two serving-men in case that should be useful but they hardly came into the cabin, only knocking occasionally to ask if their mistress was still sick or wanted for anything.

The afternoon of the fourth day, the weather finally eased. The rain cleared, the wind dropped and the motion of the ship calmed. Finally relieved of sickness, Maria Padilla fell into exhausted sleep. I went up on deck to look around and breathe in some blessed fresh air. We should reach Leigh by nightfall if the weather held, so this was my last day on board and my last chance to recover the papers.

The river was wider around us than I had ever seen in London, stretching out on either side to flat, marshy land. Birds cried from the reeds in high, curling notes that struck me as the loneliest sound in the world. The sky above was huge, a high-up wind still pushing endless ranks of white cloud across the horizon. The water shimmered with light. I had never been in such a wide, open space. It made me feel tiny, a dust-mote. I took the bronze bird from my pocket and looked at it in that vast light. Perhaps my mother had done the same on our original voyage as a reminder of home.

As I looked, I saw beyond its neat head a dark shape moving on the water. It was coming out from the marshes towards the ship, slow and steady. In the diamond light I could not tell for some time what it was: a seal, a river-bird? At last it came close enough for me to see it was a small rowing-boat with one man at the oars and one passenger, but the sun shining off the water still made it impossible to make out more than an outline of their bodies.

When it was within hailing distance the man at the oars cried out: "Ho! Throw us a ladder down!" One of the sailors, who had been watching beside me, hurried to roll down a rope-ladder to the water-line as the boat drew alongside. Clearly this visitor was expected, but I had thought I was the last to board. Could it be another of Maria Padilla's servants? I squinted down as he stepped up onto the ladder and began to scramble up the side, and as he emerged from the shadow cast by the ship I almost dropped my mother's heirloom into the water. It was Domingo.

CHAPTER 36

He was as shocked to find me on board as I was to see him. When he came face to face with me he cursed in Spanish and slipped back down the ladder, pulling himself back up and over the edge of the ship with an effort. He called down to the man below, who pushed the little boat away from the ship and set off back towards the marshes. Then he turned to me, his expression bleak.

"Why are you here, mistress?" he said. "What in God's name is your purpose?"

"Come," I said, "walk with me a little further from the cabins," and I steered him across to the other side of the deck, away from Maria Padilla's berth.

"I am fleeing England," I said quietly as we walked. "John is in the Tower. I am sharing a cabin with a Spanish woman, but she doesn't know who I am. Please, don't tell her. Why have you come aboard?"

I stopped by the forecastle, in a corner out of earshot of any crew. He shook his head, looking down at the boards of the ship.

"This is folly," he said. "Such folly. You should be safe in London, not here. Not sailing over the seas to God knows where."

"I have no choice!" I said. "Please—" but he made a warning gesture and I broke off. Derickson was approaching. He bowed to Domingo. "Good day to you sir," he said, "I am glad we had a fair wind for you to join us. You will share my cabin. Your pardon, mistress, I must show your countryman his berth."

"He is not my countryman," I said, but neither man heard me. Domingo moved swiftly away with him, leaving me alone. I stood fuming by the forecastle, watching them go. He must be caught up in this plot somehow. What was I to do? This threw all my plans into disarray.

He did not come back on deck after the captain led him away, but I stayed as twilight came in, watching Leigh approach and putting off the moment when I must turn back to my self-appointed quest. It was full dark by the time we reached the harbour in the mouth of the great river and we anchored far out from the shore where other, smaller boats bobbed. The lights of the little port town blinked at me from the shore and seagulls mourned overhead. I girded up my resolve at last. I must find the papers tonight or leave everything to Rob and chance.

The captain had asked us to dine with him as was his custom, but when I entered the cabin only Domingo was seated at the small table, picking over a plate of chicken. He rose when I entered and bowed, but without smiling.

"He's in conference with the mate, below," he said. "Some rope, or sail, or other underpinning has gone wrong. There is wine. May I serve you?"

"Please," I said, and sat opposite him. My thoughts were in a blizzard. There was no time. I must discover his purpose here but he was like a locked chest. How could I prise him open? I thought all this as he poured the wine, a deep red filling my cup. The *memento mori* ring on his hand winked in the candlelight. Campion's ring. He wore his black velvet doublet again, the white silk puffed through the sleeve-slashes. Such richness. I had not seen him for months, until he passed me at the Bull. The Bull, on the very night that we were arrested. The night the papers were taken. I looked at him with new suspicion.

"Canary," he said, nodding at my cup. "From the Señora's store." I tasted its warmth as the wind moaned against the port-holes and the ship's timbers sounded. The groan and yawp sounded melancholy to me, like a far-off cry. Outside the Thames rolled on, deep and old and fat with secrets. Now it flowed out with the tide, running to the sea. In a few hours time it would turn and push back to London, past the tower where John lay. I must find out Domingo's purpose here.

"My mother came this way with me," I said, putting down my wine-cup. "when we first came into England."

He paused for a second with his own cup at his lips, then drank.

"With Hawkins?" he said.

"No, he was in Plymouth still, We were sent to London to be fitted out with clothes and things, before we went to Sussex."

He nodded, turning his cup around and around on the table.

"Did they treat you well, in Sussex?" he asked.

"Oh, with such love and kindness," I said. "I was a sister, a daughter." My eyes filled as they always did when I thought of Anne, my lady, my childhood. The love I thought I had known, but sometimes doubted.

"Then how did you come to leave?"

"My sister died. My lady ran mad and my lord was taken to prison for harbouring priests."

It sounded so stark when I said the words. My voice sounded bitter.

"You could not have stayed?"

"If I had married my lord's cousin. A Protestant. A viper."

Domingo nodded. He looked at me with such a strange expression. He almost looked angry.

"So you were married instead to a London printer. There was no-one more suitable—no other place for you?"

"There was not," I said, and found my voice still more choked, full of thorns. "He is a good man, John Charlewood. A good husband, a kind man."

"Oh I know, I know he is a good man," said Domingo. "I have dealt with him, remember? He is a good man, for what he is, for a Guild man who has never travelled further than the cart-ride from Suffolk to London. For a man who has no Latin, no Greek, who learns Italian from a petty tutor. He is an astute businessman and a brave Catholic."

"And why do you praise him, then, in a voice that has no praise in it?" I asked. "Has he offended you? "

Domingo sat back, shrugged.

"His low birth does not offend me in itself," he said. "But as a match for someone of nobility in their own country? That is not right. That offends me."

"It is no business of yours to be offended," I said bitterly, "either by my high birth or his low one. I took the path God laid out for me. What is it to you? Were you from a noble family, in the Gambra? Does it offend you, that you were a slave and are now brought into service like any commoner?"

He did not reply, only drank more wine, but his look was murderous. Outside the ship the sound of the wind softened as it dropped, and the strain and knock of the ship around us also slowed and ceased. Now I was angry with him, and hurt. I wanted to talk with him as I had before, with that deep understanding, but he was hurtful and unfriendly and I could not trust him.

"Are you nobility?" I insisted, my voice sounding louder against the calm. "Don't you remember? Do you know nothing of your family, like me?"

"I told you what I remember," he said, and his voice was rough with pain. "I remember my parting from my mother. You stayed with your mother, yes? But she died?"

I nodded. "When I was three."

He was still for a moment. He looked as if he too were listening to the gentling wind. At last he said: "Did your mother give you anything—was anything left of your home?"

I stared at him, unsure whether to tell the truth. His voice was softer and his eyes were hopeful. Whatever he was—whoever he was—he had lost his mother, as I had. I felt in my pockets for the little bronze objects and slowly placed them on the table in front of him. He stared for a moment in absolute silence. The air bristled. He reached out a hand and touched the bird, so gently, as if it were alive and he was greeting it.

Then he took something from his own pocket and laid it on the table beside my two heirlooms. Another bronze block, about the size of the ladder block. I reached and picked it up and looked at the image stamped in relief. It was a raised cross, with a dot at the end of each arm.

My heart and my breath stopped together. The ship rose and fell and I was a stillness. Then my senses scattered like a swarm of snowflakes, a blizzard that whirled in the air and settled at last on that small bronze square. My whole being rushed to the block. I ran my fingers over it, feeling the shape of the cross and gradually coming to each layer of its meaning as my senses gathered themselves again.

"This is the dotted cross," I said. "This was your sign." He nodded, watching me intently.

"I should have known," I said. "I should have known. It was you, passing messages to Mendoza. And that is why you are here. Oh God, but I'm a fool. But what else is this? It comes from my mother's kingdom? But you are from Gambra. How did you come by it? Do you know what they are?"

"*Djayobwe*," he said. "Proverb stones. Some are weights, for measuring a quantity of gold dust." His voice sounded different when he spoke the Guinea tongue, more emphatic than his usual light diplomat's tone. It rested on the strange word almost reverently.

I took up all three and held them.

"Not royal symbols."

He shook his head. "They have their own meanings. They are symbols, of a kind—"

He broke off and shook his head again. There were tears in his eyes and he brushed them away, then he leaned forward and cupped his own hands around mine, so that we both held the three objects. His hands were cold on mine and the blocks were warm.

"Nsowah," he said, and his voice broke as he said the word. The word like a hush; sugar melting into butter, grain pouring in a bowl, my birth name. I felt the power of my name before I understood what it meant. My gaze flew to him and I looked in his eyes. His eyes, darker than mine, a shining dark like my baby's, and the same shape as my own. Drawn up a little at the corners, wide set, and looking at me with such love.

"You are my brother," I said. "You are my brother!"

He nodded and clasped his hands tighter around mine, then lifted them and kissed my hands. He rested his forehead against them.

"Little sister," he said. "Little sister. Nsowah. I used to carry you. I used to throw you up and catch you. I stopped you swallowing stones. You slept in my arms and you were so warm and fat, such a fat baby! We could not understand how you came to be so fat, but you were blessed. How we loved you! Do you remember me at all? Do you remember your brother Kofi?"

"No," I said, and found I was crying too. "No, I am sorry, I am sorry—I remember nothing. Nothing at all, not even our mother's face."

"Your face is her face," he said. "I thought it as soon as I saw you but I could not believe it, and I could not tell you. Oh sister." He opened his hands again and let mine go, showing the heirlooms. "I thought you were dead. They lied to me. They told me you died on board ship, before ever you reached England. I thought myself completely alone."

He covered his face with his hands, as if closing himself back in that dark time. "I would have come for you. If I had known the truth! I would have fought my way to England, whatever it cost me. I am so sorry, so sorry. I failed you both."

He broke down then and sobbed into his hands, his shoulders shaking.

I put the weights back on the table carefully and took his hands again. I wanted to hold them. I didn't remember him, but he had cared for me. I knew just how he would have cared for a baby sister, how I would have clutched his fingers with my own hands.

"We were told you had died too," I said to him. "Brother—what happened? What happened to us?" I clasped his hands tight, willing him to take comfort from me. In a while he grew quieter and raised his face up, wiping his eyes. He picked up the dotted cross again and held it up to me. His cheeks were still shiny with tears as he spoke.

"I was weighing gold when they came for us. You were asleep on Ma's back. There were so many of them—they must have known the men were sleeping. They took us all and they burned the houses and they marched us to the coast. We thought surely, surely our father would hear and come for us and save us, but if he came he was too late. The men that took us were Akan too—they knew who we were. They knew what they were doing. My uncle had a feud with them and they took their revenge. There was no pleading with them. We were sold to the Portuguese at their cursed tower on the coast. Our mother, Nsowah, the Omanhene's sister, and I his nephew! Sold like cattle."

His voice was full of disgust. He dropped the weight back onto the table, discarding it. "They told the Portuguese who we were and got a good price for us. We were treated better than the others. We were kept above decks, not with the others in the hold. Those poor damned souls in their chains. We never knew. I never knew that was how the Portuguese served them. We had slaves in our family and we never treated our people so. They were packed in that hold like salt fish. The stink, and the sound of their crying—ah, sister. We were lucky. Despite all our suffering, we are blessed to have been spared that."

"Did Captain Hawkins treat them better," I asked, "when he took the ship?"

He rolled his eyes and snorted. "The famous Hawkins! Of course not. We were all a cargo to him, though we were still better treated than the rest. And then he gave me away."

He looked at me and swallowed, shaking his head. "My little sister. I was a gift. A bribe for some fat merchant, and I never even reached him. They dressed me in that suit and told me I could go ashore with the men to fetch oranges, oranges for you and me. I believed them. The stupidity. I was old enough to guess. I was a man, not a child! And I didn't. I didn't suspect. You were crying and reaching for me, both of you. My little Nsowah!" His voice broke and he wept again, helplessly. I reached out to him again and stroked his head, this man who now was my brother.

"I tried to go back," he said at last. He rested his head on his arms and stared at the weights. "I ran away while I was in Seville, twice. I thought I could hide on board a ship bound for Guinea, but there are always people looking out for runaways. I was sent back and whipped for my trouble. The third time I made it onto a ship and they found me and beat me unconscious and threw me off at La Palma. The monks there looked after me and it was there I found God. They showed me that my fate was a test from God and that I could find purpose in his service. I remember lying in the sanatorium staring at the white wall and the sun coming through it. I realised I must leave my old life behind, if I was to live at all. By then I thought you were dead and I often thought—I thought of committing mortal sin and taking my own life."

He rubbed his hand over his face and closed his eyes. All his sheen and his careful, deliberate carriage had softened and collapsed. He looked younger, as young as he might have been on board ship. My own eyes prickled with tears. I wished I could remember him.

"We were told you had died too," I said to him. "Your letter found me at last, five years too late. But why, brother—why did you say nothing before? Why, if you guessed I was your sister and we might have been reunited?"

He lifted his head and dried his tears, sitting upright again.

"Because I am not Domingo, the bookseller and servant of Jeronimo Lopes, who came to Spain as an infant," he said. "I am Francis Enriquez, who serves Bernadino Mendoza, who served Conversos, who studied under Edmund Campion in the Jesuit college in Prague. You know who I am now, and what my purpose has been."

I nodded slowly.

"I didn't dare tell you the truth," he said. "I could not tell a soul my true purpose. I feared putting you in danger. And—I was not sure. I felt, but I could not quite believe it was really true. I left a letter for you at your house in London, I hoped I might return one day."

"Well, I am in enough danger now," I said.

We looked at each other. For a few moments we had been at the warm centre of our original natures. Brother and sister, Kofi and Nsowah, as we had been twenty years ago in our birthplace. We had talked as brother and sister, and there was love between us. Now the clothing of life, which obliterates, hides, conceals and protects, was drawing between us again. He was an intelligencer, carrying papers of a great invasion plot to the Spanish ambassador. I was Susan Charlewood, charged with taking those papers back, to save my husband and my country. How could any of this be reconciled?

"I don't know what to call you," I said. "Are you Domingo, or Francis, or Kofi?"

"I don't know myself," he said. "Call me brother, that is what I am to you."

"Then brother," I said. "Please—in our mother's name, and for her sake—please give me the papers you are taking to Mendoza. If they go to Walsingham he will free John. If you take them, John will die and I may too."

"You made a bargain with Walsingham?" he said. "I thought you a staunch Catholic."

"To save John's life!" I said.

"He will be a martyr, if he dies," said my brother. "His name will be glorious in memory, as Campion's is."

"You don't understand," I said. My brother was a Catholic and a citizen of Spain. He did not have to answer the Bloody Question Topcliffe had addressed to me: did I value my faith or my country more? The truth was I valued both. I had never wanted war. I did not want to see England part of the Spanish empire. I wanted the faith restored without war and that meant retrieving the papers.

And of course I had other, less noble reasons. If I went with Rob but could save John it would make my betrayal less stark. I was ashamed of myself, sick with guilt at my own actions. The world heaved and swung again as the reality of it shook me. Could I really go with Rob?

"He is my husband," I said. "He has done so much for the cause. He has done so much for you! He passed you the papers, when he could have taken them to Walsingham himself. I told him to give them up. I begged him. I tried to stop him. I would have stopped him at the Bull if I knew what he was doing. It's because of his loyalty he's in the Tower now. He has done everything you asked of him and now he is in the Tower ready to die for you—for you, sitting in this ship, drinking your Canary wine, going home to your master to be hung about with ribbons and praise like a horse that wins the race. Please, brother! It will cost you nothing. Tell Mendoza they were taken by force."

As I spoke a chill went through me. I had remembered Rob's plan. Tonight, in the dark, the river-pirates would come, and how was I to stop them killing my brother? If he would not give up the papers now, they would be taken by force. But I couldn't risk telling him what was to come, in case he alerted the captain and the men made ready. Rob might be killed in the action and I would lose all chance of finding the papers. I was caught, trapped.

I looked again at the gold weights on the table between us: the bird, the ladder and the cross. They were the only fixed points in this whirlwind.

"What are their meanings?" I asked suddenly.

"Meanings?" he said, following my gaze.

"You said the weights are symbols, of a kind. What do they mean?"

"Such a long time," he said. "So many years. They are like an alphabet. They have many meanings, depending on who gives them away and who receives them. Meanings and messages. I don't know all the meanings, I was too young when they took us. Our mother was teaching me. They should be with others, gathered in a package with gold dust and scales. The family *dja*. In Guinea, it is a holy thing. These weights alone say that the *dja* is lost, gone."

He picked up the bird again.

"This one is simple. This I always loved, because of the bird shape. It is called *sankofa*. One meaning is: do not be afraid to go back and fetch what you forgot. Do not be afraid to learn from your mistakes, from what has gone before. Your past. You see how the bird looks over its shoulder? But there are many other meanings."

"And the ladder?"

"I remember this too. All men climb the ladder to death. We must all die, it says, a kind of *memento mori*."

A *memento mori*. I turned it over in my hand and put it back down again. Last, I picked up the weight marked with a cross, each arm of the cross finishing in a circle. My brother's mark. He took it from me and sighed.

"You must understand these are not Christian objects. This meaning is blasphemous. It comes from the Akan religion, which I renounced many years ago, and it is about the Akan God, who is not our God."

"Please try. I want to know as much as I can."

"Very well. So. The deep meaning of this, is, if God dies, I will die too."

"If God dies?"

"Yes. You see how it sounds blasphemous. We know God never dies, we know he is immortal. But the message is backwards. The real meaning is: if all men die, then God dies too. Because it is men that give God a shape. The stone says that God has never said anything about himself, or written anything about himself. We think of God. We speak of him and give him a shape. So if we all die, that God we spoke of dies too. But the real God, *Nyame*, who is in everything and has no shape, does not die."

"So our people have a God? All the books say they have none."

"Nyame is the one God and he is also in everything and everybody. There are other, smaller Gods but he is the God this weight speaks of."

He put it slowly back on the table again. "These are heathen articles. I kept the weight for love of you and our mother. I used it as my sign half hoping it might be recognised, one day. Not in remembrance of idolatry, or in reverence of it."

"Thank you," I said. "Thank you for telling me." I took a breath in. "Now please, brother—"

But before I could finish, there was a shout from the deck and a thud, a sound of scratching and scraping and a horrible scream, and then the whole deck above our heads was booming with the sound of boots and men yelling. Rob had launched the attack early. Domingo leaped up from his seat.

"Don't go up!" I said and went to him. "Don't go up. It's Rob—they have come to take the papers by force."

"What! You knew this?"

"Yes, but before I knew you were my brother! This was our only hope to save John. Please, now brother—please, please give me the papers. If I have them they won't hurt you. I'll make them let you go—I'll tell Rob you're my brother."

He stared at me, not with love now but in anger and I saw again the stranger I met at Lopes's house. A man working at the limits of life and death, in as desperate a state as my own.

"Did you keep me talking here, knowing they would come? "

"No! They weren't supposed to come till past midnight. I hoped you would give me the papers and I could help you escape. I still can! I don't care if you go to Mendoza, I only want you to be safe."

"I don't have the papers," he said.

"What?!"

"Maria has them."

And with that he opened the lantern that lit the cabin and blew out the candle within. At once we were in darkness, and a thread of smoke curled past me. I blinked and waited for my vision to return as colder air rushed in and the sounds from the deck rolled in. He must have left the cabin. I felt around the table, hoping to feel my way in the dark, and put my hands on the little weights. They were precious; they must not be lost. I gathered them up and put them in my pocket. Then came a thump and a curse as someone stumbled into the room. Two men, by the sound of it.

"Who's there?" I said in a fright.

"Mistress?" said Rob's voice in the dark, and I gasped in relief. Next minute, moonlight came in through the window and I could see him by the door along with another man. Both were hooded and muffled, their faces swathed up so only their eyes were visible. I came over to him quickly.

"Rob—Domingo is on board. He mustn't be killed, you must tell the men."

"What?" he said. "Lopes's man? Why is he here?"

"It doesn't matter but he mustn't be harmed."

"Does he have the papers?"

"No, the woman does, Maria Padilla, but I don't know where she keeps them."

"Come quick to her cabin then. We've hauled her out and she's safe below. "

"Yes, but Domingo—"

"Yes, yes, not to be harmed. Will, tell the men and nail the hatches shut. Keep the bastards all below."

Will nodded and ducked back out of the cabin door. Rob took my arm and followed him, leading us out onto the deck and into a shifting, tricksy light. Clouds scudded over the moon, plunging us in and out of darkness. The ship swaying and the flickering light put the world in a perpetual, galloping motion that made it hard to balance. My brother was nowhere to be seen.

CHAPTER 37

Maria Padilla's cabin was littered with her bedding and books. There had been a struggle. The moon through the little porthole picked out the silver threads of her psalter, splayed on the floor, and I pounced on it.

"Rob—she kept this closest to her."

I handed it to him and he turned it over, weighing it, before drawing out a knife. He dug the point of the knife into the binding and ripped it open.

"Nothing," he said. "Now we must be quick. Search the bed and I'll try that chest beneath. There was nothing in her shift, I felt her up and down when we pulled her out."

He hauled the chest out from under the bed and worked some clicking magic with the lock. I turned over the bed, looking under the mattress and shaking out the sheets and blankets, then ripping open the mattress and emptying out the straw inside.

Noise rose up from below decks then, men shouting "Help, ho! Help!" and banging on the boards. The pirates had blocked the hatches to trap the men below. Their shouts gave more urgency to the search but I found nothing except handfuls of Maria Padilla's long, black hair.

Desperate, I peered under the bed and pulled out the sack with her bloody clouts in. I shook it out, emptying it on the floor, but there was nothing inside it but bloodstained rag-rolls.

Meanwhile Rob went through the chest: ripping, tearing, upending boxes, rending stitches, putting some objects in his pockets.

"Spanish bitch, where has she stowed it?"

"There were two men serving her," I said. "Perhaps they or the captain have it?"

"We'll search them," he said. "Damn them to hell, we've nailed shut the hatches. We'll have to open them up again and find these men. Come, you'll have to tell me which they are."

He lead me out on deck again. From beneath us came more banging and roaring from the men trapped below, but we were anchored away from the other ships and even if they could hear it, no-one was coming to help. The moon behind the clouds was bright and hard, clean and round as a white stone. The sight of it suddenly pulled me up short as we went toward the hatches.

"Rob, wait! Wait here." I turned and ran back to the cabin, wrenched open the door and knelt down by the bloody rag-rolls scattered by the bed, just as the moon went in again.

"Oh, Jesus," I said, half prayer and half blasphemy. I could have sworn I saw a clean roll, unused, among all this stinking litter. What better place to hide something, as a woman on a ship full of men, than this most private of places?

In the dark I had to feel around among stiff, dried rags and those still sticky with terms until I found it: a dry wad, thicker than the others and unused. It was stitched into a roll but when I gripped it in my hand I felt a thickness inside it, a hardness the very shape of a roll of pages.

The moon flickered through again and I caught sight of Maria Padilla's knife shining on the bed. Impatiently I took it up and found the row of stitches. I ripped it open, almost slashing my own shaking hand, and the roll uncurled. There it was. The wadded rag concealed a folded sheaf of papers. Could it be?

I squinted at the pages while the moon lasted—it was handwriting on what looked like plain pot paper. There was the list of names, the sketched map. The light left again but I had seen enough to recognise it. My shoulders slumped in relief and I looked up to Heaven and gave thanks to God before wrapping the book up again. I pushed the prize into my skirt pocket and felt my way towards the cabin door.

I pulled it open and stumbled out. The deck before me was flooded in blanched moonlight. The scene was suddenly full of men: stark black and white etchings, frozen where they stood, like insects in a suddenly upturned woodpile. I saw Rob nearby and ran to him, feeling my pocket to be sure the papers were still there. I grabbed his arm and he turned, startled, as I whispered to him: "Rob, I have it. I have it in my pocket."

"You're sure?" His voice and his breath were warm on my cheek. I nodded.

"Then we can go. Come."

Rob led me to the side of the ship where Will was standing. "We're done here," said Rob, softly. "Lower Mistress Charlewood down and take us in to shore. Tell the rest of them to take what they have and be off. Leave Derickson in his cabin. Is that fellow in the boat?"

Will nodded. "I slung him over. But Rob—someone's taken the other dinghy. Cut the ropes and gone."

"What?" Rob peered over the side and cursed, but I shuddered with relief.

"It must be Domingo," I said.

"He'll raise the watch. We must go after him!"

"He won't—Rob, I swear he won't. Please, let us go. I'll tell you everything when we're ashore."

"God's blood—very well. I'll go first. Will, send Susan over next."

Next minute he had hauled himself over the side. I peered down after him and saw him going hand over hand down a rope ladder, until he reached a small rowing boat below.

Will turned to me. "Hold on, mistress," he said, and helped me over the side. I clung to the rope ladder and climbed down. The pitiless moon-silvered water below waited to receive me if I slipped. I bit my lip and tasted blood as Rob reached up for me and caught me around the waist, swinging me down into the boat and onto a seat.

There was something warm and heavy beside me. I looked down and saw a man lying over the seat beside me, his eyes and his mouth wide open and a black mess boiling in his neck, like flies on meat. Someone had cut his throat.

A few moments later Will landed in the boat, tipping it, and the corpse's head turned towards me. His eyes stared straight at me. The blank stare accused me.

"Oh God," I said, and leaned over the side of the boat—hot, sour bile rushing up my throat and out into the water.

"Stay hearty, mistress," said Will. "He's going soon."

Will and Rob took an oar each, hauling us through the water with long strokes.

"What happened to him?" I said as I wiped my mouth. "Who is he?"

"Watchman," said Rob, with effort. "It's a pity. Don't mourn for him, I did it quickly. If you do it right, they don't know it's even happened."

"Bet you never knew your 'prentice was so handy with a knife," said Will, with grim humour.

"No," I said. Rob was certainly no apprentice in bloodshed.

I hesitated to name what he was to these men. Pirate, hired knife, killer. Was this how our books came to us? At night, over the bodies of dead men?

"God have mercy," I said, and I reached over and closed the man's eyes with my thumbs. I couldn't stand him staring at me.

Will laughed. "Mercy? God's mercy don't extend to these waters, any more than the judge's. Never you fear, mistress, he'll go out of sight and sound and we'll get you safe to the Crooked Billet. You won't need anyone's mercy."

I couldn't stop shivering. It came over me in great gusts that chattered my teeth in my head.

"What will happen to the people in the boat?" I asked.

"They'll stay there till someone comes in the morning," said Rob. "If you're anchored in Leigh you don't go rushing to help a neighbour when you hear shouts at midnight. It's not worth risking your own crew."

After a while, Will held up a hand and rested his oars.

"Keep rowing, Rob, or we'll drift out with him," he said. Then he stood and gripped the corpse, heaving the body over the side with a splash. For a moment the dead man hung in the water, face down and arms spread out like some blasphemous crucifix, the moon lovingly painting his skin silver, then the current tugged him away and the water swallowed him up. I gripped onto the seat, trembling, as Will sat and began rowing with as little concern as if the dead man were a fish he had thrown back into the water.

The night was dark again now. Clouds blanketed the moon. There was no light anywhere except one small, winking yellow eye in the distance. I watched it as we moved over the water, shivering from cold now as well as fright. When we were a good distance from the ship, far from where the body went in, I leaned my hand over the side and scooped up a handful of salt water to wash out my sour-tasting mouth.

The little yellow light drew closer. At length there was the sound of water lapping on shore and we came to a pebble beach. Rob jumped out and pulled the boat up and Will helped me out onto big, smooth stones that shifted and clinked under my feet.

Now I could see that the yellow light came from a lantern hanging from the wall of a house standing right above us. Steps led up from the beach to a door, and the lantern hung from a nail beside it, casting warm, homely candlelight over the unfriendly stones.

It had all happened faster than I could take it in. I was on solid land with pebbles under my feet. Rob helped me up the beach and then up the steps to the door. He knocked gently four times and after a while the door opened. A man with short, bristly grey hair and an equally grizzled beard, dressed in his nightshirt and cap, led us into a wide cellar stacked with barrels, pallets, ham hanging from the ceilings. It smelled of ale and pepper and safety.

"Thanks, Thomas," said Rob in a whisper. "Have you a room to spare for us till morning? We need paper and ink and something for a thirst. Water, and more?"

"I have," said the man. "You'll need to stay quiet, though. You're not precisely legal guests."

He led us through the cellar to a door at the side. Inside was a very small room, barely bigger than the ship's cabin, with a small bed, a chest, a joint-stool, and a little window with a jug and ewer on the sill.

I collapsed onto the bed and Rob went back out with the man. He returned alone with a flask and two earthenware cups, paper tucked under his arm, and ink and a quill sticking out of each pocket. He shut the door behind him, drew the stool up in front of the bed, set down the things, and sat beside me. I was clutching onto the bed, my heart still fluttering like a finch. There was blood on my dress and on my hands.

I went over to the jug and poured out water to wash my shaking hands. The grime and the dried blood flaked off into the water, dirtying it. I wished there was water enough for my whole body. When I turned back to Rob, he had poured out two small measures of liquid from the flask. He held one up to me.

I shook the water from my hands and went back to sit beside him.

"*Aquae vitae*," he said. "You'll be in need of that. It's been a bad night."

He threw back his own measure. I sipped mine and a fiery splutter coughed through me. God knows what it was: the dregs of the Thames. I sneezed, abandoned everything, and drank up the rest. Warmth flooded my chest. I nudged the dead man to the back of my mind. He would float up to me again, later.

"Let us see what that man died for, then," said Rob. "Is it the thing we sought?"

Carefully, I took the pages from my pocket and flattened them out, trying to straighten the curl. The papers were stained and damp, and familiar. A sketched coastline, a list of Sussex havens, and a list of names. All Sussex men, all gentlemen, all Catholics, and my master's name—Sir Thomas Framfield. I closed my eyes.

"What is it?" said Rob.

"The papers that John handed over at the Bull" I said, and passed them to Rob. He glanced briefly at the names, studied the sketch for longer.

"Someone knows the Sussex coastline well," he said.

"If I give this to Walsingham, they'll hang my master," I said.

"What do you care for him? He turned you out."

"He never wanted to—he was forced to it by his wife. He was good to me. He has been good to me even since I left him. How can I turn him over to Walsingham?"

"If you don't," said Rob, leaning back against the rough wall, "they'll hang your husband. But perhaps you don't care so much for him?"

I looked at the paper again.

"Do you know the names of the gentlemen on the list that Walsingham already has?" I asked.

"Some of them," said Rob. "Some have already been arrested—some have fled."

There were five names on this list, with my master's name second from the bottom. I got up and fetched the water jug from beneath the window. Rob watched me curiously. Then I rolled the paper up, opened up the lantern, and held the paper to the rush-light, watching it burn up.

"The devil!" said Rob, jumping up. "What are you doing?"

Before the flame bit my fingers, I dropped the burning paper into the jug, where it hissed and sent up foul smoke.

"I will give Walsingham the map," I said. "We will tell him the other paper was lost in our flight from the ship, but that I had a glimpse of it. It was a duplicate of the one in his possession. Here. Write down the names that you know."

I held out the pen and a fresh sheet of paper to Rob, daring him to say anything. He shook his head at me but took them and scribbled down a new list of names. These men were already condemned, our action would make no difference to them.

"It's your husband's life you're risking, mistress," said Rob, putting the list aside to dry. "Walsingham is the sharpest blade in the Queen's armoury. I don't know if he will believe you. But my cup is full. You are coming with me—are you not? And in Spain and Guinea we will win everything I want. All the riches of the New World."

He reached for the bottle and poured us another tot of spirits. I drank this one back without even thinking. Now the time had come. We were at the fulcrum. I had to decide whether I would go with Rob or return home. From this inn, I might leave behind my whole life and become an exile, a lost woman. Rob's eyes shone in the lantern-light.

"All the riches of the New World," he said again. "Rubies, emeralds, diamonds. None as rare as you."

"Rob—" I said, but my breath caught in my throat.

"You can't stop my tongue now," he said. "All this time, watching you with him. To think that you come from Guinea, from the land of gold itself, where I'd give my soul to go; where a man can run gold dust through his fingers. All of me burns for it. What does he burn for? Nothing. Paper. Words. Look at you. If you were mine I'd dress you in gold every day. I'd put pearls in your hair, I'd put diamonds round your neck. I'd lay you down in silks and satins, and cloth-of-gold, Susan—"

He touched me as he spoke: a hand to my hair, a hand at my neck. In the jewelled dark of the room, with the black silk of the Thames slipping by outside, dead men in our wake, and a knife at his hip, his words set the air aglow with colour. His words transformed me into what he said I was, a rare and precious thing. I felt myself shining.

I stayed still while he touched me, my eyes on his eyes. Any second I could say stop. Stop. Stop. I did not. I thought of John in the tower, our dead child, and the silence between us. I'd had my fill of intrigues and secrecy and martyrdom and words. All I wanted, in that moment, was to be freed from thought, from responsibility, faith, and loyalty. I leaned forward and kissed Rob and his hunger became my hunger. My desires became his. All at once I was ablaze and I forget everything—time, London, John, duty.

I saw the air strung with diamonds, I felt my nipple turn to a pearl under his hands. My sweat shone like gold dust. We fell back onto the mattress and I laughed; it was ridiculous. Then he kissed me again and the world flew away. He pushed up my skirt and I helped him. I never wanted anything so much. I was burning for him. I was fucking him in a web of gold strung somewhere in the deep sky over Africa, burning, burning, burning.

CHAPTER 38

All fires die. When we were done, panting and trembling, tangled in the cramped space—when stars had become candlelight again and I was back in my own small body and not loose in some scattered bright universe—we lay together for a moment in peace. There was a singing in my ears, like the sea. Then Rob sat up, his dark hair ruffled and his green eyes sleepy.

"I forgot," he said. "Domingo. Why am I not to fear him?"

I gathered myself together and sat up too, smoothing down my skirt and feeling in my pocket for the weights. They were all there. The bird, the ladder, the cross. I took the cross out and looked at it in the candlelight.

"He is my brother," I said.

"What!" Rob was awake now. "How can that be?"

"He changed his name. He has been working for Mendoza in secret. The dotted cross was his mark. Here—it comes from this. From my mother's country."

He took the little block in his hand and studied it. I placed the other two beside it in his palm and he turned them about. Watching them in his hand made me shiver, as if he was touching me again.

As he studied them I traced a line from my wrist to my collarbone, where his kisses travelled. Now I knew what it was like to lie with someone who made my heart jump. How could I ever go back to John?

"I remember this one," Rob said, holding up the bird. "Your royal crest."

I shook my head. I was still struggling to understand exactly what these things were. The importance that my brother vested in them. I couldn't explain the meanings to Rob, so I said, "A weight. It was used for weighing gold dust. I did not know before. I said it was a royal symbol because I was ashamed—I was ashamed I did not know what it really meant."

"So—you may not truly be royalty after all?"

"My mother and brother said we were. John Hawkins too. Could you love me even if I was not a princess?"

He didn't reply for a moment, and suddenly I really was afraid. Then he smiled again. "Royalty doesn't make a girl any prettier. I've seen the Queen, close enough to count the wrinkles, and she's not what the poets sing her to be. Now—I must go out and wait for the messenger who will take the papers back to Walsingham. I have to walk along the beach a little. You stay here and sleep—you may not find such a comfortable berth again for a while."

He clambered out of bed and went to the window where he set the lantern, taking the light away from the bed and leaving me in shadow. Then he came back and kissed me once on the mouth.

"I'll wake you at dawn," he said, and left me. I lay down in the tumbled bed, thinking I would never sleep after all that had happened, but the warmth left by Rob's body and my exhaustion after all those nights on the cabin floor conspired to close my eyes within minutes.

I woke when a bird called close outside the window. The lantern had burned down and the air was bitter, with that deep, lonely cold that comes just before dawn. I went to the window, wrapped in blankets, and opened it. The moon had gone down and there was just a glimmer on the horizon. All the pirates from last night had vanished into the creeks and inlets, swallowed up in the marshes.

An invisible bird scythed across the water again, yawping. It was so open here that I felt I had come to the edge of the world. It was the edge of my world. In a few hours the Dassell's ship would take its leave and I, I would be on board. My choice was made. I was leaving for a new place; a new life. I was committing a mortal sin, and at that moment all I felt was a great peace and lightness of heart.

As the light began to grey, I leaned out of the window and looked along the shore, hoping to see Rob returning. The shoreline dipped and humped, and all that came along it were more sea-birds, and then a slowly drifting sea-fret that hid the pebbled beach, the sea, and the boats beyond in white mist. It was bone-cold and the air smelled of snow.

A little breeze blew along the shore, nudging the mist, and it started to clear westward. As it dissipated I saw shadows in the East, running over the pebbles. First I thought it a trick of the light, dawn ghosts, then the shadows thickened and solidified and became two men running silently along the shoreline. It was Rob in pursuit of my brother, and in his hand was something that shone. A knife.

I cast the blankets off from around my shoulders and ran from the room out into the cellar and through the door to the beach. They were almost at the shore in front of the inn. If I flew I might catch them.

Down by the water's edge, Rob was running to kill. In the dawn light he did not look human: shoulders hunched, running low and light over the stones. My brother had the advantage of him, but now I could see what he was trying to reach. A small craft was rowing in to shore, coming to land where we beached last night. The mist was peeling away in strips and scarves now, white bandages uncurling from the water, and my brother was trying to reach the little boat before Rob could catch him. I gathered up my skirts and ran over the pebbles as fast as I could in my bare feet, directly down to the waterline. I could not scream or I would rouse the people of Leigh, but I ran as if the Devil was behind me.

My brother reached the place where the boat would make landfall, but it was still too far away. I saw the man's shoulders pulling, the oars beating the water. My brother turned to face Rob, a knife in his own hand. I kept running, slipping on the great stones, pulling myself along with clawed fingers, until I reached his side. I faced Rob too, standing as close to my brother as I could and breathing hard. I was trembling with effort.

Rob stopped within a foot of us. In one hand was his knife, in the other a stone.

"Let him go," I said fiercely, between gasps of breath. "Let him go!"

"He has the papers, mistress. He took it from me. Come here!"

"Please brother," I said. "Please, give me the papers."

I glanced at the water. The boat was only feet away and it was speckled white. Something was falling from the sky. Snow. Little, bitter flakes galloped down and Rob moved a step closer.

"Stand just there Master Roberdine, or I will kill you," said my brother. "Not one move."

"Please!" I begged him. "Please, please—brother, the papers! If you ever loved me—if you loved your little sister Nsowah—for your sister, for your mother, please."

He cast a look at me: one wild look, and threw his head back, giving a long shout of fury and despair up to the sky. There was a crunch of pebbles and the boat drew onto the shore. My brother thrust the papers into my hand, saying fiercely into my ear, "Take them yourself. Don't trust him!"

He leapt for the boat but Rob jumped at him, knocking me onto the stones. The boat tipped as Rob and my brother struggled against it and they both tumbled into the water. The oarsman steadied the boat then leaped after them. He drew a short dagger but the two men were fighting too close together in the thrashing water for him to strike.

Snowflakes landed on my face, my eyelashes. I didn't dare run in to save my brother. Suddenly one of the men slumped into the water. The other rose and beat him on the head once, twice. It was Rob and he had struck my brother down. The oarsman came at Rob and Rob pushed my brother toward him, wading back out of the water.

"Take him," he said. "Take him! Go now, and you live."

The oarsman heaved my brother up and into the boat and leapt in after him, spitting in Rob's direction as he grabbed the oars and started off. "Hell is waiting for you, devil," he called back over the water as the boat moved away, snow veiling it. Dip, dip, dip went the oars as the mist curled around the boat with its white arms. In a minute the boat was gone.

I stood at the water's edge, staring at the rocking wake left by the boat's departure. Gradually the curls of foam settled and vanished and very soon the water was calm again. There was no trace left of the boat; no trace left of my brother. Rob stood beside me, panting and bleeding from his leg and shoulder.

"You have killed him," I said. "You have killed my brother."

"He may live," said Rob. "What should I have done? He came on me in the dark and snatched the papers. I had to do it. Come, Suky," and he tried to take my arm and pull me out of the water.

"No," I said. My brother's eyes were the same shape as mine, the same shape as my little baby's eyes. His hair was soft under my fingers.

"We must go," said Rob, urgently. "We must go before the tide turns," and he pulled at me again.

"No!" I said, but Rob was stronger than me and he lifted me up and carried me out of the water. I struggled against him. I scratched at his arm and kicked at his ankles but he held my arms firm against my body and carried me over the stones.

"When Will comes back," he said,"he'll take us to the Dassell's ship."

"I am not going with you," I said. "I am not going with you!" And the hate I felt for him gave me the strength to struggle hard enough to overbalance him. We fell down onto the stones and Rob gave a shout. He had landed hard on his injured leg.

I managed to push myself away from him, finding my own place on the stones. The snow was still falling but I didn't feel the cold. I was on fire with hate. I hated Rob and I would never forgive him for this.

"I am not going with you," I repeated calmly.

He wiped blood away from his eyes. It came trickling down from a cut on his forehead.

"What will you do?" he said. "Go back to him? To the hole in the ground, printing in the dark?"

"You killed my brother."

"Mendoza's snake. Walsingham's snake. He knew he was your brother and never told you—surely he betrayed you to Walsingham. What sort of love is that?"

"Better than yours. Anything would be better than yours."

"Mistress—please—"

For a moment the belief, the restless anger that drove him, the defiance and push, was gone entirely. He looked lost. He had done all this because he wanted me—because he loved me?

This was not love.

"Please," he said, and held out his hand. "I have worked so, crafted and turned the wheels. I have made all things work toward this. Can't you see how this should be? You will be someone quite different, out of England I will be. We can marry."

"How, Rob? How can we marry? I am already a wife! Even if I were a maid, where could we go? We can't go to Spain—not now, not after what we've done here." It was folly. It was unreal. He was unreal. I saw it at last.

"Not Spain then, but Antwerp," he said. "Or Douai. Somewhere Catholics are welcome. We can marry, have children. I will go to sea and come back rich."

I shook my head. My brother was gone, dead or lost to me, and I was not going over the sea. Not to Guinea. Not to Antwerp, to be Rob's whore. I knew what he hoped. He hoped John would die and I would be free. It was surely him who betrayed John.

"No," I said. "I will not come with you. You may kill me too if you wish, but I will not come with you. You betrayed John, not my brother. Did you not? You! You call him snake! It was you, it was you."

"Look at me," he said, but I would not. He came over the stones to me, reached a hand to my face and tried to turn it towards him, but I would not look.

"Susan," he said, trying my name one last time. "Please. Will is here."

I didn't reply, and I didn't look at him.

"Be damned to you, then," he said, and sprung up. "I am going. Will can take you upriver, when he comes back."

"I'll not go with him," I said. "I will find my own way home."

I watched the water as Will came into shore and sprung out. I stared at the ripples as I heard Rob's footsteps crunching over the pebbles and down to the river that might be my brother's grave. I hoped with all my heart that John Roberdine found his grave in the water too. Let a storm strike him and send him to the bottom of the sea. Let him find his gold and pearls and diamonds scattered there and scrabble his hands about trying to scrape them up before the water filled his gullet and took his bones for sea-treasure. Let him know as he drowns that I am smiling.

CHAPTER 39

I paid money to the innkeeper of the Crooked Billet to find me a ship that would take me home. It was supposed to be a fishing boat taking a catch in but was clearly another small pirate vessel. With the wind behind us we set off up the river. I was alone in a boatful of men and I didn't know how far I trusted them, but I had little choice in the matter.

I slept on deck for the two nights it took to make the journey back. The men gave me blankets and I lay bundled up beside the captain, who did not lay a finger on me. The wind was behind us again on the morning of the third day, giving us a good run into the City.

Now I was making the journey I took before, when my mother came into England. Even though I didn't remember it, my child's eyes saw this. On either side of the banks London rose up. The walls of the Tower, gentlemen's long gardens with their own jetties, the wharves full of ships bringing in cargo. Cranes stood, delicate as birds, at Three Cranes Wharf, pecking and lifting. The air smelled of rain.

I stood looking at all this beauty, wondering how God made

such a man as Rob and why, or if, he was all the Devil's.

At Billingsgate steps, the Virgin Mary was waiting for me. She stood at the top of the stairs in a long blue cloak, her hands folded and strands of her dark hair fluttering in the wind. The early light shone on her like a blessing. I was so worn out, thin as a skeleton leaf, that I didn't question her presence. I stepped out of the boat and up the stairs, hoping she would gather me into her arms and let me sleep there. I was at the limits of my endurance. When I reached her I saw she was Lopes' servant, Sofia. She was not smiling.

"I am come to take you to Mr Lopes," she said.

"I don't understand," I said. "How did you know?"

I meant, how did she know I would be there, but she seemed to understand.

"The Dassells sent word up the river," she said. Of course. Rob's lights in the marshes, sending the message of death and betrayal. And she had come to help me, in the guise of the Virgin.

"Please come," she said.

I went with her in a daze. Nothing made sense to me any more. As we walked, I asked Sofia something that had been on my mind since she first opened the door to me, but that I had been too careful of her dignity to ask. Now I didn't care if I offended her, I was too tired.

"How does it feel to be a slave?" I said. She looked at me with those dark river-eyes.

"To be a man's possession," she said. "To be owned, and not at liberty?"

I nodded. She took a while to answer, looking down the street as we walked slowly together.

"It is as if you are chained all the time," she said, "weighed down with irons even when you are free to walk about. I remember the liberty of my childhood, when I belonged to no man and worked only to help my mother and father."

"What happened to your family?" I asked.

"My father and brothers died in the uprising. The Inquisition took my mother and I was sold."

I glanced at her as she spoke. Her face was composed and her tone matter-of-fact. Nevertheless, something in her voice brought the tears up into my eyes.

"All of us suffer," she said. "Some lose their family in war, some through sickness. But I have never forgotten when they came for my mother."

"But you are free now?"

She nodded. "I have been free these 15 years since we came here. I might go to serve another master if I wished—but I don't wish it. I am doubly removed from my homeland. This family is all I know. So I am bound, not in law, but bound still."

We had reached Lopes's house. As we went into the hall I put my hand on her arm and stopped her a moment. She looked at me in surprise.

"You said once that your kitchen maid knows how to work African hair—that she could plait mine, the way she does yours?"

"Beatriz? Yes. But—" she glanced along the hall to the library door. "I must take you to the master first."

She led me into the library, where Lopes was sitting. He looked up as I came in but did not smile.

"Sit, please," he said, so I took the chair opposite him.

"I suppose you have been laughing at us behind your hand, all these months," he said, leaning back in his chair. His voice was low and furious. "You and your brother and your traitorous husband."

I stared at him. His words made no sense to me at all. I wondered if I had somehow returned from the ship to another city—London's double, but not my home.

"I and my brother?" I said, bewildered.

He leaned across the table, his dark eyes bitter as sloes. He took a folded letter from his pocket and laid it out on the table between us, turning it so I could read it. The top half of the paper was filled with sentences written in black ink, the bottom with the fawn-coloured letters of invisible ink revealed. *Tomorrow in Paternoster Row, at noon, by the Star* it read. Beneath it was the little dotted cross. Lopes tapped it with his finger.

"Your brother wrote this. He has been in Mendoza's pocket these past three years, sending out messages, letters, spinning plots and writing ciphers for Mendoza and the Duc de Guise and that damned Scotswoman. And you and your husband have been helping him. Blood of Christ, I see the resemblance now. Your great wide smiles, your lying teeth, God curse the pair of you."

"You are mistaken," I said. "I had nothing to do with these plots."

"They sent you to reel me in," he continued in a passion, "and so you did. Royal blood! And so you have told Mendoza every thing that passed here: Dom Antonio's trade agreement, and the plans for Guinea. And now Philip of Spain is forewarned and all our cargoes and traders are endangered. You are shameless, madam. You are shameless and you risk my life and the life of my family! We are conversos, do you understand what that means? New Christians, old Jews, I know what people say. We are always watched, always suspected. We are libelled and slandered. Now the Queen knows I have had an agent of Spain in my household, do you think she will look on me so kindly? Or will she think: these Conversos, these *old Jews*, of course they are not to be trusted. Ah! You understand nothing. Take this!"

He flung the letter at me. It was only paper but the action was violent. I flinched from it and it fluttered onto the floor by my skirts.

"I swear to you," I said, "on my mother's grave, on everything most sacred to me, that none of this is true. I never knew he was my brother till a few days gone and now he is dead... I will prove to you that I knew nothing of this," I said. "I will prove it to you anon."

"How can you prove it?"

"You may ask the Dassells," I said. "I was supposed to take ship with them out to Seville, to find my brother there. Why would I go to Spain willingly to look for my brother if I knew he was here in London? Ask Anthony and Thomas Dassell. I don't care. I don't care what you do. I don't care whether or not you believe me. I am going now."

I walked back home alone by Bishopsgate and Finsbury Fields to avoid neighbours and friends, red-eyed and staring like a lunatic. The print room was empty and I let myself in there quietly. The workroom felt like a safe haven after the chaos of the past week. Everything in there was in order and had a place. I knew how every part of it fit together.

The wooden cases and the type sorts were blessedly familiar and solid. I sat down beside one of the type-cases and took out the sorts and spaces. I tucked them into the composing-stick one by one. When I finished, I looked at the letters sitting side by side, like siblings. *Requiem aeternam dona eis, Domine. Et lux perpetua luceat eis.* Rest eternal grant to them, Oh Lord, and light perpetual shine upon them. I stared at the words for a long time.

CHAPTER 40

The next day I took the map with my own hands to Walsingham's house. I refused to give them to his servant but sat in the hall until the man himself returned, swathed in dark furs.

I stood up when he came to me and looked him in the eye. Little dark eyes, he had, but they were not entirely cold. I saw a spark in them. I held the papers out to him.

"I have brought these to you as you asked, Sir, and now I ask that you release my husband to me."

He took them and unfolded them, his hands protected from the cold air by black lambskin gloves. They must be wonderfully soft. I watched as he looked over each page, unhurried and intent. When he read the list of names Rob had written down, the paper clean and fresh beside the crumpled, stained map, he looked up at me. Then I felt the power of those eyes. They were dark and sharp as Maria Padilla's, but more dangerous. I remembered then that this was Topcliffe's master, that Topcliffe himself was only an instrument in Walsingham's hands, and I had to clasp my hands together hard to stop myself shivering in revulsion.

"We wrote the list anew," I said. "The paper was lost in the taking. I am sorry."

He folded the papers up again.

"A pity," he said, "but it tallies. You may go. Your husband will return home tomorrow."

No thanks, then, for the Papist's wife. I curtsied and lowered my eyes as he set off to his private rooms, hoping that would be the last time mine and Walsingham's worlds ever spun together.

John did come back the next day, helped home by Wolfe. They had used the manacles on him and his hands were badly swollen. His cell had been filthy and he had barely slept, but they had not extinguished his spirit. The physician thought his limbs would recover, given rest, though he was prone to stiffness and rheumatics afterwards.

I put him to bed and he slept a good twelve hours through. I sat beside him a while, watching him sleep and waiting for guilt at my infidelity to suddenly crash down on my head. It never did. Lying with Rob had not felt like a choice but an inevitability, as if I was under a spell. John looked a very different man from the wild soul who had locked me in the print room the night before the Bull. He looked spent, but oddly peaceful. There were new lines on his face and new silver threads in his hair. He was still my husband—could I be reconciled to him?

When John woke at last I brought him up some broth and spooned it into his mouth, slowly. His open mouth, gaping for each spoonful, made him look like a child or an old man, but he was too exhausted to be angry at being brought so low. He opened his mouth and swallowed, lay back to rest, sat up again.

"So Rob has gone, then," he said. I nodded. I did not trust myself to speak.

"No more than I expected, eventually," said John. "There's too much of the villain in him and too much of the sailor. I shall miss him. I think he knew every smugglers bolt-hole in London."

"Do you think we are safe now?" I asked.

He moved restlessly on the pillow.

"God knows. I have been told they will not take me into prison again. If I live from now on as a good citizen and if I keep feeding Walsingham titbits of news the way you are feeding me. We will do what we must. I cannot continue in the same way as before. I used to throw them words that meant nothing, those texts of Munday's, and all the while do exactly as I pleased. They have the upper hand now. They will always be watching me."

We sat in silence for a while. I felt almost at peace sitting quietly with John. It felt like a safe haven after a storm. When I thought of Rob I felt nothing but turmoil, in my mind, my gut and my skin, a curdling mess of desire and hatred.

I started when John opened his eyes again and began to try and move his arm from under the coverlet, cursing at his weakness. At last he wrestled it free.

"What do you want? Stay there, John, the physician said to rest."

"Give me your hand. Put your hand on mine, Suky."

I laid aside the bowl and put my hand over his swollen fingers.

"Do you understand why I acted as I did?" he said. "You must understand. No, no, listen to me. I told you how I felt, after what they did to Campion, I know what I did to Campion, printing those stinking lies Munday wrote. I sickened myself. Working for my faith with one hand and against it with the other, cancelling out everything I did. Then Campion died—and our son died. I felt I was cursed. I felt like Job."

I remembered him saying those very words after the baby's funeral: *God has cursed me.* I remembered the flat despair in his voice.

"Did you do it as penance?" I asked.

"Of a kind," he said. "I prayed for help. I asked God what I should do to make amends, how I could wipe out whatever sin stained me. Howard asked if I could help with a secret enterprise, and I thought that was my answer. I received Mendoza's messages, I deciphered them and then I would meet Howard's man in Paul's and whisper to him as I passed him books. I understood what I was part of, but I thought, it is God's will. It is time to choose. Not only to make amends, but to act for my faith. All the words, all the books, have done nothing—nothing—to convert the Queen. Not our words. She only sees Luther's words, Tyndall's words. That battle is lost. Even when that man came with Throckmorton's papers. I saw the maps and the names and I understood it meant death, slaughter. I had to go on. Do you understand? For our souls, for Campion, for my children—our children." His voice cracked.

"Yes, sir," I said. "Be at peace. Lie still. I understand."

I did understand. It was the impossible choice we faced: to follow the Pope's ruling to the letter, to go to with the murderous purity of absolute faith and allow that men should die to win England back to Rome, or to live in a softer fog of compromise and self-deception and see our religion in this country suffocate slowly. I had lived with that dilemma my whole life and I could not blame John for choosing that path.

"And I am sorry for the way I treated you, that night—before the Bull," he said. "I was half mad."

"You only spoke the truth," I said. "I am no beauty. And I understand why you were afraid. I understand why you acted as you did."

"But it was not true," he said in agitation. "I said it to wound you because I was angry. Would I have married you if I thought you ugly? You are lovely in my eyes, Susan."

I did not believe him, but I kept my hand on his.

"Let's wipe it out," I said. "I have forgotten it."

"No," he said, clutching at my fingers. "No, there are too many things kept in silence. It poisoned my first marriage. I am too old to let silence kill another. Faith splits families, let it not split us. I love you, Susan, and I mourn our son every day. Let us be reconciled. I will not deal with such great matters again, I swear to you. I am done. I am done. If I have not done enough for God now, I can do no more."

I leaned in and kissed his forehead.

"We're both alive," I said. "Let us live."

I could not say I loved him. I had told enough lies in the past week.

"I found my brother," I said.

He looked up again. "Where? Alive?"

I shook my head. "He was alive until last week. Now I think he is dead. He had been in England for three years and I never knew, and now it is too late." I stopped a moment, tears thickening my voice. "Domingo. Lopes's man. He was working for Mendoza. He was the man you corresponded with, wasn't he."

John stared at me and his grey face turned greyer, as grey as goose-feathers. "God's blood, Suky. It can't be. But he was Domingo, your brother was Francis?"

"He went under an alias," I said. "I don't know why, perhaps so people would not know he came from a Converso family."

"Yes," said John. "I see. My God. But Domingo—he devised our cipher. He came here once, he saw the typecases and thought—I didn't know who he was then, I didn't know how he worked, I thought he was only a clerk, a scribe—"

He broke off, casting his eyes at me sideways as he realised he had given me a clue to the typecase code. He still did not know that I had broken it.

"We used your wedding present for the cipher," he said. "Piemontese. A foolish joke. I thought you guessed it, when I hurt you in the cellar. I am ashamed I did so, Suky. I am ashamed."

I cared little enough for that now, for any of it. I put my hand in my pocket, where I kept the bronze block my brother had given me. The mind behind the cipher was my brother's. He had walked into the print room and seen the typecases and turned those boxes of letters into a mask, a concealment for treason. Where I saw the raw materials for enlightenment, he saw a puzzle, a maze, a labyrinth where he could lose his enemies. But I had followed him in and found the centre, the Minotaur—betrayal and death.

I had been mourning a brother I did not know, but I did know him in a way. I knew that his mind was capable of devising a set of interlocking boxes and that mine was capable of unlocking them. We had been working against one another, but our minds worked in the same way.

I thumbed the cross that stood out from the top of the bronze block. I knew quite suddenly and certainly that he had rubbed the cross in the same way, had kept it in his pocket like this and turned it about, worrying at it.

"The mark he used on his letters—that cross—it came from a bronze block, like mine that my mother left me," I said.

John's hand moved under mine. This time I could not meet his eyes. I couldn't bear to feel the full weight of my grief, not with John. I didn't want to cry in the presence of the husband I had cuckolded. I could not fathom it myself, that Fate had split me and my brother, then brought us together so briefly. I had seen that dotted cross on letters and books for two years, trying to uncover its meaning, and all the time it had meant family. It was too cruel and too strange to be borne.

"I am so sorry," he said. "I am so sorry."

"It is as God wills," I said. "I am at peace with it." I picked up the bowl and spoon again, but he turned his head away, exhausted, and was asleep again in moments.

Later that day I went up into the attic to strip Rob's pallet and see what things he had left behind. Rob kept his space tidy and the space felt very bare and unlived in.

I opened the small chest where he kept his clothes. It was empty except for a psalter and a blue ribbon that must have come from some girl's hair. Not mine, maybe a Sussex maid. I stood for a while turning the ribbon in my hands. I had carried a quiet certainty with me since I lay with Rob at the inn, a little spark. The body knows, sometimes. It would prove itself in the next few weeks but I had no doubt I was pregnant with Rob's child.

At length I closed the chest again and took the ribbon downstairs to burn. This baby would grow up as John's and I hoped his real father never, ever returned home.

When I told John I was pregnant again he nodded and smiled, with tears in his eyes, but said nothing. We had learned not to hope but only to pray, as the days went by and I grew bigger. When I had recovered a little from the shock of things I wrote a letter to Lopes, setting out the story of my brother and telling as much as I could without betraying John's involvement in the plot. He must have written to the Dassells as I suggested and repented of his accusations, for he wrote back thanking me and wishing me well, but I knew our dealings were at an end. I was of no use to him now—nor he to me.

I went into confinement early, in June the next year, to keep myself away from shocks or disturbances. We lay there together, the baby and I, in the warm summer darkness of 1584. I read book after book while the child growing in my belly turned in slow circles, kicking like a dancer. It was a slow, thoughtful month. His movements formed a conversation with me as his questioning hands and feet tested the space around him, asking *who am I?* I placed my own hand on my belly in reply, saying, *you are mine.*

Sometimes when my eyes grew too tired I put the books down and let my thoughts wander. I tried not to think of Rob. I lay in the small room with my mind roaming about the universe, as I had when I was young in Sussex. While my body lay in confinement my mind broke its allotted bounds and stepped out into the stars. If I was free to walk in such a space, I was free to forget. Up among the planets, I let John Roberdine go. I let my brother and my mother go. I thought about my baby and the universe and I let everything in between blow away like dust in the wind.

Did those thoughts help form my child? My little questioner, curious one. He has always been a thinker, a watcher. Observing the world out of eyes that looked hazel when he was born but turned green over the years, a lovely colour against his tan skin and curling black hair.

My first baby would have been a brawler. I could see it in his angry face and his little bunched fists. Yet he died, and Tom, who spent most of his first year quietly looking around at the world, has thrived. All his mischief is caused by curiosity—falling off things, burning himself, getting scratched by the cat, asking impossible questions that no-one can answer.

None of our other children have lived longer than a day. Two little girls, Grace and Mary, one more boy who died before he could be baptised and many nights of slipped blood and pain. No brothers and sisters for Tom in these nine years. Nine years watching his eyes grow greener and wondering if John was also studying those green eyes and considering their origins. An unspoken question between us. If he did suspect, he never said a thing. Tom has been too precious to him.

I have spent every day of my son's life waiting for him to be snatched away from me again, but when the moment came I was not ready for it. I still am not.

Enough. No-one can hold back the sun from rising and no-one can take me from this earth and put me on another one. My story is catching up with time, my words approaching this moment. When the two meet I will put down my pen. *The stars move still, time runs, the clock will strike*. Write on, Widow Charlewood.

PART V

LONDON
1593

CHAPTER 41

Here I am then, in the print room where I have spent so many hours of my life, day and night. I still have my riddle to solve and my choice to make. *Ten culver, ten robin, 15 a bird.* The house is sleeping, full of the quiet breath of the young people under my care. I am often awake late, working or thinking in the quiet hours I have to myself, wrapped up in shawls and housecoats against the night cold or with a lapful of sleeping cat. In these hours I wonder where all the heat from our breath goes. This great lake of cold night air, flickering with the little warm fish of our breath.

Tom is sleeping peacefully up in the attic where Rob used to lie. Next to him is Geoffrey, John's nephew and our apprentice. Juliette, our little maid, is in Grace's old room. Everyone asleep but me, turning over my past, trying to find a shield for my household.

This is my domain now. My work-room. Our books bear the imprint of the Widow Charlewood. Since John died last year I choose which books we print. I register them at Stationers' Hall. I take the risks and add up the money, putting most of it in store for Tom's future.

John's death came so quickly I barely realised he was dying until he was gone. March was bitter, with grey skies and snow hanging over us, so when he caught a cold I thought nothing of it. Then the cold went to his chest, he turned feverish and within a week he was dead. He left no last words for any of us. He even left a text half-finished.

On the last day of his life the sleet whistled over Finsbury Fields and birds building nests shouted in the cold. The press downstairs was still and everyone in the house was quiet. I sat and held his hand, listening to his breath rattle and stir in his lungs, and understood at last that he was going to die.

His face was grey as his hair and his always vital spirit was utterly submerged. He looked suddenly a man in his dotage, shrunk to a husk, when two weeks before he had seemed hale and robust as ever. John always looked younger than his age. He was actually near fifty when I married him, and near sixty when he died.

None of us could quite believe that he was gone. After his breath finally stopped we all stayed watching in silence until Grace went to open the window and let his soul out into the raw day. The bleak air poured in and woke us up, shivering. I closed his eyes with my own hands, his eyelids still warm, and said a prayer over him.

Joan Wolfe came to help me lay John out. As I washed him and made his body ready for the winding-sheet, I did not see the corpse on the bed but the man I had lived with for a decade. My hands went over his short grey hair and the moles bumping up over his chest and back, and I remembered my first sight of him: the laughter-lines at his eyes and the bravado of his speech.

My heart ached for him because he loved all the things of the world. Food and drink, the affairs of his fellow men, and the struggle to leave this life richer than he came into it. He would not miss them now but I would miss his worldliness, the way he savoured life and wanted to wring the best out of it. And my heart sang because I was glad beyond measure to be alive; glad that it was not me laid out on the bed and John thinking back over our days together.

I washed him with the guilty tenderness of gratitude, with thanks to him for dying in proper time and giving me the gift of widowhood. Generous John Charlewood, generous to the last. When he was clean, before we wrapped him in the shroud, I bent and kissed his forehead. His hair still smelled faintly of the oil he used on it.

I have been a widow for more than a year and I am happier now than I have been since I left Framfield. What woman would not find pleasure in this state? I am head of the household. I sleep alone, if I wish to, and roll about the bed all night kicking blankets as I please.

I am executor of John's print catalogue. I go to the Guild dinners in my own right, not as a wife. Four other Stationers so far have proposed marriage to me and I tell them I am still in mourning, but truly, I think I may stay in mourning forever. I have lovers. I am careful, but a widow may court until she marries and so I do.

Now everything I have built is under storm and lightning-strike. A few weeks ago, all was still sunshine. I turned my face to the blue May sky as I walked through Finsbury Fields to the Barber-Surgeon's Hall, to watch them perform their annual dissection of a corpse. I went alone, the first time I had done so. I used to go with John, who never understood my interest in the dissections. He went in case he could pick up news, but he could not see what drew me.

"You can watch an execution every day or go and look at the pirates rotting down at Wapping stairs. What can those hooded crows show you of the human body that you can't see for free at Tyburn?"

I always told him I went for the learning—the anatomical lectures they give as they cut and saw and slice—but the truth is that I go to consider the place of the soul in the body. I have never found an answer to the question my brother posed in the attic, more than a decade ago now, but I keep searching.

I don't know what my faith is now. I am not a good Catholic, and I am surely no Protestant. Like many people in this country, like my old master, I balance uncertainly between the two. And since we printed Giordano Bruno's work, which some would call atheist, I find I also take an interest in even more dangerous philosophies. I am a convert to Copernican thought. The shape of my universe has changed, placing the sun at the centre of our infinite cosmos, rather than the earth.

Worse than this, I have questioned the Resurrection. I read what Bruno writes about the soul being intermingled with the body, about the whole universe being made up of tiny atoms that eternally dissolve and reform and never die—and I wonder if it can be true. These are not thoughts that should be shared, especially by a woman, so I keep them locked away and look at them when I am alone, carefully, like jewels or knives.

The Barber-Surgeons' hall is near Cripplegate. They cut up the bodies in the kitchen of the hall, which is big but not large enough for everyone who wants to watch. You have to arrive early and stand your ground or you will be shoved aside, while those who come too late crowd round outside, peering in through the windows and blocking out the light.

This year they were anatomising a robber hanged at Tyburn. I found myself a space perched on a sideboard next to two other small women. One looked with sympathy at my black mourning dress. I have worn black since John died last year. As well as discouraging unwanted marriage proposals it tells people I have—or had—enough money to afford an expensive colour. I returned the woman's glance with a smile and watched as the barber-surgeons filed in to begin their work.

The robber lay out naked on the table. His body was white, his face a dirty purple from where the rope had choked him. His tongue protruded black as a rotten plum, as if he were mocking all the people who had come to peer at him and get a closer look at the death waiting for us. His feet were covered in yellow callouses and his legs and body furred with black hair. Nothing looks less holy than a dead body. Nothing looks less like God's temple.

The senior barber-surgeon, a man with a head like a cannon-ball dusted with grey stubble, held up his cutting knife and positioned it over the stomach. The blade slipped effortlessly into the flesh and the skin parted cleanly in its wake as he cut up in a line towards the chest. The stench of the man's innards sighed out and wafted over the people nearest the corpse, who turned aside and grimaced despite the handkerchiefs held over their noses.

I watched intently, trying to guess how the sacred invisible soul mingled with the corrupt body. Whether its elements were still contained in the corpse of this man or whether they had already fled elsewhere, taken up into the air at the moment of death.

Looking at the bloody lumps tugged out by the strong fingers of the barber-surgeons, it seemed impossible they had ever hosted a soul at all. We are made of the same stuff as animals, to look at; the same stuff as a Sunday stew-pot. Meat, bone-marrow, gristle, and fat. No mysterious, pure caverns where a whole soul might rest but no tiny channels for scattered particles of spirit, either.

I walked home through Finsbury Fields, enjoying the sun on my face despite the knowledge it might awake the Plague again any day now. We suffered last year when the playhouses closed and we are suffering again this year. The last playbill we printed was for Kit Marlowe's *Massacre at Paris*, for Lord Strange's men in January, and since then I have been cursing the Mayor and casting through our back catalogue for work to keep us afloat—but who can turn away from the first warm sun of Summer even if it heralds approaching death?

My eyes are still in a dazzle from the sun when I step into the house. I hear voices in the kitchen, but when I come in all I can see for a moment is the outline of two figures. Tom, standing by the table, and a man sitting down. I blink and step into the room, and then I recognise him.

"Oh—" I say, and my hand flies up in a pointless, revealing movement, like a bird startled from its nest. There is a thick scar knitted across his left cheek, right up to the eye-socket. Whatever blade split the skin also took the eye out, leaving the wrinkled eyelid useless and empty, but his right eye is green as ever. It is John Roberdine.

He smiles at me, teeth still white in an elaborate black beard. As the sun-blindness clears from my eyes I see gold and pearl in his ear, velvet and gold embroidery on his doublet, and gold again on the brown hand that rests on the table. The ring finger is missing. He stands and holds his other hand out to me. I stare at him, disbelieving.

"Madam," says Tom, "this is Mr Roberdine come home from sea and he has brought a gold nugget with him as big as a tooth, look."

Tom's cap is pushed back on his head and his thick black hair curls out from beneath it. People sometimes take him for a little Spanish or Italian boy, with that hair and his light tan skin. He has had to learn to defend himself against the Spanish slurs in particular.

I look between Tom and Roberdine. Green eyes, dark hair, the two of them together at last. Even something in the shape of Tom's face, the way he stands. There is no doubt. Tom is Rob's son. I feel as if my child is standing next to a wild dog that might rip him with its teeth any minute and I must not anger it.

"Tom," I say, "I have remembered something. James Roberts lent me the manuscript of the *History of the Jews* and he wanted it back today. It is on the side in the print room. Will you run over and take it to him? You can stay there to dine, if they have enough for you."

He looks from me to Roberdine.

"Now, Tom!"

"Yes, Mother."

He bows to Roberdine and trots away down the hall. When the front door slams behind him the house is very silent. His father and I face one another across the table. Roberdine's one green eye is unblinking and his face gives nothing away. Did he see the resemblance too? Does he know?

He walks over to me, moving more stiffly than of old. His movements were always so quick and fluid but now he drags his left foot a little. He holds out his right hand again. His good hand. I put my own in it, disbelieving, touching him partly to be sure that he is flesh and blood. He smells of something exotic, ambergris or sandalwood.

"You thought I was dead," he says. His voice is light and mocking, but it breaks a little on the word dead. His palm is tough with callouses. The feel of it hurts my heart. I used to long for his hands on me. What has happened to him?

"Yes," I say, unable to stop myself staring at his missing eye. My voice is rough with fear and anger. The sight of him brings all the bitter feelings from ten years ago rushing up again, so powerful I can taste them like gall on my tongue, along with all the words I never had a chance to fling at him. I can smell the salt marshes and the Thames estuary water; I can see the empty pebbled shore and the white sea-fret, all suffused with hurt and rage.

I want to spit in his face, push him out of the house and slam the door, but I count up the new things about Roberdine and I say to myself, careful, careful. Damage, injury, wealth. A good deal of wealth. This is not just sailor's swagger. Those clothes are new, with the nap still on them. They are merchant's clothes.

"Why are you here?" I ask.

He smiles. "To make amends," he says.

I turn my head away and laugh, bitterly. As if a snake that bit me spoke up and promised to heal me with more poison.

"Let me bring you ale," I say. "It will be a long speech, I'm sure, and your throat will be dry."

I leave him for a moment, my hands shaking, and go to fetch ale from the kitchen. I lean on the table and take a few breaths, composing myself. I stare at my hands. There is my gold wedding ring, the heart between two hands. I stroke the fine wool of my black dress. I touch the crisp white coif on my head, the neat braids beneath that Beatriz plaited for me last week. I am sure of myself and of my place in the world. I pour the ale into two cups, put my shoulders back and my head up and go back to the parlour.

I hand Roberdine a cup and sit down opposite him. He lifts his cup to me. I do not respond. He drinks, and his good eye watches me over the cup rim. Then he leans back in his chair and spreads his hands out on the table, displaying the jewels on his fingers, the gorgeousness of his doublet.

"I hear you are a widow," he says.

"Yes," I say. "John died last March."

"I am sorry. He was a good master. As you were a kind mistress." He flicks a sly look at me, his one good eye still green and tawny-flecked, translucent. I let my own eyes travel to his empty eye-socket.

"He was a good husband," I say.

CHAPTER 42

"He was a good husband," I repeat to Roberdine, "and a far, far better man than you could ever hope to be." Suddenly I can't hold my anger in any longer, overwhelmed with fury at him and at myself, still, for cuckolding John with this villain.

"You sent me to Topcliffe," I say. "You told Walsingham John was passing those papers on at the Bull. You killed my brother. Did you always hate me?"

"I never hated you. I did what had to be done," he says. "And I never sent you to Topcliffe. I don't know who betrayed the master. If anyone did it, I think it was your brother. It bought him time to escape."

There is not a trace of regret or guilt in his expression. He is as calm as if we were debating a shop bill.

"It was you," I say, with absolute conviction and disgust. "It was you. You lied to me. Everything you told me was a cup of lies."

"I meant all the sweet words, at the moment I said them," he says. "The gold, the diamonds—your beauty. As much as any lover means his marriage vows."

I stare at his slashed face. I can see nothing of the wilful, adventurous apprentice he once was. The wildness has burned away leaving scar tissue, something harder and more ruthless, and the flare of warmth he had about him is stone cold now. This is not the boy who shared my sadness when my baby died.

"Would you have me do penance for my sins?" he says. "I have done it. I have served it in prison, at sea, and by the sword." He gestures at his eye. "It has been a very long journey. I am rich now. I said I would come back weighted down with gold. Well, here I am. I have suffered for it, enough to please even you." He takes something from his pocket and holds it up: a nub of yellow gold, soft and buttery in the light from the window.

"I suffered for this nugget that your boy Tom liked so much," he says quietly. I flinch at the mention of Tom's name. I must not let him see my fear.

"Tell me of your suffering, then," I say, "and please me. I care nothing for your riches."

He smiles into his cup and his husked eyelid flickers.

"The riches and the suffering came together. I won most of the gold by taking it from Spaniards and Portuguese who didn't deserve it, on voyages to Senegambia and Barbary with Thomas Dassell. I sent my share of the booty home to my brother. Then I took ship with a friend of Dassell's in '87 and that vessel was taken by Barbary pirates. They took my eye and my finger, too. Still no pity for me, mistress?"

I shake my head. "An eye for an eye. You killed my brother. You killed the watchman in Ratcliffe. What else should a privateer expect?"

"Ah, your hard heart," he says. "Grace was always kinder to me." He drinks again and I see his hand trembles just a little, a leaf-tremor.

"I found the Dassells again in Seville, when I was ready to take ship again," he says, "and we went out on a joint-stock venture to

Guinea. I won a treasure-trove from a Spaniard and at last I set sail for England with a treasure-ship and two pinnaces. Then the God-damned dog-fucking Spanish took me and my ship and stashed me in prison. They missed my treasure-ship though; it was ahead and escaped. They had me kicking my heels for three months with no clue if my gold had got home safely or if my men had parcelled it out between them. I had no money to pay a ransom to the Spanish till my ships got home, but by the Grace of God they set me and ten others free in exchange for a parcel of Spanish prisoners sent out from England. Now I can call myself a merchant venturer, if I want to. My ships waited for me at Flanders. My men proved honest for the most part, and my fortune is made."

"If you hope to buy my forgiveness with your treasure, you are a fool as well as a villain." I say. "I would not touch a penny of your damned gold."

"No?" he says. "It comes from your homeland. I tell you, you were fortunate to find yourself a place in England. Guinea is a very Hell in places. Hot and dripping. Forests everywhere. The people come out of the forests and trade on the sands—or shoot arrows at you, depending whether they have an agreement with the Portuguese, and they mostly do. You can't trust half of them either. We made a deal with one village and then found out they were still trading with the Portuguese. They'll think twice about double-crossing the English again, though. We burnt that village to the ground. We had skirmishes with five or six Portuguese and Spanish ships, too. It's not an easy place to make money. I wouldn't go back but if England can ever get a foothold, there's great profit to be made from slaves and from Guinea gold. All their chiefs are poxy with it."

"You burned their village," I say. "Did the people burn, in their houses?"

"None that I saw," he says. "They were all hiding in the forests.

What do you care? You've been in England thirty years now, no? They are not your people, not any more."

I look away from him. Not my people? Does being wrenched from your homeland mean its people are no longer yours? I don't know what the Guinea villages look like, but in my mind's eye I see the tenant cottages at Framfield burning and people running into the Wealden woods from the men torching their homes. Fifty years ago the French sailed in to Brighthelmstone and burned it and if the Spanish come one day, they will come with fire.

"So you would buy and sell slaves," I say, "even though you know what sorrow it brought me and my family?"

Rob shrugs. "If God wills people to find themselves in chains, so be it. We are slaves or free, damned or saved according to his design. The market is there, and I would profit by it. We are such a little country, Susan, in this great world. When you see what the Spaniards have—what riches they've won from these lands. We could make London a New Jerusalem with Guinea gold."

I stare at him. "You have turned to Protestant predestination, then?"

"I have turned towards the Queen," he says. "Have you?"

I blink and do not reply. He smiles, looking around him at the parlour, the old furniture and new wall-hangings. I sense we still have not reached the pith of his visit, the meat of the matter. He is rich now. There was no need to come back here.

I recognise it fully now, that hunger of his. I understand it as I did not ten years ago, when I thought it the hunger of desire for me, a lust for beauty and sensation, feeling and knowledge. I understand now it is the colder, narrower hunger of possession.

"So you have prospered in the years since I have been gone?" he says, nodding at the bright wall-hangings. I answer warily, unwilling to give away much of our business.

"We have the privilege to print all playbills so we are in league with the players. That has given us a good income, though this year is bad for us with the theatres closed for the plague. Grace is married now and lives up at Aldgate with her boys, but we keep a maid still."

"Your boy told me he is at Paul's," he says. "It must be hard to find the money for fees."

"I manage," I say, tightly. "He is a scholar. He will go to Oxford, after Paul's."

I do not tell him where the money comes from. A few months before John died I received a letter from Sussex, from my old master's lawyer. Even though we rarely corresponded I thought of him often; I thought of the house, of everything continuing as it always had. Now my lord is dead and my lady too, released at last from her long, mourning madness.

Much of my lord's wealth has been eaten up by recusancy fines and his cousin, who inherits the estate, plans to sell it, but Sir Thomas did not forget me. He left me enough to pay for Tom's schooling, for tutors and books and good clothes. I can send him to Paul's Grammar where he will learn Greek and Latin, and to Oxford after.

"An Oxford scholar? A bright boy, then," says Rob. "Well, he must come and see my new house. I am setting up home in London. I've had enough of seafaring for a while. Now I can pay men to captain my ships and I can put my money into goods and gear and this fair city. I have already pledged a good part of my treasure to the Queen, at which she is very pleased, and my next aim is at a portrait in the Royal Exchange." He stops abruptly, reaches into his coat pocket, and takes out a small cloth bag. He empties it out and stones spill onto the table. More gold nuggets and a handful of dull, round pebbles.

"Gold and diamonds," he says. "Uncut." He pushes them over the table to me. "Hold one."

I pick up one of the pebbles. It looks completely ordinary.

"All this and more," he says, "waiting in the warehouses at Paul's Wharf. Silks and satins and cloth-of-gold, Susan."

I look up at him sharply. His words at Leigh that seduced me. He has turned words into real things.

"All yours," he says, and I see there is still warmth about him. He is not quite stone. His one green eye still has light in it, like grass in summertime. "If you want them," he says. "I've done all I said I would. All these riches—from your country. Marry me, and they are all yours. Forget the past. I can give you the world, the whole world, Susan!"

There he is, the old Rob. The same slightly husky, urgent voice, watching me intently. For a few seconds—no more than five—his look hits home and I remember how sweet it was to kiss him. How much I wanted him. I tighten my hand around the pebble—the diamond—and the stone feels cold on my skin. A warning. I remember other kisses I have had, since John died. I have kissed better and rarer men, whose minds encompass heights and depths of thought that Rob, with his narrow earthly focus, cannot match.

"No," I say flatly. "You think to buy me with stolen treasure? To win me by telling me how you burned the homes of my people? Pirate. You should be hanging in the water at Wapping Wharf, not building houses on London Bridge. Get out of my house." I push the stones back across the table to him, repulsed by them, and one of the diamonds rolls to the edge and drops sharply onto the stone floor with a ringing crack. The sound is violent. We watch it roll to the table leg. Rob reaches down and picks it up. Carefully, he gathers all the stones together and drops them back into the little bag, taking a moment to pull the drawstring tight.

When he looks up at me he is John Roberdine the merchant again. The warmth has died.

"Is your Tom a good boy?" he asks, and his words make the hairs on my neck stand up. An innocent question, spoken like a threat.

"As good as a boy should be," I reply, cautiously. "He breaks everything he touches; he grows like a thistle and comes home covered in mud."

"If he's as able as you say, you should send him to me. I heard you had a son. I am glad I was able to meet him. A handsome child. He would be apprenticed soon, anyway, if he does not go on to university?"

"Yes. Even if he does go to Oxford he will be apprenticed on his return so he can take over the business when he is of age."

"If he comes to live with me I can promise great advancement. More than he, or you, could ever expect."

I keep my hands folded on the table. I keep my eyes on his.

"If this is another attempt to make amends, I have no use for it. This is his father's company. John wanted him to take it over. If he is not apprenticed to a Stationer I must marry one or lose the business."

Now he leans forward over the table, his hands close to mine, his eye flickering over my face.

"You're still a lovely woman, Susan. Why would you not marry again, even if I am no longer to your taste? Who would live a widow, without a man to warm the bed? Not you, Suky, you are not a girl to lie alone. Or do you plan to be a very merry widow? People talk about such things, you know. A woman's reputation, once lost, will never be got back. You told me that yourself."

I was right to sense danger. John Roberdine has grown into a very dangerous man. His voice is warm and low but he will strike at me like a snake if I let him. I wait until I am sure I can speak steadily.

"It is my business whether I marry or do not marry. It is my business where my son is apprenticed or not apprenticed."

"Now that his father is dead?"

"Now that his father is dead."

Roberdine smiles. His teeth are the only part of him not scarred or damaged. They are still whole and white and his smile would be merry if the anger behind it was not so menacing.

"Let's end this play. That boy is mine. You and John had no other children, and your only son looks at me with my face. My very eyes, as fair as ever they were when I had two. That is my son."

I can hardly breathe from fear and fury. "He is my son. He is to be a printer. He is not yours. Nothing about him is yours. He is not deceitful, or cruel, or avaricious."

"He is mine," says Roberdine. "He is my son. Why are you angry with me? I'm offering him the greatest chance of his life. I'm a thousand times richer than John ever was. And how many men would take their bastard into their household? I would not shame you. I will tell nobody who he really is. I won't even tell him. I'll say I'm taking him out of respect for my former master, to make amends for running away from my apprenticeship. But I want him in my house. I made him. He is my son."

I rise from my chair and lean on the table, my palms flat, staring across it at my enemy. "You can't have him," I say. "Get out of my house. I never should have let you in. He is my child and you won't take him."

Roberdine pushes his chair back and stands up too. He fills a room now, like John Wolfe. He is quite changed from the boy who worked in the shadows at the side of the Thames. Now he has stepped out midstream and is ready to build dams, divert water, burn villages, to send the flow of life in his direction.

"Think on it," he says. "I can't stay longer. I have business elsewhere. I will be back in London in a month's time and we can talk further. Don't think that I will change my mind. I am giving you the chance to change yours."

"Do you threaten me?" I say. "Why should I change my mind?

What can you do to hurt me? Throw ancient slander at me? Name me an adulteress? My husband is dead and you can prove nothing."

"I still have friends in London, on the river and among the printers," he said, "and I know more dark things about you than the colour of your cunt. Take warning of it now."

I have to press one hand down on the table with the other to stop myself smacking him across the face. I will not let him provoke me to lashing out. I will hold myself in until I can strike him through the heart.

"Go," I say. "We are done."

He gives me a small bow, turns on his heel and goes out into the hall. When I hear the door close behind him I collapse back into my seat, staring at nothing.

My first feeling was the right one. I should have slammed the door in his face. What does he know about me? Is he bluffing? He will not take Tom. My only child, that I have brought up so carefully. My little one, grown nearly as tall as I am, who might one day be a royal printer.

At the very least I must try and show him I am not afraid. He has changed. Well, so have I. I am not a young wife finding her place, blind to the world's badness. I am a widow with a business in my own right, equipped with a woman's armour and weapons, and I will find a way to fight him.

I count the things John Roberdine does not know about me. He does not know how much John grew to rely on me, in recent years. He does not know that I have as many secret contacts at my fingertips as John ever did. John kept nothing from me, after the Throckmorton plot. I knew all his networks and I helped him keep up the bargain he made with Walsingham, feeding the hungry, open mouth that demands intelligence on Papists. We passed on titbits. When John died I let that drop—I was only his wife, after all, and could not be expected to perform such work—but I use those networks for other things.

Now I write a list of useful men and I send out a flurry of notes across London and beyond. To Rob's boyhood town of Rye, to Flanders, and to Spain. I owe John Roberdine a debt and I want to repay it in full. He may dress like a merchant now but that man could never live clean. He is a pirate through and through. There must be something he has done, some atrocity he has perpetrated, that would wipe out the value of treasure he has given the Queen. If there is anything at all, I will dig it out and I will use it.

CHAPTER 43

A week after Roberdine's visit, our neighbour Helen, a Flemish widow and a weaver, comes to see me almost in tears. Someone has pushed a printed pamphlet under her door overnight, threatening violence to the French and Fleming immigrants.

"Another one," she says. "Ten years I lived in London now! Ten years working and raising my family, helping my neighbours and giving alms to people not much poorer than we were. We came here running from a massacre! These people, they forget everything what happened before today. People get hungry and their belly growls out old friendships."

I study the paper to see if I can learn anything from it but it is a common enough thing—smudged sentences put together from a mixed bag of type sorts, boasting that more than two thousand apprentices will rise if the Flemings and French do not depart the city. Others very like it were sent round a few months ago.

"These are fine, inflated words," I say, crumpling the paper up. "Schoolboys pissing up the wall. I doubt these boys have the iron in them and I don't believe there's 2000 of them. You are too right to talk of their bellies. This is the grumbling of an empty stomach and nothing more."

That makes her laugh, but when she has gone I unfold the paper and read it through again, smoothing out the thin grey sheet with my fingers until the smudged words are clear. These little gobbets of hate. They have been coming all this year. Early this month someone wrote up a poem on the wall of the Dutch Church, telling all foreigners to leave England, and just this week Kit Marlowe has been arrested for that and other crimes. None of us believe he did it—he has been falsely accused—but someone in our midst took up that pen. I have been in the city more than ten years and I am not a Fleming or a Huguenot, but I am a stranger. I bar my doors carefully at night. I make sure all my household are home before curfew and I watch for crowds and large gatherings as I go through the streets.

London feels wormy and dangerous. Plague and famine haunt us. The harvests have been stillborn, black, and rotten. There are more men sleeping on Finsbury Fields at night, soldiers back from war in Ireland, huddled in clumps. The Watch moves them on and they drift to another place at the edge of the city, moving in endless slow progress beyond the walls like blown leaves till they arrive back again.

It is the same all over London. Too many masterless men coming back from war and food growing more and more expensive. The long embargo on trade with Spain has hurt many people. There are still fine fair houses lining the streets around us, the homes of merchants kept clean and prosperous, but on corners and around taverns and bowling alleys there seem always to be clusters of people with no purpose, gathering only to be moved on. This circulation of lost people, these bubbles of hatred coming to the surface. The city churns like a stewpot heating on the fire. One day soon it will boil over.

And into this turmoil has come John Roberdine, bringing his

gold and his stories from the New World. Flaunting his wealth in a country that has been eking out poor wheat for a year. I am not starving because I live very carefully and I have Sir Thomas's money for Tom, but even so I go hungry often to feed the rest of my household. Has Roberdine come as punishment for my sins—for my adultery?

While I sit stirring up my guilt, there is a knock at the door and a "Hullo!" and in comes Grace, shaking raindrops from her hood.

"It's coming down like Noah's Flood," she says. She is married now with three small boys and living near her sister in Aldgate. I miss her in the house. Juliette, our maid whose parents fled Paris after the Bartholomew's Day massacre (yes, I am harbouring a Protestant refugee), is quick to learn and her dark eyes miss nothing, but no-one could replace Grace's wit.

"Tell me about Rob, mistress," she says without preamble as she takes off her cloak and hangs it on the door-hook. "Henry met Tom somewhere about and brought me home such stories. He is stone blind and has stripped Africa clean of gold. His shoes are golden, his coach is gold—his house is gold. Is any of this half-way true? I thought he was dead at the bottom of the sea and good riddance to him."

I shake my head and stand up to fetch her a drink, casting Helen's note into the fire as I go. I try to speak calmly and without bitterness or fear marring my voice.

"He is alive. He has lost an eye but sees well enough, and he is certainly rich. He is razing the traces of his old life and putting the fear of God into his old companions."

Grace sits at the table and watches me, all eyes. The years have softened her sharp face a little, but not her eyes. They are as fierce as ever.

"Why? What does he want?"

"To sit at the Queen's table. But his boots are not quite clean enough for that yet."

"Ha!" says Grace. "They never were. He was a knife, that boy. Kept the blade hidden while he lived here, but I saw it. Who has he killed?"

I never told Grace about my brother. I told no-one but John. It was too strange. I found him and lost him all in a day, and the secret of his true nature was like a gift given only to me. I held it close because it was all I had left of him. My brother Kofi, who was tricked away from the ship to buy oranges for his little sister and dragged away into a new life. Roberdine cut him and killed him and left me doubly alone,

A year or so after that day at Leigh, when Tom was a few months old, someone sent me my brother's *memento mori* ring. It came wrapped in a square of blue silk, inside a sealed paper. When I untwisted the fine stuff the ring rolled out onto the table and stared at me, amber eyes shining like little fires. I hissed in fright and drew back from it, my heart thudding at my ribs. Then I searched the paper it came in with my fingers shaking, hunting for a little dotted cross—a few words—anything that would tell me it came direct from my brother. I held the paper to a candle, I brushed copperas over it.

No words rose up to bring me hope. The paper was blank. If it was from him, surely he would have marked it with his sign. There was nothing. A flood of grief and anger welled up in me. I wept and beat at the kitchen door-frame with my hands and arms until they were bruised. When I was empty of tears I folded the paper away and put the ring above my wedding ring,with a little thread wrapped around it to make it fit. I have worn it ever since, either on my finger or around my neck on a silver chain.

I look at it now while Grace waits for me to speak, turning the skull to catch the light.

"As far as I know, he has not murdered anyone on English soil,"

I say at last. "But he has been summoned to the High Court of the Admiralty with two other merchants—the Dassell brothers. Dom Antonio, the Portuguese king in exile, has filed a lawsuit against them for failing to pay the duty on their imports from Guinea."

"Oh indeed," says Grace. "Her Majesty looks ill on men that don't pay their dues, I hear."

"She does," I say. "And they are accused further of bringing the sons of Guinea chiefs to England against their will, and thus harming the Guinea trade for all the merchants."

"Guinea chiefs? From your own country?"

"So they are accused. I don't know the truth of it. I don't see how it would benefit them, to bring men here against their will, but I believe Rob would do it if he saw profit in it."

None of this information is secret. It is all out in public, so I have not had to work to find it. And it is not enough to keep Roberdine from my door. If he is as rich as he says he is, then I am sure a few large bribes in the right hands will buy him out of trouble. So I am still hunting for something worse, hunting as the days go by with a gnawing fear in my stomach. Waiting for replies to my letters and burning them as they come back with scraps, feathers, and wisps. Not enough to build a nest that will keep me and my child safe.

I watch Grace as she drinks from her cup, the same pewter ware she used to wash and dry when she lived here. She is paler and thinner, the legacy of this past starveling year. Her hands are capable and quick as ever but her knuckles are swollen and red from her life of work. I look down at my own hands. Not as smooth as they were when I first came to London but marked with their own tally of the years. Burns, callouses, ink. No-one would take me for a lady's maid now.

"He wants to take Tom into his household," I say to Grace.

She looks puzzled momentarily, a dip of confusion. Her eyes go over my face, studying my own eyes, my mouth, then she nods.

"I always wondered," she says.

"He will make Tom the image of himself," I say. "He will make him a cold villain. He will turn him against me and I will lose him. I won't let him. I won't let him go." My fear is strangling me, my throat tight with unshed tears.

"No," says Grace. She reaches across the table for my hand and holds it a moment. Her fingers are chilly from the pewter. "Any help you need, madam, we'll give it."

"Thank you, Grace."

We talk of other things, Grace's children and the shuttered playhouses, until the rain stops and Grace can walk back to Aldgate. When she is gone I stand in the empty kitchen for a while, imagining the house without Tom in it. I know he would go away to be apprenticed. I know he would leave me soon anyway, but the air here is so warm with his presence. His constant questions, his feet racketing up and down the stairs though I shout at him not to run in the house a hundred times a day. His pallet up in the garret, where he sleeps rolled in his blankets like a puppy, one arm flung out into the cold air.

Often I go up to him before I go to bed, to make sure he is comfortable and sleeping peacefully. He looks younger asleep, his mouth and the nape of his neck still recalling their baby curves. Grace guessed he was Rob's son. His eyes are Rob's, but his nose and his mouth are mine. I am grateful to Grace for offering me help but Grace has no power. Nor have I. My best weapon against Rob is intelligence, but can I harness any power to help me?

The thought brings me to Jeronimo Lopes. I see Sofia often, when Beatriz does my hair or when they gather with other Portuguese servants at fairs and festivals. They are my friends now too, a clutch of women from Africa by way of Portugal. Even a few from Guinea, who were taken as children like me. They have taught me Portuguese and given me another kind of home within London.

Another family. So I am often at Lopes's house but I rarely see him. If we pass each other, he nods, but does not speak. Now I began to consider him again.

The Lopeses are close to Dom Antonio, the pretender to the Portuguese throne. Roberdine has encroached directly on the exiled king's rights by failing to pay him duty. If there is anything I could do to help it will surely be welcomed, so I put on my best dress and set out to Lopes's house.

Sofia opens the door and smiles at me. I kiss her cheek and take her hand briefly, then she shows me through to the library. Lopes's hair is greyer and his beard quite white but he is as slim and elegant as ever.

"Mistress Charlewood," he says cordially, as if we had parted on the best of terms. "It has been too long. So many years. How are you?"

"I am well, in parts," I say. "My husband died this year, but I and my son are very hearty."

I see his eyes narrow when he hears that John is dead. He must assume I have come to beg for money.

"I have not come to ask for charity, sir," I say. "I am here because a man knocked at my door the other day, when I thought he was dead these ten years and safe under the sea. I understand John Roberdine and the Dassells have caused annoyance to Dom Antonio."

"They have," says Lopes, his face giving nothing away.

"There is no love lost between myself and Roberdine," I say. "He was my husband's apprentice and he is now a cold villain, through and through. He has not scrupled to threaten me—a widow, with a young son—because of a grudge he bears my dead husband. I would be glad to see him locked away. If I can help you put him in prison, I will."

Lopes waves his hand. "It is unlikely this Roberdine will see a prison sentence," he says, "if he will only pay what is owed and prove to us that these Guinea princes came here of their own volition. I have no wish to chain him up. All I want, all Dom Antonio wants, is for trade to continue smoothly and the dues to be paid as agreed. I know he has the money. He has been spending it like water. He is building himself a house in this street. He has bought a great house and an ironworks in Sussex. I don't need a battle with a neighbour. I only ask for what is owed."

The hairs on my neck have risen and there is a chill at the pit of my stomach. "Sussex?" I say. "Do you know which house—which ironworks?"

Lopes turns to a table scattered with papers and leafs through them, drawing out a letter. "My man made enquiries," he said. "Let me see. Here. Framfield. A house and ironworks in the Sussex Weald. Ah! Now I recall. That was your master's house, yes? Sir Thomas."

"Yes," I say. "That was my home."

The thought of John Roberdine in the library at Framfield, sitting in my master's chair, playing lord of the estate when he is nothing better than a common pirate, a killer, and a thief. I cannot swallow this. He is setting out to take everything I love. My son, my business, my old home. This man will eat me whole if I don't stop him. My fear is turning into something hotter. I am suddenly flushed all over with anger. He will not do this to me.

"Perhaps I can help you secure the money," I say. "I have friends in Sussex still and there are a few small things I know that may convince him it would be better to pay the dues and keep the peace. Let me see what I can discover."

"That is very kind of you," says Lopes, studying me. "And what do you want in return? I take it there is a price for this assistance."

"Only your protection," I say. "You are powerful and I am not. At this moment, if John Roberdine wished me dead, he could have his wish very easily. All I ask is that if I come to you or send my son to you, seeking protection from him, you will give it."

Lopes nods. "He is a man to be feared then? That, too, is good to know." He rose from his chair, pulling his robe around him. "Agreed, Goody Charlewood. If you can bring this Roberdine to heel, I will be a shield against him."

"Thank you, sir," I said, and I go back home through Cripplegate. I feel like a walking flame, my rage clothing me like fire. That fire will destroy John Roberdine. I will burn him and I will burn his new-found wealth. He will be sorry he ever walked back through my door and tried to take my life away from me.

CHAPTER 44

Next day the city spills into violence when a silkweaver is arrested and carried off to Bedlam for accusing the Mayor of fixing prices. A crowd of apprentices surge up to Bedlam and break him out again, pushing the gates open and bearing him away on their shoulders, and a few days later there are further disturbances and someone sets up a gallows outside the Lord Mayor's house.

The troubles keep our press busy as we turn out pamphlets with the news, desperate to fill the hole left by the playbills. I am glad of the work, for every minute I am out of the printroom I am thinking about Roberdine and Framfield. I write to Kate, my dear Kate who now lives in the village by the estate, in a cottage with her niece. She is no longer housekeeper—she suffers badly with the ague. I write to her straight after my visit to Lopes, asking her to tell me if Roberdine visits and to send me news of any guests, especially strangers. Her reply, dictated to the letter-writer and scribed in his plain hand, comes in a few days.

"I meant to write before your letter came," she says. "I remembered the name Roberdine. He came to the house last week and brought a Blackamoor man with him. A man from Guinea. He suffers with the climate here and is shut up in the porter's lodge with a spiteful cold. Mr Roberdine is gone now. He had business up near Coventry next, it seems. His man has been to measure and fit the house and there is a great stir, he is ordering in furniture and stuffs and wants a new gardener to come in. I will write again when he returns."

Her letter decides me. I am going to Framfield. I will meet this Guinea man and I will find out what I can about Roberdine. If he is gone to Coventry he will surely go straight to London from there. I have two weeks. Grace offers to take Tom, and James Roberts from down the road agrees to mind the press and the house while I am gone. I will go to Framfield.

I write ahead to warn Kate I am coming, and ask her to be ready to receive me late at night. I don't care if Roberdine finds out I have been at Framfield, but I must be gone before he returns. I want no-one alerting him before I have a chance to speak to this Guinea man.

Tom is desperate to come with me but I forbid it. He knows this journey has a quality of adventure, though I have not told him my true purpose. He must see I am restless and stirred up and he knows Framfield is my old home.

"Is it near the sea?" he asks again as I pack up my bundle. "Can you get up onto the roof? Is the ironworks at the house, and do they make cannons?"

I know what he sees in his head. A great house steaming with furnaces and a cannon pointing out of every window to fire over the sea at the Spanish.

"Enough questions," I say. "Come. Time to go to Grace. I will tell you more when I am home again."

I travel clandestinely, in a covered cart transporting books. The books are quite legal but the carter will be returning in a day's time with an illicit cargo, travelling at night along the smugglers' holloways that cut through the Weald. That journey will be risky, but my quickest way back to London if I need to use it.

We leave London in the afternoon and arrive at Framfield village before midnight. The carter is breaking his journey here before driving on to deliver his books next morning. The roads are long and it rains, a steady drizzle pattering on the cart covering and veiling the fields around us. I know what rain can do to the Wealden roads and am dreading a morass of clay, but it stops before we reach Sussex.

As the sun goes down the air starts to smell of home. The carter's lantern swings, lighting familiar roads. Small birds sing in the hedges and I can hear the wind up in the Weald, stirring the trees. Thinner now, than in the old days. The Wealden forests have been stripped for timber and iron, feeding our many wars, and I am shocked at the patches of bare earth left by ancient oaks. But I am going back to Framfield. Ghosts walk beside me as we approach. My master and mistress, Anne, my mother.

It is the thick of night by the time we reach Kate's house, a neat cottage at the edge of the village. One candle burns in the window—every other house is in darkness. I clamber out of the cart with my bundle, thanking the carter as he carries on his way. The May night smells of cold air and blossom, and somewhere up on the hill a sheep bleats. That lonely sound, the music of my childhood. For a moment I am in a panic that I am at the wrong house, but before I have even knocked the door swings open and there is Kate's niece, Sarah, with a lantern.

"Come in—come in!" she says. "Quick, out of the cold."

She shuts and locks the door behind us and there is Kate in a chair by the fire, sitting up to wait for me. Her hair is thin and I can see her hands shaking in her lap, but when she smiles I run to her and hug her tight. She rocks me to and fro and I find I am crying into her shoulder like a child.

"There now, lamb," she says and her voice is just the same, all warm Sussex. She puts me away from her. "Let me see you."

Her eyes search my face, resting on my mouth, my eyes, the new lines. She nods as she looks at me, acknowledging the years that have passed. When I left I was a girl: a lover of stories, unworldly and green. Now I am a mother. I have done things that my young self could never have imagined. I am a story myself.

"Beautiful," says Kate, and kisses me. "Welcome home, my dear," she says to me, and grasps my hand. I kneel and lie with my head in her lap, in the warmth from the fire, and I am home. I am. For a few kind moments, I am at peace.

Next morning we sit in the kitchen with the door open, watching the sun on the grass. I have grown so used to the close-packed streets of London that this house feels almost like a burrow or a squirrel's dray, tucked so close into the greenery. The beech trees hang over us and dew dries on the grasses. Sarah is up at the house working and her son Sam squats on the hearth playing marbles while we talk.

"I want to speak with the Guinea gentleman," I say to Kate. "Do you think he would see a visitor?"

"He's kept close in the porter's lodge," says Kate. "This Roberdine brought men of his own and they tend to him, or keep a watch on him. They fetch his food and dine with him. Our servants barely see him."

"Does he walk out in the grounds at all?"

"Not since he caught this cold. You might try taking him a remedy while the men are riding out—in the afternoons they often leave him an hour or two. They don't sit so close to him now he's ill. You remember Arthur—the porter's son? He's grown now and taken over from his father. I'll send Sam to him and have him bring us notice if the men go out. Then Arthur can take you in, secretly."

"I'll try this afternoon. Has Roberdine any other visitors?" I say to Kate. "Any strangers—anyone talking of Spain, or tariffs, or imported goods?"

Sam laughs, a sudden squawk from the hearth that makes me jump. I had forgotten he was there.

"Birds, mostly," he says, and Kate and I turn to him.

"What do you mean, birds?" says Kate. "Speak up."

"They talk about birds," he says. "Him and that man who came last week. I was up in the big beech down there, and they were talking underneath. Ten culver, he says, and ten robin, and fifteen pounds a bird. I would have laughed but I didn't want them to hear me. *Who sells a robin at fifteen pound? Must be made of gold*, I thought.

"Who was selling, Sam?" I ask. "Was it Roberdine, or the other man?"

Sam thinks for a minute. "I don't know. Sounded like they were selling to someone else. The new master said, 'You tell him. Ten culver, ten robin, fifteen pounds a bird, and we'll send them out to John someone.'"

"Can you remember the surname?"

"No. The wind was blowing the leaves and I couldn't hear any more."

Ten doves and ten robins? This could be nothing so innocent as a list of songbirds for order. There is a humming in my ears, my whole body tuned to the note this has struck. This is the thing I am seeking, the thing that will give me power over Roberdine if I can only discover it.

"What did the man look like?" I ask Sam.

"Dark hair—a leather doublet. His voice wasn't Sussex. He looked like he might be a sailor, of sorts."

"Thank you Sam. Thank you for your good eyes and ears," I say. "This is a gift to me."

Sam blushes and coughs. I turn to Kate. "May I pick herbs in the garden? I'll make up the remedy now and take it to the house later."

CHAPTER 45

The walk up the long drive to the house takes me into another life. My young self is with me, within me. Walking in my shoes that tread over tree-roots, looking through my eyes at the wide grassy lawns. The house is older as I am older, and not kept as it was in my master's day. The grass is long and unscythed, and as I come closer to the house I see signs of neglect. A cracked chimney pot, missing roof-tiles.

The porter's lodge is still imposing, its two towers standing up on either side of the great gate. Arthur, waiting for me by the gate, is imposing too. He was only 14 when I left, a stripling, and now has his father's bulk and strength, but he smiles when he sees me and beckons me in quickly.

"They've gone hawking," he says. "You've a clear hour or two. He's in the top room, up there. Don't expect kind words, mind, he's hateful with this cold."

Carefully I step up the spiral staircase, timbers creaking beneath my feet. The little tower smells of damp, dogs, and very faint lavender from the old rushes. Sir Thomas' cousin never married and whoever is housekeeper now does not have Kate's skill. When I come into the little room that was mine through my sickness, I smell no perfumes and the wall-hangings are dusty.

There is a man sitting up in bed, swathed in furs and rugs, his draperies too rich for this room. He looks nothing like me, or my brother. His face is heavier, his eyes larger. They are also watery with cold, his skin ashy. He stares at me and sneezes, curses aloud in a strange tongue, and then asks me a question in the same language.

"I don't speak that language," I say. "Do you speak English?"

He shakes his head. "Very little," he says in a voice thick with phlegm. "*Português*?"

Praise be. The hours I have spent conversing with Sofia and Beatriz were well spent. I have gained more than a neatly braided head of hair.

"*Sim eu falo português*," I reply, and he raises himself up a little to reply to me in the same language.

"Who are you? Where is Roberdine? I will die if I stay here. I will die!" He emphasises each word, beating the counterpane with his hand, then falls into a coughing fit. When it ends he sighs and leans his head back on the pillows. "Who are you?" he repeats.

I come closer to the bed. He stiffens as I approach, pulling the furs closer around him as if he thinks I am an assassin. Perhaps he does. Perhaps Roberdine has threatened harm to him.

"I grew up in this house as a servant," I say. "I was brought from Guinea as a baby and Roberdine was my husband's apprentice—"

"Stop," he says, holding up his hand. "Enough. Have you come to take me away from here?"

"If I can," I say. "I know a man who may be able to help you. And I have brought you something for the cold. This will clear your nostrils—your nose."

I offer him the cup and he stares at it with suspicion. "Is it poison? He thinks to poison me? I am already half dead."

"No poison, I swear it," I say and take a sip myself before placing it by the bed. "Only herbs. I would not poison a countryman. You are from Guinea?"

He nods, studying my face, then he sighs again and turns his head away to look out of the little window where the sun falls on the beech-leaves.

"Did he—did Roberdine bring you here against your will?" I ask.

"Against my will?"

"Are you a prisoner here? Did you want to come to England?"

He coughs again, a deep hacking sound, and shakes his head. When the cough ends he reaches for the cup and drinks cautiously before making a face.

"Faugh! If it is poison I may as well die. No. I did not want to come to England. Not in that way. We came on the ship to talk trade. They shut us in and sailed away. I thought to come here one day, maybe, but not like this. I was to be married soon! My mother was sick. Now I am not married. Is my mother well, or dead? This Roberdine keeps me here—so kindly, with many good things—but he will not let me go. I must go home. You must help me."

"I will do my best, I promise," I say. "My mother and I were taken against our will also. And my brother—but he died."

He nods. The story must be familiar.

"What is your name?" I ask.

"Nana Kwasi Katakyie Boa Aponsem," he says. "Kwasi, you may call me. And yours?"

His name is as many-footed as a centipede. I will never remember it and feel ashamed to have so small a name to lay before him.

"Susan Charlewood. My Guinea name was Nsowah."

"Hm," he says. "Only that? What was your mother's *abusua*?"

"Her—what?"

"Her *abusua*. Her family name."

"I don't know anything," I say. "I don't know the name of her town, her family, anything."

"If I knew your *abusua* I would know more," he says impatiently. "Your name tells me you are the seventh child of your family, and of the Akan people—like me. We are strong in Guinea. "

I put my hands over my mouth. "Seventh child? I had six brothers and sisters?"

"Seventh born," he says. "Not all may be living."

I have lost four living children myself and four more to miscarriages. I knew I had one brother. Now I discover I am the youngest of seven children. What became of them all, my brothers and sisters? Are they dead, living, enslaved, free? Kofi didn't speak of them—the slavers only took us three. Perhaps they are all still alive in Guinea! The thought brings tears to my eyes.

"You did not know?" says Kwasi. I shake my head.

"What else?" I say, hungry now for more knowledge. "What else can you tell me?"

He coughs again and takes another sip of my remedy. "I hope your poison works, sister," he says. He seems less hostile now he knows we are of the same people.

"If you knew your *abusua* I could tell you more. Your *abusua* is your mother's line. Like family, but bigger. I am Agona. Perhaps you know your *abusua* totem—the Agona totem is the parrot. There will be a bird or an animal for your family. Perhaps your mother knew it?"

For a moment I cannot think. Then I remember my *sankofa* bird. I brought the weights with me in the hope they might help me talk to the Guinea prince. I take the bird from my pocket to show him.

"Is it this? I know it is a weight, and it has its own meaning, but is it part of my family too?"

He takes the figurine, turns it over in his hands slowly. His expression is regretful and interested as he hands it back to me.

"No. The totem birds and animals are different. I do not know them all in Portuguese. Parrot, hawk, crow..."

"Crows," I say, in a flush of feeling, the hairs on the back of my neck prickling. I remember the sight that greeted me when I first came to London: the bird perched on a traitor's leg at Southwark, tearing off flesh.

"My mother told me crows were lucky. Here they are birds of ill omen but she told me that for us they were lucky. Could it be a crow?"

"Ah." He smiles. "*Yaa Asaonaa*! You are Asona. The crow is your totem. I should have guessed from your beauty. The Asona are very beautiful and their women are strong. The women can rule, like your Queen here."

I laugh aloud at being called beautiful, at the notion that women can be rulers in Guinea, at being given a family to belong to.

"My mother used to say she was a princess."

"It is possible. There are many Asona rulers. I cannot tell for certain though, unless you know your full name or your mother's full name."

I shake my head. "She was christened Katherine, after my lady. I don't know her Guinea name. What else? Where do they live, the Asona? What does it mean, to be one?"

He shakes his head, trying to catch the rush of my speech. "Questions! It is an old *abusua*—one of the three oldest. The first Asona were led out of a cave by a snake, back in the beginning time. Where do they live? Many places. What does it mean? It tells you who are your ancestors, back and back along your mother's line to the very beginning."

"Along my mother's line? Not my father's?"

"Yes. The Akan line comes down through the mother. I understand here it is from father to son? If you did the Akan way, your son would inherit from your brother, his uncle. And he would, ah, he would look his family back along your line, not his father's line."

"My line." Not Roberdine's or John's. My son, my line. My brother's line. Slowly I take the other two weights from my pocket and hold all three together, touching them with my fingertips.

The lines stand up like the raised letters on pieces of type. Messages from my mother. I press my palm to the image of the cross, hard, till it hurts, as if it were a brand. I am overwhelmed. I cannot remember my mother's voice and she will never again speak to me directly. All I know of her and her country has come to me through other people. That brief hour with my brother at Leigh. Books, stories, sailor's gossip. Even these three weights are tiny scraps of a whole language, as if I had only three letters from which to make an alphabet or to write a book. There are tears spilling down my cheeks and I let them fall. They run over my lips, tasting of salt. After a long while I look up again.

He is sitting patiently, watching me, his hands folded on the counterpane. Suddenly his presence astonishes me. He looks like a painting, sitting up in bed with light from the window picking out the shine of his furs, the landscape of his face. I feel our differences and similarities like a chord of music, clashing individual notes making a harmony I want to hear played again and again. With an ache, I want him to be family. I want him to be my brother.

"Thank you," I say. "Thank you."

He inclines his head. "It is good to speak with you," he says. "I don't know where my companions are kept, the Dassells took them." He shivers. "This country! The land of the dead. When I came in to Dover it was raining. Grey stone, grey sky, grey river. This cold, cold rain that did not fall but hugged me like a ghost. Everything grey and white and cold. No colour. I was cold in my bones! I cannot get warm. How can you live here?"

"I am used to it," I say. "I suppose I would find Guinea like a fire to me."

"But the dirt of the people!" he bursts out. "On board the ship they threw their filth into the bilges at the bottom and it stank. And people do not take off their shoes in the house. They do not wash. They do not care that they are dirty. And men and women kiss in the street! I have seen this."

He stops abruptly, having run through this torrent of observations he must have been storing up since his arrival.

"I have offended you?" he asks.

"Not at all. Not at all. It tells me what my mother might have felt."

He nods, but says nothing more, perhaps thinking he has said too much despite my protest. He looks about the room again, the plain white walls, the little fireplace, the chest under the window. Perhaps this house seems dirty to him too.

We smile at one another, ill at ease, the spring of talk drying up. Suddenly I feel exhausted. He is not my brother. He is a foreigner, a stranger. We were born in the same place but that does not mean we can understand one another. No matter. I know what I must do.

"Are you well enough to travel?" I ask.

"If it takes me away from here, then yes," he says.

"I am going back to London tonight," I say. "It will be a rough journey in a smugglers cart. But once we are there I will take you to Jeronimo Lopes. He is a great merchant with an interest in the Guinea trade and he will look after you well, I promise. If you are willing, I will ask the porter to bring you to the back gate before midnight."

"I am willing," he says. "I am very willing."

"Good," I say and my heart is glad. Still one dark journey to make through the Wealden forest, but I am so much closer to victory. And perhaps I have made a friend from my country. Not someone to replace my brother, but still a kinsman in his own way.

"Thank-you," I say. "Wait. What is 'thank-you' in the Guinea tongue—I mean, the Akan tongue?"

"Thank-you? For you to give thanks to me, you should say: '*Meda wo ase—nyame nhyira_wo*'. That is to say, thank you and God bless you."

I repeat it slowly. "*Meda wo ase, nyame nhyira wo*." He smiles at my stumbling pronunciation. The words feel round and good in my mouth; they taste of rain.

That night's journey through the Weald is full of fear. Anne and I always loved and feared equally those goblin-haunted woods where we were forbidden to walk alone. The cart comes to Kate's as arranged just before midnight, wheels and lantern muffled. No-one in the village would report it. Everyone here has in interest in smuggling, but I am still shivering as I climb in. The night is perfect for such a journey, cloudy without rain. The porter brings Kwasi to the little gate at the back wall of the estate, as arranged. He is so swathed in furs that he looks half-bear, but he is still shivering beneath them.

I thank Arthur, who has risked his employment by delivering Kwasi to me, though we plan to say that he was drugged and fast asleep, unable to prevent the escape. He helps Kwasi into the cart, where the carter has made a makeshift bed in between barrels and boxes. Kwasi lies down uncomfortably on the piled rugs, groaning. I sit beside him on a box. I doubt I will sleep much tonight. We whisper our goodbyes and off starts the horse along the lane, on a midnight path to London. A dark echo of my journey thirteen years ago.

Kwasi falls asleep quickly despite the jolting of the cart, exhausted by his walk from the lodge to the gate. I watch alone as we turn off from the main path into the woodland and onto the sunken track. These paths are well-worn and deeply rutted. In wet weather they are impassable. Luckily it has been fine for the past week, but I still hold my breath at every lurch and bump, fearing a stuck wheel will strand us here and stop my plan. The horse pants and works, tugging hard in the shafts as the path winds uphill. Somewhere in the woods we will stop and meet the carter's friends, who will take our cargo to its next destination. Once it is gone we can rejoin the main road to London, but until then we must struggle on in darkness, lit only by the swinging circle of lantern-light. I can't even see the charcoal-burner fires that glow red in the Wealden night. The holloway walls bank above my head on either side. All I can see are tree-roots, burrows, ferns, and the stones on the path ahead. The smell of earth and moss envelops me and owls call overhead. Sussex, my home.

I turn my thoughts back to the words that Sam overheard in the beech-tree. *Ten culver, ten robin, fifteen pounds a bird.* What do these birds represent? Little red-breasted robins that hop and shout from twigs, their voices bigger than their bodies. White doves, white culvers, their soft crooning making the air a feather-nest of song.

Culvers. The word pecks at something buried deep in my memory. Something to do with Sussex, but not the soft white doves in the Framfield culverhouse. Roberdine owns Framfield now. The dovecot belongs to him, the woodland where the robins sing too. What is he planning to do here? Go hunting birds in the deep rutted paths of the Weald, that lead to ironworks burning deep among the ancient trees that feed them?

Iron. That is the key. I sit upright, cold certainty flooding me like moonlight. Culvers and robins and the bright ore that seams the Wealden clay, the metal that made my master's fortune. I have him, oh, I have him. I have Roberdine in my hand, as surely as any finch that perches on a birdcatcher's limed branch, and I will not let him go.

My elation sustains me all the way to London, despite the cold, the black night, and the fear of hounds on our trail. I deliver Kwasi to Lopes's house early in the morning, bringing him in to an astonished Sofia and bidding her find him a bath and warm clothes, and further remedies for a heavy cold. Then I go to Grace's and find Tom. Roberdine will be burning with rage when he finds I have stolen his Guinea prince. He will come back to London ready to strike me down, but I have my own weapons now. Doves and robins coo and stir in the air, rustling about my head and shoulders. On my arm sits a hooded crow, black and glossy. My mother's bird is ready, and it is watching Roberdine's one good eye.

CHAPTER 46

"A coach, a coach!" Tom comes shouting into the kitchen. "Blue and gold and four grey horses!"

Juliette leaves the dough she is kneading and runs after him as he goes back out through the hall, and I follow them both, calling Juliette back to sweep up the flour she has scattered. Out of the front door into the bright sunlight and there it is. Dark blue and gilt, with four greys leading it and the footman dressed in the same blue and gold livery. A collection of neighbourhood children and some adults have gathered to stare at it. The door opens and out steps Roberdine onto the worn stones of Barbican. A patch now covers his missing eye and his cloak is a swirl of rich yellow wool, trimmed with fur. He has come early—it is not yet three weeks. He smiles at me.

"Susan," he says. "Good morning. It's baking day, I see? May I come in?"

I am conscious of my workaday blue dress and my floured apron. He has come early to wrong-foot me. I meant to meet him in my best blacks, with my jewelled hairnet, showing him what my business has bought me. What if I refuse him? Tell him to return in three days? Another three days of imagining this meeting, of seeing him in my sleep. I want him gone. I want to be done with this.

"Come in," I say. "Tom, Juliette—take the bread down to the bakers now. Wait there till it's done, then you may come home. Go now!"

I lead Roberdine into the house. I had planned to talk to him in the parlour, bring cakes and wine. More show. What was I thinking? He is no honoured guest. I take him to the kitchen and point to the table bench. I bring ale for him. I unfasten my apron and hang it up, then slowly I unpin my coif and put it on the side. I sit down on the old settle-back chair and face him exactly as I am. Susan Charlewood, bareheaded, in her work dress. Nsowah, who comes from a line of chieftains in a land where women may rule.

He looks at his ease in his fine leather boots, his brocaded doublet and white linen, resting one leg up on his knee. His scarred face somehow doubles the effect of all that finery, rather than seeming at odds with it. He looks like a man who has fought hard for his wealth and feels he thoroughly deserves it.

I remember my first sight of him thirteen years ago, jumping down from the carrier's cart in Sussex: slim, sunburned, and vital. A young apprentice and a young wife. I felt the danger of him straight away. I wish to God I had stayed so wary of him.

"I've come from Milk Street," he says. "I'm building my house there. Your house at the Barbican will fit into one wing and the garden will be the envy of every man who comes to supper. Tom will dine there with Lords and Earls and the wealthiest men in England, he will walk in the gardens with their daughters. Perhaps Lopes told you about my house? I know he has my Blackamoor prince. That was neatly done. Poor man, he's still in bed. I think our climate may kill him. It makes no difference though. I've paid Lopes off and I'll pay off Dom Antonio too. Did you think stealing him away would put me in prison? Look."

He draws off his gloves and takes a small silk bag from his pocket. He empties it into his palm, then holds his hand out to me. More jewels. Two dull, red, uncut rubies rested there and one cut diamond that glitters in the light through the window.

"I gave Lopes one of the best rubies," he says, "and one of the best diamonds, and some Guinea gold besides. And I told him how much I have already given the Queen and what good standing that has put me in at Court."

"Gold and diamonds," I say.

"Gold and diamonds."

He closes his hand around them and puts them back in his pocket. A man so wealthy he can carry stones like that around with him on his person, scattering them here and there like small coin.

"Other men might be angry with you," he says, "for creeping into their houses and spiriting away their guests. I'm not angry. My wishes haven't changed. I still want Tom. I am his father. I can give him an education—a university education. I can make him a gentleman. I am not stopping here. I plan to have land, titles, houses, power. Why would you deny me my son? Why would you deny him this chance? You were never selfish before, Susan."

"I am Mistress Charlewood to you," I say, "and I can give him a chance as good as yours. I have sent him to Paul's school on purpose so that he can learn all a gentleman's accomplishments. He is quick and bright. He can go to Oxford as a scholar and there he will meet as many gentlemen and merchants as you might introduce to him."

"Not on the same footing, though," says Roberdine. "In my house he will be a rich merchant's ward and at Oxford he will sit with the sons of gentlemen. If he goes as a poor sizar scholar he will be serving them, clearing their plates and sitting at table with the thick-necked sons of yeomen farmers."

I ignore his interruption and continue as if he has not spoken.

"I will look after the business for him and when he comes down from university it will be here ready for him to step in and manage it, to rise in the ranks of the Guild and perhaps one day to be Queen's printer or printer to the City."

He smiles at me. "You are so determined to choose the path of pain. Why would a woman choose to run a business all alone, as a widow, when she might marry and have a man's protection? It is unnatural, Susan, and wanton foolishness. Times are hard. I am offering you feathers for your nest and you spit at me and go to line it with thorns you have plucked yourself."

"Because I love this trade," I say. "I would rather work as a widow and choose how I manage my house and which books I publish, than put my neck in yoke with a man again and bend to his will and his choices. And besides, how in God's name am I to trust you, after what you did to me before? After what you did to my brother? How can I trust that you will keep your promise and send Tom to Oxford and have him walk in your garden with earls and ladies? When you marry and have children in wedlock, will your lovely new wife, your merchant's daughter, want a half-Blackamoor boy running about your house and soaking up the light of your favour? She will suspect who he is and she will hate him for it, I guarantee it. Then you will turn him into some kind of second-hand servant. You will forget your promises. You will put off Oxford and turn him into a household valet so your wife can sit at the top table with her own brood and feel safe watching him eat with your footmen, while he reads his books by candlelight in the small hours because he can get learning no other way."

He studies me, still sitting back apparently at his ease. I cannot keep my own countenance and I know my voice is bitter and passionate, but I can see it all so clearly as I speak.

"You have forgotten what I know," he says. "If you will not send him to me willingly, what is to stop me telling the world you are a sixpenny slut who gave me use of your body in an alehouse and that he is my son to take? You cannot keep the business for him if he is a bastard. And what is to stop me telling Walsingham that you destroyed that paper at Leigh, that you are a traitor and you deserve to burn?"

I actually laugh aloud at that. He has laid his hand clear on the table. He has shown me the edge of the blade he can use to cut me, and he does not think I have any defence against it.

I can see he is taken aback by my laughter. I face him, eye to eye across the table, close enough to lean over for a kiss.

"So, now we are done with the sweet words," I say. "Thank you for honouring me with the truth. I had not forgotten but I thought the years might have taught you compassion. Now I see I must treat you like a lawyer if I am to deal with you at all.

"Yes, you could ruin me if you spoke out, but I know things that you would rather not have broadcast. I know what business you have been at with the iron furnaces in Sussex since your return into England, helping smuggle cannon and shot to the Spanish that will be used against our own people in the Netherlands. The Queen may be well pleased with the treasure you have already given her, but remember that if she finds you are a traitor she is free not only to take your head but to seize all your gold and assets, from the fair land where your new house will stand to the damned bricks it is built with."

His face does not change, to do him credit. He does not betray his feelings even by a twitch of the mouth. That is not to say he is smiling. If I were a man I am middling sure he would knife me.

"People gossip about successful men," he says. "Riches breed envy. I'm surprised you've been opening your ears to such poison."

"It is no slander," I say. "I have written proof, which is deposited very safely somewhere, laying out the exact details. Ten culverin cannons, ten small robinets and fifteen rounds of shot for each gun, cast by the Framfield furnace and going out to Spain via Jean de

Luz next Tuesday week, in the *Bartholomew*. I understand it was the bargain you made for your release from prison in Seville, the first of many such deliveries. If I die unexpectedly, I have left instructions for the proof to be delivered where it will be most appreciated."

He studies me closely. For a moment I see him quite plain, the calculation in his one green eye. Cold, cold, cold. He is considering whether to risk killing me, weighing his chances in the balance. Then he blinks and moves, and the calculation turns to shock. Fear, even. He stares at my neck and he looks afraid. I glance down and see my brother's *memento mori* ring on its silver chain. The amber eyes spark in the sunlight through the kitchen window, the little skull grinning warmly at Roberdine. He could not have seen the ring when he came here the first time, it was tucked under my partlet. He looks from the ring to my face and back again and I see he is wondering if my brother could possibly still be alive. And if he is alive, and in Spain, what else might he be able to tell me about John Roberdine? Perhaps there is more to it even than the smuggling.

I stare back at him, my brother's ring giving me power. Even in death, he is with me. My family are here with me, my brother and mother, shielding me from Roberdine and striking at him. Something shifts between us. He looks away from me as I stare him down.

"I would marry you if I could, mistress," he says at last. "A wife with your wits is worth her weight in gold. But I want the gold more, and I could never be sure you might not cut my throat in my sleep. I think we are at stalemate. I do think I could talk or buy my way out of such trouble as might arise from your written proof. Greater men than me have done that kind of business with the enemy and survived, but I would rather not run into rocky waters so early in my career. And you would prefer not to die. So what can we do to safeguard ourselves, other than drawing up a marriage contract?"

"I want a different kind of contract," I say. "I want you to sign a bond guaranteeing that you will pay to put Tom through Oxford, that he will live in your house as your honoured ward and that you will provide all the education and training he needs to walk among gentlemen as their equal. And that he will spend every holiday with me, in my house, so that he does not forget his mother."

He thinks for a moment, then places his palm on the table. "Done. My lawyer will write it up."

"No, I will have the man who drew up John's will do it," I say. "Then we shall sign it in the presence of both lawyers."

"Agreed," he says. "I will do it."

He stands up, pulling on his gloves. Yellow kid, soft as butter.

"There is one more condition," I say. He pauses with one glove on and the other still in his hand. "You will leave Tom Framfield and the estate, for him to inherit when he is 21."

There is no calculation in his eyes this time. They speak pure murder.

"You ask too much," he says.

"I am not asking," I say. "Bring your will to the lawyers meeting and write Framfield into it, or I will tell all I know."

Slowly he pulls on the other glove, taking time stretching the material over his hand and fingers. I wonder if I have gone too far and he will kill me anyway and take the consequences.

"Very well," he says. "I will sign away the house and the estate. I wanted the ironworks more than that clay-mired pile anyway."

"You may go now," I say. I lead him to the front door. He turns with his hand on the handle and leans to kiss me goodbye, but I turn my face away.

"Not quite a clean victory for you," he says, "but nonetheless, mistress, you play a good game. I'll wait for your lawyer's note. God keep you."

I watch him walk away down the Barbican in his bright-coloured clothes, my arms folded. I am trembling. I tell myself to be proud of keeping my nerve in battle. I had gone over the thing in my head a dozen times. Placing Tom in Roberdine's household would help protect us from Walsingham, and ensure Tom was fed and clothed in these hungry times. I would be a fool not to use Roberdine's wealth as shelter for myself and my son. I am in a precarious position and I need strong allies. But what is an ally if you do not—cannot—trust them? I have no trust whatsoever in Roberdine, so in place of trust I must have insurance. I tell my heart to be glad at what I have clawed back for my son. But a heart is not a dog, to be called to heel and whipped into obedience, and mine just now feels like a very wolf, wild and hungry and howling.

CHAPTER 47

When Roberdine is gone I fetch my mother's weights from my chest and set them on the table in front of me. I put my hands on them and think of my brother and mother. I remember my brother saying my name on board the ship at Leigh, with such love. Nsowah. Nsowah. I say it to myself. I call my mother to me. I thank them for saving me. I thank them for the weights and for the ring. I promise they will never be forgotten. I feel them near me and I sit in the warmth of their presence. My family, my home.

I close my eyes, and in my mind I walk the rooms at Framfield. I go up and down the Long Gallery where my lady used to walk, her low heels clipping the floor. Light through the windows turns the floor-timbers silver in patches, and I tread through these sunlit places with care, suddenly twinned with my shadow.

I go past the great fireplace where Anne and I roasted chestnuts in the winter, our skirts puffed around us like two mushrooms. Burnt fingers and tongues. I told her stories and she peeled away chestnut-skins to get at the sweet kernels.

I go past the window-seat where I would read, stopping sometimes to look out over the lawns and the Weald beyond. In the sky over the trees I built cities and continents: Rome, Athens, Venice, Africa.

I go past the portrait of my lady, Anne, and I. Anne to the fore and me solemn behind her. The space where my mother should be, filled with a swathe of richly patterned tapestry.

The house is silent. It should be full of servants. Kate, busy in the linen cupboard, Nicholas the cook screaming orders in the kitchen, the footman in his best suit swinging up the stairs to find my master. My master in his favourite chair by the library fire, cutting the pages of a new volume with his paper-knife.

In this vision the house is empty. I walk the halls like a ghost, counting my steps, making it ready for Tom. Where I walk I leave a track of golden footprints, invisible to anyone who does not know how to look for them. My fingers trail gold-dust along the panelling and the wall-hangings. I leave my message in a language Tom can read. I have made a home for him, my little heart, and no-one shall take it from him.

I am still sitting with my hands on the weights when I hear Tom come back in. He walks past the door, whistling.

"Tom," I say, "come here." The whistling stops and he pokes his head through the door and sees me at the table. I have never shown him the weights before.

"What are these things?" he says, his eyes bright and interested. My mother cannot speak to me, but I can speak to him. I don't have to leave him to pick out scraps and pinches of knowledge from other people.

"Bring up a stool and sit down," I say.

He fetches a stool and drags it over so we are sitting side by side.

"May I touch them, madam?" he asks.

"Yes." I watch as he looks at them. He reaches for the bird first, of course, standing on its little pyramid. He turns it about in his hand, testing the weight and the feel of it the way he tests a stone for his slingshot.

"They come from Guinea," I tell him. "My mother left them to me and one day they will be yours too. They are a kind of alphabet, with secret meanings. They were made by our Guinea ancestors. Our grandfathers and great-grandfathers, who were great philosophers."

He smiles; secrets please him. "Do I have to try and guess?" he says. "Like a riddle?"

"No, I will tell you some of them. This bird is called *Sankofa*. It means *go back and fetch what you forgot*. You see how it bends its bill backwards? It means that you should not forget your past. It is telling us we should never forget my mother or where she came from. Some people will tell you that the Guinea people—our people, the Akan—are heathens and savages and know nothing. That isn't true. My mother was wise and brave. It is thanks to her that I came over the sea safely, so we must never forget her. Do you understand?"

He nods, turning the bird over and over. Eventually he puts it back on the table and picks up the weight with the ladder on.

"What does this one mean?"

"That one reminds us that we will all die one day. All men must climb up the ladder to death. So you must live well while you can. Be good to people of all stations, learn your lessons and work hard. Tom—Mr Roberdine, who visited the other day, would like to take you into his household. He is a wealthy merchant and you will learn all kinds of things in his house. Falconry, how to ride and hunt, how to fence. He will send you to Oxford and bring you up as a gentleman."

He says nothing in response. I thought he would be either delighted or upset. I expected he would smile, or cry, or ask a dozen questions. Children never do the things you imagine they will. He sits in uncomfortable silence, turning the ladder weight in his hand, as if he knows I am waiting for him to say or do something but he cannot think what it is.

"You may take the bird with you," I say at last, putting it back in front of him. "Keep it very, very carefully. He is yours now and he will go wherever you go."

"May I have the ladder too?" he asks, holding one weight in each hand.

"Not yet," I say, taking it back from him. "I must keep this one for a while."

"But I like that one," he says.

"You will have it one day," I say. He frowns. "Tom, be patient. It's not yours to ask for. You must not beg for things when you go to Roberdine's house, either. You must wait for them to be offered to you."

Still he says nothing about going to live with Roberdine. Instead he reaches for the last weight, the dotted cross, and picks it up.

"What does this one mean?"

I think for a moment. "I can't tell you yet. You must wait till you are older." He makes a face, but doesn't protest. He looks at the bird again, turning the figure round in his hand, feeling the shape of the beak and the textured wings. He hates it when I stroke his hair, but for a minute I draw him in, stroking and kissing the side of his neatly-shaped head and the hair that I keep soft with almond oil, as Kate kept mine.

I breathe in his smell and listen to his breathing, a little snuffly with cold. The nap of his jacket collar is rubbed away where he sucks on it, though I slap him whenever I catch him at it. I can feel the impatience in his body. He wants to be away and looking at the bird by himself, making it part of his own small life, but I cling on a little longer, remembering when he used to cling to me.

My dear son. I remember when he was small enough to sleep in my arms, curled up on my breast with his little hands furling and unfurling against my skin. I held him until my arms and shoulders ached with his weight, all so that he would sleep in peace. I broke my own sleep to feed him at night. I kept vigil over him, watching his every breath. Each morning when I woke I expected to find him pale and dead in his cradle like the others, and each morning when he yelped and waved his fat fists in the air I felt as if it were the first day of summer. He is my dearest love.

"Go and put the bird in your chest upstairs," I say. "Keep him safe. Don't let anyone take him from you."

Then I give him a push and watch him run upstairs with the bird clutched in his fist. I feel the tug in my chest as if he is going away for good. My little heart, my own heart, gone out into the world. But I have passed on my mother's knowledge. I have given him something to take with him—more than I had when I was small. And in time he will know the truth of his genesis. His real father, the man who will see him through the next years of his life, is rapacious, deceitful, and without conscience. A man who would not scruple to turn a profit from the very trade that tore my mother and I from our homeland in the first place; a trade that is built on suffering.

By the time Tom is a grown man, will he be more Roberdine's child or mine?

The candles are burning low. The cases of type are silent around me, waiting to be formed into words. The letters glitter at me like music, like stars to be formed into constellations. I can make them or scatter them. Here in the print room I am a little god and the universe of words is mine.

Dawn is edging in and I must make my choices. I won't condemn Roberdine to death. I haven't the heart for it, despite what he has done to me. It is enough, knowing I have the power to do it. Besides—what might he say about me, to keep himself from the gallows? We know too much about one another.

It is not safe for me to live alone in London, unanchored. A widow-woman. A Blackamoor and a Catholic, in a time of anger that turns out towards the un-English, the strangers. I stand on the edge of the cliff. It would take a very little shove to send me over. If Tom is not to be a printer, by the Stationers' laws I have no choice but to give up the business or marry again, some other printing man, forgoing my independence as a widow.

I will marry again. Someone with children. Someone of my choosing. This is my world now and I am hungry to print more books, poems, plays and sermons—fierce, beautiful words that sell across England. And I would rather be run ragged mothering and helping with a business than sit waiting for the guards to call again.

What if I were to marry Kwasi instead? He is young and strong, and of my people. I could go back to Guinea with him. Find my brothers and sisters and live there like royalty in the forests that perhaps are not so different from the Weald.

Go to Guinea and leave my son behind. Leave my trade and my books. Start anew in a country that is strange to me. That is no choice, either.

My ties are all in England, whatever earth I sprang from originally. I am a stone in London wall, a part of the city. When I die my atoms will mingle with London soil—the soil where my children are buried—and grow again in grass and flowers.

And Tom is a true citizen of London, by birth and blood. A child of mixed parentage who will most likely marry an Englishwoman and mingle himself even further with this country, his children carrying in them my blood, a Guinea ribbon, a secret history. For all the misfortunes and cruelties that brought me here, for all the sin that made him, Tom is my best legacy.

I put the remaining weights together on the table and trace the shape of the ladder and the dotted cross with my fingers. All men must climb the ladder to death. If God dies, I die too. Such solemn meanings treasured up in such small things. So easily lost. We pass our knowledge from mind to mind, from hand to hand. Even sacred knowledge comes to us along a human chain. One broken link and it is lost forever.

If I had not spoken to my brother on board that ship, the meaning would be lost to me, to Tom, to Tom's children. Would another soul in England understand the meaning of that dotted cross?

It has given me an urge I never had before. A feeling, a distinct feeling. I want the paper under my hand and the quill in the other. I want to write something more than a letter. I want to write down what my brother told me, and what Kwasi told me, about the place where I was born. I want to write down the story of what carried me here. My mother, myself. I want to write. In pen and ink, and then in type on the compositors stick, and then as words clear on the page to be carried out across London. I have seen the power of words. I might not put my name to this, but I want to write.

We women are told from birth how and where we may speak, and to whom. We are told to keep a guard on our tongues and our thoughts. Who are you, to speak? Who are you, to think? Stop your wagging tongue. Break off that thought, before it flowers. We have carved you a canal of thought; we have laid out a straight road for you to follow. Why must you keep looking out to sea? Why do you leave our road and run barefoot out into the grasses, into the rough heather where adders curl around roots and sharp rocks will cut your soft feet?

And we who are out of harmony with the tune the State wants to play are also silenced. Our hands cut off, our windpipes crushed, our bodies torn into pieces, all so that we shall not speak. So the polyphony of thought and speech becomes one line, a single thin strand of melody.

Here I am, thinking in heavy discord. Wild words. Here I am making chaos, hacking down fences, letting my words run about like colts in spring. In private.

Tomorrow—today—I will be in order again. Tom will go to Roberdine. I will wear my milk-and-water coif, speak in straight lines and marry another printer, because I don't want to die. It is that simple: conform or die. The *memento mori* ring sits on my finger, the skull facing towards me with its jaw resting on the heart of my wedding ring.

I am not a martyr. I want to live. I myself may not be remembered but that's no matter. One thing lights up another. Outwardly I conform, but my thoughts are free to go where they will. Let my thoughts and words echo in other peoples' minds, secretly, until the day comes when they can be spoken aloud without fear and the whole world rings to the music.

EPILOGUE

Ama stands on deck with Nsowah in her arms, lifting her to see the great river at sunrise and the ships coming in to dock. Gulls fret the air overhead, sailors shout, the masts around them are like the forests of home. The wind is fresh but Nsowah is wrapped close in her shawl and she waves her hands and babbles at the birds, the ships, the water below them and the gold in the sky.

Ama is only a little piece of her old self. A finger, an eye. These men have cut away the rest of her. They cut away her home, her children. They cut her son away before her eyes as they led him down the gangplank in Seville. They have cut her heart into bloody ribbons. She holds Nsowah tight to her all the time. She never lets her go for a minute. She is the only thing Ama still breathes for. She lies beside her at night, Nsowah's head resting on her arm and her little body turned towards Ama, curled like a nut in its shell. Ama rests a hand on her ribs to feel her quick breathing: in, out, in, out. She lies for hours at a time feeling that in, out, in, out; feeling the little warm breaths that Nsowah breathes. Her baby gives her life. Her baby's heartbeat feeds her own. Without it she thinks her heart would stop with grief, so she keeps her close. Nsowah is her protection as much as she is hers.

Together they look at London, rising all around them. Bells ring out and the sun is up.

"*M'akoma*," says Ama to Nsowah as the water rushes past them and they draw nearer to their destination. "*M'akoma*." My heart, my heart. She feels her strength fail as they approach the dock. While they were at sea, on their journey, she still had some wild hope they might be returned home. The boat might be attacked again. They might sail back home on a raft, on a sea monster's tail. Be carried there by an eagle. She told these stories to Nsowah night after night, hoping in the telling they might become true. Now the journey is ending. She is not going home. The red earth, the forests, her family, are burning away in this sunrise. She holds Nsowah tighter, closes her eyes and sucks in her daughter's scent in a kind of desperation. Please, please, hold me up. Don't let me fail her, don't let me lose her. My heart, my heart.

There is a bump and she opens her eyes. Nsowah squeaks. They are at the landing place and below her is a sea of white faces staring up at her from the dock. A forest of ghosts, black-mouthed, arms reaching up for her baby. Nsowah is not afraid. She waves at the people below and sings her babble of sounds. Ama takes courage from her. She is a warrior. She is sister to the Omanhene. She is an Asona woman and these ghosts will not defeat her. In among the gulls a black wing turns, spreads and carves the air. A crow is coming. It flies down to the yard-arm above them and shouts. It has come to attend her. Ama stands straight and tall and meets London with fierce eyes and her daughter clutched to her heart. Behind her the Thames runs to the sea, plunging on and on, and the bones of the city acknowledge her. Here is another life.

A NOTE FROM THE AUTHOR

Historical context

This is a work of fiction based on fact. The most important fact is that Africans lived and worked in Tudor England, in domestic service and as craftsmen and women. Africans married English people and had children with them, owned property, were involved in lawsuits. The evidence of their presence is in church registers, court records, wills and other archive documents.

Around this, I have built a story that weaves real people and events with fiction. Nsowah/Susan is a fictional character, and Framfield is also a fictional creation. The rambunctious world of the Stationers was very real, as were John Hawkin's voyages to Ghana (then known as Guinea), the secret Catholic presses, inn-house theatres, Jesuit missions and plots against Elizabeth I. Some historical dates and details have been changed to fit the story and these are noted below.

John Charlewood was a real—and very interesting—person, as were the other printers and authors mentioned including John Wolfe, Anthony Munday and Joan Jugge. Charlewood may have been responsible for helping print the works of Robert Southwell, the Catholic poet. His wife was actually an Englishwoman named Alice who continued to print after he died in 1593 and in that same year married James Roberts, who registered and printed several Shakespeare plays including *Titus Andronicus.*

There is no evidence that *Campion's Brag*, or *Challenge to the Privy Council*, was ever set to be printed. Persons's press printed every publication by Campion and there is no evidence that other printers ever took a part in the production.

The Throckmorton plot was very real and it is documented that some papers were spirited away from Throckmorton's house when he was arrested. These were never traced, so the account of their journey with Maria Padilla is pure speculation.

Jeronimo Lopes and the Dassells were also real people, although the incident with the Dassells allegedly bringing Ghanian princes back to England against their will occurred in 1592 rather than 1593.

It's also important to make the distinction between the different kinds of slavery in this period. Slavery was not legally enforceable in England at this time, however the status of those who would have been slaves in Spain and Portugal before they came to England with their masters is unclear. As mentioned, Akan people also kept slaves during this period. The difference is that freedom could be earned and slaves were often absorbed into the family system by marriage. It was entirely different from the uniquely horrific form of chattel slavery forced upon African people by the transatlantic slave trade, which denied their humanity and condemned generations to enslavement.

ACKNOWLEDGEMENTS

Part of my original motivation in writing a Black character in Elizabethan England was to give the lie to those myth-makers who use a fantasy all-white English past to feed into far-right white supremacist narratives. However, good intentions don't always justify actions. I understand that an author can empathise, research, and build a character around a human experience that is not their own, but that it is also not theirs to claim. I hope I have achieved this delicate balance.

It has taken me 15 years to finish writing this book, since I began in the summer of 2003. This book spans many subjects and research areas and I have an army of people to thank. I hope I have done the research justice—any errors are my own.

Taking it chronologically, thanks to Nick Monu for first opening my eyes to the presence of Africans in Tudor England. Thanks to Arts Council England for a grant that gave me 6 months to complete the first draft.

Thanks to Damian Barr for letting me pitch the idea for the book to a panel of editors and agents at a Brighton Fringe event, which gave me the confidence to keep on with the idea.

Thanks to Ros Barber for mentoring me through the writing of that first draft, particularly for patiently explaining why my childbirth scene was completely unrealistic despite my extensive research into 16th Century midwifery.

Thanks to Esua Goldsmith for giving me so much of her time and insight into life growing up as a mixed heritage British-Ghanaian girl in 1970s England and what it meant to find her Fante kin and roots.

Thanks to Marika Sherwood and to Onyeka Nubia and Miranda Kaufmann for sharing their then unpublished research into Black Tudors. Particular thanks to Miranda who shared her full thesis text, read drafts, and gave me notes. She has been a fellow-soldier in the fight to write a book while parenting small children. Thanks also to the rest of the team at What's Happening in Black British History—Philip Murphy and Michael Ohajuru.

Thanks to all at Bath Spa University's Book, Text and Place research centre 1550–1700, especially Tracey Hill and Ian Gadd. Thanks also to Paul Nash at the Bodleian Library print room, for letting me try my hand at typesetting and patiently fielding technical questions.

Thanks to Judith Murray, my brilliant agent, for herself playing midwife to this book; for being passionate about it from reading the first chapters, helping shape the narrative and keeping the faith. Thanks to all at Greene & Heaton for representing me as an author.

Thanks to everyone at my publishers Jacaranda who has worked on the book—Valerie Brandes, Laure Deprez, Jazzmine Breary, Cherise Lopes-Baker and Kamillah Brandes. I arrived at my first meeting with Jacaranda with my six-week baby in a sling and felt immediately welcomed and hopeful. Jacaranda is more than a publisher, it is on a mission to increase inclusivity and representation in UK publishing. I'm honoured to be on its author list. Thanks for your invaluable editorial guidance, your patience and forbearance.

Thanks to Helen Smith for notes on women printers, Ian Friel for his insights into Elizabethan naval history and Earle Havens for sharing notes on recusant book-smuggling in the Marshalsea.

For fact-checking my research into Akan history and culture I must thank the Ghana Society of Great Britain, Tom McCaskie & the British Library for giving me access to the Universe of Akan Gold-weights by Georges Niangouran-Bouah. Thanks to Nadine Akkerman for pointing me to letterlocking videos and early modern female intelligencers.

I am indebted to the work of scholars who have researched the presence of Africans in early modern Europe, including Kim F Hall, Peter Fryer, Kathy Chater, Imtiaz Habib, Rosalyn Knutson and Gustav Ungerer.

Thanks to the dear souls at the BFN writing group; Harriet Kline, Penny Price, Tannith Perry, Ken Elkes, Emma Smith-Barton, Amy Wilson, Ilana Winterstein, Agnes Halvorssen, especially Harriet who read the whole thing and gave me feedback. Thanks to Rex Obano for guiding me back onto the right path when I felt lost and to Fiorella Nash for giving the manuscript a Catholic reading. Thanks to those who helped my thinking about voice—Heather Agyepong, Tarik Elmoutawakil, Heather Marks—and to Colin Grant for reading and understanding my aims.

Thanks to my family and dear friends for picking me up on the many times I tripped on this long quest, especially my parents, my brother Jim; Hazel, Vicky, Eleanor, Lucy, Helen, Emma, Katie. Thanks to Jo, Luke and Vicky who read drafts and gave feedback.

So much love and thanks to my husband Jonny for believing in me and holding the household together while I worked late on yet another draft. And to my children who have made the logistics of writing 100 times harder but compensated by giving me a bigger heart.

About the Author

Kate Morrison is a British debut novelist who studied English Literature at New Hall College, Cambridge and worked as a journalist and a press officer. She currently lives in West Sussex with her family.

Morrison was mentored by Ros Barber, the award-winning author of *The Marlowe Papers* and *Devotion*. She was a visiting scholar with the Book, Text, and Place 1500-1700 Research Centre at Bath Spa University. Her short story "Sam Brown" won second prize in the 2011 Asham Award and is in the Asham Award Anthology, *Something was There. A Book of Secrets* was longlisted for the Mslexia Unpublished Novel Award in 2015.